# A TRIAL OF FATE

J.E. LARSON

Map Design by J.E. Larson
Copy Editing by Jen Boles
Proofreading by Eleanor Smith
Cover Design by cheriefox.com
Interior Design by J.E. Larson

ISBN: **979-8-9900411-1-0**

## DEDICATION

This story is dedicated to all who are brave enough to dream and transform it into a *reality*.

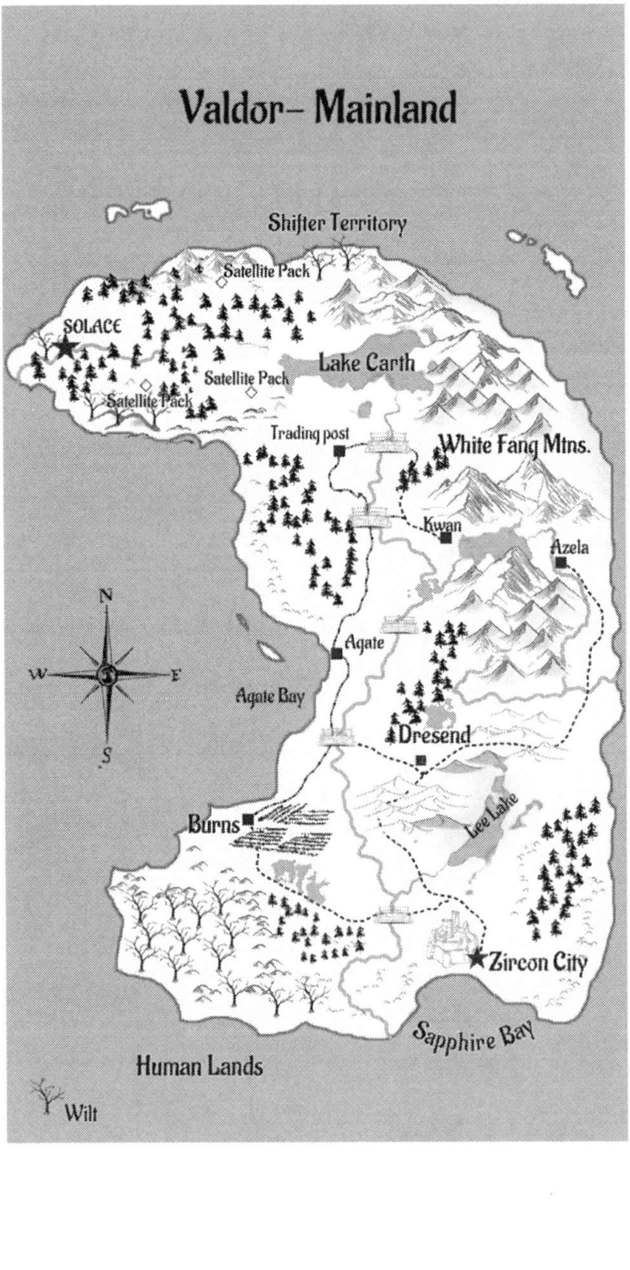

Valdor– Mainland
Shifter Territory
Satellite Pack
SOLACE
Lake Carth
Satellite Pack
Satellite Pack
Trading post
White Fang Mtns.
Kwan
Azela
N
W
E
S
Agate
Agate Bay
Dresend
Burns
Lee Lake
Zircon City
Sapphire Bay
Human Lands
Wilt

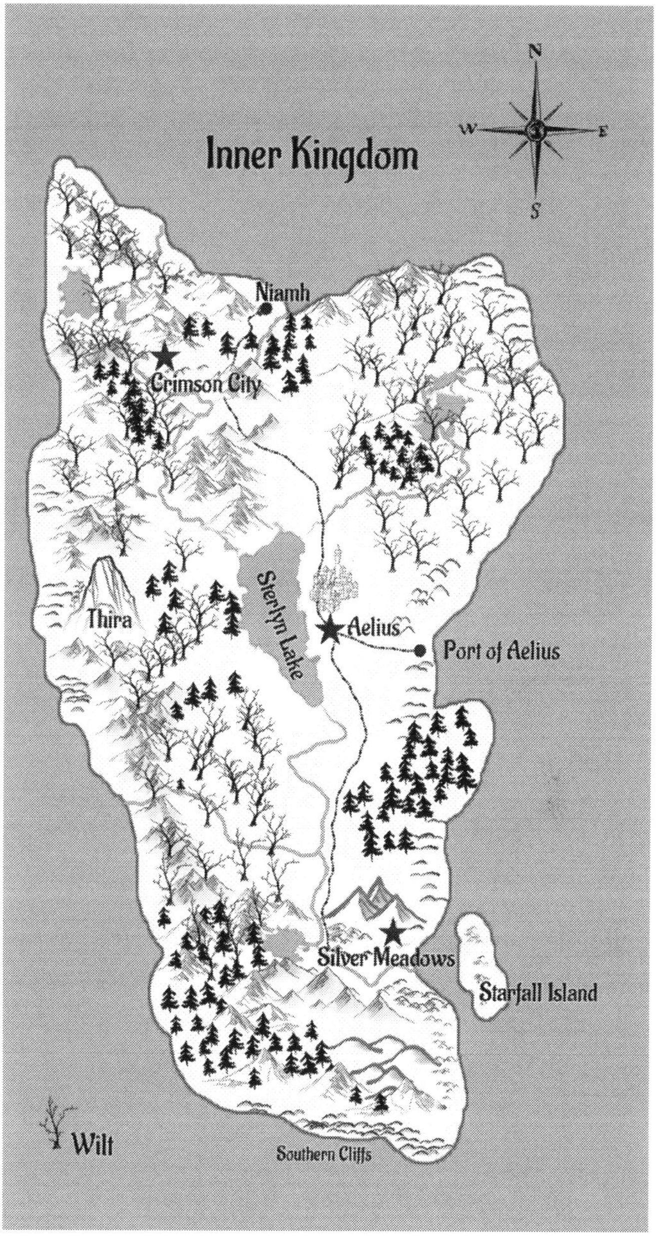

Inner Kingdom
N
W
E
S
Niamh
Crimson City
Sterlyn Lake
Thira
Aelius
Port of Aelius
Silver Meadows
Starfall Island
Wilt
Southern Cliffs

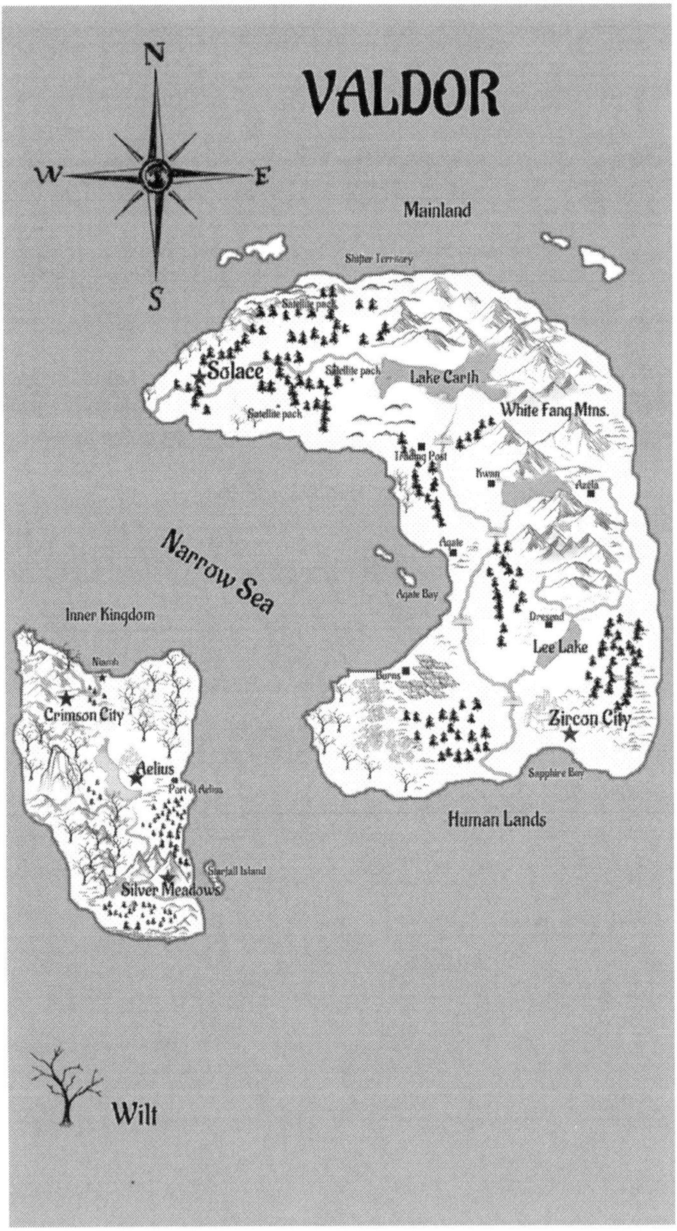
VALDOR
N
W
E
S
Mainland
Shifter Territory
Satellite pack
Solace
Satellite pack
Satellite pack
Lake Carth
White Fang Mtns.
Trading Post
Kwan
Aeela
Agate
Agate Bay
Narrow Sea
Inner Kingdom
Lee Lake
Burns
Zircon City
Sapphire Bay
Human Lands
Crimson City
Aelius
Starfall Island
Silver Meadows
Wilt

## ACKNOWLEDGMENTS

First, I will always thank my husband. There is not enough whiskey in the world to say thank you, and I know I can hear you scoff at my mention of this … even though it is 100 percent true. Thank you for being there through this wild ride of anxious nerves and encouraging me to be brave. Also, being a caring father to our little princess and special unicorn.

Second, I must thank my beta readers. KD, you were there from the start … giving me essential feedback to buff up Skylar's story and making it relatable and authentic. My mom and aunts for reading and always being willing to answer my next question or just give me the encouragement I needed. And to my friend Sarah, who found the time to read between running a business and being a bad-A mama herself. You all have my immense gratitude for giving me your valuable time to help me on this journey.

Third, I have an amazingly strong team of ladies with me that helped make this story sparkle and shine. Jen, my copy editor, gave me endless feedback and went above and beyond with her guidance and support. Cherie, my cover artist who brought tears to my eyes by bringing my cover and characters to life. And my proofreader Eleanor, thank you for helping finish this project and making sure it was ready for the next step.

I also wanted to say a special thank you … to my high school English teacher. Thank you for inspiring me to write. For not giving up on the dyslexic student striving to be the best she can be. For giving me the opportunity to find my voice and every week, write you a story.

And finally, *I thank you, the reader*. For without you, this story wouldn't have breath, or come to life. I hope you enjoy this journey. There is more to come.

Welcome … to Valdor.

# Chapter One

Sitting on the crystalized shores of the green sand beach, I stretched out my long limbs and basked in the warming sun. My golden-brown hair draped over my shoulder, waving in the breeze skittering over the open ocean.

If anyone were to ask themselves, "Where is Skylar?" The answer would be here with a book or two as my only companions. The Solace Shifter Pack didn't have the most extensive library, but new collections ventured in from the southern human kingdom often enough to keep me intrigued.

Today's waves were calm and relaxing, gently rolling and shifting the olivine sand along the isolated alcove. The tall cliffs surrounding this secluded beach were the remnants of an ancient volcano's caldera.

I loved my hideaway and the solitude it often brought me when I needed a break from my shifter pack life. *Don't get me wrong, I care deeply for my kin and would do anything to defend them.* I wouldn't hesitate to die protecting my people—none of us would. That was the shifter charm for ya, right there. And even though I wasn't a full-blooded shifter, they were my pack.

A splash caught my attention, and along the outer corner of the caldera, I could see a group of young shifters diving off the cliffside. I smiled, closed one of my favorite romance books, and sat up to watch the daring teens test their bravery among their friends. This was an old tradition among the Solace pack—a test of their nerves and to see who among them was aware of their animal awakening within.

As shifters, we shared the spirit of an animal that gifted us with heightened abilities and allowed us to change into another form at will. In our early teenage years, tied with puberty, our animal spirit awakened, and we became aware of their presence. It wasn't until early adulthood, however, that we manifested the ability and harnessed enough control over our magic to shift into our animal form, which was unique to each individual shifter.

"I'm surprised you haven't joined them already," a familiar voice called out behind me.

I couldn't help the girlish grin from spreading across my face or the blushing in my cheeks, no matter how hard I tried to stop it. I could feel his power pulsing and vibrating over my skin, delicately caressing my senses with the mere sound of him.

"Gilen Warrick." I fixed my gaze on the teens jumping into the open water. I wouldn't be the first to turn and look, happily continuing to play the dance of dominance with him.

"Skylar Cathal," he whispered, saying my name slowly and announcing each syllable in an inquisitive tone, moving to stand behind me.

The warmth of his body seeped into my own, and I couldn't help leaning back into him. I tilted my head up and flashed him a large, playful grin with far too many of my teeth showing. "And how are you doing today?" I asked, knowing exactly why he had come. "I see you found me in my hideout."

"It wasn't hard to guess where you were." His warm honey-colored hazel eyes softened as a smirk teased the corner of his mouth, complementing his comely expression. "Why didn't you show up for training today?"

"Oh, did the alpha call us?" I asked, trying to avoid getting into trouble. "I had no idea. I'm sorry. I guess I didn't hear it. Human interference, yet again."

Gilen sighed heavily and ran a hand through his mid-length wavy golden hair. "Come on, Sky. Don't play the pretty, clueless damsel role with me … It's beneath you. I know you're smarter than that."

"Whatever do you mean?" I exaggerated with a heavy sigh, flinging my arms outward and folding them over my chest as I slumped back into the sand. "Wait," I said, arching my brow and turning to give him a playful half-smile. "Did you just call me pretty?" I added a wink just to seal everything in.

Gilen rolled his thick shoulders and sank down next to me in the green sand. "You're telling me you didn't hear our alpha's call? Again?" His hardened rule-following stare bore into mine, and I had to bite my lip to stop from confessing the truth.

"Sky, come on. It's me. Tell me why you didn't come to training today." He paused, furrowing his brow. "Are the others picking on you again?"

"No," I snapped. "That hasn't happened in a long time." I absently rubbed my arms, recalling the taunting and bullying I took from the other shifters our age when we were kids … all because I was half-human. My station in the pack improved when my animal's presence emerged, but I was still far from a favorite.

"What is it then?"

Oh no. I was cornered.

The truth was that I had heard the alpha's command earlier today, but I chose to ignore it. That was the secret I was deathly afraid to tell Gilen. It was the fact that I could ignore our alpha's command, not that I simply didn't hear it. Even though Gilen was one of my closest friends, no one besides my family knew about this special ability. I was afraid of what others would think if they knew.

Well, first, I know they would be pissed off that I had lied to them all these years. Blaming my human side was an all too easily convincing lie, but after that, I had no idea. Would they be scared? Would they call me a freak and shun me like some of the members of our pack? Would our alpha see it as a threat to our safety and force me to leave? I think that last question scared me the most, but it also gave me a thrill imagining what other kind of life I could have outside the pack.

Just to add some trouble, over the past few weeks, my animal had been sending random pulses of strong magic through me, making me extremely anxious. All my senses were on high alert, but I had no fucking clue what it was. All I knew was that it was giving me the worst headaches in the world, and I needed space. That was why I ignored the alpha's call and came here to my green sand beach today.

"I don't know what to tell you," I said as I rolled over onto my stomach to break his piercing gaze. "I didn't hear the alpha's call. Must be my human side running interference again."

"Right." Gilen huffed in annoyance, shaking his head.

I could hear the disappointment in his voice as guilt ripped through my heart. Gilen and I had grown up together. From day one, we were inseparable friends, and I trusted him. If I were to open up and be my true self with anyone, I believed it could be him.

Gilen knew I was hiding something. But he would never push me to tell him, and that was one of the biggest downfalls in our friendship. He didn't challenge me and expected me to fall in line with formalities and the pecking order of the pack. The difference was that I liked to push those set rules he loved and create my own.

The problem wasn't him, though; it was me. I knew that I was different.

A piercing scream erupted from the cliffs as one of the young girls in a group of teenage shifters leaped into the ocean.

"Come on now … that's not how it's done," I scolded, making Gilen laugh. "You can't expect the boys to give you any respect if you squeal like a pig while jumping off the edge. They'll assume that's what your animal is, and then no one will ever respect you."

"Oh, really?" Gilen asked. His carefree laughter set me at ease for the moment. "Do you even remember what sounds came out of your mouth the first time you jumped?"

"I sure as hell didn't squeal." I kicked some sand at Gilen, but he reacted in time to block it from hitting his face. Darn those quick shifter reflexes; it was hard to get anything past him.

He casually brushed the sand off his shoulders and gave me a gentle smile that had me curling my toes. "Care to test out your memory and show me what you can do?"

"Is that a challenge?" A faint growl sounded at the back of my throat. Shifters were competitive by nature, and my instinct was always to win.

"You bet your lazy ass it's a challenge." My eyes grew wide with excitement. This was a new twist to how these situations typically went. "How else am I going to assess your potential for our pack? You need to start showing up to the group sessions. I can't keep training you privately and playing catch-up." Gilen arose from the sand and grabbed the bottom of his tan tunic, pulling it over his head before dropping it onto the beach, readying himself for a sparring match.

As shifters, we grew accustomed to nudity at an early age, but I couldn't help the warmth in my middle from spreading whenever I looked at Gilen. Strong muscular arms framed a chiseled chest and stomach that could only come from years of training and fighting to protect our people and lands. I couldn't stop myself from admiring his physique for a moment longer, but I quickly averted my gaze when Gilen's half-smile hinted that he caught me lingering longer than I probably should have.

"Come on, Sky," he taunted in a sing-song voice.

After surviving through our teenage years, he filled his tall frame with a taut muscular build. His thick, dark blond hair swayed loosely around his face, brushing against dark brows that framed honey-hazel eyes. His tanned skin was kissed by the weathering sun, defining his high cheekbones and remarkably unscathed facial features. He was the epitome of handsome, a golden boy, and the constant trail of willing females vying for their chance to become his mate only grew with each passing year.

"Challenge accepted," I answered as I jumped up from the sand and tried to wrestle him to the ground. "It'll be fun showing you what a *real* female can do."

Gilen was stronger than me, but I was faster.

I jumped at him and tried to wrap my legs around his torso, but he anticipated my move and threw me back against the ground. I recovered, spinning around to strike at him with a punch, which he dodged, but wasn't quite fast enough to evade my kick that followed. I collided with his shin, and he backed up a step, giving me a small opening that I wouldn't let go to waste. We continued back and forth, exchanging blows, testing each other's weak points, and pushing one another until both of us had sweat dripping from our brows. I cursed under my breath as a coy smile curved at the side of Gilen's mouth—the bastard was toying with me.

"If you only came to our lesson today."

*We'll see about that.*

I lunged for him at a blistering speed I knew he would have difficulty matching. I made a connection with my fist on his jaw, but sadly, that was only the bait to lure me in. Gilen took the hit—losing the battle only to earn his victory in the war. He followed the momentum of my punch, moving backward as he ducked under me and grabbed my wrist, bending it behind my back and twisting my arm.

Ouch. "Dammit," I cursed. With one move, he could dislocate my arm from its socket. I was stubborn … But I also had enough sense to know when to bow out. "I yield," I said as I hung my head and gritted my teeth. I did not like to lose.

"Good … Now, next time come to the training session." His dark brow arched with a cunning half-smirk that made me want to turn around and punch him in his smug, handsome face. My animal sent a pulsing wave of power, agreeing with me, even though I knew it was pointless.

Losing was one thing, but I refused to be a sore loser.

Gilen released me, and I moved away, stripping off my now sweat-soaked loose shirt and pants. My black undergarments were all I kept on my body, enjoying the sea breeze on this warm, late summer day. The winds suddenly shifted, lifting my hair off my shoulders, and gently cooling my neck. It encircled my nearly six-foot frame before dancing off in the other direction, where Gilen stood in the shallow rolling waves.

Suddenly, Gilen's entire body stiffened. His eyes darkened and locked onto my gaze as I threw my clothes on the sand next to his. The intensity of his stare made my hands tremble, and my body shake. Danger. My animal stirred inside my chest, acutely aware of him, but she didn't encourage me to run away.

I closed my amber-colored eyes and lifted my chin, detecting a faint change in the air from Gilen's scent. My eyes snapped to meet his as my breath caught in my chest.

I swallowed nervously. "Gilen?"

Bravely or stupidly—I was not quite sure which one yet—I stepped toward him to try and help, but it seemed to do the opposite. His nostrils flared, and his fists clenched so hard at his side that his knuckles turned white.

"Skylar … Back. The. Fuck. Up. Now!" Gilen was visibly shaking, but he remained frozen where he stood. His eyes looked more feral than human right now, and I could feel his power, his magic, rising around him.

Oh no. His animal was trying to break free. Questions danced inside my mind. What caused this sudden change? Why was Gilen holding back? Why was his animal trying to break free now?

"Gilen. Come back. Come back to me …" I don't know where my commanding voice came from. Some spark inside of me was pushing my instincts into overdrive. It wasn't the time for his animal to emerge—not yet.

Gilen shook his head and forced himself to turn away from me. His blond hair fell in front of his face as his shoulders hunched forward. Every muscle in his body flexed, trying to fight the urge to shift.

"Gilen!" I didn't yell, but my voice deepened. My power pulsed, begging to break free. Without thinking, I moved in front of Gilen and flung my arms around his neck. I pulled him in close and pushed my body up against his. I could feel his resistance as I tightened my hold on him. He was a solid wall of muscle, and I was naively asking him to soften and bend to my hold. If his animal broke free right now, he would be in grave danger. There was no full moon. No one was here to guide him through his first shift. Gilen could lose himself forever to his animal form.

Desperation pulled at me, and I released my own power from its internal cage. "Do not shift. Release him." My words thrummed with my animal's magic; my eyes glowing. But I had no choice. I would not lose him.

Gilen turned his head and inhaled a deep breath against the nape of my neck, sending chills of excitement down each vertebra of my spine into my toes. He was marking my scent, putting the smell and feel of my power into memory. Strong arms wrapped around my waist as he picked me up and held me closer to him. He rubbed his nose along my collarbone, and his lips hovered over my skin, daring to make contact.

Deep, slow breaths countered my own racing heart. Gilen slowly released me back onto the shore, his hands moving down my lower back, his touch lighter, but still a burning presence. A low growl emerged from deep within his chest that made the hairs on my neck stand at attention. Gilen's scent surrounded my senses, causing my stomach to flip.

I dared to pull myself away and release my arms from around his shoulders, allowing my hands to trace the bulging muscles on his chest and arms. I couldn't bring myself to pull away from him just yet, though. I didn't have the courage to look at him. What would he think of me now that he felt a taste of the true power I had tried to keep hidden?

"Look at me." Gilen's voice was deep and raspy. Almost like the claws of his animal had scrapped at his insides, trying to break free. I hesitated … afraid of how he would react or what he would say. "Now."

My head turned, and my eyes snapped open to meet his.

Fire.

I knew he would see the fire glowing in my eyes from the well of magic I kept caged inside my soul. My amber eyes were rare, even among the High Fae and human races. When I allowed my power to break through the surface, my eyes danced to the freedom of the ignited blaze contained within.

Neither one of us moved, or uttered a sound. It felt like days, even months, in those few seconds together on the shifting sand. Gilen's right hand reached up to cup the nape of my neck. His fingers laced through my long, wild hair, gently pulling it to his nose as his cheek brushed against mine. He inhaled a deep breath, closing his eyes for a moment before snapping them open once more.

The fire, the hunger, I saw lingering in his golden depths took my breath away. Gilen had never looked at me like that before.

I didn't know what to do, and I don't think he knew either. This gesture of memorizing another's scent was only reserved for mating among shifters. To allow another's presence to mold into our memory so they were an extension of ourselves.

Gilen bent to whisper in my ear, "Your fire does not scare me, Skylar. I always knew it was there. It just needed to come out and find its match to help tame it."

Holy, shit. If only he knew this was just a taste of what I fought to contain. What my animal held. Shifters respected power. It was irrefutable, undeniable, with our alpha always holding the deepest wells of it. But to reveal how much I truly had … as a half-breed. Well, I wasn't brave enough to test how that theory would pan out with our pack.

A rush of heat danced across the surface of my skin where our half-naked bodies were still entangled together. I could sense his desire rise in turn with my own, causing a deep pulsing sensation to build between the apex of my legs. The thought of being with Gilen had crossed my mind more than a few times, but this reality held little to no comparison. I shifted in his arms to press my brow to his and felt myself sink deeper into his hold.

"I'm not a helpless, dainty female that you can easily claim," I challenged as my amber eyes snapped open to meet his. "You'll have to fight for me." Gilen's lips curled into a smile, mere breaths away from my own. I huffed a laugh and easily slithered out of his grasp. If he wanted to, I knew he could keep me there, but he allowed me to slip away.

"Race you to the cliffs," I yelled as I took off at a sprint, knowing he was not far behind me.

# Chapter Two

As expected, I reached the top of the cliff lengths ahead of Gilen. A beaming smile crossed my face as I saw our pack mates waiting at the top. I could have guessed the young ones were not jumping unsupervised, and our group loved doing this almost as much as they did. Rhea, Shaw, and Talon lounged near the edge of the overhang, waiting for us to join.

"Ha! Pay up," Rhea taunted as she reached out her hand toward Shaw and Talon. "And … don't whimper or complain. I don't give two licks about your pride in this. I told you my girl Sky would win. You never should've doubted her, *or me.*" Neither of them acknowledged her demand, forcing Rhea to jump to her feet and strut over to them.

Rhea's long, auburn-brown locks that curled at the middle of her back swayed in rhythm with her affirmative march. She had dark blue eyes paired with delicate freckles on her cheeks that enhanced her remarkable, cunning beauty. She swung her hair to the side before bending forward to whisper something in Talon's ear. His own pale blue eyes widened, and he quickly reached over into his adopted brother Shaw's pocket, retrieving one gold coin to pair with his own.

"Here," Talon grunted, his dark brows narrowing as he glared at Rhea. "No need to start that fight up again."

Talon was the stable, loyal peacemaker of the group and could always be found by his best friend Gilen's side. Actually, when any of us needed him, Talon was there. He looked after us, added in a joke to lighten a mood, or tried to settle any disagreements in our inner circle. But recently, one female shifter in particular was able to get under his skin.

"You know it's not ladylike to gloat," Talon mumbled as he plopped the coins into Rhea's outstretched hand, scuffing his crooked nose that was broken more than a few times in his youth.

"Who are you trying to fool? I'm a shifter, not some pampered highbrow *lady.*" Satisfied with her bounty, Rhea spun herself around and gave me a triumphant grin. "Sky, we are celebrating tonight! And

I'm buying."

"Only fair, seeing that I earned it," I added as I cooled myself on the breeze by the cliff face. I glanced back to see Gilen slow his pace and leisurely walk the remaining distance to the top.

"But my wisdom earned us this trove." The ever-confident Rhea flaunted her victory in front of Talon and Shaw, shamelessly continuing to gloat.

That was a part of Rhea's unique outspoken charm.

When we were kids, Rhea was the one who encouraged me to formally challenge the female shifter who teased me for my half-blood. She told me to never put up with their shit, that they were just jealous of what I could do. What I could become. Even though I lost that first challenge, she never let me stop fighting, and helped me pick myself up and try again.

"Where would I be without you, Rhea?" I asked sarcastically.

"Richer," Talon scoffed quietly, knowing that we could all hear him with our enhanced hearing abilities as shifters.

Rhea pivoted around to face him, shooting her own challenging glare right back at him. Completely unafraid. And if it was possible, I admired her even more.

"What's got your mangy fur twisted in knots, Talon?" I asked, continuing to push the tension. There was something brewing between these two, and everyone was ready for them to finally figure it out.

"Yeah … don't pout, Talon Black," Rhea countered. "It's ill-becoming of a male. Not the best way to attract a worthy female as a mate … if that's what you intend to accomplish one of these days now that you've shifted."

Talon crossed his arms and glared at Rhea with a menacing scowl. Whatever Rhea had whispered to him earlier must have hit a nerve, and that was hard to do with the two Black brothers.

"When you see a worthy female," Talon said with a forbidding gleam in his frosted gaze. "Let me know, and I'll be sure to turn on the charm."

I cautiously took a step backward. I liked to push the envelope, but this was one of those situations where I did not want to get mixed up in whatever was going on between them.

I glanced over at Shaw, who gave me a nod, telling me that he was thinking the same thing. We didn't want any part of this. Over the past few months, Talon and Rhea had been arguing with each other non-stop. We all stopped keeping count of the number of disagreements because there were simply too many to keep track of.

Shaw, Talon's adopted brother, was taken in by the Black family when he was only seven years old. We formed a friendship through our love of reading and in competition to be the brightest students in our schooling years. Shaw was the ever-watchful, calculating member of our circle. His clever mind and caution helped our group out of trouble that I and, at times, Rhea, unfortunately, got us into.

Gilen finally joined us near the cliff as Shaw wisely stepped away from his brother's side. "And this is where I bow out," Shaw announced. "See y'all at the bottom." With those last words, he took three swift steps and launched himself off the cliff and into the waters below.

"Watch yourself, Talon," Rhea growled. "We all know how well this turned out last time …" Her eyes shone with a vengeance. Even I was skeptical about approaching Rhea when she got in this mood, and somehow, Talon had a knack for pushing the right buttons to get her there.

Talon grinned, flashing a cocky smile he recently held only for her as he crossed his toned, tanned arms across his chest. Shifting on his feet, he said, "Care to share our secrets with the rest of the group? I know I'm anxious to find out more for myself."

Rhea's cheeks flushed red, and she lashed out with her balled fists, throwing a mean right hook. "You mangy … low-life … dog!" she snarled.

Without hesitation, Talon caught her fist in his hand, spun her around, and pulled Rhea tightly into his arms, holding her steady. Her back was against Talon's bare chest, and he grinned, keeping a firm hold on his prize. His speed was remarkable and unmatched by anyone else in our circle because Talon was the first among us to shift.

I felt Gilen's power stir like untamed wind, responding to their scuffle, but he remained where he was at my side. Rhea was not one to go down easy. On cue, she bent her head forward and bit Talon's hand so hard that he yelped—quickly releasing her.

"Dammit, Rhea!" Talon yelled, shaking his hand and examining the teeth marks etched in his skin. "I think you drew blood!"

"Don't fuck around with a female if you can't handle what she can throw at you," Rhea spat back at Talon.

"Don't test me …" Talon taunted, glaring at her with heat building behind his strae. Without another word, Rhea turned toward the cliff and dove head-first into the waters below.

"Can't you command her not to fight dirty or something, Gilen?" Talon asked. "Being the best friend of the future alpha has to have some perks, right?"

Gilen shifted and discreetly brushed a hand across the small of my back before folding it casually behind his head. "Find a more docile female to curb your needs then, Talon. I hear Daphanie has been eyeing you since you shifted." Talon narrowed his eyes, darting between Gilen and me.

Did he sense something between us? Was there a change in our scents only his evolved shifter abilities could detect? I didn't dare bring up what had just happened between us on the beach. I don't think either of us really understood it enough to talk about it with the others. This was unchartered territory between Gilen and me.

"Right," Talon huffed with a cutting laugh. "Anything new you two care to share with the rest of us today?"

Gilen dropped his hands from behind his head as his expression turned cold and stern. He stepped toward his friend, a deep, rumbling growl protruding from his chest. With a pulse of his power, Gilen snarled at Talon, "As Rhea would say … choose your words wisely."

There was some unspoken exchange between them that only shifters would understand. We couldn't communicate with words to our other half; it was more of feeling and connection with our emotions, kind of like a sixth sense combined with enhanced instincts.

This was an animalistic dance of dominance and power, sniffing out the pecking order between the two of them. Even though Talon was stronger as a full shifter, the power of an alpha always shone through, impossible for any shifter, well aside from me, to ignore. Gilen was next in line to become our pack's leader—the only son and heir to our current alpha, Alistar.

"Okay, ease up, you two. Time to simmer down." I wiggled myself between them and placed a hand on both their chests. I didn't wait to give either of them a chance to say another word, so I shoved them backward, causing them to tumble over the cliff and into the water below. Not wanting to be left out of the fun, I leaped in after them. The free fall into the water was short-lived but exhilarating. I splashed down next to Gilen just as he pushed himself to the surface.

I dove down toward the reef, where colorful fish darted in and out of their protected homes. The currents under the rolling waves above carried me, giving me a warm embrace as I drifted toward the sandy bottom. Majestic sea creatures casually swam around me, adjusting to my presence in the underwater world. The home of these animals was, sadly, not as beautiful as it once was. Large sections of the once colorful reef were stark white and slowly dying. The acceptance of our world withering away into nothing was difficult, but the evidence was hard to miss. The worst part was that we didn't know why or how to stop it from progressing.

The waters I sank into muffled the commotion above the surface, and it allowed my mind to drift. My animal was still restless, and this quiet allowed me to calm the anxiety rushing through me. Our relationship and soul connection had always been strong. She never pressured me for dominance or control. Instead, we held a symbiotic relationship that I treasured.

We were one being.

She gave me strength when I needed a push, and I gave her stability when she was teetering on the edge of control. I could only imagine what our first shift would be like. To embody the other half of my soul would complete the missing piece of the puzzle of who I really was. I often dreamed of what animal I would become, but regardless of what type it was … I knew it would be magnificent.

The young ones who leaped into the waters before us were busy splashing and taking turns diving down to the bottom to retrieve shells. I watched a few swim past and gave a friendly wave as they retrieved their various trinkets from the depths below. Feeling my lungs begin to burn, I kicked off the sandy bottom and rocketed upward to join the others at the surface. Breaching the water, I inhaled a deep breath of fresh air that filled my lungs with cool relief.

"I thought you drowned," Rhea teased.

"Well, glad to know you'd come looking for me, at least," I answered. "Where did Gilen and the others go?"

"Talon challenged them all to swim out to the rocks."

"And you didn't join them? Not like you to back down."

Rhea rolled her eyes. "Not with you being a potential drowning victim. I had to stay behind to make sure you came back up alive."

"Again … I am so lucky to have you, Rhea." We both laughed and moved to float on our backs, resting head to toe in the gentle rolling waves.

As young children, before we were aware of our animal spirits, some of the others in the pack looked down on me for being half-human. Saying I would never truly be one of them because I was a late bloomer and that I would never be able to control my power enough to shift. Rhea stepped in right away and stood up for me. Making it clear with her words, and possibly her fists, that regardless of my bloodline, I was pack.

"What do you think they're talking about?" I asked out of curiosity.

"Always with the questions. Can't you just sit and relax without your mind spinning?" I silently grinned. We both knew the answer to that was a clear no. "Typical male nonsense," Rhea answered with a heavy sigh. "They are a mystery … And honestly, I'm not sure I want to know."

I circled my arms in the water, mulling over the interaction between Gilen and me on the beach earlier. Maybe he wasn't even asking Talon about it at all? Regardless, I needed answers.

The sun was beginning to lower along the horizon. "We better start heading in soon," I said to Rhea.

"Five more minutes."

"You always say that," I argued as I tilted my head up out of the water.

"And it's usually a good idea."

The males were still out on the rocks, but the younger ones were beginning to head toward the shoreline for the trek home. They didn't need us to follow them the short distance back to the main village, but I wanted to ensure they stayed out of trouble.

"Come on," I murmured as I splashed Rhea with water. "You know what tomorrow night is. We should prepare back at home with the others." I turned in the water and began swimming toward the shoreline.

"Fine. You win." Rhea spun around and followed my lead.

Gilen, Talon, and Shaw were all still on the outer rocks, and from the looks of it, they were still deep in conversation.

"They know the way back," Rhea added as we reached the shore. "Besides, we have two gold coins to burn at the tavern. I foresee two large and well-deserved spirits for us tonight. Maybe even whiskey."

I nodded. "With the ascension and the full moon tomorrow night, I don't see why not."

"That's the spirit." Rhea beamed as she looped an arm around my shoulder.

"I'll meet you back at the village," I said, suddenly remembering

I left my belongings on the other shoreline. "I need to go back to the green sand beach and get my books and clothes."

"We are shifters." Rhea laughed, gesturing at her fair skinned half-naked body. "You know the adults just walk around nude half the time anyway from their shifts back and forth between their animal and human forms."

"My books are there!"

Rhea threw up her hands in defeat. She knew I would never risk the safety of those books. "Say no more. Go. I'll meet you in one hour at the tavern. Don't be late."

I nodded. "I'll see you then, my friend." I wouldn't forgive myself if I left my books at the mercy of the washing waves. Solace's library needed all the material it could get, and I wasn't going to be the one to take away stories for others to read.

My clothes were right where I had left them, with the books stacked inside my bag—safe from the damaging rough sand. I reached for my clothes and noticed Gilen's shirt lying beside mine. I quickly dressed and then paused, looking down at his belongings. I didn't think he would return for his shirt, so I decided it would be kind of me to bring it back to town for him.

I scooped it up, brought it close to my chest, and inhaled deeply, smelling his scent in his clothing. I don't know why I suddenly had the urge to do this. When in doubt, blame my other half—a shifter trait, I guess …

The crisp aroma of salty air, the spicy scent of sand dunes, and the open wild skies flooded my senses. However, there was no spark of electricity. Instead, a calming presence of safety and serenity, like being wrapped up in a warm blanket in front of a burning fire in the hearth.

But … Hmm.

I didn't feel any kind of heightened emotion stirring from my animal. It did, however, hold some elements that Julia, my aunt and surrogate mother, told me about when she first felt the mating bond with Uncle Magnus.

I lingered for a moment in contemplation before chalking it up to the fact that I was simply not ready to shift just yet. Gilen clearly was, though, so maybe he was able to sense something I was not. Annoyed by my lack of understanding and even more questions spinning in my head, I stuffed Gilen's shirt in my pack and headed for home.

# Chapter Three

I walked onto the porch of my family home and gently turned the handle of the door to enter. Due to my uncle's standing in the pack, we were more fortunate than most. The rustic two-story house held three bedrooms upstairs, with an enclosed kitchen, study, and family room downstairs. Large windows were in every room, keeping the connection to the surrounding nature that we and our animals craved. The elaborate garden in the back just outside the kitchen was a masterpiece that we all enjoyed from the hard work of my dear cousin, Neera.

The smell of the decadent stew brewing from the kitchen filled the house, and my mouth was already beginning to water. Julia was the heart and soul of this family—and man, could she cook. I tried my best to take after her in the kitchen, but some recipes never turned out the same. Baking, however, now that was where I shinned.

I turned the corner and placed my bag on the nearby chair as Julia called out to me, "I'm sorry I started without you. Magnus and Neera were starving, and I didn't know when you'd return."

I scurried over to the fire and examined the boiling pot over the open flames. "Seems like you did just fine without me. It smells amazing!"

Julia blushed against the freckles on her tanned cheeks. Her luscious brown curls fell freely over her headband as she brushed a bead of sweat from her brow due to the heat of the boiling stew pot. "Thanks. I could still use some help with the bread, though. Mind checking on it for me?"

"Sure thing," I answered as I snuck a spoonful of the stew into my mouth without her noticing. I rationalized that it needed to be taste tested before serving it to the others, and I had no problem being the tester when it came to Julia's cooking. "Anything else you need? What type of meat did you decide to use in this one? Did the carrots get added last, or did you put the celery in before?"

Julia rolled her eyes at my continuous questions. She was used to it at least and didn't seem to mind when it centered around what was cooking in the kitchen. "Just focus your special touch on the bread … I will fill you in as you work."

"Where are Neera and Magnus anyway?" I asked as I left the delicious pot of stew and moved toward the oven.

I noticed Julia eyeing my spoon full of stew, but she smiled sweetly, ignoring my impatient, growling stomach.

Shifters were always hungry, and I mean always. Our metabolisms ran higher compared to humans, and our body temperatures were on the warmer side as well. It came in handy when the adults shifted, and they didn't have a scrap of clothing on them. They didn't need it to stay warm, even in the colder months of winter.

"Neera was tired, so I sent her upstairs to rest before dinner," Julia said, glancing up toward the second floor where our rooms were located. "And Alistar called Magnus to his quarters in the main house before you arrived. It seemed urgent."

Our pack lands encompassed the northern section of the mainland of Valdor, hosting the entire population of shifters in our world. Alistar, as our alpha, oversaw and protected hundreds … maybe close to a few thousand of us now. An alpha was comparable to a king or queen in the fae or human customs, and my uncle Magnus was his second—his beta.

"Huh, that's weird." I wondered what would cause Alistar to call his beta in such haste. Gilen and the others didn't seem pressed by anything besides being tired from a training session that I managed to meander away from. Hmm. Maybe I should have attended the group training session after all. "Magnus didn't say why?"

"Nothing. Just that he would be back as soon as he could." Julia didn't seem worried or upset, and it helped put me at ease.

"I imagine he will, considering the delicious feast you were preparing in the kitchen."

Julia's kind brown eyes shone with a spark of pride and gratitude at my compliment. "It would have been better with my trusty assistant in the kitchen with me."

I smiled as I turned the bread in the open oven and sprinkled chunks of butter into the cuts on top of the loaf. It would crisp in a few minutes, giving it a crunchy texture I knew my cousin Neera couldn't get enough of. "I'm sorry," I said. "Gilen found me on the beach, and we ended up cliff diving with the others."

"Not surprising," Julia muttered unkindly to herself. It took me by surprise, so I turned and gave her a curious eyebrow raise. "He stopped by today, looking for you. I told him you had a new batch of books to read, and that was all the hint he needed to find you, I guess." Julia slowly turned the ladle and glanced up at the top shelf. "Reach that for me, please?"

I wasn't done interrogating her soured tone when I mentioned Gilen. "Sure thing," I replied as I shuffled over to the cabinet and easily reached the spice rack on the top shelf.

"Thank the gods you were blessed with a height advantage from your father. I would never get this recipe right without you."

Emery, my father, was the former alpha of the Solace pack. Former due to the fact that he died fighting for the land treaty with the current human king, Taran, before I was born. My mother, well, there was not much to tell or know about her besides the fact that she was human.

Twenty-two years ago, I was abandoned, wrapped in a purple blanket that I still had tucked under my pillow, on the outskirts of the Solace pack lands. Thankfully, my uncle Magnus found me and instantly knew I was his kin—an extension of his family—sensing my father, his lost brother's, scent on me. There was no questioning that I was coming home with him—half-shifter or not. I was family. I was a part of the pack.

Towering just under six feet tall, I was almost a foot over Julia's barely five-foot-three stature. "Happy to oblige," I said as I handed her the spices and watched Julia calculate which ones to add to the stew to make it just right. "Oh, before I forget to tell you. Rhea wants me to meet her at the tavern tonight. Did you need anything before I go meet her?"

"No, but I do appreciate you checking in with me. Even though you're old enough to be living out on your own," Julia added with a wink. "Come on, Skylar … any males tickling your fancy lately? You are almost at the prime mating age with your shift likely happening sooner rather than later." Julia couldn't help gossiping. She and my younger cousin Neera both, actually. I held an adventurous, independent spirit and found myself in the middle of things often, but gossip was something I tried to avoid.

"And leave this paradise?" I laughed, gesturing to the room. "Not a chance. Can't get rid of me that easily."

"And we wouldn't want to," Julia replied with a genuine motherly smile. "Your shift will come all too soon for us, Skylar. I'm excited for you … but also …" Julia sniffled.

"Don't get emotional on me now," I said, trying to comfort my aunt. "I don't plan on leaving anytime soon. Where else would I go that could even remotely compete with my home?"

"You're just as wild as your animal, Skylar. With all the books you read and the time you spend daydreaming of adventures, you're not meant to be caged. You are meant to leave our quiet life here for something worthy of that special magic I feel from you." Tears pooled in Julia's eyes, blurring her vision, and she missed the placement of her ladle. "Ahh!" Julia gasped as the hot iron of the pot burned her hand. I could see her skin bubble and turn bright red in an instant.

I reached out to inspect her. "This is a good one," I said, moving her hand over gently in my own, careful not to inflict any more damage caused by the hot cast iron.

Closing my eyes, I concentrated on the ever-present pool of magic that spiraled around in my chest. I steadied myself and released a small burst of my power, magically healing the burn on my aunt's hand.

"And thank the gods for your mother's gifts," Julia said as she examined her hand.

Shifters naturally healed quickly, but I had a special gift thanks to my mother's human bloodline. An ability that helped raise my status in the pack despite being only a half-shifter.

Some humans, defined as mages, had an innate ability to access the magic embedded in this world. The human king, Taran, highly coveted these mages and protected them by any means necessary. Some, like me, and we believe my mother, had a healing magical gift, while others dabbled in various crafting spells that varied from love potions to poisons, and even weapons. I mean … it was magic, right? So anything was possible with enough connection to the right power source.

My healing magic was an inherited trait from my mother that I cherished. It was a special piece of her that I was able to carry with me, similar to the gift of sharing my life with an animal spirit that I received from my father. I always saw it as their protection, a way to carry them with me even if they were never physically at my side.

"Lucky is an understatement," I said. "I'm pretty sure it's the reason why Alistar keeps me on the scouting party lines with Gilen and the others. I'm a twenty-two-year-old, unmated half-breed who hasn't shifted yet. Everyone else my age is showing signs of shifting during tomorrow's full moon, while I'm still a mystery. My healing abilities are my only asset as of now until I shift. I'm sure of it."

"Magnus says your father was a late bloomer like you, and he was an alpha. Don't take that into account for the power you will have once you are able to shift. You've shown potential in your combat training and especially archery … when you *decide* to show up." Julia left the final comment hanging between us for a moment. She knew of my ability to disregard the alpha's command.

"Yes … Well, it still doesn't answer my questions."

"Which ones? You never stop having them." Julia smiled and rose up onto her toes to kiss my cheek. She paused and stiffened her stance as she slowly moved a step back.

"Julia? Is everything okay?" I was suddenly worried. She had a peculiar look on her face that was laced with uncertainty—very uncharacteristic of her typical easygoing demeanor.

"You said Gilen found you on the beach today?" The coldness in her tone had my animal perking up inside me.

"Yes?" I answered, my voice unnaturally quivering as I squinched my expression.

That didn't sound good. Did this have to do with what happened on the beach? My senses were not keen enough to detect anything compared to an adult shifter. What did Julia smell on me?

Julia pursed her lips around a clenched jaw. "That stupid, idiotic boy! I won't even give him the courtesy of saying male, because he was clearly not thinking this through as a male should." She began tapping her foot, her mind clearly spinning. "He did not … No … This is *not* okay." Her eyes radiated with a hint of green shimmer that spiraled around her. Whatever made her upset, her animal was raging as well.

"Slow down, Julia. You're rambling, and no one can understand you when you do that." I could see her revert inward as she grabbed the ladle and aggressively continued to stir the stew. Julia rarely got this upset. Like her daughter Neera, she was a gentle soul. But then again, when Julia was angry, we all knew to clear the way. Something was going on, and my curiosity was not going to let this go.

"Spill it, Julia. What's got your cat's fur standing on end? You know I'll only continue to pester you until you spill the beans." Julia's animal form was a fiercely cunning mountain lion, an animal that you did not want to ever mess with.

"I can smell him," she snapped with a low feline growl attached.

"Him? Him … who?" Julia spun around, narrowing her dark brown eyes and glaring so hard at me that I could barely see the whites of her eyeballs. "Gilen?"

Julia scoffed and turned away from me as she continued to stir the stew. "I shouldn't be able to smell him on you, Skylar. Not like this—"

"I can't smell anything different," I admitted as I scrambled to look for my bag. Reaching inside, I grabbed Gilen's discarded shirt and presented it to Julia with an arm cocked out on my hip. "Is this what you smell?"

Julia sniffed the shirt and firmly shook her head. "No. It's more than that."

"Then enlighten me."

Julia sighed heavily, setting the spoon aside and firmly pressing her palm to her forehead. "Neither of you has shifted yet. You don't understand the mark he is starting to place on you—it … it's a warning, Skylar."

"A warning? From Gilen? Okay … Okay. I only have more questions now."

"Naturally," Julia mumbled as she grabbed a bowl from the shelf. "Sit and eat," she commanded. "I will tell you more once you have some food in your rumbling stomach."

"Can't I just wait until I get back from the tavern?" I asked.

"Not the best idea. You need to stay out for a bit longer tonight. I don't want Magnus coming home and discovering what I smelled on you."

I grunted in disappointment, unhappy with the lack of information Julia was willing to share. It was never this difficult to get answers from her, so this had my head spinning even more. A bowl full of stew slid across the kitchen island, and my growling stomach won the glaring battle I had begun with my aunt. I grabbed the spoon and proceeded to silence at least one of my needs for the time being.

"Gilen will likely shift during tomorrow's full moon," Julia said as she walked over to the oven to remove the baking bread. She cut me a slice and set it next to my already half-eaten bowl of stew. "In fact, I would bet my entire recipe book that he will. It's practically a guarantee."

"Yeah, I could have guessed that," I answered with a mouth half full of food. Everyone could sense his rising powers. I was surprised it hadn't happened already.

"And have you thought about what else occurs when we shift for the first time? When our animals emerge, and we are able to find and feel our mate bond?"

"I …" *To be honest, I hadn't thought about that part.* Gods be damned … Why hadn't I thought about that?

"The scent that Gilen has faintly marked on you is a warning to all other shifters to basically *back off.* It is a clear sign that he intends to claim you as his mate … Nothing in an official capacity, but—"

"But one that is pretty damn close to official." I angrily sank my teeth into my bread and allowed the delicious buttery crisp crust to bring a hint of goodness into my life. "I didn't … We didn't." I was beginning to panic as my cheeks flushed a dark crimson color.

"I know," Julia blurted, almost laughing to herself. "Trust me … if *that* had happened, I wouldn't have to kiss your cheek to smell him on you. I would have sensed it before you opened the door."

I sighed with relief—I think.

I would be lying to myself if I said I never secretly hoped that maybe, just maybe, Gilen and I were mates. It made no logical sense due to the fact that I was a half-breed, and Gilen was the heir of our alpha. But then again, my father had been an alpha. My most recent love affair, I thought, could have been the one until he shifted and then promptly dumped me, never really giving me a reason why.

"So stay out until … Is there a time frame I should stick to?"

Julia put a hand on her chin to think. "Tomorrow, you should be fine. Gilen's scent should be gone by the morning."

"It's not *that* strong, is it?" I asked with uneasiness.

"No, only a full shifter with close proximity to you would be able to detect it." Now Talon's reaction on the cliffs made sense.

I nodded and quickly devoured the rest of my bowl before using the bread to wipe up the yummy bits hidden at the bottom. "Right, so don't run into Magnus until tomorrow morning. You are sure, that no one else would be able to smell this marking Gilen put on me?"

"Again, only adult shifters, and they would have to be very close to you. It is faint, but it is still there," Julia warned.

"Good. I never asked him … I mean, ugh. This is—"

"I know." Julia's kind smile somehow made it feel like everything would be all right.

I placed my bowl in the sink and washed it before returning it to the cupboard. "I'll see you tomorrow then."

"Try not to make too much noise when you stumble back home," Julia teased.

"Can't make any promises." I laughed. "I swear to the gods I am as quiet as a mouse!"

"No, my dear Skylar. You are most certainly not. The more you try to be quiet, the louder you are. You're just as bad as your father and Magnus. I wouldn't be surprised if your animal turned out to be a bear, just like them."

There was no guarantee for what type of animal we would

eventually shift into. It was a special secret, the hidden truth to a piece of your identity. Even if both parents were hawks or bears, there was no promise the offspring would follow suit. There were trends, of course. Wolves were the primary animal, followed by other large predators of the land and sky. When we were kids, we used to love guessing what type of animals lived within our souls.

I couldn't help but grin. "Are you saying I lack your grace and elegance? That I won't be shifting into a type of predatory cat?"

Julia's animal was a large, deadly mountain lion. She might be small and seem docile in her human form, cooking up a storm in the kitchen like a tamed housewife, but when she needed to … Julia unleashed hell itself. Her animal form was utterly terrifying if you crossed her. It was enough to even force Magnus, who, by the way, was a giant grizzly bear standing taller than a horse on all fours, to bend to her will.

"Not a chance." Julia grinned with a feline glimmer in her dark, predatory eyes. "Now hurry along. We'll see you tomorrow."

I turned on my heels and left the same way I came in. Julia's uneasiness was nothing to be taken lightly, and now my head was spinning again with all kinds of questions. What was Gilen thinking? What in the gods' names did this mean? He was an alpha's heir, and I was a nerdy, impatient, at times reckless … half-human shifter.

In shifter mating rituals, males physically marked their intended females with a bite mark at the base of their neck, but it was mutual with the female doing the same. Their scents also combining, intertwining as one. Sure, I dabbled in romantic relationships with other males in our pack, but nothing ever lasted.

But Gilen and me had never even kissed.

I decided to take the scenic route to the tavern to meet Rhea. The main street was paved with cobblestone, while other pathways off to the side leading to smaller cottages and shops were packed down with dirt. The thick collection of white spruce and birch trees outlining the pathways provided cover, and the smell of wild nature surrounding me softened my anxiety.

The fewer shifters I interacted with, the better. Since our pack's alpha, Alistar, called Magnus and likely other leaders to his home, that meant our tavern's typical attendees would be absent.

I stepped out of the woods and walked the dirt pathway toward my destination. The tavern's heavy wooden door swung open, and I ducked quickly inside to inspect who was there. Luckily, it was early, and the normal occupants seemed to be absent. In the oil lamps and candles on various tables, I spotted Rhea off in the corner, waving her arm to get my attention. She already had multiple drinks sitting on the table in front of her, waiting for us to enjoy. I sank into the wooden corner bench and eagerly reached for the cup of wine she coaxed in my direction.

"All right … spill. What happened?" Rhea sighed, swallowing a hefty swig out of her own glass.

Damn Rhea and her annoyingly accurate intuition. "How'd you know something happened?" I snapped, perhaps with a little too much bite. Lucky for me, though, she didn't seem to even blink at the tone I threw her way.

"Don't dodge my question with another question." She slid a smaller glass into my hand and raised her own. "You know the drill." She threw her head back, swallowed the rest of her strong, oaky whiskey, and turned the glass upside down on the table. She arched her brow at me, a sign that I was supposed to follow her lead.

"Fine." Grumbling under my breath, I tilted my head back, reached for the whiskey, and drained my own glass. I squirmed as the liquid sprouted fire in the back of my throat and forcefully slammed it on the wooden table as a tavern maid wandered past us.

"Going to need another, Elain," Rhea said, grabbing our empty glasses.

Elain, the barkeep, smiled sweetly as she cocked an arm on her curvy waist and approached our table. "You two at it again, I see."

"It's all *her* fault," I exclaimed, pointing at Rhea. "I'm the innocent one here. I'm only a half-shifter, so I burn through the effects of this stuff slower than she does."

Elain laughed to herself as she gathered our glasses from the table. "Whatever you say, Skylar. The customer is always right." She gave me a playful wink that I was sure was mastered over the years to pull at the heartstrings of the males who still fawned over her beauty.

Elain had dark blond hair paired with warm chocolate-brown eyes that made you melt. Her animal form was a beautiful white fox that you couldn't miss even if you tried. Elain was only a handful of years older than us and, thankfully, always treated me just like anyone else. She had no idea how much it meant to me, but every time we came to the tavern, I made sure we gave her an extra coin on our tab.

"Don't pout," Rhea said as she sipped another helping of the earthy-scented drink. Elain looked at me, and I shook my head, indicating I was fine with the one I already regretted drinking and would be content with the remaining glass of wine. "You cheat," Rhea hissed. "You know you can heal a hangover, right? Just like a wound. You have the magic to heal literally anything."

"Not for myself," I countered. "Wait, is this why you drag me out to the taverns with you? So I can heal you after a night of overindulging in liquor?"

She grinned. "I always said you were the clever one between the two of us."

I took a long sip of the wine, the warmth of the drink churning my stomach and loosening the cage of my inhibitions. I never was able to hold my liquor well. At least not when I compared it to any other shifter in the pack who could easily drink me under the table.

"So," Rhea said, "what was going on today with you and Gilen?" She always had a clever way of striking straight to the heart of a topic.

"Was it that obvious?" I sighed, sinking my rosy cheeks into the palms of my hands and leaning onto the wooden bar table. "Dear. Gods, Mother and Father … Do we really have to talk about this right now?"

"There you go with the questions again. Yes, it is obvious. And yes, we are going to talk about it. It's the whole reason why I made you come to the tavern and force-fed you whiskey. I know it's already working its magic, so … tell me everything."

I took another gulp of my wine and began to divulge all the details Julia told me in the kitchen about what Gilen did on the beach and how I apparently now have his scent on me. Being the amazing friend Rhea was, she sat in silence as I told her everything. She did not interrupt once and kept quiet until I finished telling my story.

"So, want me to kick his ass for you?"

"What?" I exclaimed, nearly spitting out my drink. "Rhea!"

"I bet Shaw or even Talon could help. They would gladly help, actually."

"No!" I protested. "I do not want or need you to kick his ass for me. I'm perfectly capable of doing that myself."

Rhea cocked a brow and slanted her blue eyes in my direction. She leaned back on the wooden bench, looking unimpressed. "Uh-huh. Yeah, calling bullshit right now."

"I can handle myself, Rhea. I don't need you or anyone else to do anything."

"I still call bullshit. With anyone else, yes. You are more than capable of handling yourself. But … when it comes to Gilen. No. No, you cannot."

I grunted with annoyance and sipped my glass. She had always known about the crush I had on Gilen, but thankfully never spoke openly about it or shared it with the others.

"Elain, I need another!" I shouted without delay. Elain glided through the near-empty tavern with not one but two refills, anticipating our needs as she always did. "Thank you." I nodded. "I owe you one. Now, back to you." I whirled my head toward Rhea. "What the actual fuck kind of response was that?"

"Harsh language, Sky—very unlike you." Rhea kept a straight expression as she took a long sip from her glass. "He's not the right match for you. I know you've liked the male since we were teenagers, but in the long run, I vote no. Actually, hell no." The joking, fun-loving nature of the evening was beginning to take a turn.

"Elaborate. Now, please."

My worst fears and insecurities were rattling inside my brain. My self-confidence shattered with the thought that I wasn't *good enough* for a male like Gilen. Tainted blood. A male who was going to be the next alpha of our pack needed someone, pure.

"Stop your spiraling," Rhea demanded. "It's not you. It's him." I clamped my lips shut, not asking the questions I was squirming to keep inside. "You are not meant to be caged, Skylar. As the mate of the alpha, you would be shackled to his will. He would be in charge of every aspect of your life and force you to follow in his command more than anyone else. It would be expected of you. It's not a fault of his, but it's just the way he was raised. It's how Alistar is with his mate, Helen. Gilen would try to own you when you are meant to fly free. Your power is too special to keep hidden in this place or behind his shadow."

"Gilen is not the type of male to—"

"Have you thought about what else happens when mates claim each other?" Rhea asked, and I silently stared back at her, cursing the whiskey shot she had me drink. "With a shared claiming mark and bond, you also share your power. Your healing magic would provide the best protection and ability for Gilen to be a true and unmatched alpha. It makes sense why he would want to keep you around."

"I want to protect our pack just as much as anyone else," I argued. "So why would this be a bad thing?"

"I know you do—but some of us are just meant for more. The world is calling to you, Skylar. It always has been … You just haven't woken up and heard it yet."

"What're you saying?" I knew that everything Rhea was telling me was from the heart and how she truly felt.

"I'm not a seer. I don't have magic powers to predict the future … but I have always known you were special. You, my dear friend, would be trapped and suffocated being the mate of a male like Gilen. He will force your hand, expect you to extend his bloodline, and take away your voice. He is not a bad shifter or male by any means. He's my friend too, but …" Rhea pursed her lips.

"But … but what if we are fated mates?" I dared to ask the question I had been pondering since I was a teenager. "What if our animals recognize the bond in each other and we are mates?"

"Then you can tell your animal to stick it where the sun does not shine." Shaw's gravelly voice was unmistakable. "Because she picked the wrong male."

Rhea and I whipped our heads to the seat behind us. "When did you get here?"

"How many of those have you two downed tonight?" Shaw asked as he casually sipped his own drink.

"Apparently not enough," Rhea answered with a sly smirk. "I can still only see one Shaw."

I pulled up a chair and encouraged Shaw to join us. "Come on. Don't be the creeper in the corner and act like you don't know who we are," I teased. "Because, like it or not … you're stuck with us, buddy." After a moment of quiet contemplation, he shook his head and stood up to join our table.

Shaw, like me, was adopted and raised by parents who were not his own. Talon's family took him in after Shaw's parents were captured and killed by a radical, magically altered group of humans called hunters. Shaw was unfortunately not spared from their grasp. The hunters tortured him, slicing his hands and forearms to shreds before releasing him back into the woods of our pack lands. His scars still lingered to this day.

We still didn't know why they let him go, and Shaw refused to talk about the horrors he endured while he was with the hunters. None of us pushed him to do so, either. Hunters were still known to wander into our lands and capture shifters for mere sport.

"What do you have to add?" I asked Shaw, knowing he had been listening in this whole time.

He brushed back his raven hair that shone with hints of blue in the candlelight and glanced at Rhea with his keen dark eyes. Shaw was careful, always watching and calculating his steps ten paces before the rest of us. I could tell from his shared expression with Rhea that they both definitely knew more than I did.

"You two know something!" I shouted. "Tell me!"

In his own defense, Shaw threw up his scarred hands, his palms facing me. "All I know is that Rhea is more familiar with the mating bond than she would care to admit."

I raised my brows in utter shock, my jaw practically dropping to the table as I turned back to my other friend. "What, really? Rhea, you have been holding out on me!"

She narrowed her eyes. "He told you … didn't he? Gods-damned prick—"

Shaw nodded, flashing a hint of smugness in his grin. "Of course he did."

"Oh my Gods. Talon," I exclaimed and nearly jumped up out of my seat. "Talon! Talon! It has to be." Those two were like an old, mated couple, bickering every chance they got. They challenged each other, and somehow, their spicy mixture of personalities blended perfectly.

"Mother," Rhea cursed. "Shaw, I know Talon's family took you in, and you two are basically brothers … But why did he share that with you?" Rhea buried her face into her hand and signaled to Elain for another round.

"It's what we were discussing while out on the rocks today. Gilen was the one to bring it up, and Talon told him all he knew from his experience with Rhea," Shaw said in his defense. "Even though it was the second time I'd heard it."

"Back to Skylar, please," Rhea groaned, burying her face in her hands.

My heart sank in my chest, and my insides tightened. Gilen was the one asking about the mating bond.

Also … the news that Talon had felt something with Rhea was mind-blowing. But since she hadn't yet shifted, the bond wouldn't completely take root until her animal form was released. She would be able to feel traces of it, though. Like a whisper at the tips of their tongues, but nothing concrete. Now, all their bickering was beginning to make sense.

"Well, what do you think?" I asked Shaw, and I could detect his uneasiness as he shifted in his seat.

"Talon is my brother, and Gilen is my friend." My shoulders sank a little as Shaw paused for a moment, carefully thinking about what to say. "But you are also my friend, Skylar, and I won't lie to you. Gilen is a worthy male … I would be proud to one day call him my alpha and be in his pack. But, as much as it pains me to admit it, Rhea is right. When it comes to you, I'm afraid he would try to cage your fire instead of letting it burn."

"Neither of you are helping."

"You didn't ask for our help. You asked our opinions," Shaw replied calmly. "The real question is how do you feel about him? What are your thoughts?"

I took another long draw from my glass until it was empty. This was a question I asked myself over and over again. How did I feel about Gilen? I was obviously attracted to him, and we had been close companions our entire lives. There wasn't a female around who would deny how handsome, strong, and caring Gilen was. But, was all that enough?

As stupid or foolish as it sounded, I didn't just dream of a mate bond linking me to someone. I needed to feel true love. And I blamed my human side for this fact.

"I think I ..."

My words were cut short by the sound of the tavern door being shoved open by two large wolf paws armed with claws. A massive midnight-black wolf the size of a small horse filled the door frame with pale blue eyes that shone like stars against his ebony fur coat.

Talon.

Rhea kicked her chair back and stood at attention, her stare locking with his from across the tavern. Shaw moved around the table to my right while none other than Gilen emerged at the black wolf's side. His head stood at Talon's shoulder, armed to the teeth with a sword, bow, and various daggers strapped to his frame.

"There you three are," Gilen said with a sigh of relief. "Come with me. My father is calling in every able-bodied shifter to help patrol the borders."

"What's going on?" Shaw asked. I scoffed loudly, annoyed that he beat me to the question.

"Our borders have been breached. We believe *hunters* have entered our pack lands."

That one word sobered every drop of liquor from our bodies. I stood ready to fight, fire blazing brightly in my amber eyes with my animal coming to attention. The *hunters* would pay with their lives if they dared to step foot in our lands.

"Lead the way," I growled with resentment burning in my soul.

# Chapter Four

The night before the full moon gave us the advantage, our powers naturally rising with the phase of the full moon. I didn't know why the hunters thought tonight was a good idea to try their hand at invading our territory, but not much they did made sense to me.

Hunters were a group of magically altered humans that were elite members of the human king Taran's personal army. They were supposed to only protect and defend. Alas, that was not the case. With their increased speed, stealth, strength, and heightened senses, they were the perfect weapon to extinguish the human's greatest threat to their territory—shifters. And, like us, they could see in the dark.

Shifters are not immortal, but we live two or three times the human lifespan. The High Fae, and perhaps other fae subspecies of the Inner Kingdom, were the only beings in Valdor known to be immortal. But none of them have been seen outside their territory for nearly five centuries. They played no part in the dynamics of our daily lives, and frankly, there was enough going on in the mainland of Valdor to keep us busy.

Entering the training grounds behind the alpha's house, we all glanced at Alistar from across the way, watching him become the eye at the center of the storm that engulfed our pack.

Our alpha, Alistar, took the form of a large tan wolf with a gray face with haunting hazel-brown eyes. He diligently watched over his gathering warriors, meticulously calculating and plotting our defenses behind his golden stare. Alistar had the same dark blond hair as his son, Gilen, curling around the nape of his neck and blowing gently in the light breeze that whipped through the open area.

When Alistar looked at you, there was no doubt about his position in our pack. He was our alpha, our leader. He remained calm in the center of all the chaos, keeping a stern but relaxed demeanor among everything spinning around him.

I knew he was telepathically sending out his alpha commands to his various leads, preparing them to advance into the darkening night. No doubt, Magnus had already taken a legion of his bears and was patrolling the southern perimeter.

Everyone was busy gathering weapons or shifting into their animal forms, preparing for a hunt of our own. Gilen led our group to the back of the compound, where a gathering of shifter warriors prepared different scouting parties under Alistar's command. I couldn't help but notice that there was a difference in the way Gilen was walking. His shoulders were pulled back, and the gleam in his golden eyes was focused and calculating. He was beginning to embody the role of alpha, and everyone we passed seemed to notice it as well.

"Arm yourselves." Gilen's deep voice directed the three of us toward the table. It thrummed with power, making it difficult to disobey even if the others wanted to. "Those of you who cannot shift, make sure your fighting leathers are secured and you have enough weapons."

Rhea and I quickly checked the straps of our brown leathers, made sure they were in place, and outfitted ourselves each with a bow and quiver of arrows. I strapped twin daggers to my thighs while Rhea selected a short, curved sword that hung from her hip. Shaw added long twin blades to his back, already wearing an assortment of daggers hidden on his person in various locations. Since he was once caught off guard and unarmed, he had vowed he would never do it again.

"Put these in your quivers," Gilen commanded as he handed Rhea and me a different set of arrows. "And tonight, don't wander far from the group." The last statement I knew was meant specifically for me. He was always the rule follower. Never one to question a command from our alpha, and always first to point out how I made a mistake or didn't do things just the right way.

"Well, what if I see something?" I couldn't help but ask.

Gilen's eyes narrowed and flicked to mine, his annoyance at my question now unmistakable. "Then you report to me, and we investigate it together." Gilen turned and tightened his sword belt before leaning in closer to whisper in my ear, "My father won't tell me exactly what's out there, but I have a strong feeling it's more than just hunters. Please, for me, Sky … don't try to handle a threat without someone with you. Follow the rules I am setting and don't set off on your own."

His plea hit me hard and fast in the center of my chest. I softened my gaze, submitting to his request. I felt my animal stir inside me, not liking the fact that I was backing down without more of a fight. I pushed her influence to the side, knowing that, in this instance, it was better not to pick a fight.

"Fine," I growled with discontentment.

"Fine? Fine is all I get?" Gilen furrowed his brow and crossed his arms in front of his chest.

"*Fine* is the best I can give you right now, Gilen," I huffed as I stuffed the new arrows in my quiver.

The duty to protect our home was the priority, but I was still confused and a bit pissed off when it came to the topic of him and me. We needed to talk, or at the very least, I needed to yell.

"What's wrong?" Gilen asked, daring to take another step closer. His chest brushed up against my arm, his proximity causing goosebumps to trail along the base of my neck.

"This is most certainly not the time or place for this kind of conversation." I motioned around the yard at the gathering shifters. Gilen tilted his head to the side, pursed his lips, and then, out of nowhere, firmly grabbed my arm.

"Hey!" I yelped, pushing back against him.

"Stop," he snarled, dragging me along toward the nearby willow trees. "Come with me, Skylar … Please?"

I gritted my teeth but reluctantly gave in to his plea, following him once he loosened his grip on my arm. I stole a glance back at Rhea, who was holding her arms up, silently asking, *What the hell are you doing*?

I motioned back, *I have no clue,* I added with a melodramatic sigh and an eye roll that I knew Gilen would notice.

Gilen guided me into a collection of willow trees lining the creek at the northern side of the training field. Darting around groups of shifters, he led us into the thick layer of western hemlock that surrounded the alpha's main residence, his home. He knew this route like the back of his hand because this was our secret hideaway.

As children, we would play endless games of hide-and-seek in these woods. Talon, Rhea, and Shaw would join us, but Gilen and I somehow always managed to win. It was where we would tell each other our secrets, whisper our greatest desires, and also share some of our darkest fears. I told him about being afraid I would never feel my animal, and he shared his concern about not being strong enough to become the alpha that fate had thrown onto his shoulders.

When we were older, it was here that Gilen showed me the first painting he had ever dared to create on the surface of a small rock. He always had a passion for recreating the beauty of the world around him, and over the years, between his duties as the alpha's son and vigorous combat training, he had gotten pretty damn good. Alistar even allowed Gilen to paint his portrait for the alpha's mural that hung in the hallway of the manor with our past leaders.

The willow trees provided enough of a divide for us to speak privately with one another and hear anyone if they called out for us. Once we ventured under the thick covering of leaved branches, I crossed my arms in defiance, waiting for Gilen to begin. I leaned my back against the trunk of the willow tree, impatiently tapping my foot against the wild, overgrown root system that peeked up through the dirt. Gilen was the one who had some explaining to do, and I was not going to give him an inch until he started giving me some answers.

"You know, don't you?" His ruffled hair fell in front of his face as he deeply sighed, looking down at his feet. He reached up his hand and fisted his hair in frustration, clutching it tightly as the muscles in his arms flexed. He was nervous. I had never seen him stumble and fidget like this before. I fought back my instinct to try and comfort him … desperate to understand what was going on inside his head.

"I believe *you* have some explaining to do," I stated as firmly as I could.

He turned away from me and growled into the open night air. "Not like this, Sky. I didn't want to have *this* conversation right now—"

"Excuse me?" I wasn't going to allow him to turn away from me, so I boldly blocked his escape path. I didn't care if he was conflicted. I was prepared to beat the answer out of him if I needed to. "What is going on, Gilen? You marked me with your scent on the beach today and somehow memorized mine?"

"It was out of my control," he countered, looking even more nervous than he had before. "It was my animal!"

"What was?" I spat back at him, narrowing my dark brows with venomous anger lacing my words.

Gilen swallowed heavily, stammering as he spoke. "I-I'm losing control, and I don't know what is happening." This took me by surprise. Gilen was always the confident one, the most grounded between the two of us. Never questioning who or what he was.

He reached out his hand and brushed his fingers across my cheek. Startled, I staggered backward a step, but he countered, matching my movements perfectly. Looking at him, I couldn't help succumbing to the openness etched in Gilen's stare.

"I'm going to shift tomorrow," he whispered.

"You don't say?" I raised my brows at him as he huffed a humorous laugh. I could feel the thrum of his animal's power pulsing like the wild wind. Begging to break free. I knew his skin itched with the need to shed his human form and embrace the other half of his soul. It was like that for all shifters.

"So what does this all mean, Gilen? You have never shown this type of interest in me before. Why now?"

"I don't have an answer for you, Sky. As I said, I'm losing control, when it concerns *you*. My animal, well …" He paused for a moment before beginning again, wrestling with a truth I was dying to hear.

"Well?"

"I don't have an answer for you right now," he said, and even in the dark, I could see the creased lines of his brow, the tension building in his shoulders, as he shut his eyes tightly, fighting with himself.

I turned to the side, creating some much-needed space between us. With him this close to me, it was hard to breathe, let alone think straight. Summoning courage from the depths of my animal soul, I bravely admitted what I needed to hear.

"You need to tell me before your shift, Gilen," I said. "I need to know how you really feel about me."

I remember the exact moment that my world changed, and I realized my feelings for Gilen went beyond just friendship. It was the morning I woke up and, for the first time, felt my animal's presence stir inside my chest. I raced as fast as I could to tell Gilen the news first. When I found him on the training grounds sparring with his father, I couldn't help blushing as I watched him. From that moment on, my heart raced whenever he entered a room, and he stole my breath away with the simple ease of his smile or the sound of his laughter. He was more than just my friend.

A tingling sensation crept into my mind, and the pull of my attention turned from Gilen to the booming voice inside my head. *Move out and cover your areas.* It was Alistar. He had sent out his command to his pack members, a unique gift only an alpha could control.

"Fuck. This is not how I wanted to do this. I needed more time!" Gilen snarled as he turned to release his anger, punching an indent into the trunk of the tree. The bark shattered from the indent made by his fist, but I merely rolled my eyes in annoyance, unflinching at his sudden outburst of violence.

When shifters were pushed past our tolerance, our animals took over, which at times resulted in rash outbursts. I knew I was guilty of them, and Gilen was no exception.

"Gilen … Look, I—"

Before I could say another word, Gilen crossed the distance between us, grabbed the base of my neck, and pulled my lips to his. The feeling of our bodies colliding was intense, all-consuming, and everything I ever dreamed it could be. The smell and taste of his lips were so sweet that it made me want to devour every inch of him.

I was not a complete novice in romance, though still holding onto my virginity, but this, this kiss, was different.

Desire rolled through me like liquid fire, and my body instinctively reacted to his dominating hold on me. I could smell a discreet shift in the aroma around us, and there was no mistaking what it was. The scent of Gilen's arousal was tantalizing, and it increased the rising pulse of heat through my middle. My stomach twisted and did a backflip as Gilen kissed me with reckless abandon.

My lips parted, inviting his tongue inside my mouth as my hands wrapped around his strong arms, possessively pulling him closer to me. His grip tightened on the base of my neck while his other hand migrated down my curves to cup my backside. He squeezed it, and I pushed my hips forward in response, grinding into his hardening length. A soft moan escaped my mouth as my tongue parted Gilen's lips to explore his mouth further. With his sculpted body pressed against mine, I could feel every inch of muscle that formed his delicious physique.

*I said move out now!* The alpha's command rang loud and clear in our minds. This was the absolute worst gods-damned timing. Just my luck, it seemed.

My heart was racing, paired with rapid and uneven breaths, as the spark throbbing in my middle blazed to life. Gilen's breathing was ragged and unhinged. I could feel him trying to fight the pull of the alpha command, but he could not will himself to disobey. Even this level of hesitation was astonishing for him. I reluctantly pulled away from his kiss, our lips separated only by a thin layer of breath.

He clung to me like I was the only thing keeping him grounded in this world. "I … We need to …" His voice was shaking along with his hands. Refusing the command from his father was physically hurting him.

"Later," I whispered. "I will have more questions later."

He released a slight laugh with his teeth clenched. I shifted my weight and grabbed his hand to lead him back toward the others. I didn't tremble or shake like Gilen did. I had heard our alpha's command but didn't have to follow it. I chalked it up to another lovely gift from my human half. *Thanks, Mom.*

Rejoining the others, I gave Rhea a weary look as we paired off together to scout the southern area of our pack's territory. I made a conscious effort not to reach up and touch my swollen lips. I knew I couldn't hide the flush of my cheeks, but anyone could assume it was from arguing or a brush of cold air from the brisk evening chill. No one would believe it. Hell, I was still shocked and questioning the reality of what had just happened. It was hard to fathom that my swollen lips and flushed red cheeks were due to a passionate kiss from Gilen. The heir of our alpha.

"Not now. I promise I will tell you everything," I whispered to Rhea, and she nodded, content with the fact that I would divulge every detail soon.

I steadied my breath, clutching my bow in my left hand and sprinting off through the forest on our patrol. The nearly full moon hung high in the clear night sky, allowing us to see perfectly into the depths of the woods. Shifters naturally had exceptional eyesight. Even in the darkness of the night, we could see every detail of the woods like it was high noon.

Gilen and Shaw took the lead, with Talon in his wolf form following close behind, leaving Rhea and me at the rear. With Talon as a wolf, he was able to communicate with other members of the pack, giving our scouting party free rein to investigate a section of the territory on our own.

As we arrived at our rendezvous point, Gilen sent us out in different directions to look for any sign of hunters. Before I had a chance to leave for my area, Gilen reached out and grabbed my hand. Frozen by his touch, I didn't say anything at first, and neither did he.

"Remember, if you see something, come find one of us. I don't care if you are one of the best archers we have … Don't engage anything alone, Skylar."

"Understood." Smiling softly, I squeezed his hand before running toward the meadow he assigned me to watch.

Green spruce along the outskirts of the grassy field were wilted brown and stripped bare of any sign of life. The once bright, colorful birch trees full of life now held whispers of their once whimsical state. The forest was strong, but the wilt was stronger. The essence of this meadow shifted from a beaming home bursting with vivacity to a mere shadow of its former self.

We didn't know why, but as shifters, we could feel the change in the nature surrounding us. Glancing around the open grass field, I found the perfect tree to climb that would conceal my presence as I watched the night unfold below. I strapped my bow across my chest and climbed onto the bottom limbs that were still shielded with a thick array of branches covered with needles. It was the perfect camouflage. Not even the wind could sneak through and touch me, so I leaned back and waited to see what would come.

And waited …

As the night dragged on, I caught myself dozing in the comfort of my hideaway tree stand. To be honest, I was a terrible scout. Sitting still was not a strength of mine, and I struggled to remain in one place for long periods of time. I blamed my shifter side for that lovely trait. It was obvious that my animal was not meant for any type of cage, and that translated into my consistent fidgeting. At least, that's what I told myself anyway.

*Snap.*

My ears twitched, hearing the sound of someone approaching off to my left. I froze, waiting for the creature or person to reveal themselves in the glowing moonlight. Only silence followed. I kept my sight locked on where I heard the sound. Whoever was entering the meadow was stealthy, and the snap from before was not intentional. I couldn't hear or detect the scent of anything in the air. If I hadn't caught that first hint of noise, I wouldn't have known anyone was there.

Slowly, a silhouette along the tree line at the edge of the meadow appeared. The stranger's identity was concealed beneath a heavy dark cloak, but with my shifter eyesight, I could make out features that were draped in shadow.

This was definitely a male. A large hand clutched the pommel of a long silver sword resting on his shoulder, while the other hung all too casually at his side. He paused at the edge of the clearing and straightened to his full height. Looking at the surrounding tree line, I could infer that he towered over my nearly six-foot stance, with strong, broad shoulders filling his frame. Judging by the defined muscled arm that escaped his black cloak, I assessed that this male had experience using the sword clutched in his grasp.

*Please, for me … don't venture off alone and try to handle a threat without someone going with you.* Gilen's words tugged at my conscience, trying to pull me away from investigating any further, but I couldn't just sit here.

*Sorry, Gilen.*

I moved into a crouched position and silently readied my bow. I retrieved an arrow out from my quiver, my fingers delicately curling around the fletching.

The male quietly stalked out from the trees, tilting his chin toward the sky, revealing a trimmed black beard along a squared jawline. A breeze danced around him, circling under his cloak and carrying his scent straight toward my hiding place. I crinkled my nose at the strange foreign scent of this male. Fresh evergreen pine paired with a frost that reminded me of snowcapped mountains. My animal coiled inside my chest, thrumming with power and shooting prickles of fire through my veins.

*This is different.*

The stranger moved, sheathing his sword along his back, before tugging his hood and covering his face. I knew he was not our kind. He didn't move like a shifter or radiate any type of familiar power. There was no doubt in my mind that this was a hunter, and I was determined to strike first.

Soundlessly, I drew back on my bowstring, inhaling a long, steadying breath, ready to take aim. In one swift movement, I leaped out of the tree, landing balanced on the ground as I lined up my target. The male heard me and spun his shrouded face in my direction. I released my breath as my arrow soared through the night, aiming straight for the heart of the hunter.

A silver shimmer flashed, and my arrow impaled the trees behind my mark.

"What the?" I stammered, turning my head left, right, and left again. Searching for the hunter I'd seen in the meadow. "Where the hell did, he go?" I cursed as I retrieved another arrow and carefully stalked around the base of the tree. I kept the trunk at my back so nothing could come up from behind and surprise me. He couldn't have just *vanished.* That was impossible.

I might have been afraid, but I could not panic.

No, panicking would surely get me killed, and I refused to allow myself to become prey to those beings. I focused my hearing and other senses on detecting what my eyes could not yet see. An unnatural silence fell in the forest, warning all those listening that something was here. My heart rate slowed. The rhythm matched my breathing—calm and steady as I waited. I called upon my animal's instinct and seeped into an acute awareness of the world around me. I was the predator here, not the prey.

Nocking another arrow, I noticed the difference in how the shaft felt against my fingers, and I realized it was one of the new arrows Gilen had placed in my quiver earlier this evening.

A shift in the wind alerted me to look right, and as I turned, I released a blind shot from my bow. A solid thud and a roaring curse echoing through the night indicated that my aim was true. Rustling sounds echoed along the forest floor, followed by grunts and groans of pain, which helped guide me to my prize. I leaped over the shrubbery to find the cloaked male lying on the ground with my arrow embedded through his left shoulder, just inches above his heart.

"What are you doing on our lands?" I growled, nocking another arrow. "Your kind are not welcome here."

The male was doubled over on the dirt with blood staining the earth below him. He grunted as he shifted his body to face me, trying to grasp the head of the arrow that was just out of his reach.

"*Iron?*" His voice was deep and laced with a screaming internal agony. Collapsing onto his side, I noted his rapid, uneven, staggered breaths paired with the blood pooling under his limp body.

I quickly pulled back on another arrow and stalked to his front. "Want to add another? I missed my mark the first time. And … Trust me, that doesn't happen. It would be a shame to leave you unbalanced. Shall I even you out?"

A deep, thundering sound echoed from the depths of his chest, causing him to shudder, and I could have sworn he was *laughing*. I had no clue what to make of that, but I was not waiting around to find out. I took one final step forward, and with the tip of my arrow, I flung his hood back to unveil his identity.

My jaw practically fell to the ground as a face even the gods themselves would be envious of appeared in the moonlight. His eyes were clenched shut beneath heavy jet-black brows that were framed by high cheekbones and a flawless complexion. A dark, neatly trimmed beard and mustache followed a strong, angular jawline, framing sultry, lustful lips that were pressed tightly together. His silver, black-streaked shoulder-length hair was half tied back, revealing the elegant, handsome contours of his face and pointed ears.

*Pointed … ears.*

My eyes widened with disbelief and shock. There was no mistaking what the male was.

*High. Fae.*

*This was a High Fae!*

The male groaned and fell backward, collapsing onto his back as his breathing became erratic and his coloring began to fade.

"*Iron …*" the male rasped once more.

"Fuck!" I gasped, suddenly realizing the gravity of what I had just done.

I'd shot a High Fae with an iron-tipped arrow. Iron repelled magic and interfered with our magically heightened abilities, including our rapid healing. The arrow I fired at him penetrated through his left shoulder, just breaths above his heart.

"Gods Above! No … no … no." I was officially panicking now.

My animal stirred inside my chest, flooding me with her presence and power so I could get a grip on my emotions and try to focus. "Don't die!" I shouted at him, my power pulsing through my limbs and flowing through my words.

I immediately dropped my bow to the ground and moved to straddle his torso with my knees on either side of his hips. The lean, solid mass of muscle beneath my body tensed but didn't move away. I quickly wrapped my left fingers around the shaft of the arrow and reached my right hand toward the arrowhead protruding through to his back. If I could snap the head of the arrow clean, I could remove the entire thing in one swift pull. Rising onto my knees, I bent forward and tugged on the arrow with one hand while I tried to push it through his skin.

Faster than I thought possible, the High Fae male opened his mouth, turned his head to the side, and bit down *hard* on my arm, right below my wrist.

"Shit!" I screamed, instinctively fighting back and elbowing him in the nose so hard that he thumped backward against the ground. "That's fucking deep! I can see my gods-damned bone through the wound!" Blood dripped down my arm, but luckily, my shifter healing was already starting to kick in. Nothing compared to adults who had successfully shifted, but it was better than nothing. I tore at the bottom of my shirt tucked underneath my leathers and wrapped it around my wrist. "You High Fae have fucking fangs for teeth or something?" I sneered, tying my makeshift bandage. "I can't imagine how painful foreplay is for your kind."

His eyes remained closed, but the deep rumble once again echoed through his chest. Realizing it was most definitely a laugh, I squeezed my legs tightly around his torso to try and make my point.

"Not funny," I grumbled, but it only seemed to encourage him.

Moving my body backward, I shifted my weight onto his hips to try and get his attention. I felt him twitch and stiffen, so I knew it had worked. He was listening. And I now had his undivided attention.

"Look … I know I shot you with this arrow and tried to kill you, but that was a mistake. My bad. I was actually told not to try and investigate threats on my own, but as my luck would have it, here we are. Honestly, I'm just trying to help fix this mess." I spoke softly as I gestured to his mangled chest and shoulder.

His pointed ears seemed to twitch at the sound of my voice, and for the first time, he opened his eyes to look at me.

An awe-inspiring gray stare that mimicked the raging storm

clouds over a mountain pass bore deep into my soul. Distant and dark, but yet … strangely, anything but cold. I felt a shock of warmth seer into my center as my animal danced in my chest, pulsing with power to match the swell of strength dwelling in his eyes.

There was a deep-rooted sadness echoing in his stormy gaze, paired with anger and violence. I was not scared, however. Quite the opposite. The intensity of his gaze drew me in, granting me an alluring invitation and desire to sink into his world and never ask to be released. Seconds seemed like hours as his eyes refused to move from mine.

I blinked and shook myself, remembering where I was and what I was supposed to be doing.

"Bite me again, and I'll blacken your eye. Got it?" I didn't mean it as a threat, but more of a promise. There was no way I was helping him if he was going to use those sharp canine teeth on me again. I refused to buckle or back down as I held his stare with my own fiery amber gaze. "So, are you going to let me help you or not?"

He narrowed his brows, and I could feel his body begin to tremble beneath. Oh no. The iron in his system was already beginning to shut his body down. Was I too late?

"You don't have much time," I whispered, trying to pull back the aggression in my tone. "I fired a clean shot. That iron is too close to your heart to stay in there for much longer. You will die if I don't take it out." He went utterly still for a moment. Those luminous eyes calculating his options, still debating if he would accept my offer to help.

Stubborn male.

"Please," I asked softly.

His eyes darted to his wound, and then he snapped them back up to me. He didn't say a word but gave me one firm nod.

"All right, then … here we go. Hold onto whatever grit you have. This is going to be a bitch to get free."

I reached my bleeding arm behind his back once more, and the High Fae closed his eyes, inhaling a deep breath to brace himself. I felt his body tremble beneath me and watched his hands clench into tight fists.

I knew I needed to be quick. I snapped the head off the arrow and then braced my palm on his chest while grasping the shaft of the arrow with the other.

"And now the easy part but unfortunately the more painful one." Rooting my toes in the ground and squeezing my knees tightly around his torso, I swiftly pulled the arrow out of his flesh. He allowed a small gasp to escape his lips as I jerked forward, pressing a hand to his open wound to try and slow the bleeding.

"There … All—whoo!" A hand grabbed the nape of my brown leathers, and I was flung backward off the male High Fae and thrown onto the ground. A snarl erupted from another cloaked figure, and before I could utter a word, a long, curved blade appeared, angled directly at my throat.

*Well, this is definitely not good.*

"Leave the … Spitfire … alone," the injured High Fae grumbled as he struggled but somehow managed to sit up.

Fuck. I couldn't believe he was conscious, let alone managing to sit up on his own.

The newest addition to our little party flung back his hood as he sheathed his curved blade and rushed to his injured comrade's side.

*Holy … Gods! Another High Fae!* I gazed at them both in complete shock and awe.

This new male had a slimmer build compared to the one I struck with my arrow. His hair was shorter but longer along one side and folded over the top of his head with a deep, pure silver color, paired with dark brown eyes. My gaze darted back and forth between the two of them, and the similarities were far too obvious to ignore. The angles of the nose and jawline were identical, despite the silver one having a clean-shaven face. Even the shape of their eyes was the same despite the difference in color. I would bet my life on the fact that these two were related in some capacity.

Before I had time to think, a large midnight-black wolf, leaped from the brush of devil's club and protectively placed itself between the two High Fae males and me. Talon. I would recognize that mangy coat of fur paired with those pale-blue eyes anywhere.

Not a second later, Gilen crashed through the branches with his sword drawn as well.

The two High Fae seemed to ignore the three of us as the silver-haired one meticulously examined the wound on the other. I carefully watched their interactions and how they seemed to understand one another without ever speaking a word. This was a trait developed over time spent together, formed by a long-lasting bond that stretched over lifespans.

They began whispering to one another, and the most shocking and unexpected thing happened next. The silver-haired male burst out in a loud barrel of uncontrolled laughter, almost falling over onto the ground.

I couldn't help releasing my own chuckle, but Gilen shot me a look over his shoulder that forced me to cover my mouth quickly and regain my composure.

"You can't be serious!" The silver-haired High Fae exclaimed as he stood slapping his knee. The darker-haired male held a firm grimace as he stared off into the woods. "You mean to tell me … that the female shifter over there managed to strike you with an iron arrow to the heart? The Silver Shadow of the Inner Kingdom was almost slain … *unintentionally*?" His body convulsed, doubling over in laughter.

What kind of twisted sense of humor did these High Fae have? I didn't find amusement in near-death situations, but somehow, this was funny to them?

Gilen and Talon both straightened with similar looks of confusion on their faces. I, for once, wasn't confused, but I wisely decided to keep my mouth shut while the fae I struck with the arrow attempted to stand.

"Nope. Not happening," the silver fae scolded, wagging his finger. "You," he called out, pointing to Gilen, "help me escort him back to your village. The High Fae queen is already in audience with your alpha, and she would not appreciate hearing the news that one of her high princes has been attacked and killed accidentally in your woods." His dark eyes flickered to find mine. "Iron arrow … clever but not enough, I'm afraid."

High prince? Silver Shadow? The queen of the High Fae was here on Solace's pack lands? What did all that mean? I glanced down at the arrows in my quiver. I didn't want to believe it, but it seemed that Gilen had known more than he let on.

The injured male, who was referred to as the Silver Shadow, pointlessly fought against his companion's aid. The iron had already mixed with his blood, and I knew the wound would take time to heal regardless of his strength and obvious stubbornness—typical male.

"I can help," I said as I crossed the distance between myself and the two newcomers.

"I believe you have helped enough," the silver one shot at me. The other High Fae male seemed to release a small growl of discontent, but he brushed off his response.

Deciding to try and push my luck, I moved past Talon as four sets of eyes immediately locked onto me. There was a mixture of confusion and annoyance—mainly from Gilen—but also a sense of curiosity or intrigue from the Silver Shadow. As I brushed past Gilen, he released a low, menacing growl, and my progress quickly came to a halt. He forcibly grabbed my uninjured arm and thrust me behind him.

"Hey!" I protested, but Gilen snarled, baring his teeth at me. His dark, ominous glare had me hesitate, but not for long.

*No fucking way*, I thought as I bit my lip, trying to steady my shaking nerves.

I could see Silver Shadow tense as he watched me closely. I countered, grabbing Gilen's wrist and twisting it around until he released his hold on me. Once I was free of his grasp, I marched right past Talon and stood face to face with the two High Fae.

"Spitfire?" The silver-haired male murmured with a sense of amusement, giving me a cocky smile that I mentally brushed to the side. "You seem to have named her well enough."

I could have sworn I heard the same deep chuckle from before emerge from the Silver Shadow, followed by a grimace of pain and clenched fists at his efforts.

"Serves you right," I taunted. "I didn't know I was such a comedian. That's not the first time I have amused you tonight, apparently."

Dark gray eyes shot open as he looked straight at me, making the world surrounding us disappear into the darkening night. "You. Attacked. Me!" he roared at me; his deep, enchanting voice made it hard to focus my attention on anything else. "And somehow …" He gritted his teeth, fighting back a twinge of pain. "Somehow … you have the audacity and the nerve to taunt *me*? I have killed others for less."

"Look, I know we don't know each other, but asking the questions is sort of my thing. And if you haven't noticed, I'm not afraid of threats. I'm a shifter, after all."

"Skylar," Gilen growled. "Get behind me. Now."

I could feel the power in Gilen's command, and instead of giving away any glimpses of my unique abilities, I reluctantly obeyed. Still in his wolf form, Talon tilted his head in my direction, wordlessly asking, *What in the gods' names are you doing?*

To be honest, I didn't know. There were too many questions spinning around in my head for me to plan my next move properly. I was reacting out of pure instinct, and that, unfortunately, had a tendency to lead me into trouble. There were High Fae here … on our lands. They never ventured out of the Inner Kingdom. It was unheard of to see them.

Gilen moved toward the two High Fae and bent to offer his help to carry the injured male. The Silver Shadow abruptly brushed off his offer, insisting on making a stand either by his own sheer willpower or stubborn streak. Standing up straight, he was taller than both Gilen and his companion, but the silver-haired male was able to adjust his weight and help his wounded friend move his feet.

"Talon," Gilen commanded, "take Skylar home first. Then find Shaw and Rhea and escort the others back to the village. I will take the High Fae males to the alpha's house. Meet me there when you are finished." Talon was never one to question his alpha and nudged me with his snout in the opposite direction, toward home.

I reluctantly obeyed, much to both my and my animal's dismay. Still, I couldn't help but glance back over my shoulder at the wounded fae, and to my surprise, I discovered that he was already watching me.

# Chapter Five

*I absolutely hated sitting and waiting.*

The rain steadily fell from the blackened night sky as Talon escorted me home, taking away my chance to talk with Rhea about what happened in the woods. I stripped out of my brown fighting leathers and back into my fitted pants and tunic, restlessly pacing back and forth across the hardwood floor in the living area. My mind raced with more questions than I had answers as the rain continued steadily pattering against the windows. A part of me still didn't believe everything that had happened tonight. It was unfathomable that there were High Fae in our pack lands—let alone that I shot one with an iron arrow.

Lost in my endless train of thoughts, I almost didn't notice Neera's delicate steps as she descended the stairs from her bedroom. "What's up with you?" she asked, wiping the sleep from her eyes and yawning loudly.

I snapped my head in her direction, genuinely surprised to see her awake at this hour. "I could ask you the same thing," I replied. "I'm sorry. Did I wake you? It's still early, or late. The sun hasn't risen yet. Julia mentioned that you weren't feeling well today?"

"No, it's fine," she said, waving away my concerned look. "Just the lovely bi-annual bleeding and cramps females get to enjoy."

"Ah yes, that lovely, charming perk. Oh, the joys of being female." I gave her a sideways smile as she descended the final steps into our living room. "You have been a little short-tempered recently."

She glared, narrowing her eyes and scrunching her face at me as best she could manage. "And *you,* are practically a feral beast when it is your time."

"Feral is a bit harsh, but I have been known to break down a door or two when the mood strikes me."

Neera rolled her eyes at me as she gracefully stretched out her arms and glided across the living room to the large, cushioned chair in the corner. Shifter females fortunately only had our cycles twice a year. However, when a mate bond was formed, we entered frequent cycles of heat that typically resulted in the birth of a child nine months later.

"Well, I'm awake now, and there seems to be something on your mind. Want to talk about it?" Neera asked with a sleepy yet somehow still beautiful look on her face.

Neera had this innate calmness and caring capacity for others that was unmatched by any shifter in our pack, along with her effortless beauty. She had long, slender limbs with a slightly taller stature than her mother, and she carried a graceful nature that I could never hope to achieve in my lifetime. Her midnight-black hair cascaded into natural voluptuous curls along her mid-back, framing the delicate features of her face. The freckles on her tanned cheeks were kisses from the gods themselves that highlighted her beautiful green eyes gifted from her father.

I often teased Magnus that he would have his hands full when Neera was older, scaring away males who wanted to stake their claim and steal her away. Lucky for all of us, though … Neera wouldn't settle for anything but a mating bond.

Shifters were able to recognize a mate bond once the sun rose after our first shift. Some could sense the connection to their mate beforehand, but the bond was not sealed until our animal souls recognized it as well. Not every union in our pack, however, was the result of a mated pairing. Alistar, our alpha, claimed his mate, Helen, without the presence of the bond.

At the ripe age of eighteen, Neera was a hopeless romantic, and there were countless males eager to whisk her away from our home and claim her as their own.

I dabbled in romance, but nothing ever truly felt right. My most recent relationship was with a bear shifter named Xander, which lasted just shy of the six-month mark. Uncle Magnus was convinced we could be a mated pair, but once Xander shifted, he quickly broke things off. I never really received a good explanation as to why, but Rhea and Shaw wouldn't let me sulk for long. He was the first male I thought I would give myself to, but fate apparently had other plans in store for me.

"Come over here and sit with me." I said, as Neera scooted over in the large, cushioned seat, patting the pillows with her dainty hand.

While growing up, Neera loved to tend to the gardens outside the window next to this loveseat while I read. She would sometimes ask me to read aloud and tell her about all the heroic tales and worlds of the characters I would lose myself in time and time again. She was especially interested in the love stories and the adventurous trials characters would overcome for true love to prevail. This place was our little nook—our sanctuary together.

I sighed and slumped my shoulders forward, joining her on the loveseat. "How could I turn my nose up at that offer?" Neera smiled, draping a blanket over the two of us as I settled in next to her. I waited with bated breath to see if she noticed any changes to my scent from Gilen, or even Silver Shadow. She hadn't shifted, so her senses were not as acute as Julia's. As my moments of silence ticked by, I sighed in relief and relaxed when she didn't seem to notice anything different.

"Well?" Neera asked.

Pursing my lips, I decided to take Rhea's approach to this situation and just rip the bandage right off. "There are High Fae in Valdor."

Neera tensed and turned toward me, her eyes wide and her mouth hanging open. "What? They … they never leave the Inner Kingdom."

I raised my brows and flashed a sarcastic grin. "Never say never." I couldn't help teasing her just a little.

"Clearly," she huffed, rolling her eyes at me. "Is that why Mom and Dad are gone?"

"I imagine Alistar wanted his beta by his side when he met with the high queen of the fae. Apparently, her *high prince* is the one I met in the woods tonight," I said, leaving some of the finer details about me shooting him quiet for now. I couldn't help but wonder what else Gilen was hiding. What more did he know about the reason why they were here? He was the alpha's heir … He had to know more.

"Wait, w-what!" she stammered, sitting cross-legged on the seat and facing me. "You could've led with the fact that you met one of them!" She gasped. "Wait a second. Do you think … Could they be here because of the wilt?" Neera asked.

Her question was the same one I dreaded asking myself. "It might be the only reason they would leave their Inner Kingdom and venture into the mainland of Valdor," I said.

"Because it could be happening there as well." I never gave Neera enough credit for her sharp mind.

"Very true. But why now? The wilt has been around for our entire lives," I wondered aloud. "Why not yesterday, last year, or last month? Why have they decided to return now?"

Long ago, longer than any of our current elders or ancestors could recall, shifters and High Fae lived together in the Inner Kingdom and all throughout Valdor. Humans were the newest occupants of our world, arriving on ships that crossed the vast unknown eastern sea. The divide between shifters, humans, and High Fae was the result of a bloody war of power between the three species. Eventually, after countless battles with no clear victory and so much death, the lands were divided.

The veil, a magical barrier, isolated the High Fae's territory called the Inner Kingdom from the rest of Valdor, while shifters and humans divided the mainland. I wasn't really sure why the veil was created, but everyone assumed that the High Fae constructed it to protect their lands from any intruders. Of course, this was all assumed because no one had heard of or even seen one of their kind in centuries.

Until now.

"Oh, and I forgot to add," I said shyly, twirling a strand of hair in my fingers and glancing out the window, "I shot one of the high princes with an iron arrow." Neera whipped her arm out and firmly slapped me on the side of the head. "Hey," I yelped. "What was that for?"

"For not thinking before acting! Are you serious, Skylar? You shot one of them with an *iron* arrow? How did you even manage that?"

"I thought it was a hunter!" I exclaimed in my own defense, rubbing my head. "Once I realized it wasn't, I tried to help him. He did get me back for it though …" I held up my bandaged arm to show the evidence of the male's retaliation. "He bit me. Right down to the bone, so I guess he and I are even on that count." I paused for a moment, my thoughts circling around the high prince. "You know, I have no idea who he was. I don't even know his name."

"What *do* you know about him?" Neera asked, giving me a peculiar expression that reminded me of her mother, Julia, and made her seem much older than she was.

*You mean besides immense stubbornness, a twisted sense of humor paired with beautiful, alluring gray eyes that mimicked a raging mountain storm*, I thought to myself.

My animal stirred inside my chest at the thought of him, but I immediately forced her presence back down. "The other one called him *Silver Shadow*, I think."

My cousin's eyes widened, and this time, she promptly smacked the wound on my bandaged arm. "Neera! Gods be damned, that hurt!" I growled at her. "There's a dressing here for a reason, you know!"

"For someone so smart you are very dull at times, Skylar!" she scoffed and threw the blanket to the side, storming off toward her father's study while muttering to herself.

*That was very uncharacteristic of her.*

In between the grunts and murmurs, I could hear her rummaging through a trunk, trying to find something. I wisely decided to let her be for now.

My mind drifted as I waited for Neera to return. I didn't intentionally allow my thoughts to meander toward him, but I also didn't stop them. I found myself thinking solely about the mysterious male I had shot in the woods, Silver Shadow.

From my memory, I recalled his enticing yet rugged handsomeness paired with his body's predator-like movements that allowed him to sneak through the meadow undetected. I remembered how the moonlight danced across his fair skin, which contrasted against his thick, shoulder-length silver hair streaked with black. I remembered the sound of his deep, authoritative voice when he finally spoke and challenged me about my taunting remarks.

On the contrary, I was impressed that he managed to stand only moments after knocking on death's door. It was a testament to how powerful he truly was.

I believe that was what triggered my animal's sudden alertness. She was never one to shy away from a challenge. It was annoying and inconvenient at times, but I had learned to just go with it and accept her dominating nature as my own.

"You're sure his name was *Silver Shadow*?" Neera hollered, reentering the living area and interrupting my daydream with an open book in her arms.

"Yes …" I tried to tilt my head to the side and read the title of the book Neera was holding.

"Silver … Shadow," she repeated.

"*Yes.*" I dragged out the word so she would get the hint.

"I still can't believe his name is not ringing a bell in that thick head of yours. I thought you prided yourself on being the brightest of your class." I squinted my eyes and promptly stuck out my tongue at her. "Aren't you supposed to be the mature adult around here?"

"Lighten up," I barked back at her while I turned the book around and scanned over the title.

"Read," she demanded.

*The Great War* was etched in bold lettering along the front, and my memory was jogged. It was a historical war book chronicling the final battles of the three races of Valdor. It described the appearance of the veil and the separation of the Inner Kingdom and the area of the mainland in Valdor. No wonder I didn't recognize the title. This was not my favorite genre to casually read, and one we all studied early on as children in school. Understandably, I might have forgotten some of the details.

Neera bent over and gently turned to the page she wanted me to look over. The rain fell over the glass windows of the house, causing the pitter-patter of the drops to echo across our home. "This is from my father's collection. The humans wrote it, but it's still good enough, I guess."

"Ouch. Nice burn there. Do you have any salt you want to rub in the wound you smacked tonight?" I commented with a scowl. "I'm half-human, remember?"

"I know," she answered with a soft smirk and a sly wink that could get her out of any trouble she found herself in. "That's why it is good *enough* and not worthless. Now read here." Neera guided me to a passage that described various High Fae warriors who fought in the final battle.

"N-no way …" I stammered as my mouth suddenly became dry, and my stomach dropped to the ground. The sound of the rain rumbled against the frame of the house, with a clash of thunder that seemed to shake the floor beneath our feet.

Neera arched her dark brows, whipping her head around with a worried look. "Yes—that thunder was normal, right?"

I didn't give her fears any weight and kept my gaze firmly on the passage in the book. It depicted one of the most feared High Fae warriors of the Inner Kingdom, nicknamed Silver Shadow—a powerful high prince hailing from Silver Meadows. This specific account was from a young human boy who was a squire for one of the human generals.

*Our human forces fought gallantly against the High Fae, but once the Silver Meadows warriors rejoined the fight, we were gravely outmatched. Their forces pushed us to retreat to the shores nearest to the mainland. The constant bombardment of High Fae relentlessly attacking our lines was terrifying. We could hold them off with the magic of our own mages, but one warrior in particular, leading their bloody assault, no one could defeat.*

*I was just a boy, but I remember him. I would recall his face in my nightmares for the rest of my mortal life.*

*The Silver Shadow—more lethal than a hundred of our soldiers combined and more powerful than a line of mages uniting with their own magic. He effortlessly slaughtered countless numbers on the battlefield, never once stopping or relenting in his attack. His silver sword sliced through the armor of our men like butter. In a flash of silver light, he was bombarding one side of our line and then magically appeared on the other. The blood of his enemies splattered his face and armor as a badge of honor for his countless victories won on the battlefield that day, and the countless days of battle that followed. There was no telling where his next strike would be—only the bloodied trail he left in his wake.*

*I was scrambling to follow my charge, our general, across the Inner Kingdom's beach toward the boats. The ships were just beyond the sand dunes, and we were so close to safety that I was crying silent tears of gratitude to have made it here alive. Suddenly, my charge stopped, and my insides churned at who stood in our way.*

*Blood streaked his black and silver armor, and storm-cloud-gray eyes locked onto us as he reached up to slowly remove his helm. The silver and black-streaked hair paired with killing gray eyes were unmistakable—the Silver Shadow stood between us and our retreat.*

*My charge was one of the most skilled generals fighting in our army, but even he was no match for the Shadow's speed and power. The ground seemed to freeze beneath our feet as the High Fae prince moved in fluid, effortless movement, attacking my charge head-on without remorse. Their blades collided as they fought one another, but I could see that Silver Shadow was only toying with him. With a flick of his wrist, the silver sword in the fae's hand circled around, and with one clean swipe, he severed the head of my charge clean from his shoulders.*

*Blood spattered across the now-frozen sand, and I tried to scream, but unbridled fear kept my voice locked in my throat. His stone stare then turned to me, and I felt the pulse of his magic strike my middle, freezing the breath in my lungs. His raw, unrelenting power emanated in waves from where he stood, and it felt like drowning on dry land. He stalked toward me, his silver sword dripping with the blood of my charge.*

*He knelt down and, I swear, I saw my short-lived life flash before my eyes.*

*"Run," he commanded in a deep, authoritative voice.*

*At first, I didn't understand or even comprehend what he had said.*

*Then, the Shadow shifted and sheathed his sword on his back as he stood over me, blocking out the sun with his towering height and broad frame. "Run … and never return to our shores again."*

*This time, I didn't hesitate as I willed my legs to carry me away, thanking the gods that I somehow survived an encounter with Silver Shadow because no one ever had before me.*

My breathing became rapid as my hands trembled. "I knew he was a warrior. Just by the looks of him, I guessed that much," I stated. "There was no questioning that. But I had no idea he was *this* warrior. He's one of the most powerful High Fae in history."

"And *you* somehow almost managed to kill him!" Neera exclaimed, her green eyes flaring. "You better go apologize and try to heal him with your magic."

"I tried," I replied, "but he wouldn't let me, Gilen wouldn't let me." I pursed my lips, still disgruntled by how Gilen tried to physically force me to stand aside and order me around.

"Then you try again. You owe him that much, at least. The reason for them being here must be important if both Silver Shadow and the high queen of the fae are here. They would be honored, if not slightly feared, guests. You need to make amends."

"I have no idea where they are staying," I countered.

Okay, that wasn't entirely true, but after reading the squire's account of Silver Shadow in battle, I was hesitant to face him again.

"Seriously? You do, too." Neera half laughed and took the book back from me. "Not scared, are you? Since when is Skylar Cathal scared and not willing to push the boundaries of the rules."

"I am not scared," I snapped. "Gah, fine." I huffed, slumping my shoulders forward and closing the book. "I know where they would likely be … but I don't want to get into any more trouble. Gilen is not happy with me right now. I may have challenged him and didn't exactly follow his command while on patrol."

"And since when does that stop you, Skylar?"

I smiled at my cousin's response. She knew me so well.

"You have always been able to bend the rules and stand on your own. I think it's time you started doing just that and realized you are stronger than you think."

"And breaking into the alpha's home would benefit me how, Neera?"

"Because you *want* to see Silver Shadow again." Her alluring eyes seemed to sparkle with her own amusement.

"Neera!" I gasped.

"You want answers, and this male has to know something."

I mulled over Neera's logic, and I had to admit she wasn't wrong. But it didn't change how I hated her just a little bit in spite of how right she was. Knowing me well enough to manipulate my curiosity was clever; I'd give her that.

"Go … and find out all you can. Then come straight back here and tell me everything," she said, smirking and practically pushing me out the door.

"Oh, I see how it is." I narrowed my gaze at her with a mischievous grin. "You're invested now, too. You're curious."

"Hurry along, would you?" Neera scolded as she shoved me out the open door and into the falling rain.

# Chapter Six

The rain was falling harder than ever, almost like combined winds from the sea and the nearby mountains united to create a superstorm over our heads. Despite the rain, the specks of moonlight helped guide me through the forest, keeping off the main paved roads and even packed-down dirt trails along the outer edge of town.

In the distance, I could see the firelight lanterns in the main sections of town with silhouettes of lampposts that would burn throughout the evening. I stayed on the outskirts of the city center, dodging through various smaller cottages and yards of villagers who were luckily sound asleep. I didn't want to attract any more unwanted attention for the night.

The annoyingly consistent rainfall thankfully helped conceal my scent and cover my tracks as I ran through the forest, but I was completely soaked to the bone. As the alpha's house came into view, I carefully assessed the areas around the large compound and the land surrounding it.

Alistar's home was a gigantic log cabin structure reinforced with decorative gray and white stone. There were three main levels with various side staircases that led to each floor and different hallways that connected the numerous rooms throughout the structure, with towers on either side. Large windows adorned each area of the central section of the building, allowing the natural surroundings to shine through the interior.

Each new alpha of our pack created their own addition to the main structure during their time as our leader. Even though my father's time as the alpha was shorter than most, he added his own touch of elegance before I was born. He constructed a vast library on the bottom floor that was open to all shifters to come and borrow as they pleased. It was one of the reasons I loved to read as much as I did. I believed this was a connection I had with him—our shared love of literature and creativity, along with the gift of my animal spirit.

I crouched in the nearby brush of hemlock and devil's club, hiding from the light emanating from the gaping A-frame windows.

Through the clear glass, I could see the large center mantle was roaring, and candles illuminated the corners of the gathering room. It was an open area, larger than our whole house, where Alistar and past alphas conducted their pack business and gatherings.

I recognized the burly, tall figure to Alistar's left with his small but fierce mate at his side—Magnus and Julia. Elders from the Satellite pack regions were also gathered, with a lone cloaked figure that had their back turned to the window. Judging by the slender, curved silhouette alone, I assessed that they were female. Commotion stirred along the hallway as a dark-blond-haired shifter joined them, and I knew without a doubt that it was Gilen.

I swallowed a twinge of regret watching him from outside the cabin. Pack members were allowed to enter the alpha's residence, but Gilen had specifically ordered me to return home when Talon dropped me off—and to stay there. Lucky for me, however, he didn't say for how long.

The healers' quarters, which I knew by heart, were toward the left side of the complex, closest to the nearby creek and training field. Since my healing magic was well known in our pack, I was a frequent visitor to this section of the compound. If the lead healer, Latte, had an injury or illness she couldn't fix, I was called in to assist. I didn't make it a habit to interfere with her craft, and I believe she respected me for it. We assumed I inherited my powerful healing abilities from my mother's bloodline, but I didn't understand the complex knowledge the healers possessed from years of work and experience. I was learning, though. Between bouts in the training fields honing my archery skills and whatever time I could spare, I would also sit and learn from the healers.

To be honest, I was in awe of their caring nature paired with iron-clad nerves of steel. I enjoyed helping people, and this was a unique way to honor my mother's memory by using my magic to strengthen my pack. It was a gift I cherished and never took for granted.

The lanterns inside the healing room were still lit, so I cautiously opened the door and crept inside. Glancing around the room, there was scattered evidence of its use earlier this evening. I could already hear Latte's roaring threats of death and dismemberment at the mess left behind. Bloodstained clothes and a dirty wash bowl were just a few indications of the High Fae's presence here tonight. Inhaling a deep breath, I could smell his unique aroma of pine and fresh, cold mountain air, reminding me of an early spring day full of life and hopes of a bountiful summer ahead. It was definitely fresh; they were here not too long ago.

"Well, they must've gone to the guest wing on the third floor near the eastern tower."

I followed the winding stone staircase all the way up to the third floor and stepped out into the open hallway. It was late—or early, however you wanted to look at it—and this area of the house was deathly silent. Only the thundering rain could be heard in the quiet of the night. I knew the main residents in the rest of the house were wide awake downstairs, but up here, it was deadly calm and often vacant. I wandered along the corridor, trusting my shifter senses to guide me, trying to be extra careful not to make a sound. The scent of pine and snow drifted past me, and I eagerly followed the trail, my animal nudging me toward the end of the hallway.

I didn't know how to describe it, but my animal seemed almost *eager.*

I assumed the guilt of almost killing him was weighing heavily on us both—wanting to right our wrong. Shooting and almost killing a high prince, who would have been welcomed as an honored guest in our lands, was not one of my finest moments.

Stopping at the last door on the third floor, the scent trail ended. He was definitely inside. It surprised me that he was in here, though. Rhea and I often slept here when we didn't have the energy to return home or wanted to get a night away to hang out with our friends. It wasn't very large or grand, not very fitting for a high prince of fae royalty in my mind.

I reached up to lightly knock on the wooden door frame, but the handle turned on its own before I could close my fist.

"For a shifter, you're not as light on your feet as I would have expected." It was the handsome silver-haired High Fae male standing in the door frame.

I tried to conceal the look of shock from my expression and mustered my courage to speak. "I'm here to help …"

"Yes, *Spitfire,*" he said with an amused tone in his voice and a half-cocked grin. "He said you were coming … and as annoying as he may be at times, here you are. Right on schedule." His eyes traced over me from head to toe like he was examining a piece of meat, and I managed to give him a warning scowl as his eyes finally wandered back up to mine.

"He?" I asked, but I already knew the answer. Silver Shadow.

The silver-haired male stepped aside and graciously invited me in while continuing to glance me over, disregarding my earlier warning.

I growled as I brushed past him and inhaled a deep breath, drawing in his scent for the first time. His smell was wilder than that of Silver Shadow's. The faint aroma of fresh cold air was there but also a sweet, rich flavor that reminded me of spice or a glass of fine red wine. The similarities in their scent only confirmed my suspicion that they were kin. They clearly lived in similar locations but possibly led different lifestyles.

"Don't even think about it," I warned.

"Wouldn't dream of it, love. I value my life, but you can't blame me for admiring beauty. Nothing compared to my own, but still, I must admit it is refreshing."

"Enough," a deep, snarling voice boomed.

I noticed the silver-haired fae's coy grin fade, and his posture immediately straightened. My eyes wandered toward the open window on the far side of the room, finding none other than Silver Shadow.

He sat in the chair next to a raging fire in the mantle, flames dancing across his fair-colored skin, highlighting the hard yet comely contours of his face. His wavy, silver, black-streaked hair was loose, falling just below his bearded jaw, with stray pieces draping across his face. He didn't bother turning his head as I approached. Instead, he seemed indifferent to my presence, which I hated to admit annoyed me—and my animal—to no end.

To anyone else, Silver Shadow embodied a persona that defined him as *deathly terrifying*. Even in this seated position with his hard stone-like stare and stoic expression, he was a formidable warrior few would even approach.

But I saw this as a challenge and refused to sulk away in fear. Instead, I bucked up my chin, steadied myself, and walked toward him.

"You're dripping water all over the floor," he said, keeping his gaze fixed on the world outside the window. His deep, electrifying voice vibrated my senses, sending a chilling feeling along my spine before encircling my chest. *Fuck. Talk about intimidating.*

I glanced down at the water pooling beneath my feet from my wet clothing. "Obviously—it's raining outside. Does the rain fall sideways or something in your alluring Inner Kingdom, and people don't get soaking wet?"

He cocked his head in my direction with his eyes narrowed as he silently looked me over from head to toe. His gaze lingered far longer than I had anticipated, almost like he was sizing me up.

"What?" I spat at him with a little more fire than I had intended.

"The rain helps dilute your scent," Silver Shadow said. "I imagine the alpha's son would be displeased if he knew you did not follow his command … *again.*" He raised his dark brows at me as he turned his head back toward the fire, revealing a smug, amused look that told me he knew there was a dance of dominance between Gilen and me.

"Okay, someone is apparently very observant—good to note." I steadied my shaking limbs and stepped forward. "How is the wound?" I dared to ask.

"Tolerable for now." His voice was rough and rich, laced with a deep-seated pain that I couldn't help but notice hiding behind his mask of indifference. "The healer did what she could, but due to the iron tip of your arrow, it will take longer to heal."

"That's why I'm here," I said as I boldly moved to his side.

A breeze whipped through the window, circling around him before flying directly toward me. The fresh mountain breeze tingled my senses, giving me a feeling of comfort and tranquility, with a bit of wildness that stirred the animal in my chest. It spiraled around me before darting back outside the window next to Silver Shadow.

I watched as he tensed, inhaling deeply and closing his eyes tight while resting his head back against the chair.

"He puts on a brave face," the silver-haired male said, diverting my attention. "But he's in excruciating pain … as you can see."

"Right," I said, not entirely buying what he was telling me. "As I said, that's why I'm here." I didn't know how many more times I needed to tell them before they would listen.

"Enlighten me then. What can a mere shifter do to heal his wound?" silver hair snapped.

"She is not *just* a shifter." Shadow opened his eyes, looking directly at me as he spoke. "She's … more than that."

The intensity of his stare left me speechless, causing me to shudder slightly with goosebumps crawling along my exposed skin. With just one look, I was somehow instinctively drawn to him, and for a split second, I noticed his hard eyes soften as he held my attention. I lightly shook my head to try and right myself. This had to be some weird type of alluring High Fae magic playing tricks with my senses.

"Lucky for you, I'm half-human," I said. "And by the fate of the gods themselves, I inherited, well I believe I inherited, my mother's healing magic. So please, for probably the fifth time now, let me help. I feel bad enough for almost killing you. I'm just trying to atone for my mistake."

The silver-haired male leaned back against the nearby mantel and crossed his arms with a cocky smirk, his dark eyes darting between me and Shadow. "She is *more* … is she?" I could tell the question was not directed at me but instead at the other High Fae. He was acting like I wasn't even here, and my patience was beginning to reach its limit.

Silver Shadow shot the other male a look that silenced the room and made me take a small step backward from where he was sitting. The other male huffed a laugh, and suddenly, the nature of their relationship made perfect sense.

"So, now I understand the similarities in your scents." I grinned, cocking a hip and resting a hand there while I bucked up my chin with a wide-set grin. "The appearances alone made me suspect it, but that look you threw at him was the dead giveaway. He's your younger brother."

"Spitfire, indeed. You named her well, *brother*," silver-hair replied, granting me a mocking fake clap of applause. Terrific, a jokester was here with us today.

"Clever, Spitfire," Silver Shadow grunted. "Now, let's see what else you can do." He reached up to unbutton the collar of his shirt and pulled it to the side, granting me access to examine his wound.

"Besides being one of the deadliest archers in all of Valdor, apparently?" I asked with a bold smugness and an inkling of humor. "Gladly."

I caught the hint of an amused smile in his expression before it disappeared behind a mask of stone. I imagined he had practiced disguising his emotions from the world, and I was lucky to catch this glimpse just before it faded behind his warrior's facade once more.

"How do your healing abilities work?" Silver Shadow asked as I pulled his shirt further to the side, revealing the wound.

"It's pretty simple. All I have to do is activate my magic, and it does its own thing. But I will need direct contact with the site of your wound if that's okay?"

The silver male chuckled to himself, and Shadow cut him an even colder glare. "Do you need to leave?"

"No. I am perfectly content to remain right where I am," he said with a muffled chuckle.

I rolled my eyes at them both. "You two might be ancient, but you still act like the young ones."

Shadow's tone was firm and hard once more. "Very brave to insult princes of the Inner Kingdom, Spitfire."

"Thanks for the compliment," I said.

"Or very naive when it comes to understanding the severity of a situation, it seems." His eyes burned with a challenge, and my animal flooded me with strength to meet it.

"I meant it as a testament to your relationship with one another," I interjected quickly, trying to interpret what was brewing underneath his stone-cold expression. "With the world only seeing our mask of iron, those who know us best are able to strip it aside. They allow us to be our most vulnerable and open selves."

"*Iron?*" Shadow tilted his head and arched his brow at me, his expression softening for the briefest of moments. "A little early for that reference, I believe …"

"Oh, Sorry. Probably not the best example."

I had to admit I admired his quick wit and the light-hearted banter he was showing me. It softened him a bit, giving me confidence as I moved closer to examine him. His scent hit me like a brick wall, and my heart began thundering inside my chest.

"May … may I begin?" I stammered, trying to steady my shaking nerves. *Get a grip, Sky*, I cursed. *This is not proper etiquette for healing.* I hated it when my animal instincts flooded me for dominance, especially now. Something about this fae's power riled her up, and I needed to get a hold of her pronto.

Silver Shadow nodded. "Intriguing way to perceive the world," he added as he leaned back.

"You need to relax your shoulders," I scolded, using my firm healer's voice.

I watched him turn his head away to the side and close his eyes once more, but thankfully, his shoulders dropped. I began tracing my hands over the exquisite muscle concealed under the fabric of his shirt. His skin felt electric as my fingers touched his broad chest and shoulder, trying my best not to blush. I prayed to the gods that he didn't notice how fast my heart was racing because there was little, I could do about that.

"We each have a role to play in this life," I said as I meticulously moved my hands closer to the wound. "I'll need you to remain still. Wait, Silver Shadow isn't your real name, is it? I usually know the names of all my patients. Latte, our lead healer, says it's proper bedside manner."

"Daxton Aegaeon, High Prince of Silver Meadows," he said plainly, almost like it was an extension of who he was and what he stood for in this life.

"Okay, that's longer and way more complicated than Silver Shadow."

His eyes flashed open to meet mine, and I swore I was about to receive the retribution for shooting him with my iron arrow. "Daxton is fine," he murmured. "And what pray tell do others call you, Spitfire?"

"Skylar Cathal of the Solace Shifter Pack." I couldn't help but flash him a wide grin that I knew he would shrug off. "Skylar for short, though. Nice to meet you, Daxton."

"I believe our first meeting was not *nice*. You almost killed me." Disdain laced his deep, vibrating voice, but I was determined not to be intimidated by him. I had enough of that happening to me when I was younger, and I thankfully learned how to stand up for myself.

"I said *nice* to meet you. Not … the *first* time," I countered.

A toothless half-grin curved at the side of his trimmed bearded chin, revealing the faint hint of a dimple on his cheek. "Well played, *Skylar*." He spoke my name for the first time, and thankfully, with less venom in his tone. Letting the *S* roll on his tongue for a moment longer than necessary.

"I promise to leave you unharmed after this rendezvous," I said with reassurance.

There it was again—the deep, muffled chuckle that rumbled under the fingers I braced on his chest. Was I somehow amusing to this high prince? In the few moments of knowing him, he was quiet, deathly terrifying one moment and then bantering with me the next. He was a male that spoke more with his actions than with his words. His brother, on the other hand, was definitely the outspoken charmer of the two.

I untied the bandage on Daxton's shoulder and gently placed my palms on either side of the wound. I could feel his heart thumping beneath my hands—steady and strong like a warrior marching on a battlefield. Closing my eyes, I fell into a trance with the rhythm of his strength to help me concentrate. Drawing from the well of power that stirred in me, I released the healing magic that flowed out through my palms and into his skin. My hands emitted a warm golden glow against my fair skin that transferred my energy, mending what was broken and reforming what needed to be rebuilt. It took seconds for my magic to heal him, and I could feel his strength return as the skin stitched together. Regardless of the iron's damage, my healing magic somehow surpassed that barrier. Always had.

"There," I said proudly. "You should feel good as new now." I removed my hands from his shoulder and took a step back so he could examine my handiwork.

"I'm genuinely impressed," Daxton said as he moved about the room, circling his arm to test his mobility. "And that does not happen often."

"Is that yet another compliment from you tonight?" I smirked, dramatically planting my hand to my chest and sighing. "I'm genuinely touched."

"Don't push your luck, *Spitfire*," Daxton added, flashing a hint of amusement in his deep gray eyes.

"And, by the way, I … am Castor Aegaeon," the silver-haired male added from the mantle, watching his brother carefully. "The second son … but still titled as a prince of Silver Meadows. Dax usually has better manners than this and should have introduced me, so please don't judge our kind by his lack of proper etiquette."

Daxton rolled his eyes, continuing to assess the mobility of his shoulder. He was a few inches taller than his brother, with a wider frame that supported a thick, sculpted, muscular physique. I was tall for a female, my final growth spurt raising me to just under six feet tall, but Daxton still had a full head over me. He moved like a warrior, graceful yet powerful, and for the life of me, I couldn't seem to take my eyes off him. I didn't think the human records of the wars he fought in did him any justice. His obvious strength combined with the waves of power I felt emanating from him were unlike anything I had ever experienced.

"Now that I've healed your wound … there's something I need from you." That seemed to get his attention. Daxton whipped his head around and arched his eyebrows with a questioning look. His brother, Castor, gave a smug yet entertained expression.

"Why are you here? How did you venture past the veil and leave the Inner Kingdom?"

Castor rested an elbow on the mantel near the fire and leaned in toward Daxton. He seemed to be on the verge of answering me but stopped to check in and assess his brother's opinion.

"We should just tell her, Dax. I mean, what are the chances the queen will choose her? They will all find out sooner or later why we are here if they don't suspect already."

Daxton stared at the roaring fire and placed his hands on the mantel, bracing his weight onto his arms.

"Please," I asked again, "is it because of the wilt?"

"The wilt?" Castor questioned.

Daxton tilted his head toward his brother. "That is what they call the decay of the land." Castor nodded, but neither of them said anything more, nor did it look like they were going to.

I didn't like how this conversation was going, and I intended to do something about it. "I won't leave until you give me some answers.

If this involves my pack, I deserve to know. We all deserve to know."

"This should come from your elders and your alpha," Daxton said. "It's not our place to tell you."

The high prince's fingers flexed against the brick as a cold chill entered the room, freezing my breath as it exited my lungs. It was not yet the winter season, and the cold southern winds were not due for another few months. I had no idea where this icy breeze was coming from or how. With a raging fire burning, I could see my breath laced with frost.

"Well, I guess I'm here all night then." I plopped myself down onto the chair by the warmth of the fire and casually laced my hands behind my head. "I won't leave until I get my answers." Making myself comfortable in uncomfortable situations was something I strived to achieve.

I was about to say something when the two males suddenly went stiff. A grim look of pain etched into their expressions as they tensed in discomfort. I watched Daxton's fingers practically dig into the brick, ice forming at his hands and cascading through the top of the mantel.

Had he just created a sheet of ice with his bare hands? He had ice magic?

Castor's eyes widened in a look of surprise. "Dax—" He cautioned.

"What's wrong?" I asked. They were both the epitome of strength. Whatever was causing them to cringe like this was something worth noting.

"You need to leave." Castor's once airy sing-song demeanor suddenly changed. He no longer held a light, carefree expression—but one of fear.

I turned my attention to Daxton, feeling his tension and uneasiness continuing to rise. "Daxton?"

Suddenly, his body was towering over me in the chair in a flash of silver light. Daxton's eyes were dark and ominous—embodying fear itself captured inside a glass bottle, ready to shatter and break free with just the right prick.

I was acutely aware of every inch of my skin as he stood over me. The proximity of his body covering mine sent chills down my spine combined with a warmth spreading in my core. The strength and the power I felt from Daxton was intoxicating. My animal stirred inside my chest, answering his call of power with our own rush of magic. My blazing amber eyes sprang to life, meeting his challenge without hesitation.

"There seems to be *more* to you … than I expected," Daxton whispered in a low tone that vibrated through all my senses. It was like a lover's caress without ever touching my skin. Deep and delicious. Dammit, this High Fae's magic was intense.

"How did you do that?" I asked. One second, he was forming icicles on top of the fireplace, and the next, he was standing over me and crossing the span of the room in the blink of an eye.

"Later," he whispered as he grasped my hand.

His touch wasn't as forceful as I anticipated it to be. The callouses on his palms and fingers from countless years of holding a sword were rough but oddly gentle. He paused for a moment, examining the way in which his fingers intertwined with mine.

"Right now," he said with a hesitant, raspy voice, "I need to get you to safety."

What danger was I in? We were in the alpha's home, so technically, this was the safest place for me to be. Before I could respond, the world disappeared before my eyes. One moment, I was leaning back in a chair with a warrior prince straddling over me, and then the next, I was outside.

Wait, outside? How the hell did we get outside?

My feet brushed the familiar wet grass along the forest floor with rain falling from the sky. Before I toppled backward onto the soaked ground, Daxton reached out his other arm, encircling my waist, and pulled me upright against his chest.

*Electricity.* My skin ignited from his touch. From being held in his arms, our bodies flush against each other. I remained utterly still.

Keeping his arm around my waist, Daxton slowly released our laced fingers, meticulously sliding his palm down toward the bite mark he left just below my wrist. His eyes scanned over the mark that would eventually heal and leave a scar.

"Why didn't you heal this?" he asked.

It was a common question asked when people learned about my healing magic. "It's not how my magic works. I can heal others—just not myself. I will end up carrying this scar for the rest of my life." I tried to smile and laugh to release the tension building in my middle. "Didn't know you were leaving me with a souvenir, did ya?"

Daxton creased his brow. "I didn't mean to harm you. I just reacted out of instinct." He paused his gaze, never leaving his mark, and I had to admit I believed him. I couldn't explain why, I just had a feeling, and I could tell my animal agreed. "I have to go now." There was hesitation in his voice, and it almost sounded like he didn't want to leave.

"Right, and go as in … How did you get us here anyway?" This time, he didn't conceal his half-smirk, and the small dimple on his right cheek reappeared.

"You have gifts from your mother, as do I. Mine grant me the magical gift of teleportation—instantly being in one place and then another. A very powerful ability of the mind. I envision where I want to be and then appear there."

"The silver flash!" I spoke. "How far can you travel? Does the distance or frequency of the jump strain your magic? How many can you carry with you? Does this interfere with your ice magic, or do they work together?"

"Do you always have this many questions?" Daxton asked with a half-toothless grin, revealing the dimple I couldn't seem to ignore.

"Of course. As I said before, it's kind of my thing."

"Never a negative trait for a female in my opinion."

"Is that yet *another* compliment from you tonight?"

Daxton huffed a laugh. "To answer one of your endless questions … Yes. That flash of silver light is from my magic. Luckily, there is no indication of where I will go, only where I just was. It is a useful skill to have in battle or when trying to ferry a spitfire shifter from my quarters."

I felt him tense again as his grip tightened around me, pulling me in close as he forcefully shut his eyes. He cringed like he was experiencing intense agony with no known source. He abruptly angled his body away, letting me go, and shaking his head to try and regain his composure.

"Are you all right?" I asked with genuine concern, reaching out to stroke his cheek with my palm. I had no idea what drove me to reach out and touch him like this.

To my surprise, he didn't flinch or push me away. He placed his hand on top of mine and held it there, his eyes darting back toward the window of his third-floor room.

"I have no choice. I have to go." He gently pulled my hand from his face and released his hold on me. "Tomorrow, all this will be explained, I promise. This information needs to be heard from your elders and alpha."

"But, I hesitated, "it's about the wilt? Isn't it?"

"It is," he said with a nod, turning back toward me so his body brushed up against mine. "You have no reason to do so, but I'm asking you to trust me. We are doing everything in our power to stop this. We … we just need help."

A silent moment passed between us, almost like the world stopped turning so we could remain where we were for just a little longer.

I closed my eyes, feeling him lean in closer toward me, with only breath separating us. "I will find you—"

Suddenly, silver light flashed around me, the cold chill of the falling rain stung my face with the absence of his warmth, and I knew Daxton was gone.

# Chapter Seven

I was exhausted and soaked to the bone by the time I finally returned home. Dawn was fast approaching with beams of sunlight peeking over the far-off hills, framing the forest surrounding our village. It was too early for the morning shopkeepers to be awake and too late for the night owls to be lurking in the final moments of the evening. But honestly, I was too tired, wet, and utterly confused to even care if anyone saw me.

All I wanted to do was flop down onto my bed and shut my eyes for some much-needed rest. This mission I decided to take on didn't answer many of my questions, and it only ended up leaving me with more.

That and the fact that no matter how hard I tried, I couldn't seem to get that stupid, stubborn, arrogant High Fae male out of my head. Daxton Aegaeon, *High Prince of Silver Meadows.*

As I opened the front door, I saw Neera curled up on our loveseat, fast asleep. I didn't want to wake her, so I slipped off my boots and carried them as I silently crept upstairs to my own room. It wasn't anything special, but it was one place designated to me—and me alone.

Magnus and Julia still hadn't returned, and I released a heavy sigh of relief as I closed my door behind me. I crossed the small room to open the window, stripped, and wrung out my wet clothing before hanging them to dry on a hook near the opening. I flopped backward onto my bed, barely able to pull my blanket over my face before sleep finally claimed its victory with a familiar dream overtaking my mind.

*I was standing in an open meadow surrounded by mountains covered in snow and ice. My warm breath created fog as I exhaled into the frigid night air. Even though the air was cold, I didn't feel the antagonizing bite of a chill against my skin. The waning moon hung in the dark night sky, high above my head, casting beautiful beams of moonlight that illuminated the surrounding tall grass and trees in the distance. Walking forward into the meadow, I outstretched my hands to dance among the various wildflowers that engulfed the vast opening. I felt calm here. I felt peaceful …*

*Twirling my fingers around the blades of grass, I searched for a special flower I had only ever seen in my dream. Off to the side, I spotted the thick ebony stem cradling a circular cocoon of delicate midnight-black petals. A strong breeze rushed against my bare skin as the clouds up above were brushed aside, revealing the magnificent moon above.*

*I gazed upward toward the mesmerizing idol that represented one of our gods of creation, the Father. The moon … ever watchful during the night. Guarding and protecting us all from the darkness while his mate safely slumbered. The sun, which was a representation of the Mother, would take her turn watching over us against darkness and allow her mate to rest when her rays awakened during the morning. The sun and the moon represented the two gods who, together, created all of Valdor. They watched over and guided us in our life's journeys until it was our time to make the final crossing and join them again in the afterlife.*

*As shifters, we first changed into our animal forms under the power of the full moon. Once the sun rose after our first shift, it was then, if we were lucky enough, that we could recognize our fated mate bond. As young ones, we were taught to respect the balance created by the gods and strive to honor them always. I admired the dual balance of power with the gods. One could not overpower the other, and together, they were stronger than they could ever be apart.*

*I glanced down at the closed flower in my hand and anxiously awaited what I knew would happen next. The moonlight shimmered over the outer petals, and the flower immediately opened into a magnificent bloom. Silver and orange petals danced in the moonlight, with the other flowers in the meadow springing to life all around me. They were vibrant and breathtaking, fanning outward and up like it was stretching out to try and touch the sky.*

*This place always felt like home. Like a distant beacon, calling to me and my animal. I had only visited this meadow in my dreams, but it still felt so real—*

Thud–thud–thud.

"Skylar …" Magnus's voice bellowed from beyond the wooden door frame.

I groaned and turned over in my bed, burying my face underneath the pillow to try and ignore my uncle.

"Skylar, the entire day has practically passed by. Are you just going to let it go to waste?"

"Magnus," I grumbled. "Come on, don't guilt trip me." I could feel his disappointing glare through the layers of pillows, sheets and beyond my door.

"May I come in?"

"It's your house … I don't see why not."

I could hear him chuckle as the handle of the knob turned. We both knew he wouldn't enter unless I gave him permission to do so. Even if this was his house, Magnus always respected my privacy.

My bed shifted under his weight as he sat down next to my feet. Magnus had a stocky warrior's build, and stood just taller than me, with thick, short wavy brown hair and a full beard that covered his pale complexion. His green eyes were the exact same as my father's and Neera's. The Cathal green eyes that passed through our bloodline for generations.

*And skipped right over me. Oh, joy.*

"Not easy staying up on patrol all night, is it?" Magnus said.

"You and Julia seem to manage just fine." I yawned and moved my feet so he could sit more comfortably.

"Raising children helps prepare you for sleepless nights," he chuckled. "And you were kept busy … coming into contact with a High Fae," Magnus added with a fatherly tone that told me he knew everything. "Now that must have been exciting. Care to tell me about it?"

"Define exciting," I said, still buried beneath my pillow. "And don't forget accidentally almost killing him. Did Gilen leave that part out?"

"No, he did not." Magnus's deep voice rumbled with amusement. There was no doubt that his animal was a bear; all you had to do was hear him laugh or yell and the roar was unmistakable. "I was glad he ordered Talon to bring you straight home."

"I guess." I rolled my eyes, still hidden under the pillow, but I knew he could read my tone. I was not pleased.

"Very mature," Magnus grumbled. "And you, being you … followed Gilen's command without question and remained here all night?"

I reached up and moved the pillow off my face. I was too tired to play interrogator right now. All I wanted to do was sleep. "Yup," I said, giving him a thumbs-up, then promptly thumped my head back against the feathered bedding, looking up to the ceiling.

"I'm sorry to keep you up. I won't be much longer, I promise," he said with an all-too knowing chuckle, "you must be exhausted from your run-in with the High Fae."

"Exactly."

"So, my next question is … was this before you were taken home? Or after you snuck into Alistar's manor?"

My eyes darted to meet his, and the smug grin on his face was something only a father could give. I sat up straight in my bed, scrambling to think of something through my fog of exhaustion. "Umm."

The gleam in Magnus's eyes was mixed with amusement but also a twinge of disappointment. He stroked his beard with one hand, his brows furrowing as he mulled over my response.

I often imagined if he and my father would have held similar expressions whenever scolding me about something, and this was no exception. Magnus had a gritty, shaggy roughness that perfectly mimicked his grizzly bear form.

"Skylar." His deep voice rumbled with authority. I didn't know if he was demanding answers or just waiting for me to confess what I was thinking.

"Gods. Above." I narrowed my eyes and crossed my arms in front of my chest. "Neera."

"Don't blame her. You know she can't tell a lie to save her life, and she was asleep downstairs when we came home this morning. Julia and I both knew something was going on."

I rolled my eyes and scoffed loudly, curling my knees to my chest and hugging my legs. I knew she wouldn't be able to lie to her mom and dad. She was too pure-hearted and kind to step out of line and do something like that.

"You used a beta command on her, though, right?"

"Unfortunately, yes."

I smiled to myself at the thought of Magnus having to use his animal's power to force Neera to fess up about what happened.

As shifters, we followed and obeyed the dynamic of power. The alpha was always the strongest among us, with his beta following close behind. When either of them gave a command, power flowed into their words. It was hard to describe, but it was like a compulsion was placed over the shifter, and they couldn't resist the pull to follow their leader's order.

Me, on the other hand, I had a special ability to resist Magnus's and even Alistar's commands. I played it off as a hindrance, blaming my human half for not "hearing" them, but that was not the case at all. I heard them loud and clear. I just didn't always have to obey. My animal didn't want to submit, and I had free will to resist the compulsion.

"Well, even Neera doesn't know the whole story about what happened after I left. I didn't wake her up when I returned. So, logically, I assume you are here to get the rest of the story."

Magnus sighed heavily, his head bending forward as he reached out his other hand to pat my foot. "We both know you will have to tell me willingly. I can't force it out of you."

"I could be bribed," I teased.

Magnus smiled, and it made me relax. I respected my uncle and didn't want to hide anything from him intentionally. I knew he only had my best interests at heart.

"What would be your price?"

That got my attention. I lifted myself up so I could sit cross-legged on the bed. "Information."

"Such as?" he asked, arching his dark brows and scrunching his face to the side, having no idea what he was getting himself into with this type of bargain.

"I answer one question, then you do the same."

He paused to consider the arrangement before answering. "Deal. Now, get dressed and come downstairs. Julia is making a very late breakfast … Well, dinner now? Or late lunch? Regardless, she is again cooking alone without her favorite helper, so hurry up." Magnus patted my leg, stood up, and marched out of my room, closing the door behind him.

"Coming right up." I grinned and sprang out of bed. Luckily, my clothes had dried from my nighttime excursions, but I decided a fresh shirt and pants wouldn't be the worst thing in the world.

Hurtling down the stairs, I turned the corner to the kitchen, where Julia had a stack of potatoes waiting for me to start dicing.

As I entered, she gave me a soft, loving smile. "Neera and Magnus are gathering a few herbs and peppers from the garden. Get started on the potatoes while I work on the eggs."

I grabbed the knife, spun it around in my palm, and quickly began working on dicing the potatoes into bite-sized cubes. "Are we feeding an army today?"

"Our house has two full adult shifters, potentially one more after tonight's full moon and one on the verge of shifting in the next few years. We were *all* awake for most if not all night. I'm not sure I have enough food to fuel us for another night of antics."

I blinked and stopped chopping. "Oh right, the full moon gathering tonight."

How had that slipped my mind? Dammit, I needed to get my head on straight and stop thinking about the stupid High Fae. Regardless of the reasons why they were here, the shifter's moon held the higher priority.

"Yes, dear," Julia lovingly replied. "Will tonight be your time to finally join us?"

I didn't have the heart to tell her that this time, along with all the others, I was not going to shift. I couldn't explain why I wasn't going to—just that I, well, *we*, weren't ready. My animal was content with not revealing herself, and I was not going to push her to do it.

"Never know until it happens, right?" I smiled weakly and returned to my chopping.

Magnus and Neera entered the kitchen from the back door and sat down around the large island in the center. Neera looked at me and then turned her gaze away quickly. I could tell she felt horrible for telling Magnus.

"Don't feel bad, Neera. I'm not mad."

The tension in her shoulders slackened as a bright smile crossed her freckled cheeks. She slid next to me, helping me work on the giant stack of potatoes in the center of the island. I couldn't be mad at her for long anyway. I knew Neera would never do anything to cause harm intentionally. Her gentle-natured heart was a rarity in this world, and I knew I would do anything to protect her.

"All right," Magnus announced as he pulled up a stool across from me. "Time to begin."

"You want to go first?" I offered. "Age before beauty, right?"

I heard Julia chuckle off to the side as Magnus scoffed a humorless laugh.

"Sure …" he said, flexing a hand around a dagger on his belt, casually thrumming his fingers along the sheath.

Shifters carried weapons we could easily unclip or disengage when needed. While in our animal forms, we didn't have a need for blades or a bow because *we* were the weapons.

"Where did you go inside the alpha's home?" Magnus asked, narrowing his gaze.

*Getting right to the heart of it. Fantastic.* One thing I learned from Magnus and Rhea was to not dance around the topic when trying to get information.

"I went to the healers' quarters and then to the third floor." He never asked me who I saw or what I did. So, I purposely left those details out.

"My turn. Why are the High Fae here?"

Magnus accepted a cup of hot tea from Julia, and they exchanged an uneasy look before he answered. "They are here to ask for help."

Bastard. He was using my own tricks against me, and he knew it. The grin on his face was cocky and calculating.

*Oh … let the games begin, Uncle.*

Magnus took a long sip of his tea before asking another. "Who did you see last night inside the alpha's home?"

He was getting more specific now—good. I wasn't a fan of boredom. "I saw you, Julia, Alistar, some elders, and Gilen," I answered as I gathered the diced potatoes in a bowl to season before Julia fried them in the pan of oil. I raised my brows with a smirk. He never asked who I talked to, just who I saw.

"My turn." I could see a hint of pride shine in his eyes despite the lack of information he was getting out of me. Magnus had trained me since I was little to ask questions, always encouraging my curiosity and helping me grow my mind. "Why did the High Fae come here to ask for help?"

"Because shifters are the only ones who can give them aid. Now, who did you interact with while in the alpha's house last night?"

I mulled over how to answer this one. Should I use their nicknames or their true identities? There was so much I didn't know about the fae, but I also wanted to gauge his reaction. "Daxton Aegaeon, High Prince of Silver Meadows, and his brother, Castor."

Magnus's expression remained stoic, but Julia's fumble with the spatula gave a window into what her mate was truly feeling on the inside. They could sense each other's emotions through their mate bond, similar to how we could feel our animals. Although Julia was not as skilled at masking her emotions as Magnus.

"What did you do while you were with them?"

I held up a finger and wagged it from side to side. "Wait, it's my turn. What help are the High Fae asking for?"

This time, Magnus tried to answer, but he couldn't. "I-I can't answer that, Skylar."

I knew he wanted to, but this clearly wasn't a choice for him. It dawned on me that the alpha must have given a gag order for this particular piece of information. "What can you tell me?"

He tapped his fingers on the tabletop, thinking about what details he could share with me. "I can tell you that tonight, everything will come to light. This is something Alistar wants to address with all of us himself. It is not my place to overstep his command."

Dammit. I knew it.

"Well, this game is over then," I announced as I finished dicing the final potato. With Magnus unable to answer my questions, I was not obligated to answer any of his. "But I'll give you a bonus just because I love you." I bent over, batting my eyes playfully at Magnus, who gave me an unimpressed look that made me chuckle on the inside. "I went to heal the male I shot with the iron-tipped arrow. I felt horrible about almost killing him and wanted to make sure he was all right."

"And you healed him?" Julia asked.

"I did," I said with a firm nod.

I left out the fact that I already knew the High Fae were here because of the wilt. I knew everything I had asked Magnus. I just wanted to make sure they were aware of it as well. I also chose to leave out the details I learned about Daxton. His power and strength were unlike anything I had ever experienced before. I didn't know what it meant, but I knew they were important.

Julia finished preparing the meal, and the four of us ate like ravaged, starving beasts. There was no scrap to spare. If there was one thing shifters did well, that was eating. I cleaned my plate and grabbed the bag I left by the doorway the other day.

Scanning through the contents, I stopped as my fingers grasped the soft fabric of Gilen's shirt. I glanced around to see if anyone had followed me or was watching what I was doing. To my surprise, I was alone for the moment, so I lifted the fabric to my nose and inhaled a deep, steady breath. The salty sea air was sweet and wild. I waited to see if my animal would have any reaction, but she remained calm and content. I didn't know what I was expecting, to be honest. I placed the tan tunic back in the sack and counted the books inside.

"Oh no." One of the books was missing.

I must have left it on the green sand beach. I hated the thought of that book weathered and destroyed by the waves and sand. I had to retrieve it before the gathering tonight.

"Magnus, Julia," I hollered. "I have to go back to the beach and retrieve a book I left behind."

Magnus peeked his head around the corner. "You have to be at the alpha's before the full moon gathering tonight, Skylar. That is not an option." I could sense a wave of power coming through his words … It wasn't a command, but, instead, a stern parental warning.

"I know … I know," I reassured him. "Trust me. I have questions, and if you are telling me that tonight I am going to get my answers, you bet your ass I'll be there on time. Even early if I can help it!"

Neera giggled near the sink as she helped Julia with the dishes. I didn't wait for Magnus to remind me again about the gathering and dashed out of the house with my bag strapped to my back.

I took off at a slow jog. Most of the day had passed, but there was still plenty of time to return from the beach before the moon was high in the sky.

The trail to the green sand beach was one of my favorites. I loved how the specks of green were subtly scattered along the tanned pathway, hinting at the treasure hidden in the nearby cove. I slowed my jog and began to walk, allowing the fresh sea breeze to cool my brow and fill my spirits with a sense of freedom.

I loved the feel of the wind and the beauty of the sky. The openness of the world above, with no shackles holding you down, was a dream. My animal stirred inside me, enjoying the feel of the breeze across my skin. I knew she craved the wind, too.

I approached the cliffside leading down to the beach, and without giving it a second thought, I began the descent to my sanctuary below. Landing firmly in the olivine particles, I stood in awe of what I saw. It wasn't until I scaled the final drop that I even noticed *him.*

How was *he* here?

Daxton, High Prince of Silver Meadows, was casually wading in the waters along the shore of the green sand beach—my beach. This was *my* hidden sanctuary. How in the gods' names did he even know this place was here? It wasn't a location that many knew of or even cared to venture to.

I licked my lips and fidgeted with the strap on my bag while ducking behind a divot along the cliff. What would I even say? What should I do? Should I just walk up and say hello with an awkward wave?

Glancing around the corner, I watched him closely. He appeared to be deep in thought, allowing the water to guide his footsteps as he walked with his back toward me. He was barefoot, wading in and out of the rolling waves, with his dark gray pants rolled up to his knees. The black shirt he wore was casual, but it still had a trace of elegance with silver threading along the neckline and the center. It was open at the top, revealing a hint of his muscular physique underneath that I had to admit I remembered a little too fondly.

The breeze swept past me, and I inhaled his sweetened scent of pine and cold. I continued to watch him, unable to or maybe not wanting to turn away. He was mesmerizing and not just because of his magic or strength—it was more than that. It was the way he made me feel in his presence that intrigued me the most. Like me, Daxton was … different.

I watched as he reached the end of the shoreline near the surrounding cliff and abruptly turned around to continue walking toward my hideaway. He clasped his arms behind his back as a smug, amused expression appeared across his face. He blinked slowly, allowing his gray eyes to soften, and I could have sworn a grin slid onto his hardened exterior. The dimple on his right cheek appeared, and my stomach erupted with the feeling of butterflies.

"Hello, *Spitfire*," he announced, his husky voice echoing along the cliffs.

My eyes widened, and I froze.

His voice was like a soft velvet caress on my skin. Daxton called out to me like we had known each other for years instead of only just meeting last night. My animal flooded me with a flush of power in my chest as my cheeks flushed crimson.

How in the gods' names did I think I could hide my presence from his detection this long? *Ugh.* Had he known I was here the whole time? *This was utterly embarrassing.*

"I can sense you behind the crack in the cliffs. I said I would find you, but it seems you have found me instead," he added.

*Dammit.* I pushed my back against the divot to try and compose myself, clutching my bag to my chest and placing a palm to my forehead. I had to get a grip, but that was easier said than done. I could feel my animal stirring in response to his magic, a mere dance for dominance.

"Skylar, you can come out. I promise I won't bite … unless you have a bow paired with a quiver of iron-tipped arrows and are trying to kill me again?" Daxton's tone was softer this time, almost friendly.

I couldn't help my faint snort of amusement. Sarcasm, really? Was this ancient fae warrior actually making a joke, trying to make me feel better? Swallowing my pride, I turned around and moved out from my not-so-secret hiding place.

"Promise?" I taunted, cocking my hip to the side and placing a hand on it.

"My teeth will remain caged. It's never my intention to disrupt your world or stake claim to what clearly belongs to another."

I narrowed my eyes in annoyance. "I don't *belong* to anyone but myself," I said with a deep growl at the back of my throat.

"Really?" he asked, cocking an intrigued black eyebrow toward me, seeming surprised and also amused by my response.

I put my hands firmly on my hips, staring down at him without fear. "Really," I stated plainly.

"All right then." He smirked, and that damned dimple on his right cheek appeared again.

I didn't know what to say or do next. My mind shifted to Gilen, and I realized that Daxton must have smelled his scent on me the other night. Awkwardly, I shifted my bag on my shoulder and reached up to scratch the back of my head. Unspoken moments passed between us, with only the gentle crashing of the waves and the churning breeze filling the silence.

"I think we started off on the wrong foot," I announced, gaining his immediate attention. "So, let's try this again." I jumped down from the cliff wall and stood before him. "Hi," I said shyly, changing my demeanor to try a more friendly approach. "How are you doing today? Is your wound feeling better?"

"Hello," Daxton answered with a slight dip of his head, followed by a deep, graceful bow. "I'm feeling much better. Thank you, for asking." There was suddenly a softness in his hardened stare that I hadn't seemed to notice before. "It is astonishing what treasures you can find hidden in plain sight, is it not?" he asked, his gaze scanning over the beach before returning to look at me. "Unparalleled beauty can be missed if one does not take the time to look. But today, I'm fortunate enough to find what I have been looking for."

I gulped loudly and began to nervously fidget with a strand of my hair. This male embodied power and strength, and even in this calm, relaxing scenario, he held a natural, regal composure unmatched by any other living soul.

"And what exactly have you been looking for?" I boldly asked.

"A hidden treasure," he replied, his stare boring into me, nearly taking my breath away. A small curve of his mouth turned upward before he tilted his head to the side with an amused expression flashing across his annoyingly handsome face. "I've visited this place before, and I was ecstatic to have found it once again."

"You've been here before?" I asked, learning yet another clue to who he was. "When?"

"You have a curious nature, don't you?" Daxton rebutted, giving me a full saccharine smile.

"Surprised it took you this long to figure that out." I shrugged with a humorless laugh.

Daxton didn't speak, but his smile managed to reach both sides of his face, revealing his teeth that I remembered all too well.

"Well, am I going to get any more answers from you yet, High Prince?"

"No. Not at the moment … but soon."

"Not the first time I've heard that," I grumbled in annoyance as I averted my gaze down toward my side. I was starting to get tired of hearing that answer.

"But perhaps I can share something I have learned over nearly six centuries walking this earth."

I was immediately intrigued, raising my brows, and crossing my arms, eagerly awaiting his reply.

"Everything in life happens for a reason."

I scoffed and shook my head, flipping my hair over my shoulder and flashing him a look that said, *Really?*

He chuckled, his dimple once again appearing beneath his half-smile at the corner of his cheek. "Really," he replied. "We just don't always know the reasons why fate has guided us. Good things come to those who are patient."

"Not my strong suit. Hate to break it to ya."

"Perhaps not," he snickered. "But your other strengths are superior, matched by your cunning spitfire mind and radiant beauty." The way he looked at me sent my heart racing. With fear or something else, I didn't know just yet. "Here," Daxton said, extending his hand. "I believe this is what you were looking for. I found it over there along the shoreline and thought it best to ensure its safe return, but here you are."

Looking down, I realized he held the book I was looking for in his outstretched hand. Where he had been keeping it, I had no clue. But magically, here it was.

"Oh, thank you!" I flashed a girlish grin and reached out to happily accept the book. "Hopefully not to your surprise, I have more questions now."

"I am shocked," he teased with an amused gleam shining in his eyes. His lip curled upward, and I couldn't help myself from smiling back at him.

I reached out to grasp the book, and my fingertips lightly brushed against his skin. My animal's power surged through me, stoking the burning fire generated by just a whisper of his touch. My eyes flared to life within my amber-colored gaze, locking with his storming gray stare.

He immediately released the book and staggered backward, putting distance between us.

"I-it's my animal …" I stammered. "I must be reacting to your magic. I don't know how to describe it. It just feels, I don't know, different." Clutching the book to my chest, I dipped my chin and averted my eyes.

"You …" Daxton's voice was raspy, holding an air of uncertainty that caught me off guard. "You are so much more than what is seen on the surface, Spitfire," Daxton replied.

I forced myself to look at him and felt waves of confusion spiraling through my head and body. "It comes with the territory of being a hybrid, I guess."

"No," he said in a hushed whisper. "You intrigue me, Spitfire. Not many things in this world do that anymore."

"Maybe you should find a new hobby or something. Have you tried needlepoint? It's similar to a sword, only smaller in comparison. I hear from our elders that keeping the mind sharp in old age is crucial—"

The booming laughter that erupted from within his chest was the same as the previous night. Only this time it wasn't muffled. It made me smile, enjoying this shift in his fearsome personality from when we first met.

Daxton regained his composure and took a step closer toward me once more. "Sound advice," he murmured through his dwindling chuckle. "This visit to the mainland has inspired me unlike any others I have taken. New opportunities seem to be presenting themselves, and I would be a fool to allow them to pass by unnoticed."

"You've mentioned that you have ventured outside the veil before. What made you return?"

Daxton's narrowed smirk told me he was impressed that I picked up on that information slip. He constricted his gaze on me like he was trying to figure out the answer to the riddle. Oddly enough, it seemed to be *me.*

"I travel outside the veil to help aid my people, and I will continue to do so as long as there is a need."

I waited for him to continue, but that was apparently all the details I was going to get for now. Very vague and likes to dance around the truth—noted.

"It appears time is of the essence." Daxton tilted his head toward the orange and yellow sky with flecks of pink. The sun was beginning its descent below the horizon, and the night of the full moon was fast upon us. "It is getting late, and we both need to return to the village before nightfall."

"Oh no!" I exclaimed, anxiously stuffing the book into my bag. I knew I could make it back in time, but I couldn't casually go about it like I did getting here. Without thinking, I turned to begin scaling the cliffs. Once I reached the top, I glanced back over my shoulder, thinking a wave goodbye might suffice, but Daxton was already gone.

"Add it to the list," I said, muttering to myself.

"To what list?"

I squealed like a little girl—much to my dismay—and turned my head around to see Daxton standing on the path behind me. "What? How?"

He laughed and smiled again—a true beaming smile that could leave females everywhere weak in their knees. "My mother's gift," he replied with a slight nod of a bow. "I will find you again, Spitfire. Thank you for the lively conversation."

*Lively?* I cocked a confused brow as he vanished once more.

In a silver flash of light, he was gone. To where I had no clue. I scoffed and cursed myself for not asking if he could take me with him like he did before. It really could have saved me from the headache and exhaustion if I could magically transport myself from one place to another.

Lucky fae, unlucky shifter-human.

I started running toward Solace, my mind now changing focus to tonight's full moon gathering. The setting sun painted the sky in vibrant colors that streamed overhead, creating a beautiful display that painters tried but often fell short of recreating. If I had the time, I would stop and watch the sunset and the stars begin to appear. But, as Daxton had mentioned, time was of the essence.

I knew I would not shift tonight, but I could tell Gilen and possibly Rhea were about to change for the first time. Fate was a fickle thing. Gilen shifting tonight brought so many unknowns into my life, in addition to Alistar finally telling us all why the High Fae were here and why we were the only ones who could help them. The wilt was slowly gaining ground, and the decay of our world put us all in jeopardy.

# Chapter Eight

I made it, and just in the nick of time.

Dusk took hold of the village as the evening stars shimmered in the blackened night sky. I dropped my book off in the library of the alpha's wing and raced out toward the meadow. The trek was simple enough, and it wouldn't take much time for me to get there. I could see crowds of people gathering up ahead, with adults and young ones along the edges surrounding those of us old enough to shift for the first time. The speckled cloudy evening allowed a partial view of the stars and moon above. The instinct to shift would begin once the full moon reached its apex.

We were all taught at a young age that each one of our animals would choose when and where they would appear. This was an accepted part of our magic and not something we could control or predict. There were definitely signs, but there was no guarantee when a shifter would change for the first time.

Before I reached the tree-lined trail to the meadow, a familiar voice caught my attention. "There you are, Sky."

I stopped, frozen in my steps on the dirt trail from shock at hearing the sound of his voice again. "Xander?"

He stepped out into the clearing, and I detected his spicy aroma which always reminded me of cinnamon. His dark brown hair curled at the nape of his neck, flowing in lazy waves along his brow line with a new beard grazing his jaw. His cocoa-colored eyes were narrowed and focused solely on me. I quickly recovered from my shock and slapped on an indifferent expression that I had perfected since he ended our relationship the morning after his first shift.

"I was wondering when you were going to show up."

"Why do you care? I thought I was no longer your problem when you broke things off last year."

His mouth twisted into a firm thin line as he took in a labored breath before stuffing his hands into his loose pants pockets. "I never meant to hurt you, Sky. It's just …"

"It's just that I am only a half-shifter, right?" Xander's dark brows lifted. A look of unease flashed, before his hard-edged expression returned once more. "Save it," I said, holding my hand up and shaking my head, not wanting to hear another word out of his mouth.

I could have stormed off right then and there, but then I would be no better than he was. I didn't want to, but I turned to face him.

"Look …" I sighed, hating being the bigger person in this. "The sting of your rejection and lack of explanation last spring wasn't easy for me, but I decided a while ago to move on." It was his turn to look surprised. "How can I help you, Xander?"

He frowned, his eyes turning somber. And if I didn't know any better, I swore he seemed hurt by what I had just said. "I … Gods. Above," he cursed. "I just … I just wanted to make sure you were here tonight. That's all. I wouldn't want it to be your time to shift, and you were not here with the others …"

"Again. Why do you care, Xander?"

"I never stopped caring, Skylar," he admitted, and I felt a flicker of cold snake its way up my spine.

"Then … what?" I was completely thrown off my game. If I had any to speak of.

Xander had dumped me the morning after his first shift and, regrettably, after giving him head the night before. He had cut all ties with me, barely looking me in the eye or talking to me since then. I had always assumed it was because I was only a half-shifter. Never good enough for his pure bloodline to mix with.

After all, he was currently with a lioness shifter whose family was very outspoken against allowing half-shifters into the higher ranks within the pack. Thankfully, they didn't want to exile me, but they did not approve of my status in Gilen's patrol guard. They believed I should focus on my healing gifts and only train as a healer.

"I never stopped thinking about you. I can't explain it, but even though you were not my mate, my animal was somehow drawn to you. *Is* drawn to you."

"Okay. Not weird at all," I said with a heavy dose of sarcasm paired with an eye roll.

"You're a remarkable female, Skylar, with a sharp wit and caring heart. Plenty of males still have their eyes on you."

"Even though …" I began, but he abruptly cut me off.

"Your power shines through the bullshit politics of the elders and you know it."

This was beginning to turn uncomfortable. "All right. That's enough, Xander." I didn't need to travel down this road with him. It would only lead me into trouble.

"I know it doesn't make sense, but … I wanted you to know that I was told to leave you alone. When the mate bond wasn't there, I was ordered to back off."

*What the actual fuck?* My eyes widened with disbelief at his confession.

"Skylar!"

My head snapped around, recognizing the voice of the shifter who, only last night, had stolen my breath away with an earth-shattering kiss under the willow tree. Gilen's golden blond hair was free-flowing in the night's breeze, and his honeyed hazel eyes glowed when he saw me, before hardening as they darted back to Xander.

"I was just leaving," Xander countered, lowering his gaze and dropping his shoulders in a submissive stance toward Gilen.

It was all starting to make sense now, and I was beginning to put the pieces together as I watched the exchange between the two males. It was crazy and an utterly insane theory, but all signs were pointing to it.

Gilen had commanded Xander to end our relationship.

"Good," Gilen growled, narrowing his stare and pushing out a wave of power that made the hairs on my arm stand at attention.

My animal naturally awakened to answer the challenge, and she didn't hesitate to flush my body with her own strength.

"Glad you decided to finally show up," he said as he looped an arm around my shoulder and possessively tucked me into his side.

I couldn't help my grin spreading from ear to ear, nuzzling into the nook of his collarbone. "I made it." I felt Xander's eyes watching us, but I couldn't care less at this moment.

Gilen flashed me a wide grin. "I only doubted you … for a moment."

He reached to cup my face with his strong hand and leaned in to kiss me. It was soft, unhurried like yesterday's, hidden away in the forest. He was easy, gentle, and tender. Delicate, like a mate greeting their other half after finally coming together after time spent apart.

"Go now, Xander," Gilen commanded without even turning to look at him, and Xander quickly obeyed, darting away back into the woods. Gilen held me close as we walked down the dirt path together, joining our people in the meadow where the full moon was beginning to rise overhead.

Rhea was my best friend, but Gilen had always held a special place in my heart. Since my uncle was the beta of the pack, we practically grew up together, and I never had to taste the sting of loneliness with him by my side. He was the rule follower, always there to pull me back if I ever strayed too far. We balanced one another, and Gilen was the first person to ever witness my healing powers.

When we were small children, Alistar called Magnus to his manor to review their plans for securing the outer borders. Naturally, I begged Magnus to come so I could play with Gilen. A single day seemed like an eternity when you were separated from your friend at that age. He happily obliged, which also gave Julia a quiet moment in the house with baby Neera.

The males left us to play in the yard, and Alistar used his alpha command to ensure we didn't wander … but I had other plans. We could not leave the yard, but he never said anything about climbing above the area. I practically had to drag Gilen up into the trees that day. Everything was fun, laughter, and games until Gilen jumped and missed the branch on one of the neighboring trees. He fell … colliding with the earth and shattering the bones in his arm.

I rushed down to him to help. His screams and tears were flowing, and I knew he was badly hurt. I didn't know how to help, but instinct told me to reach out my hands and try to ease his pain. Suddenly, my palms glowed a golden color, and my powers manifested, healing his broken arm.

Any *normal* shifter would have freaked out and run for help … but not Gilen. He was amazed and praised me for my special gift, encouraging me to share it instead of hiding it away. I don't know what would have happened if I had come into my powers with anyone else but him.

Entering the meadow, we stopped when we saw our friends, and he boldly pulled me in for another soft kiss. The heat from his body wrapped around me as my desire began to build, flipping my stomach and flushing my cheeks red. I didn't want this to end. I didn't want him to ever stop kissing me.

"Ahh-hem," Rhea coughed.

Gilen pulled his luscious lips from mine, and I shot an evil glare in her direction. Rhea shrugged her shoulders and turned back to her conversation with Shaw and Talon. Her words of caution the other night flooded the logical side of my mind. I wanted to heed my best friend's warnings about Gilen, and Shaw's, but the reality of him was all too much for me to just push aside.

Thankfully, Gilen didn't break away and lightly kissed my forehead. "We will continue this later," he whispered as he kept one arm around my waist, holding me close against his side.

Butterflies danced inside me, and all I could do was nod that I heard him. The questions began spinning around in my mind with whispers of a secret hope becoming a reality. Were we fated mates? This was crazy. Me, the half-breed late-blooming shifter, bonded to the future alpha. The other females in our pack who had chased after him for years would not be pleased.

Dozens of us waiting to shift were gathered here tonight, and I could only imagine how many more were still coming. Alistar issued an order to all Satellite regions of our pack to send representation to our main stronghold for tonight. Every shifter who might transition to their animal form was here in attendance, making this one of the largest gatherings of our people.

The Solace pack held a majority of its members here in the main village, but there were also factions spread out around the northern areas of Valdor. Alistar communicated through sub-alphas he placed in positions of leadership in the other regions under his protection. If we counted each shifter in Valdor, we would be close to a few thousand of us all together. Nothing compared to the human population, but we were able to hold our own and keep a strong grip on our territory.

Humans might have the numbers and a select few with access to magic, but we had the strength of our people and fierce fighting animal forms. We were naturally faster and stronger, and once we shifted, those abilities increased tenfold, along with the rapid healing abilities similar to the fae.

Among the chaos and frenzy of Gilen's isolated attention and the large number of us here tonight, I almost missed the arrival of the High Fae Royalty.

Daxton marched out into the meadow, and every pair of shifter eyes snapped in his direction. His casual dress from before had vanished: donning leather boots with his dark gray trousers paired with ebony armor with intricate silver threading, and a cloak draped over one shoulder, with the other holding an emblem of three silver mountain peaks. He was armed to the teeth, with a long silver blade strapped to his back and daggers at his belt. He held a cold, distant expression I recognized from the descriptions written about him in the texts.

Right now, he was the Silver Shadow. A deadly warrior that struck fear into the hearts of all those who opposed him before his sword finished the job. His hair was tied back from his face, exposing his menacingly terrifying storm-cloud stare, the distinctly pointed ears, and the remarkable beauty of a High Fae.

That was one side to him, but I knew there was another. My mind drifted to our conversation on the beach and the previous night when I had healed his wound. There was a different side to him—a humorous, perhaps gentler demeanor that he had to keep hidden beneath the surface to protect himself.

Castor strutted out behind his brother, and I mean literally strutted. He wore a similar coloring to Daxton's attire but a longer dress coat instead of a cloak over a shoulder and carried far fewer weapons.

I chuckled at his casual yet authoritative presence following in Daxton's footsteps. Castor's silver hair flowed in his face, and as he reached up to casually brush it away, he flashed a brazen grin at any female he could. I swear I heard swoons from behind me as Castor paraded with more confidence than a peacock on display out toward the gathering crowds. I snickered and rolled my eyes, unimpressed by his flashy demeanor.

Gilen pulled me closer to him. "Looks like the High Fae you shot the other evening is healed."

I only nodded. There was no way I was going to ruin this moment and let him know I bent his rules. I turned to look at Gilen, but his eyes were firmly set on his father, who had entered the clearing.

The night became thick with the anticipation of our people gathered under the full moon. The trees seemed to silence themselves, listening in and watching us from their rooted stations. The winds settled as the blades of grass slowed their swaying movements in the crisp evening air. Even the songbirds and crickets were silent, waiting for something to happen. The night was unusually calm, and it made me uneasy. Something was happening, and I was dying to figure out answers to my many, many questions.

Our alpha stood tall and proud in the open area of the grass meadow. His golden hair was highlighted by a full beard that was beginning to hold streaks of white. His warm, light-hazel eyes embodied the heat of the sun, giving him a kind yet powerful persona. He was the protector of our people and did not take his role lightly.

His claimed mate, Helen, Gilen's mother, stood next to him. Her long, wavy brown hair was pulled into a braid that hung across her exposed, tanned shoulder. Her brown eyes shone with intelligence and a cunning nature. Like my aunt Julia, Helen was a mountain lion in her animal form.

The High Fae princes approached Alistar, and Daxton greeted our alpha with a firm, outstretched handshake. Their greetings seemed friendly enough, but it also could have been a faked pleasant encounter. I couldn't exactly tell. Both the males held unreadable expressions, locking away any hint of how they were really feeling deep below the surface.

I hated that they could do this so well. I couldn't hide any emotions like that if my life depended on it.

"What questions are mulling in that pretty little mind of yours?" Gilen whispered with a smirk.

"Little?" I asked with an arched brow and scoffed at him. "What do you know about all of this?" I tilted my head in the direction of Daxton and Castor.

Gilen was silent and kept his gaze forward as he shifted to move behind me. His right arm wrapped around my middle as our bodies molded together. I was keenly aware of the possessiveness he was displaying toward me, and in this moment, I honestly didn't know what to think.

Gilen brushed my hair to the side as his lips danced lightly over the skin on my neck. "I might know something," he whispered.

My breathing quickened as I reached up and laced my fingers into his hand behind my head. "You have a price, I imagine?"

"Just one."

His teeth nipped at the bottom of my neck, near the nape of my collarbone, and my undergarments were soaked in an instant.

For shifters, this is one of the most sensual and erogenous regions of our bodies. It was the place where a mate would make their claim and mark the other with their bite. A bite that connected the pair forever with an exchange of power that linked their souls for all eternity.

I melted.

"But for now, it can wait," he teased and pulled back to whisper again in my ear. "My father and High Queen Minaeve met just after dawn. They are here to seek our help to end the wilt. Shifters are the only ones who can put a stop to the decay of Valdor because we are the only ones who can unlock the magic to end it."

"How do we unlock the magic? What magic can heal our world? Why can only a shifter access it?"

Gilen laughed. "So many questions." His lip turned up as his eyes shone with amusement.

"Why does that surprise you? You had to know I would ask."

"Soon, I will be able to help tame your wild mind." Gilen's comment was said casually, but it made me nervous. I cocked my head to look at him with uncertainty hidden beneath my stare. "Ever since we were kids, Sky … I always had to make sure you stayed in line. But don't worry, soon it will all make sense. Fate has finally brought us together."

Gilen tightened his grip on my hip and nudged my head for me to look toward our alpha. I wanted to ask more questions, but instead, I ended up following his silent command. Alistar stepped out into the moonlight, and our pack unanimously gave him their undivided attention.

Well, everyone did—except for me.

I couldn't help it, or perhaps deep down, I didn't want to. My line of sight drifted past Alistar and fell to the mysterious High Fae warrior standing behind our alpha.

Daxton's gray eyes felt like they were seeing directly into my soul, and for a split second, the world disappeared within the intensity of his stare. Fire erupted through me, his scent and the feel of his magic somehow drifting through the distance between us and engulfing my senses. My stomach plummeted as my hand dropped from Gilen's. An intense wave of heat passed through my middle and flowed out through my appendages like liquid fire through my veins.

"Pay attention, Sky," Gilen muttered.

I shook myself and, to my surprise, took a small step away from Gilen's side. Something felt wrong. I placed a hand on my heart, fighting a wave of nausea as I finally broke my gaze away from Daxton.

"Hey, you okay?" Rhea moved to my other side, giving Gilen a look. "Maybe you'll shift tonight after all."

Ignoring her, I managed to catch my breath and glanced back toward Daxton, who continued to stare at me from his position in the meadow. He leaned his head slightly and arched his brows, eyes dancing from Gilen and then to me again.

I pressed my lips into a fine line and stood straight, refusing to flinch away. My animal's power surged to the surface, and for the briefest of seconds, I saw the phantom grin crack the side of his stern expression.

"Yeah, just a random hot flash, I guess." It was an easy lie, as shifters often fell prey to them. I knew it was an excuse no one would dare to question.

"She's all right," Gilen added as he reached out to try and pull me back toward him. I hesitated to follow his guidance and shook him off, remaining where I stood. I could tell by Gilen's pursed lips and furrowed brow that he wasn't happy about my decision.

Rhea, who didn't approve of our pairing, glared at Gilen, challenging him and stepping in between us to rub my shoulders.

Talon moved behind Rhea and tried to pull her away. "Let them be. They need to figure this out, Rhea," he whispered.

Before Rhea could release the smart remark butting from her lips, our alpha's voice boomed over us all. "Shifters. Thank you for answering my call. I asked you all here because …" Alistar suddenly stopped and closed his eyes to the world. His shoulders sagged as he fought against a heavy, invisible weight. Helen came to his side and placed a loving hand on his shoulder. He glanced at her, and they both nodded, giving a silent show of support.

Wow. That was unexpected. Alistar was distressed. I had never seen this side of him before. None of us had. I looked to Gilen, who seemed just as surprised as we were.

"I struggle being your leader and coming here today to ask something I cannot do myself. Our world is dying. The wilt is spreading, and soon, it will consume every inch of our land. The only way it can be stopped is through the Heart of Valdor."

*The what?* I racked my brain, trying to recall if I had heard of such a thing from our history lessons, but nothing seemed to stick.

"Shifters were created by the gods," Alistar continued, "combined with magic from a stone called the Heart of Valdor. Our people are descendants of the fae, becoming our own species that could magically transform into creatures at will. The Mother and Father sought to enhance this ability, and through their combined powers and the magic of the Heart, they created our kind. Linking our spirits to an animal's, strengthening and connecting us to Valdor beyond what previous fae or any other species could achieve."

My jaw dropped. Our people were descendants of fae? That was something the history lessons left out.

"When did this all happen?" someone from the crowd shouted.

"Long before the keepers of the archives or scholars of the world knew or understood what time really was." The voice that graced the meadow was delicately feminine yet also strikingly fierce. It commanded attention, and I knew it could only come from one being … Minaeve, High Queen of the Fae. "Our kind also progressed, thanks to the blessing and gifts from the Mother and Father. Our ancestors branched from the traditional fae and other subspecies of the Inner Kingdom and became a new race of High Fae. Gifted with a deeper and more powerful connection to the magic of Valdor than our predecessors."

The high queen glided—yes, glided—through the tall grass toward her companions, Daxton and Castor. Stunning would not accurately describe her beauty. Long, thick, wavy black hair flowed freely from a crown of gold decorated with three small shimmering translucent silver crystals draped across her brow. Her skin was a shade darker than Daxton's, but it held a magical glow that shone golden even in the moonlight. Her black dress flowed behind her, decorated in vibrant purple and silver swirling designs. The exposed back of her gown mimicked the front, flaunting the seductive feminine curves of her thin, elegant body. She was *beautiful.*

Minaeve glanced around at various shifters as she pranced through the crowd. My people parted ways, clearing a wide path for her to meander, and to my surprise, she paused when she reached me and Gilen. I swallowed a lump of anxiety as her luminous sea-green eyes, decorated with purple accents, found their way to me.

*Do not fret, young shifters. We are here to help. We will only ask for one.*

My eyes widened as I instinctively grasped Gilen's hand. He looked at me with the same shocked expression on his face. The queen had just spoken to us with her mind.

She continued forward. The rest of the shifters in the meadow were just as shocked as we were. None of us expected to hear another voice inside our minds aside from our alpha or other pack members when we were in our animal forms.

"She said, 'We will only ask for one …'" I looked to Gilen and then to Rhea with my heart pounding in my head. "What does that mean?"

"Silence, please," Alistar called out. He gave a slight bow to the high queen and moved to the side so she could speak.

"We braved passing through the magical barrier of the veil because we had no choice," Minaeve said. "The High Fae can no longer battle to keep the decay of our world at bay, and we need one of you to help end the wilt." Queen Minaeve wore a polite smile as she glanced around at the shifters standing in the meadow. My breathing was becoming erratic, hanging on every word she spoke. "One of you who has not yet shifted will be chosen to partake in the trials inside the Inner Kingdom."

The trials? Inner Kingdom? None of these things sounded good to me.

"Why is it a young one that must go? What is the reason for this?" The demand came from the older group of shifters, clutching their children tightly to their chests.

"The signature and intensity of your magic alters when you shift, and the trials will only allow an unchanged shifter presence to enter." Daxton's rugged voice boomed into the night. "We will not choose a shifter under the age of eighteen, however." I released a heavy sigh of relief for all our parents and young ones.

"Thank you, High Prince Daxton," Minaeve said, glancing over to her right, her eyes tracing over Daxton's frame head to toe.

I clenched my hands into fists, insulted for the famed warrior to be looked at with such disrespect like he was a decadent meal. I didn't like that at all, not one bit, and neither did my animal.

It was again Alistar's turn to speak. "A shifter over the age of eighteen who has not yet changed into their animal form will leave to compete in the trials in the land of the High Fae. It is there that the Heart of Valdor is hidden. Shifters are the only ones that can unlock its power."

"Yes, Alpha Alistar," Minaeve agreed. "The Heart will only reveal itself and allow access to its power for a shifter—not a High Fae. We have fought against the dark magic of the decay for as long as possible, but each century, we must ask for your people's sacrifice. We must ask you to try …"

Sacrifice? Every one hundred years? Wait, how long has this been going on?

"Why have the elders never spoken of this!" a voice cried out from the crowd.

"The elders were all given an alpha's command to never speak of the trials until the arrival of the High Fae." Alistar stepped in once more to quiet his people. "Since the divide of our races … the veil has been keeping the majority of the decay at bay. Queen Minaeve and the other royals combat this enemy as best they can, but every century, their magic weakens, and they reach out, hoping one of us can unlock the Heart and heal our world."

"Which is why we are here," Minaeve said once more. "We need one of you to do this. I will select a shifter after the full moon ceremony is complete. This is deemed a sacrifice because the shifters chosen in the past have not survived."

Murmurs and gasps echoed across the meadow.

"The life lost, however, has not been wasted. The energy and magic from the sacrifice of a shifter striving to unlock the Heart's magic is reabsorbed, and we are able to combat the decay for another century," Minaeve added.

"Who's absorbing the magic from the life freely given?" I

couldn't keep this question locked inside. If what they were saying was true, then there was a good chance that someone from my pack was going to face untold dangers and likely death. I demanded answers.

Gilen clutched my arm as Minaeve's smile curled around her lush red lips. "That is a fair question, young shifter. Fortunately, my magic is able to combat the death and darkness that plague our world. My powers are sufficient, but alas, not everlasting."

Daxton went to his high queen's side, his eyes locking on mine for a moment before scanning across others. "All royals, myself included, willingly give our magic to help empower our queen, to help keep the wilt at bay. But over time, the strength of the wilt grows, and once again, we are tasked to seek aid. Right now, the wilt has surpassed our ability to contain it—and is spreading. You can see evidence of it here on the mainland when it hasn't spread this far before." Daxton spoke to all of us, but it felt like he was speaking directly to me.

Sorrow and regret were buried deep beneath the surface, and I recognized his hidden distress. He was a strong and powerful fae warrior, but even he was frightened by what the wilt would inevitably do to our world. He did not want to come here and ask this of us. They had no choice.

Before any of us could think to ask another question, the winds above began to stir, and the clouds parted in the sky.

"It's time," Alistar announced.

I could feel the hum of magic through the air as the full moon reached its apex. I closed my eyes, basking in the feel of my animal's presence rising to the surface and power stirring through my chest. The call to shift was pounding in the hearts and souls of the pack, calling to the newest members to finally reveal their animal spirit and shift for the first time.

"Good luck," Gilen whispered as he and the others began to fan out.

Alistar and Helen guided the High Fae royals toward the opposite side of the meadow. I watched Queen Minaeve glide effortlessly after them, with Castor close behind. Daxton, however, didn't move from where he stood. I saw his head slightly turn as his gaze met mine once more.

There it was again—pure fire.

I didn't know if it was the call of the shift, my magic reacting to his, or something else entirely, but when he looked at me like he did tonight, it awakened something primal inside of me. Fire from my power flowed through me, generated by something locked inside my soul and begging to break free.

*Don't resist the call. You must shift!* Alistar's voice drew my attention from Daxton and toward the entrancing power of the moon above.

It suddenly dawned on me that our alpha was influencing this shift. His command was meant to push us all to embrace and release our animals into the world. I glanced over toward Rhea, who was ripping and tearing the clothing away from her scorching skin. She bent over on her hands and knees, her body trembling as she screamed out a cry of pain.

"Rhea!" Her auburn hair fell around her face as she clenched her eyes shut, fighting against the pain of her shift. "Rhea!" I shouted as her blue eyes snapped open to meet mine.

I could feel her agony. We all knew that the first shift was the most difficult, and painful. Her bones began to break as the joints bent and turned in on themselves. She screamed, and my heart hurt to see her in such pain.

"Don't fight it," I roared.

Rhea gritted her teeth, and I could see a green shimmer of magic rise from her naked flesh. It was happening. She was shifting.

Once Rhea stopped fighting against the shift, the transition happened in a flash. She succumbed to the power of her animal and stopped fighting the pain of her body breaking and changing. The magic was finally able to take control. I held my breath as I gawked in awe at the beauty of my friend's shifted form.

A large tan- and auburn-colored wolf stood on four strong legs, panting and looking down toward the ground. Her beautiful coat of fur danced in the light breeze, showing hints of red and gold in the underbelly. The head of the wolf raised to meet me, and the familiar blue stare of my best friend shone with happiness and freedom.

"You are beautiful." I smiled with the hint of a tear in my eyes. A long wolf howl echoed across the meadow, and Rhea turned in a flash, bounding into the woods to chase the song. I recognized the howl, and I knew in my heart it was Talon.

With Rhea gone, I turned my attention to Shaw, but unlike Rhea, he showed no signs of shifting. He looked up at the moon with a sense of longing that only a shifter would understand. He closed his dark hazel eyes and sighed. Running a hand through his ruffled black hair, he shrugged his shoulders and looked at me but didn't utter a word. It just wasn't his time yet.

That left Gilen.

# Chapter Nine

I knew Gilen was going to shift tonight.

Over the past few months, we all felt his power steadily growing. Once he embraced his animal's spirit, we knew he would become our next alpha.

Alistar's alpha command added a boost to our shifter magic that would push many of us over the edge. The raging fire coursing through my body was the result of my fight against the urge to shift. I had always felt a deep connection to my shifter half, and I knew this was not the time. Another wave of blistering heat trickled across my skin, bringing me crashing down onto my knees in the tall green grass of the meadow. The power pooling inside me continued to build, and even though I could resist the alpha's command, somehow, this night was different.

*Not yet. Not like this.* I screamed inside my head. Reaching out, I dug my finger into the cool earth, shredding through clumps of dirt and tearing blades of grass as my body convulsed in pain.

*Please … Please. No. Someone help.* "Help," I whispered between silent screams. I knew my animal was fighting to resist the call.

We were not ready.

I focused on breathing, trying my best to calm the magic raging inside my body, urging me to shed my human skin and embrace my animal. Each second ticked by like an eternity. The heat trickling along my limbs continued to rise, and I didn't know what to do. I knew I would not shift, but would this fire consume and eventually kill me?

When I didn't think I could last another second, I felt the brush of ice trickle across my flesh. The cold wind caressed the nape of my neck and sank into my body, magically cooling me from the outside. The breath of cold danced with my blazing fire, creating a balanced, harmonious melody that soothed my soul and my animal's—our connection mending as the need to shift diminished. I inhaled a deep breath, regaining control of my power once more.

*Where did that come from?*

I glanced around, searching for the source, but my attention was quickly rerouted.

A magnificent creature of the old folklore slowly stalked toward me, effortlessly wading through the tall grass of the meadow. I froze, my eyes wide in shock at what stood before me. Gasps and murmurs surrounded the field as everyone gawked in disbelief. There was no doubt in my mind who this was, but I never would have guessed this was the animal he would shift into.

Gilen had transformed into a massive roc, with breathtakingly gorgeous golden feathers that looked like rays of sunshine even in the darkness of the night. Long, sharp talons that were as large as my torso curled and gripped the dirt, paired with a deadly sharpened beak that was polished to a fine razor point. His eyes, though … They held the same honey-colored tint of hazel I knew all too well. He rolled his head backward and released an ear-shattering call before spreading his massive wings and lifting himself into the sky.

The roc was a massive legendary bird of prey, rumored to be strong enough to carry animals as large as elephants in its talons. It could fly with the speed of the wind, and its feathers were said to be as resilient as metal armor. The roc could ferry passengers on its back, and in times of need, it was known as the great protector of the skies.

This was Gilen's animal.

Without a shadow of a doubt, I knew my childhood friend had shifted into one of the most powerful birds ever to grace the sky. My heart thrummed in my chest as I watched him fly into the night. His song rang out across the land, and all other shifters in their animal forms answered his song with their own. The sound thundered with pure strength, and I knew there was no hiding Gilen's power or fate now. He would be our next alpha.

Each new shifter who embraced the change into their animal form ran, scampered, or flew around the meadow. Looking around, I could identify a handful of new wolves in the mix, including Rhea, a few new bears, which would please Magnus, a handful of smaller creatures, such as a fox and smaller songbirds, and one very large tiger. I had no idea aside from Rhea and Gilen who was who, but I was overjoyed for each of them.

Regardless of size or strength, every animal brought unique adaptations that would help protect and provide for our pack. The fox shifters might not fight with the bears and wolves along the front lines, but they were excellent spies. The songbirds were amazing at patrolling the borders and carrying messages between the outer regions of the pack lands. Everyone had their purpose and the ability to contribute. That was the way of our people and how we not only survived but thrived.

Still kneeling on the ground, I glanced down at my hands, noticing a red tint coloring my flesh from burn marks that bubbled underneath my skin. I could still feel the cooling touch of the icy breeze, and instead of questioning it, I allowed it to continue caressing my boiling skin. It still hurt like hell, but at least the pain was now tolerable and healing.

More than anything, I wanted to join Rhea running through the forest or Gilen soaring through the skies above. But the call … it wasn't right. For some reason, my animal refused the alpha's command to shift.

Footsteps behind me caught my attention as a scarred hand reached out and grasped my shoulder in support. "You all right, Sky?"

"Hey, ya. It was just … a lot." I sighed, closing my eyes to focus on my breathing as the coldness started to drift away.

"I know. Well, I guess my animal is just as stubborn as yours. I could feel the urge to shift, but, like you, I just wasn't ready."

"We can't force fate," I replied.

"Ya. Wouldn't dare fuck with that." Shaw was quiet for a minute, and I could see sadness lurking in the depths of his eyes. "When I saw you stop the shift, I don't know how to explain it, but my animal decided to follow your lead."

I gave him a peculiar look. "I'm beginning to wonder how wise that animal of yours is, Shaw."

He chuckled lightly to himself. "You and me both. He sure can be a fucking prick when he wants to be, and rarely does he push me to fall in line. I think he is an independent creature by nature."

I gave Shaw a soft, friendly smile, trying to reassure him that everything would be all right. He was three years older than me, and at the age of twenty-five, our shifter magic was known to reach a peak in its development. No one pressured or questioned why he hadn't shifted yet, though. Due to his trauma at an early age, a later shift was expected from him.

"They all seem to have a mind of their own," I teased.

Shaw nodded and gracefully knelt beside me on the ground. I admired a variety of attributes about my close group of friends, but somehow Shaw always knew what I was thinking. He was a great listener, always watching and waiting to react to situations I instinctively jumped into. The ever-calm, quiet, and steady one between the two of us. It was a trait I admired him for and one of the reasons I trusted him.

I looked over at my friend and recognized the same longing in myself reflected in his own expression. His dark hazel eyes were somber yet hard. He was holding back his pain, hiding it from others who didn't know him, but unfortunately for him, I did.

Shaw reached up to brush his hair out of his face, and I watched the scars along his arms shimmer in the moonlight. The wounds that he bore from his capture and torture by the hunters. The injuries were inflicted before I discovered my magic, or else I would have tried to heal his wounds. I wish I could heal them now, but I knew the scars were deeper than the surface of his skin.

"You all right, Shaw?" His firm nod of *yes* was all I was going to get, and I was in no condition to push for more.

"You know what this means, right?" Shaw abruptly stood and extended a hand to help me get on my feet. "The high queen could choose one of us for the trials."

The truth of his words hit me like a cold, hard punch to the face.

I frantically looked around to assess who was remaining in the meadow that hadn't shifted. Shaw and I were the oldest of the group, but that wasn't a guarantee for our selection. I grimaced, unable to stomach the thought of Shaw or any of my pack members being forced to leave. If everything they said was true, no shifter had survived these trials. This was practically a suicide mission for whoever would go, but we all knew … the wilt would eventually consume us all.

Our world was dying, and only a shifter could save it.

Queen Minaeve moved out into the open meadow while Daxton and Castor remained behind in the silhouette of the shaded trees, their gazes firmly locked onto the queen's every move. She meandered through the knee-high green grass, her long dress flowing elegantly behind her as the crown of three gems atop her head shimmered in the night.

I held my breath as she approached Shaw and me. On instinct, I reached out and grabbed his hand to try and settle his shaking nerves and my own. What were the criteria for being chosen? How would the High Fae queen know which one of us stood a chance at passing the trials and unlocking the Heart of Valdor?

Minaeve stopped in front of me, and I swore my heart skipped a beat. The cold breeze from before reappeared and wrapped itself around us. It swirled, making the air from our lungs fog as our swift, anxious breaths exited our bodies. The queen's turquoise stare bore into us, seemingly searching for something just out of her reach.

What was she seeing in us? What was she thinking? She flashed me a half-grin, blinked, and continued walking toward the others for what seemed like a never-ending time loop.

Shaw was visibly shaking now. I didn't know if it was from the unnatural cold or from the queen's attention. Regardless of the reason, I moved next to him and wrapped my arm around his shoulder to try and settle his nerves.

"It's okay, Shaw. She passed us … We were not chosen."

"It's not that." Shaw took a deep breath to try and calm his nerves. "Sky, someone has to go. I was scared it was you. Hell, I was even nervous it would be me … but it has to be someone."

Before I could think of a way to comfort Shaw and assure him it would be all right, my own nightmare unfolded before my eyes. Queen Minaeve stopped in front of the youngest group of shifters, turning eighteen only this year or the last, with her gaze set firmly on my cousin, Neera.

She raised her tan-golden glowing hand and pressed it gently onto Neera's paling cheek. "You, my young darling shifter, will be our champion and compete in the trials."

No … Not Neera!

My eyes widened, and I gripped Shaw tightly to keep myself from falling over in the meadow. Off to the side, I could see a giant bear shift and take its human form. I had never seen Magnus look more terrified in my entire life. Neera was his baby girl, and since the day she was born, he was at the mercy of his daughter. His love for her would shatter worlds. He loved and cared for me as his own, but Neera was his heart and soul. He tore through the brush, not even bothering to find his discarded clothing, and barreled toward Neera and the High Fae queen.

"No, Magnus!" In a blink of an eye, Alistar shifted out of his wolf form and stood in his beta's path. "You cannot interfere. That is an order."

Magnus's loyalty to our pack and the alpha was iron-clad. Never wavering. Even when my father Emery died in battle against the humans and Alistar took his mantle, Magnus was there to lend his support. This, however, was something different. This was Neera—and everyone knew how protective he was over his gentle, kind-hearted daughter.

Tears were streaming down Neera's cheeks as the color drained from her sweet, freckled face. Her green eyes were so wide I could see them from across the distance. She didn't want to go. She was utterly petrified.

"Father … please …" Terror radiated in her pleading voice.

The sound of his daughter in distress sent Magnus into a rage. The roar of a bear erupted from his human chest, and it made everyone in the meadow flinch. He stepped forward to press against Alistar's hand, but the alpha grabbed him around the neck and forced him back. Magnus struggled to push Alistar aside, but the power of the alpha command, combined with his strength, was not something Magnus could overcome.

"I'm sorry, my friend," Alistar said with remorse as he forced Magnus back.

A scream of pain rang across the night, and I immediately recognized that it was Julia's mountain lion cry. While Magnus's roar was filled with anger and aggression, hers was one of sorrow and loss. It was enough to break even the stone-cold heart of an emotionless hunter.

Tears dampened my cheeks and dripped onto the grass. "No. Not … Neera."

Shaw turned to me with concern etched in every creased line of his face and desperation lingering in his eyes. "She won't survive the trials, Skylar." He only confirmed what I knew we were all thinking.

There was no telling what these trials held, but … no. Not Neera. The High Fae had been extremely cryptic, but we all knew she would not survive them. She would merely be a sacrifice to hold off the wilt for another century until another shifter was called for the task.

Without thinking further, I let go of Shaw and drew my shoulders back so I could yell across the open night air. "Take me," I shouted.

Every pair of eyes snapped to me in both animal and human

form. I could feel the stares prickling across my skin, yet I knew what I had to do.

"I will compete in the trials. I will travel to the Inner Kingdom and unlock the Heart of Valdor." I didn't know if I could achieve this task, but the alternative was not an option. Neera would not be chosen.

A strange sense of calmness settled in my limbs, combined with a surge of strength swirling inside me. My animal agreed with my decision. She was balancing my fear with beats of courage that surged through my being.

"Take me." I didn't say it as an option. The High Fae would be bringing *me* instead of Neera. I walked away from Shaw, confidently standing alone in the meadow.

It was too late to get cold feet now.

Minaeve tilted her head to the side, meticulously examining me from head to toe like I was some kind of spectacle. Slowly, she released Neera from her hold and appeared in front of me in a flash of blinding speed. She circled me, like a predator stalking its prey. I had no clue what she was searching for, but I knew I could not show my fear or doubt. Despite what unknowns I had just pledged myself to, I would be strong for my people. I would be strong for my family, who raised me as their own and never made me feel like I was anything less than their own daughter.

The strikingly beautiful high queen gazed up into my eyes and spoke inside my mind, *You are more than you appear.* Her voice held a delicate air of feminine grace that made it easy to underestimate the power she held lurking beneath the surface of a divine face. *The trials will challenge your mind, body, and soul. Testing the strength of your own heart to see if you are worthy. You must be willing to sacrifice everything you have and everything you are. None before you have volunteered for this, nor have they survived. Knowing this, do you still desire to declare yourself our champion?*

She was giving me the choice to turn away, but I knew I could not take it. I could not live with the idea of Neera going instead of me … of anyone going in my place. This was my *fate*, and I would not turn back now.

"Yes," I said as a piercing scream of Gilen's roc tore through the sky.

Gliding swiftly through the air, Gilen landed in the grass forcing himself between Minaeve and me. The roc flashed its massive talons and snapped its beak toward the queen, forcing her to step back. A shimmering green tint floated around the legendary creature's massive wingspan, and in a flash, Gilen shifted back into his human form. He stared down the fae queen, his fearsome eyes glowing with anger.

"You will not take her," he growled, grasping his discarded pants from the grass and pulling them up his thick thighs.

"It's all right, Gilen," I said, rushing to his side to try and calm him. I tried to turn him to face me, but he was immovable. He wouldn't even look at me. His attention and rage were solely directed at the queen.

"Gilen," I pleaded, seeing his shoulder slightly turn in my direction.

"Get behind me, Skylar." His voice was rough, thrumming with his new dominating strength that seeped into my body.

"No, Gilen," I answered this time with a rush of my own power.

Gilen's eyes snapped to me and widened, his brows raised in surprise at my power and outright refusal to follow his command. He grabbed my arm and forced me to stand behind him. I fought to push him off me, but with his shift tonight, there was no way I would be able to out-muscle him.

"Let me go," I grunted. "Now!"

"Silence," he sneered. "There's no fucking way I'm letting you do this, Skylar. I will not lose you."

That statement alone was enough to make me stop fighting him. "Why are you doing this, Gilen? She chose Neera … Neera! I have to go."

He turned so I could finally see his face as he spoke to me. "Do you honestly still not know how I feel about you, Skylar? Do you not understand why I can't let you go? Is it not obvious what I intend to do once the morning sun breaks free from this darkened night?"

"I …" I shuddered and swallowed loudly as my hands began to tremble and shake. "Gilen … am I your mate?"

Before he could answer, Minaeve's voice interjected our conversation. "The shifter has made her choice. You must allow me to mark her as the champion."

Gilen spun his head around to turn his attention back to Minaeve. "You will not touch her."

The fae queen laughed and flashed us an unnerving grin that made my skin crawl. "You are brave, future alpha of the Solace pack.

But I'm afraid your bravery cannot release her from her promise. She has made her choice, and the decision is final."

Gilen let go of my arm and stood up straight with his shoulders rolled back and his head held high. "You will not touch her," Gilen repeated, staring at the high queen.

In a flash, Daxton and Castor appeared at their queen's side. She tilted her head to acknowledge their supportive presence but waved her hand, calling off any threat of confrontation. "We are here to ask for help. This shifter female has offered herself for the trials. Only she can speak to what her own actions will be."

"She will not be going," Gilen growled, answering for me. "Pick someone else."

*Hell no!*

I did not like this one bit. I would not be silenced and pushed aside like a damsel needing rescue by some overbearing male. I appreciated the protection Gilen was trying to give me, but no one, not even my potential mate, would silence my voice. I had the right to choose how I wanted to live my life. I knew Gilen was scared for me, but I would not allow someone else in our pack to take my place. This was my task, and I would see it done.

"No!" I announced with absolute clarity. "*I* will travel to the Inner Kingdom. *I* will face the trials for the Heart of Valdor." I marched out past Gilen.

"Skylar," he growled, but I ignored him. Determined to stand my ground, I moved before he could grab me again.

"Stop it, Gilen," I demanded. "I'm not some piece of property you can command or order around. I am going to do this. I will not only face the trials, but I intend for this to never happen again." I then turned to Queen Minaeve. "I'm ready. I will go with you. Take me."

I heard Gilen begin to argue behind me, but Alistar's other region sub-alphas grabbed him and forced him to stay back. I hated that this was hurting him, but my mind was not changing. I was ready to do this for everyone I loved and everyone in Valdor.

Off in the distance, I could hear Neera's uncontrollable cries from the other side of the meadow. Glancing in her direction, I could see Julia cradling Neera in her arms with tears flowing down their faces. I couldn't bear to look at them. Their heartbreak tore at my chest as tears welled in my eyes. Magnus stood behind them, and his forest-green gaze locked with mine. I watched him take a deep breath, holding his wife and crying daughter close to his chest. A single tear dropped from his face, landing silently in the grass.

*Regret.*

That was what he was feeling. What I knew most of our elders undoubtedly were also feeling. Regret that they could not take my place. That a young shifter who had never known their animal form had to do this.

I bucked my chin up, refusing to break down and crumble under my family's sorrow. Seeing Rhea would make this a thousand times worse, and a part of me was glad she was not here.

Queen Minaeve held out her hand and beckoned me to approach.

My feet felt like thousand-pound stones, but I somehow managed to move toward her. My heart was racing, my palms were sweating, and tears were trickling from my eyes no matter how hard I tried to keep them at bay. But I refused to turn back. This was my choice. My fate.

"Hold out your arm," the queen commanded, and I willingly obeyed. I held out my left arm as the queen grabbed it with her right. She firmly dug her nails into my skin, piercing it and allowing my blood to pool around the wounds. "Do you agree, to serve as our champion in the trials of the Heart of Valdor, Skylar Cathal?" I didn't even dare to guess how she knew my name.

Clenching against the sting of her nails digging into my flesh, I answered, "I do."

Magic flowed around us, binding me to my oath and flowing through my veins. The blood from my wound began to levitate and swirl around my arm. She released her grasp as the magical liquid danced along my forearm, creating a tattoo of three staggered open eight-point stars that swirled and connected through threads of wisping clouds.

I could feel the buzzing sounds of the woods and the animals surrounding me. The smell of the wildflowers tickled my senses, threading a memory into my mind that I would never be able to forget. This mark was a promise. One that was now etched into my flesh and sealed with my own blood. I knew it could never be broken, and that my fate was now sealed as the champion of the trials.

"It is done," Queen Minaeve announced. "The female shifter, Skylar Cathal, will leave with the High Fae and travel to the Inner

Kingdom as our champion for the trials. Let us hope she is worthy enough to unlock the Heart of Valdor … and save us all."

It was quiet amongst my people, the kind of eerie silence that followed death. My strength finally gave way, and I crumbled to the ground. I stared at the mark on my arm as the gravity of my reality sank in. I was going to leave my home, my family, and possibly, even my mate behind. All in the hope that I, a half-shifter, was enough to save us all.

A cold breeze kissed my cheek, causing me to look up. Castor and Daxton stood behind their queen, and their eyes were firmly locked onto me. From Castor, I could see a depth of gratitude that was warm and open. He mouthed the words *Thank you* to me in a silent gesture that seemed oddly genuine, unlike his playful, slanderous, carefree demeanor from before. Beneath his flippant facade, I was able to identify a layer of hardship he tried to keep hidden. Like his brother, there was more to him than what was on the surface.

I then glanced over toward Daxton, and his expression left me breathless. The world stilled as our eyes met across the distance. The silence that followed gave me an overwhelmingly calm feeling in my middle. I felt balanced with a surging strength rising inside of me that could take on the world and never cower in fear.

I could feel compassion and a sense of hope flowing from Daxton's expression, coupled with overwhelming waves of astonishment. He looked at me with unwavering confidence and assurance that inspired me to face any challenge that dared cross my path. Gods above, I realized that by volunteering for this task, I had somehow gained the respect of the high prince.

*What the fuck did I get myself into this time?*

Neither Gilen nor even Magnus had ever looked at me like that before. I watched him carefully, unable to turn away from those mesmerizing gray eyes that had entranced me since the moment we first met. He bowed his head in gratitude for my bravery.

"We will depart tomorrow evening so that you may say your goodbyes to your friends and family," the fae queen announced. "Until then, Champion." She turned and stepped toward Daxton, delicately resting a hand on his chest as she reached out toward Castor. They disappeared in a silver flash of light, transported away through Daxton's magic.

"Move it!" Rhea's voice rang across the crowd of gathered

people as she pushed her way toward me.

"Rhea!" I turned to meet her, but a part of me wished I could have run the other way.

I had to give it to her, even naked without a shred of clothing covering her body, she did not shy away from scolding me.

"You fucking idiot! How could you do this? How did you not shift … You … You …" Tears streaked down her face as she lunged forward and clung to my neck, burying her crying face into my chest.

I held onto her as tightly as I could. "I'm sorry, Rhea." There wasn't much more we could say, so she cried some more, and then I cried until we both could catch our breath.

"You are a fucking idiot," she scolded me again as she wiped tears from her face.

"You've said that," I said.

"It needed to be repeated."

"Still doesn't change this," I replied as I motioned to the mark on my arm made from my own blood.

"Yeah, that is definitely in the realm of an unbreakable vow."

"Rhea … Sky!" Talon ran up to us with a spare change of clothes in his hands for Rhea. She turned to him, and Talon kissed her tear-soaked face, clutching her tight to his chest. "Here, slip these on."

I inwardly sighed at the sight of Talon and Rhea together. The sun had not yet risen, but their mate bond was plain to see. It made me happy to know she would not be alone when I left for the trials.

"Magnus wanted me to tell you that they will see you at home … when you make your way there. Neera was a wreck, and they needed to take her away," Talon said.

I nodded. I could only imagine how hard it was going to be to say goodbye to them.

Shaw joined us, and before I could say anything, he reached out and hugged me tightly into his chest. "I agree with Rhea," he whispered, "you're a fucking idiot. But, if you hadn't done it, I would've."

I pulled away and lightly kissed his cheek, believing his confession without a shred of doubt. "I know. I just beat you to the punch. Besides, if you had left, I would annoy the hell out of everyone, asking questions and wondering what was happening in the Inner Kingdom. This way, I'll be able to get all my answers firsthand."

"Thank the gods above." Talon scoffed as he held Rhea tightly.

"I don't know if we would've survived that."

I laughed so that I wouldn't start crying again. The three of them encircled me in a warm, loving embrace that calmed my shaking nerves. I lifted my head and gazed fondly at my friends, thankful for each of them and how they had impacted my life and helped shape who I was. The only problem was that we were missing someone.

"Where's Gilen?" I asked, searching the meadow.

Talon pushed his lips into a firm, thin line. "He left," he said with a disappointing frown. "As soon as you were marked, he turned and ran from the meadow. It was too much for him, Sky."

I looked at Talon and asked the same question I asked Gilen. "Are Gilen and I mates?"

Talon bit his lip and kicked at the ground uncomfortably. "I don't know."

"But you know that Rhea is, right?" I asked, turning then to Rhea. "Is Talon your mate?"

"You know we won't have a definite answer until morning." Rhea scowled. "But, yes. I can feel the bond. It's quiet, but I can only imagine what it will feel like come sunrise when it takes full effect."

"Well, sunrise is not far off now," I murmured as I looked at the morning sun's glow along the eastern horizon. "I need to find him."

They all nodded, and I hugged them each one last time.

I sprinted in the direction Talon last saw Gilen, passing countless shifters who all thanked me for volunteering. Even those who had once looked down on me for my half-breed status had given me a respectful nod and thanks. I didn't want to ignore them, but I did have other pressing things on my mind. And time was not on my side. I needed to find Gilen before it was too late.

I took off at a run, thinking he would be down by the beach, where he often escaped when he was troubled. As the scenery began to shift from the thick wilderness to the exposed shoreline, my heart raced at the anticipation of finding him. But, to my dismay, he was nowhere to be found. I walked the shoreline alone, kicking rocks over and trying to think about where he could be. Honestly, though, he could be anywhere right now. Gilen could shift and fly off to only the gods knew where.

I sat down on a large boulder and sank my head into my hands.

*Gilen, where are you?*

Rocks tumbled from the cliffs nearby, and I turned my head up to look. "Gilen?" But there was no one there. My heart sank, and I lost myself in a swirling loophole of what-ifs and what-will-bes.

I was distracted.

I didn't notice the soft clinking sounds of the chains while the roaring waves crashed along the rocks. I was oblivious to the smell as the winds blew upwind, concealing the scent that would have alerted me to danger. I was a naive fool.

Hands grabbed me.

Iron chains shackled me.

And, my world went dark as hunters abducted me.

# Chapter Ten

I never wanted to kill anyone more than I wanted to kill my kidnappers. Even though I knew it was pointless, I kicked and fought against the iron chains that bound my limbs. Any strength advantage I had was stripped away once the iron encased my skin. A solid thump landed on the back of my head, causing my vision to blur. I was gagged, draped with a black hood over my face, and thrown into the back of a wagon inside an iron barred cage. I fought against it, but eventually, I was struck in the back of the head again and passed out. Drowning any hope that my screams for help might be heard by a member of my pack.

Fuck. Hunters had kidnapped me.

I had no idea how long I was unconscious when I finally awoke, but my unrelenting hunger and dry throat begging for relief indicated more than a day had passed.

"Assholes! Fucking bastards!" My roars were muffled, but I couldn't stop. "Let me go! Let me out!" After a while, my voice became ragged from the relentless screaming, but I still didn't relent in crying for help. Even through the gag, I tried to yell for help. To scream for anyone to save me from a fate that was worse than death.

"Enough! Quiet down, you mangy half-breed bitch!" One of the drivers reached their arm through the bars and smacked me hard across the face.

Under my hood, I could taste the blood trickling into my mouth as I tried to adjust the gag. Choking on my blood was not how I wanted to leave this world. Nope, I had other plans, and dying here was certainly not one of them.

Hunters were a magically altered human species with heightened speed and strength compared to their humble beginnings. However, the most noticeable feature about them was their eyes—every hunter had their eyes magically shined-out. The luminous opal clouded orbs gave them the advantage of seeing in the dark like shifters, but unlike our kind, it made them sensitive to light.

The magic used and then gifted to create them by the human mages also made them nearly impossible to track. Wherever they went, their footsteps seemed to disappear. I could never make heads or tails of how they managed this, but time and time again, hunters vanished without a trace. Even from horseback, I knew they would somehow manage to hide their tracks.

Specks of daylight shone through seams in my hood, and I could just make out the silhouette of trees and surrounding landmarks. The mountains were strange to me. I had never ventured this far from our pack lands before. The forest was thinner here with little to no animals flourishing along the pathway. I couldn't hear the sounds of songbirds or the typical hustle and bustle of teeming life. Bounded in the back of the iron-caged wagon pulled by horses, fear gripped my chest like the chains that shackled me to my cage. They were taking me to one of their hidden lairs that never stayed in the same place for long.

I had never experienced this depth of sheer terror before in my life, and it stole the breath out of my lungs. No one would be able to track me. The cage was undoubtedly spellbound to trap my scent so we would not be followed, and these fuckers always covered their tracks.

The mages of the human kingdom placed wards across vital areas of their territory so our kind could not decipher any scent or distinct markings. It was used in countless battles against our two species for land rights and treaties that seemed to change with each new human king or queen. Currently, King Taran was rumored to keep his hunters and mages complacent and obedient by paying them handsomely to keep his borders protected. They bounced to different locations throughout the mainland—always at the beck and call of their king.

The wagon jolted and threw me to the opposite side, my face colliding with the bars, causing my vision to blur once more. The two—well, at least I thought there were only two—sitting in the front gave no indication they knew or cared that I was being tossed around like a rag doll. I was so weak. Exhausted by the weight of the irons and the effect they had on me. But I knew I could not give up trying to escape. If the hunters were successful and brought me into their lair, I would likely not come out alive.

I tried to sit up, but the heavy chains clinked and rattled, causing too much noise to go unnoticed. Instead, I decided to find something to lift the bottom of my hood to assess my surroundings better. A piece of the wooden wagon floor splintered upward, offering me just enough of an edge to move my hood. The only problem was the damn gag that was double or even triple-knotted behind my head. There was no doubt the white cloth had turned crimson from my injuries and the slap from one of the drivers. If I ever got out of these chains … he would be the first one I went after.

Another large bump jolted the cage, giving me the push I needed to expose the bottom half of my face from my hood. I moved my tongue around the gag and gathered as much saliva and blood as I could manage. Leaning my head near the bars, I tilted my lips so they were parallel to the cage.

*Come on. One more jolt should do it.*

The gods must have been smiling at me. Or laughing because, to be honest, this situation was not a blessing.

My head bobbed with the rhythm of the wagon, my head and drops of my blood. I felt the thick liquid drip from my mouth through the gag and prayed it would land on the rocks below. I quickly pulled the hood back over my head to hide any evidence of my attempt to call for aid.

*Please let it be enough for someone to find me.*

I sent a prayer to the Mother and Father, asking them to give me the strength to fight until help arrived. To not give into death if it was offered. To be brave enough to take a breath when all I wanted to do was stop breathing. I asked them to help me so I could help all their children. I was the chosen champion of the trials. I refused to die here, wherever here was.

Another day passed on my rickety ride of silent destitution. I could feel the stillness of death slowly creep in through the surroundings, shrouded in blackness beneath my hood. The air began to thin, and I knew we were climbing high into the eastern mountains of the human territory. This place was a barren rocky desert with little to no life flourishing. The red and tan mountains of this area were isolated with no established villages or cities for miles in any direction. A perfect hideout for the hunters because no one would think of settling in this area for long. The vegetation was practically non-existent against the cliffs' salt rock top, which held endless natural tunnel systems for them to hide in.

The wheels stopped moving, and my cage was lifted from the back of the wagon. Bars on each corner extended from the top, allowing hunters in the front and back to rest the bars on their shoulders and carry me by foot. Others, who were on horseback, began dismantling the wagon and hid the evidence among the rocks.

We continued for another hour or so, finally cresting the incline and flattening our route. Through the seams of my hood and the cold feeling in the air, I could tell that the night once again caressed the sky. Suddenly, we came to a stop, and my cage was lowered to the ground. Fear settled in my gut. I knew we had finally reached the lair of the human hunters.

Hands forcibly grabbed and dragged me from my mobile prison. I kicked at them and tried to fight against their hold and squirm out of their grasp. There was no possible way I was going to escape, but I wanted them to know I was not going to go quietly or planning to make this easy.

*Fuck that.*

Another blow crashed into my face, and my nose cracked as blood gushed from my nostrils. *Ouch.* I choked on the gag as my hood was violently pulled off my head. A hand grabbed my hair and forced my head back to look upward as feet kicked the back of my knees, forcing me to kneel on the ground.

*Fantastic*, I thought. *These guys really know how to give you the royal treatment around here—forcing a bound and gagged female to kneel before them so they can feel powerful. How mighty of them.*

What kind of creatures would do this? What purpose did this serve to be so cruel and destructive? I had no idea why the hunters did these things, and I was pretty sure I would never understand why.

With a busted nose and a bloodied gag, I slowly opened my eyes and looked up to see the face of the hunters who captured me. In their typical fashion, all of them were heavily cloaked, hiding their shined-out eyes from the last remaining rays of light from the setting sun. The two hunters with their hands on my shoulders had dark hair and tanned, almost blackened skin, with rough callouses clinging to their palms. I could hear their deep chuckles of amusement as their leader stepped forward from a line of them and removed his cloak.

Opal shined-out eyes gleamed in the setting sun, but there was no light inside this man. His full beard parted into twin braids of auburn curls while his smooth, pale shaved head gleamed in the light.

My stomach flipped as he reached out and grasped my chin in his rough hand. His fingernails were cracked and caked with dirt. His scent reminded me of scum, of something unclean and twisted, just like his soul.

"Those eyes …" he purred with an amused grin. "Our mage has been looking for you, half-breed. I couldn't believe our luck when we found you sitting all alone on that beach. It was almost too easy."

One of the men who held me chuckled. "The mage loves to experiment with half-breeds. Your tainted blood cannot be cured, but we can gain knowledge on how you creatures operate."

No. How did they know I was only part shifter?

I had no idea what kind of tortuous experiments they planned to do, but I refused to cower. I refused to scream out or cry. Instead, I kicked my head back, colliding with one of my captors' faces, likely breaking the bridge of his nose.

"Hold her down," their leader shouted as the other hunter I injured roared in pain. I was forced flat on my stomach into the dirt, with a knee in my back and a boot on my neck.

"Gods … Fuck," one of the hunters swore with disgust. "She smells foul. These shifters are nothing more than animals."

I squirmed under their hold, but the pressure on my neck was starting to cut off my breathing. A hand grabbed my hair once more, forcefully turning me to look up at their leader. I stared at him with fire blazing in my amber eyes, refusing to show my fear. I would not scream. And I would *never* submit. My animal raged inside me, encouraging me to fight back.

"Lock her away in the cell until the mage is ready to begin." The cold, menacing smile the leader gave me sent a tingling chill down my spine. It was a look of pure evil, and worst of all, he seemed almost cheerful. He held a sinister kind of darkness with no thread of kindness. The man was bred … No, he was created to hunt down and kill my kind. And by the looks of it, he enjoyed it.

I could no longer smell the salty air of the sea or the rich, thick forest of my faraway home. I prayed that someone, anyone from my pack, was searching for me. That the hunters missed covering a track or that my blood was enough to leave a marker for my pack to find me.

It was my only hope.

The two hunters who carried my iron cage on foot forced me onto my feet and angled me toward a large opening in the wall of the rocks. Months, maybe even years, of carving and chipping away at the sandstone and granite created this enlarged archway. The unique features of the rock held secret cracks of misery that I knew alluded to the prison awaiting me down below.

I stilled my breath as my acute shifter hearing flared, silencing the world around me. The stillness of my final moments above ground flashed before my eyes, creating a memory for me to cling to in the darkness below. The last rays of orange and red danced along the horizon. The moon was already visible in the sky with the sun setting along the western skyline. The colors were vibrant and alive, giving me one final shred of bliss before descending into the hunters' lair.

My iron chains clinked and rubbed against open sores on my skin as I was forced to descend into the darkness. They forced my head down, pulling my hair to pin my gaze forward. I sent my final prayers to the gods and slumped my shoulders in defeat, finally accepting my fate. At the opening, only the sound of cold, hard stone and crumbled rock echoed beneath the boots on my feet.

"Bastards," I mumbled in the silence. "How's the nose?" I taunted, trying to fight back in any way I could.

The hunter on my left heard me and gave me a swift punch in the gut that caused me to double over. I lost my balance and tumbled down the stairs that led into the abyss. The heaviness of the chains pulled me down as I stumbled forward, desperately trying to catch myself. I tripped over the irons and toppled over, ducking my head, with my shoulder colliding first with the ground. I rolled over onto my side and groaned loudly. There was a loud popping sound and a blinding pain that radiated down my arm. It wasn't broken, maybe, but fuck, it hurt.

"You idiot," one of my captors scolded. "The mage wants this one fresh when he arrives to begin his work. The fall could have easily broken her neck, and we would have taken the lashings meant for her."

Lashing … great. At least one question about my torture was answered. My animal's anger boiled with my own as I grunted and groaned to try and get to my feet.

The hunter who punched me ignored the other's comment and bent to pick me up off the ground. "The bitch deserved it for headbutting me in the nose. Give me a hand. She's not a small female, and these chains are heavy."

*You're telling me.*

"Not as foul-looking as some of the others we have brought in here though," he added as his hands hauled me upward.

"Bite me," I snarled.

If I had the ability to roll my eyes and convey my disgust and annoyance, I would have. But one eye was already starting to swell shut from the impact with the ground. It wasn't worth the effort, though. I was beginning to realize that this would be a waiting game. I had to hold out for as long as I could until help arrived.

If help arrived?

No.

*Do not start going down that rabbit hole, Skylar. Help will come. They will find you … You just have to outlast the humans.* I could not give up hope.

My captors disregarded my sparkling personality and guided me down a winding staircase, leading me farther and farther from the open sky and fresh air from above. The darkness thickened as we descended farther underground.

Fifty-five.

That was the number of steps I counted as they dragged me down the path to my demise. I wasn't going to make this easy for them. I was a fighter. As shifters, we didn't bend, and we refused to break.

The putrid smell of decay and death oozed from the chambers hidden in the abyss under the rocks. I allowed a silent scream to erupt inside my head as the looming panic tried to creep inside my mind. My fear for the moment was getting the best of me as my breathing began to accelerate with sweat pouring from my brow and my fists clenched.

I didn't want to die here. No. Not like this. Not as some experimental torture victim.

The cell door swung open, and I was thrown inside yet another iron-locked cage. Could they change things up a bit? The lack of sunlight or even torches only added to the gloom and doom of this underground holding. From the stairs, I was taken to the left, but I could also see another pathway leading to the right. With only some hay and a piss bucket for company stashed away in the corner, I settled in. No other cells were here aside from mine.

Bastards. They planned this well. Shifters found strength in their pack. Here, I would be isolated and alone.

*Congratulations, Skylar. Your torment has officially begun.*

To my relief, one of the henchmen—I nicknamed Tiny—cut the gag from my mouth. The other one, whom I nicknamed Thorn, unlocked the excess chains around my legs and torso. However, the shackles on my ankles and wrists remained where they were. Thorn gave me a stern look that said if I caused trouble, the chains would return.

I nodded in silent understanding. I would play along for now.

Thorn grabbed Tiny, who was the recipient of my headbutt to the nose, by the collar of his cloak and shoved him out of my cell. The barred door slammed shut, followed by the sound of the lock turning over.

I was alone.

Well, not entirely alone.

My animal was with me. A lifelong soul companion that would never leave my side. I reached out to her, begging her not to take away any physical pain but to comfort and protect my mind. My body would be broken to pieces. I knew that … I could handle that aspect of their torture. Shifters were born with a high pain tolerance due to our bodies breaking when we transformed into our animal forms and a tendency to invoke violence—among other things.

But my mind, my soul, needed to remain intact. If I could manage that, then I could survive. I knew my body would eventually succumb to this place, but I refused to allow myself to break. I couldn't help my trembling limbs as I wondered what I would have to sacrifice in order to survive.

These questions scared me more than the pain I knew I would likely endure.

My stomach growled into the emptiness of my cage and echoed off the stone walls of the underground abyss of darkness. I tried to think about anything else. Literally anything would be better than dwelling on the pain, hunger, or upcoming hell I would be forced to endure. My shackles rubbed against the bandage on my right arm where Daxton had bitten me, and I glanced down at the mark of stars on the other.

Steadying my shaking breath, images of Daxton entered my mind. I don't know why I saw his face when I closed my eyes in the darkness of my cell or why I sought this memory out of all the others. But for whatever reason, it comforted me.

Daxton was the epitome of strength and power. Visible in every movement he made and the sound of his voice as he spoke. I recalled the last time I saw him in the meadow as I received my mark from the

High Fae queen. The pride and gratitude in his expression was heartfelt and full of honor. He looked at me like I was a ray of hope awakened inside his soul after centuries of despair.

I was his hope.

My eyes adjusted to the blackness of my cell, and I could begin to make out the marking on my left forearm. "I will keep my promise," I said aloud. "I will unlock the Heart of Valdor and save our world." I didn't know if anyone was listening, but I felt my animal surge inside my chest. The power inside me sang, and the fiery glow of my magic warmed my heart.

Time was a mystery trapped inside this iron prison. I didn't know when I fell asleep, but the sound of a key moving inside the lock startled me from my restless slumber. I sat up from the wall and leaned forward with my hands resting quietly in my lap. Tiny was the first to enter, followed by Thorn.

"Get up," Tiny barked.

This guy clearly didn't know me very well, or else he would have used his manners and said *please.* I stared him down, refusing to move an inch. The tension in the underground lair was so thick you could slice it with a knife. Hot and thick. Like the humid climate after a blistering rainfall, except there was no rain here.

Only stone … only darkness.

Only me and my captors.

"I said get up, you mixed-blood bitch."

"Do you know any other insults you could call me during our time together? I've heard that one before. And I'm worried about being bored to death. I would appreciate a more diverse vocabulary if you are intelligent enough to have one." *Well … that did it.*

Tiny lunged forward and began beating me. His larger-than-average foot for a man his size struck me in my middle while he pounded my cheek with his fist. I felt my shoulder finally pop out of place as he stood on top of me to strike me harder. I could barely make out Thorn's screams for him to stop. Finally, Thorn grabbed Tiny and held down his arms. He released one final kick to my back, making me whimper as I spat blood from my mouth.

I had been beaten up before—mostly when I was a kid—but this was different.

In my early years, I was picked on when Gilen or the others weren't around to help protect me. Eventually, I learned how to fight back, and the last time someone tried to put their hands on me, I broke them. From then on, I proved I could defend myself, and I earned respect in the pack.

"The mage will see her wounds," Thorn warned in a hushed whisper.

"Good. She deserves worse. Besides, he will heal her before the experiments begin. That's how he keeps them alive to repeat the procedures, or did you forget that part?"

Not good.

Keeps them alive? What good would that do? Their mage was a healer?

It made sense why the mage was stationed here. Hunters were born "normal" humans and altered through magic. Their eyes were shined out with the intense light of the sun through a glass that burned the backs of their eyes. Only a healer could seal those types of wounds and have the subject survive. Their senses were also altered, granting them superior speed, annoyingly undetectable stealth, and immense strength in exchange for a piece of their humanity. When magic was used to alter the reality of the world like *this*, it came at a steep price. They became creatures loyal to their maker and deadly to all who stood in their path.

My father, Emery, died defending our people against hunters. I cringed thinking about him in the hands of these creatures, but I was also thankful they never captured him. He died with honor defending our home, a task I was also willing to undertake for the sake of our pack. I sometimes wondered what would have happened if the hunters had not killed him or even if my mother had not abandoned me with the pack.

No. Abandoned was a bit harsh. A long time ago, I decided that being angry would only make things worse. I couldn't change the fact that my mother did not raise me. That type of anger would only poison my soul. I decided as a child that I would paint her in a different light, believing she had no choice but to leave me. I was a hybrid. A shifter-human at risk of being used simply because I was different. I believe she left to protect me.

My prison guards positioned themselves on either side and hoisted me to my feet. I kept my eyes forward, not giving them the pleasure of seeing the fear that lurked deep inside in my cast-off stare. The trick was not denying that I was afraid. It was being strong enough to face it head-on.

I was carried—well, dragged would be a better description—down, surprise, surprise … a dark enclosed corridor to an open room at the end of the hall, off to the right of the main staircase. The heavy wooden door swung open, and my dry throat cracked. An iron table lay in the center, surrounded by small open canals with trickling water. Chains were bolted to the floor, and the scent of this room reminded me of death.

The sound of the babbling water was oddly comforting to me—something natural and clean in this unholy gods-forsaken pit. I decided to focus on that sound when I could no longer face my fears, and allow it to wash me away and take me somewhere safe.

Tiny and Thorn moved me to the table and forced me to lay on my back, arms and legs spread apart with my shackles chained to the floor. I was still wearing the same clothes I had on when I was captured. The beatings and time in the cage ride had torn at the loose ends, exposing my stomach, parts of my back, and many holes in what were once pants. My boots were discarded, but I didn't care.

"She's not in the prime condition I asked for." The mage's voice cracked the silence of the underground hideaway.

"She gave us some trouble and needed to be set straight," Tiny said as he crossed his arms. A hint of pride beamed beneath the dark hooded cloak from his opal luminous eyes.

*Prick. Fucking slime.*

"Leave," the mage commanded.

Tiny and Thorn hesitated momentarily before a burst of magical light jetted across the room, carving a gash in the rock. That was warning enough, and they both gladly took their leave.

*Outstanding.* I sighed internally. This mage not only had healing abilities, but he could throw some weight around if needed. He had to be highly gifted and revered by King Taran, paired with a high ranking among the mage group called Constellations, who were also in service of the human king, following their leader, Istar.

"Doesn't this type of treatment against shifters violate the treaty between our two peoples?" I asked into the empty space. I could barely see out of my right eye, so I turned my head to try and see the mage with my left.

"*You* are not a shifter." His back was turned to me, and all I could see was a midnight mop of hair atop a slender-built man with dark blue robes. "You, my dear, are an abomination. It's not your fault … but the blood must be cleansed."

"What does this *cleansing* entail exactly?" I asked, my curiosity being my downfall.

The mage sighed heavily, bending over an array of knives and other devices laid out on a nearby table. "This should've been taken care of before you were even born into this world," he mumbled as he continued to study his tools.

I rattled the shackles to test the strength of my holds, but to my dismay, they didn't budge. Dammit. I wasn't going anywhere.

Igniting a candle from a torch, the mage turned around and looked at me for the first time. He peered at me with what seemed to be permanently narrowed, ominous shadowed eyes. His medium-colored skin had a tint of olive coloring that contrasted against his midnight-black hair. Royal blue robes hung from his thin frame that held speckles of stars dancing across the buttoned top that circled tightly around his neck. His pants were an even darker blue color that disappeared against the blackness surrounding the cave.

"What do they call you? Besides a half-breed? We won't be spending much time together, but for the purpose of my study, I do like to have a name for the records."

I pushed my lips together, remaining silent and stubbornly refusing to answer him.

"Maybe this will help encourage you to answer my question," he said, moving around his desk toward me, keenly examining my broken nose. "I will be addressing this with the leads. It was ordered that you not be brought to me in such condition."

The mage bent over me, opening his palm and placing it flat against my forehead. The warm, luxurious feel of his magic caressing my flesh felt like a dream. Instantly, my wounds began to heal. His magic spanned the length of my body from my bloodied nose all the way to my bruised shoulder and broken ribs. The only place his magic did not reach was the shackled areas of my ankles and wrists, bound with iron.

"I'm sorry that I cannot heal your bruised wrists and ankles, but I believe this will suffice for now." Was that a hint of kindness in his voice? Or simply a sigh of disappointment at the lack of his orders being followed?

The trickling sounds of water underneath the stone caught my attention. I braced myself and allowed the sound to create a barrier or box that I could lock myself safely inside. The babbling of the steady stream beneath the rock held a unique rhythmic tune, almost like a harmonious melody singing inside my head. I used this natural music to help ground my determination and soothe my fears. My animal answered this song with her own, protecting my mind and strengthening me for whatever was to come.

"Now what?" I spat, unwilling to fall victim to a false sense of comfort from his healing magic.

"Ah … Ah …" he said with a ticking sound as he wagged a pointed finger at me. "Answer my question first. What do they call you? I must document this for my records."

Only one name came to mind, and I smiled internally as I bit back a cunning grin. I had only recently earned this nickname, but for this situation, I felt it deserved to be used.

"Spitfire."

"What a truly unique description for your, *kind*." His condescending tone made me want to roll my eyes and punch him square in the face. Glancing over, I saw him write a note in his journal before returning his attention back to me, the pen replaced by something *new*. Something that sent my heart racing like a jackrabbit across a field.

"Now, this will hurt. You will scream. But it is all for a good cause." My eyes were glued to a long, slender knife that gleamed in his left hand.

"For the good of what?" I tried to move, but he reached down to tighten my chains, making it impossible for me to even flinch.

He effortlessly twirled the blade in his hand, like he had done this a hundred times before, and I had no doubt that he had.

"Let's begin." In a flash, the tip of the silver blade dug into the flesh of my inner thigh. Slowly—oh, so fucking slowly—he cut through layers of muscle and flesh all the way to the bone, beginning at my hip and trailing down to my knee.

I screamed so loudly that my face turned red, and my vision blurred to nothing. The world around me vanished as my voice slashed through reality and realms that were make-believe.

He raised the knife to make a second incision on the same leg, and I roared even louder in agonizing pain. Without hesitation, or even a hint of empathy, he transitioned to my other leg, mimicking the same cuts from the other side. The indescribable agony of being carved alive would be a memory I would never be able to forget. It would scar my soul and forever linger in the depths of my bones that were touched with the blade of his knife. Once finished with the wounds on my legs, he returned to his journal and rolled his raised desk close to my torture table.

I knew there was a vital artery bleeding from where he had made his cuts. Blood … my blood soaked the table and trickled out along the sides. I tried to focus on *anything* but the pain. My animal was trying to help, but the reality of this agony was overwhelming us both. The only solace I could latch onto was the music of babbling waters trickling below the table. I clung to that melody with everything I had, desperate to focus on something besides the pain.

The mage kept scribbling in his journal as I bled out, slowly fading away. "Oh no … Not yet." He tsked. Gliding over to me, he used his magic to mend my bleeding flesh. Instantly, the wounds closed, but the radiating sting of pain beneath the surface still lingered.

"Interesting … you didn't bleed out in the time a human would. So you did inherit some healing aspects from your *other* half."

I didn't answer him. Silent tears filled my eyes as I stared upward at the ceiling.

"Hmm. Let's try this one." This time, the mage withdrew an iron-tipped arrowhead and scraped it across my chest. The iron immediately mixed with my blood, causing a deep burning sensation to spiderweb across my skin. "Oh yes! That is the same reaction I get with all my full-blood shifters. Interesting … interesting," he squealed in delight.

Gods be damned … fucking *delight*? Was he seriously enjoying this?

His soul must be more damaged than the bodies of his victims chained to this table. I tried breathing through the pain. My animal was rattling inside me, pushing me to fight back, but there wasn't anything I could do. All I could do was retreat inside my mind and try to keep my body's pain from shattering my sanity.

Again, the mage healed me with his powers, and again, I was used as a cutting board for an array of weapons scattered across his table. Each time, he documented my physical reaction to different weapons used and noted my healing progress before he was forced to step in. And each time, he healed my ragged body only to begin again.

My voice was raw from screaming. I couldn't even speak if I wanted to. My mind drifted into a semiconscious state to escape the torment I was forced to endure. I followed the rhythmic sounds of the water below me, wishing it could carry me away with the current.

I thought of my pack and of my home. My family, Magnus, Julia, and Neera, whom I loved more than words could ever express. I pictured their smiling faces encouraging me not to give up and to keep going, no matter what.

I remembered Rhea, my feisty, honest, and good-natured friend who would never abandon me. Talon, the stable peacemaker of our group, who could make a joke about almost anything. Shaw, the watchful, patient scholar who searched for the beauty of the world despite witnessing such darkness, and finally, Gilen. My childhood friend who never shamed me for my mixed blood and showed me what a blessing my differences could be. My mate? Would I ever see any of them again?

"Interesting. Very interesting." The mage halted his assault for a moment, examining the bite mark on my right wrist. "This will not heal. You passed out for a minute, and I removed the iron shackle around your wrists to heal it … but it would not react to my magic. I understand you animals like to mark yourselves with ceremonial tattoos, so the other arm is obvious. But this mark is truly enticing. You're not mated, are you?"

I didn't look his way or respond. I refused to answer any of his questions, and I was still woozy from the loss of blood and searing pain.

"Oh, that's right. How could I forget? Shifters mark each other along the neck." He brushed back my hair to examine my neckline. "Hmm … nothing."

He turned back to the books stacked on his shelf as my eyes wandered to my right arm. *Daxton.* Closing my eyes, I pictured his face. The image of him was so clear to me that, for a second, I thought it was real. His storm-gray eyes, which captivated every part of my being, held such strength and unwavering courage. I clung to that courage, needing anything to find the strength to survive this. Footsteps announced the mage's return, and I squeezed my eyes tighter, trying my best to keep the image of him with me for just a moment longer.

*Hope. Don't lose hope.*

"I need more time and more sessions with you," the mage exclaimed. "Hunters, return her to her cell. I will not be able to finish the experiment today."

My wounds might have been healed, but my mind was on the verge of crumbling. I had no will to fight against the guards as they unshackled my chains and dragged me from the iron table. I called for my animal spirit to help strengthen me, to wrap me in a blanket of her power that would help keep me from faltering and giving in to this torture. I smiled to myself, sensing her there in an instant, flooding magic into my middle and saving a piece of my soul from dying right there on the table.

"You were supposed to dispose of her tonight. You know the captain does not approve of captives lasting longer than a few days. We need to move camp soon."

The mage huffed a sigh of displeasure.

Oh no, he wasn't happy? *Sorry, not sorry there, buddy. Join the motherfucking club.*

"Tell the captain it will be done the next time she is brought to me. And entice him with the offer to use his new weapon."

I didn't have to look up to know the hunters were grinning from ear to ear at hearing this news. Tiny and Thorn forced me to my feet and dragged me along the dark corridor to my cell. The water bucket wobbled as they dropped me near the far corner next to it. They turned to leave, locking it once more and leaving me alone in the darkness.

I curled my knees into my chest and allowed myself to cry. I cried until tears could no longer run down my face. I fell to my side in the strands of hay and tried to find some shred of comfort to fall asleep. As I closed my eyes, I reached out and prayed once more to the gods for strength. I asked the Mother to watch me during the day and the Father to guard me at night.

My hand traced over the scar on my right arm, and a familiar sensation of comfort curled around my chest. It stirred my animal, awakening her spirit and giving me a burst of energy that surged through my core. It wasn't enough for me to sit up from the hay and start banging on the lock of my cell, but it was enough to keep me breathing.

Enough to keep me alive—for now.

# Chapter Eleven

My kidnappers were liars. I shouldn't have expected anything different, though, so I guess that was my fault. I believed that the next time the hunters dragged me from my cell would be my last, but, surprise, it was not.

The mage summoned me again … and just for fun, a third time to really seal in the torture. I had no grip on time. The only quiet moments of solitude were between our experiment sessions together. That was what he joyfully called them, anyway. Personally, I thought sick, sadistic madness had a better ring to it.

He said I was an anomaly that needed to be studied, whatever the fuck that meant. I really didn't give two shits about what the mage wanted or what he was discovering. I was beyond caring about anything at this point. I didn't know if it was the constant cutting into my flesh that was worse or the mind-fuck of him healing me right after he did it.

There was no way of guessing how long I had been trapped in these caves. Two days, three? Maybe a week? I never saw the outside world. I never smelled the fresh air from above or felt the rays of sun on my face. I was locked in a constant void of darkness that was slowly eating away at my soul.

My body had been sliced through enough times to destroy any thread of clothing I had when I came here. I was naked and numb as I waited in the deafening silence of my cell. I did, however, still find comfort in the melody of the trickling waters as they flowed in the open room of my torment. Nature's music was singing to me. It was a lifeline I clung to. Music emanated from the different babbles of the water as it ebbed and flowed against the rocks.

This was my state of living, if I could call this living. How much longer could I hold out? What hope remained of a rescue?

I tried to be strong. I tried to be brave, but each time they came for me, I knew I was closer to reaching the limits my mind and body could endure. Shifters were strong-willed and adapted to enduring pain, but this was a true test. I hated to admit it, but I knew I was beginning to crack. It wouldn't be long now before death would come for me.

Call it stubbornness or sheer strength of my will, but I refused to break while I was still breathing. I would be stronger than this. *We* would be stronger than this. A spark of energy burned my center, awakening my animal spirit. I took comfort in knowing that she never left me. I dared to try and crack a diluted smile in the darkness of my cell. Luckily, shifters' body temperatures run hotter than any other species, so I wasn't cold. I curled my knees to my chest and rotated to my side to give myself a much-needed hug.

Dammit, I could really go for a hug right now. One of those huge, overbearing, all-consuming embraces I always got from Magnus when I needed it most. And right now, I wanted that more than anything.

Since the mage healed my body each time he tortured me, he rationalized that I didn't need to eat. Another joyous piece of the experiment he was conducting on his subject. Hey, lucky me. I managed to rock myself to sleep despite the gurgling sounds of my empty stomach that refused to stop raging.

*I was in the meadow again. Peaceful serenity surrounded me as I inhaled a cold breath of fresh mountain air. The moon hung above my head, beaming, beautiful and bright. Even though the air was cold, I didn't feel the antagonizing bite of a chill against my bare skin. Instead, I felt safe and warm. Walking forward, I stretched my hands to the wildflowers that surrounded me in the tall grass, and instantly, I recognized my favorite flower.*

*All alone, I sat and waited patiently.*

*This place was my sanctuary. Each time I managed to fall asleep since being captured, my dreams guided me here. To this place that I had never been to, but somehow, it felt like home.*

*Suddenly, the dream changed, and I was no longer alone in my meadow.*

*Footsteps slowly approached in the grass behind me. I felt my shoulders stiffen as their steps halted momentarily before continuing again. Whomever this was, they didn't seem to mind that I knew of their presence. I didn't dare look back, but my senses were on high alert. There had never been another person in this dream with me before.*

*No words were spoken as the unidentified stranger slowly approached me with graceful steps that barely skimmed across the surface of the lush green grass.*

*"Skylar." The deep, soothing velvet voice caressed the naked skin of my flesh. It sent a spark of electricity into my nerves, awakening my animal within.*

*I knew this voice.*

*"Don't give in." His plea was full of sorrow and pain. "We are on our way. You must be brave for a little longer, Spitfire. Trust that I will find you. We*

*will always find each other."*

*I couldn't turn to look at him. Instead, I reached out my hand and cradled the blooming silver and orange flower of my sanctuary. Plucking at the stem, I held it to my chest and breathed in the sweet aroma of the petals, drawing strength from anything I could.*

"Get her up and out of the cell now!" Thorn's voice was panicked. My cell door busted open with my two captors standing in the doorway. "The captain is done waiting. One week of this is enough. His other experiments typically don't last more than a day. He doesn't care what the mage wishes to uncover. We are out of time and must move camp. Now!"

One week, huh? Well, that answered my question concerning the length of time I had been trapped in this hell hole.

"Don't tell me this is our last chance to spend quality time together?" My sarcastic humor and mocking tactics were helping to keep me from going insane. It was a game I played to focus on anything else besides what the mage planned next. Thorn was more difficult and resistant to playing along, but not Tiny. I could always get a rise out of him.

"That thing is twisted and deranged beyond repair. I don't know why the mage continues." Tiny pointed a finger at my back as I rolled over to see them. "Even if she is remotely attractive for a shifter."

"Fat chance, Tiny." I narrowed my eyes and stuck my tongue out at him. "Your other point is valid, however. I agree with you there. You should simply toss me out of the caves like garbage and be on your own way. I doubt anyone would even notice—"

"Grab her, and let's go," Thorn grumbled.

Yep, he was definitely not in the mood to play today.

"On your feet," Tiny demanded.

I staggered to sit up and crossed my legs underneath me. "Come on … Can't we change the routine just this once?" I glared at him with a cocky smirk that I knew would ruffle his feathers.

As I anticipated, steam practically blew out his ears as he gritted his teeth and stomped toward me. "Get up. Have some dignity before you die."

I spewed laughter, barely able to catch my breath at his remark. I wiped the tears from my face and looked up at his hard, opal stare. "That ship has sailed, along with my clothes. Did it ever occur to you humans to give a lady a blanket or a shirt to cover herself with? Rude—" I scoffed with defiance.

He ignored me and grabbed my arm, forcing me onto my feet. I was taller than he was, but that didn't seem to stop him from throwing me around like I was only two feet tall.

"Move. Now!"

"Pushy." I gritted my teeth and tried to hold my ground to make their last haul the most difficult. If this was it, I planned to make it memorable.

Thorn groaned and ended up helping, grabbing my other arm to get me to cooperate with their hurried timeline. This was different. Usually, they didn't bother rushing me to the back to the mage's chamber. Tiny loved taunting me about all the new *toys* the mage was raving about. That was what they called the various weapons the mage used to carve into my flesh—slightly sadistic if you ask me. Then Thorn would inevitably grumble about having to be my guard and insult my very existence, finding anything not already tarnished to try and break. They both quickened their pace when I wasn't moving fast enough for their liking, grabbing my legs to carry me and sprinting down the hall.

The setting inside my room had changed with oil lamps and lanterns illuminating the space. The iron table had been removed with two solid wooden posts standing in its place. Tiny took one of the iron shackles on my wrist while Thorn grabbed the other, forcing me across the floor. Pulling tightly, they attached chains to the two wooden poles, spreading my arms out and away from my body. I stood naked, fully exposed and vulnerable to whatever the mage was concocting next.

"You know this is a shame," the mage mumbled. "You are quite a beautiful creature. I imagine if you were to have been born of pure blood, the Lords would fight over your hand. It's not just the rare amber eyes that glow like fire. Your stamina is truly remarkable. You could have borne them countless numbers of strong heirs."

I tried to hold back my sickening reaction to his poisonous words. "Are these so-called *compliments* meant to comfort or impress me? Sorry to break it to you, but neither is happening." Rattling of new tools or weapons echoed behind me, and my back stiffened. "What do you have planned for me today?"

"Sadly, this will be the end of our endeavor." He sounded genuinely disheartened, and it made me want to vomit. "I asked the captain if I could keep you as a pet, but he declined."

If I had been granted anything to eat or drink in these weeks, that comment would have sent the contents of my stomach soaring across the room. "A … *pet*?"

"Oh, yes. I find your hybrid nature fascinating, and since you are part animal, the term *pet* seemed fitting."

Rage bubbled inside me. Was this all *he* and the hunters thought we were? Animals? I clenched my fists at the belittling insult. These human trash heaps were nothing more than a speck of mud on the bottom of my foot, and my opinion of them dropped even lower than I thought possible.

I despised these creatures.

The mage moved around to face me. "This," he said as he held up a long whip with frayed straps of leather tipped with jagged shards of iron, "this is your final test."

My eyes widened as panic set in—my animal supplied me with a flush of power to try and escape, even though it was pointless. This would be one hell of a finale.

He narrowed his slanted eyes that shimmered with a spark of amusement. "Interesting …" he said as he stroked his chin. "I haven't seen this look from you before. You have the right to be afraid, you know. I have cataloged every injury you have sustained while in my care, and this will be your end."

Did he just say … *care*? "Didn't know I meant that much to you," I growled.

"Oh, yes. And that magic flowing in your blood …" I held my breath as his magnanimous smile widened and he stroked my cheek with his gangly finger. "I can feel your power. I taste it in your blood."

I jerked my face to the side and glared at the mage with everything I had, my amber eyes glowing with my inner power. "Do. Not. Touch. Me," I snarled with a burning vengeance.

He bit his lip as his head tilted, his ominous eyes scanning over my exposed chest and venturing farther down my naked body. I could feel his magic flare, and he ignored my command, stepping closer to grab ahold of my breast. His touch was worse than the carving knives digging into my flesh. I could see his desire flash in his eyes as he pinched my nipple, making it hard. I bucked against his touch, which felt like hot needles on my skin.

"Such a waste," he purred, moving one hand lower. "This has never been touched, has it?" I sucked in a breath as his grotesque fingers traced over my stomach.

He pocketed his whip and caressed himself through the outside of his robes. "Look at what you made me do … Little Pet." His eyes rolled back inside his head as he stroked himself while his other hand returned to fondling my breast.

My animal raged, urging me to do something to stop this.

*Please, no … Please.* I begged. I prayed with all my soul. I would rather his blades cut into me than endure this. I jerked my body to the side, catching him by surprise, and threw my head forward, colliding with his oh-so-delicate small nose. He immediately released me as blood gushed from his nostril while he hollered in pain.

"And here I thought you enjoyed suffering?" I taunted. "Oh wait, is it only the suffering and torment of others then? My mistake," I growled, forcing my bravery to the surface as I braced for what I knew was soon to come.

Suddenly, a horn boomed against the rocks in the underground fortress.

"Gods above be damned!" the mage cursed through his clenched hand, stomping around toward my backside. His whip dangled and chimed against the stone floor as he readied himself behind me. "If I had more time, I would at least give you one final blessing before your life was over, but perhaps this is for the best. You will pay for this insult."

I tried to brace myself for what was next, but I knew this was going to be his best work yet. I could hear the whip rise, and the mage inhaled a deep breath before grunting and bringing the leather-tipped iron points across my back.

Pain—sheer, unruly, mind-numbing agony—streaked across my backside. Blood poured down my legs as the lashing beat down against my skin. I could feel the iron tips scrape against the bones of my spine and chip at my ribs while they tore away pieces of flesh.

I didn't even know the mage's name, but I didn't dare ask it now. Like Tiny and Thorn, I would give him a nickname that embodied the dark, twisted, unnatural state of this being.

I clenched my eyes shut, trying to focus on anything but the pain. The erratic rhythm of his limited strikes left me in a constant cage of suffering. I didn't know what else I had left—what else I could cling to in order to survive. The natural rhythm of the trickling waters was somehow dormant against the thrumming beat of suffering radiating throughout my body. My legs gave way as I hung lifeless from my wrists, bound in iron chains between the wooden posts.

*You must be strong just a little longer, Spitfire. I will find you …*

The singular ray of hope in my heart reached out and clung to the memory of the voice from my dreams. It kept me from shattering to pieces and giving up the will to live. Those words combined with my animal's fighting spirit fluttering inside my chest became life rafts in a never-ending sea of death.

The lashings didn't stop until the floor was drenched with my blood, and the mage could no longer hold his weapon steady. The sound of my blood dripping to the floor echoed from all sides of the silent room.

"My masterpiece …" he whispered to himself.

His whip held pieces of my flesh, revealing my ribs through the open bleeding wounds on my back. I drifted in and out of consciousness. My animal fought for me to continue breathing , but I didn't understand why. Death was calling for me. The pull to give in and stop fighting for breath was so strong. A promise of a peaceful afterlife.

Fucking hell, any afterlife would be better than this.

The crashing sound of weapons vaguely entered my semiconscious state as Tiny barreled into the chamber. "You're not done with her yet?" he exclaimed.

"I've been busy. Look at what carnage this weapon can cause! The iron tips slow the healing process while carving out chunks of flesh." The mage's joyous voice was so psychotic I think it even made Tiny hesitate. The mage was a sick, twisted excuse of a human who did not deserve to live. I prayed for the gods to serve him justice someday, even if I would not be around to witness it.

Another blast of a horn sounded, and I felt the chains on my wrist release my weight. I collapsed lifeless onto the ground, unable to move or even try to escape. The cold stone was drenched in my blood, and I forced myself to turn my head to the side to not drown in it. Drowning in my own blood was not the way I intended to go …

"Heal her enough so I am not drenched in her blood when I move her."

The mage grumbled but obeyed Tiny's wishes and waved his magic across the open wounds on my back to close them. He didn't completely heal them, of course. He did not mend the damage beneath the skin or replenish the blood lost on the floor.

I was dying.

I could feel the heaviness in each breath my lungs dared to take, in the weakness of my limbs as I tried to move, but was unable to even flinch. I strained at the effort it took to keep my mind alert, to listen to their words, or to try to piece together what was happening. I searched for the natural babbling trickle of water in the chamber, but even that was proving difficult to find.

Tiny grabbed me by the arm and hoisted me off the stone. "Leave using the escape routes," he said to the mage. "I have been sent to see you to the kingdom safely by Istar's direct order. Go, and I will meet you."

"Leave her here!" the mage yelled. "That was the second horn. We do not have the time to dispose of her in the cell. We must escape now!"

Was that panic in his voice? Why? What was the rush? Didn't he want to see how his experiment ended?

Tiny nodded and lazily tossed my body against the far wall.

"Ouch," I managed to grunt as I rolled onto my stomach. Tiny was so panicked that he didn't acknowledge my grumbling or leave me with his traditional farewell beating to really seal in the torture. Instead, he rushed out with the mage and slammed the door shut.

My mind was screaming to move, to get up and escape, but my body would not listen. Even my animal was strangely quiet, succumbing to the fate that was now knocking at our door. After the repeated bodily torture and these final bouts of lashings, I was done. Breathing felt like an impossible task, similar to pushing a boulder up the side of a mountain.

I felt guilty that I wasn't going to be strong enough to survive this, that I would not uphold my vow and enter the trials. And then, a deeper pang of regret and guilt tugged at me, knowing Neera or someone else would likely be forced to take my place. I had failed.

The wounds on my back might have been closed, but the damage underneath still tore through me. I wheezed out a breath, tasting a metallic twinge of blood on my tongue. It wouldn't be long now. The mage was right. This was my final test. His final experiment before I would meet my welcomed end.

As my heartbeat slowed and my vision faded, I imagined what death would be like. To my surprise, I no longer felt afraid. A tranquil peacefulness washed over me while I relaxed my broken body on the dark stone floor, finally hearing the babbling waters trickle as whimsical musical notes. I might not have trained with our healer Latte for long, but I knew what death looked like. This much blood loss would eventually shut my body down. Each second ticked by in agony and felt like hours or even days.

Wait … Why was I fighting this?

Why was I continuing to linger on like this when the salvation of death was waiting on the other side? Honestly, anything would be better than struggling to breathe in a dark, endless prison with only your thoughts and dreams for company.

"Skylar!"

*Ha!* I laughed to myself. *Nice try, imagination … but this is it.* I smiled to myself as my heavy eyelids fluttered.

"Skylar!"

*Wait, was that my name being called?*

I couldn't focus enough to decipher the other sounds bouncing through the cave hallway leading to the mage's torture chamber. I was broken and battered on the floor of the hunters' prison. A captured shifter-human who endured endless torment simply because of who I was.

But, that voice.

"I'm sorry," I whimpered as my eyes finally fluttered closed.

In a flash, I saw myself lying on the cold, hard stone of my own personal hell. My naked, lifeless body was sprawled out in the open with the evidence of my floggings on full display across my back. The sight of my injuries forced a silent cry to emerge from the depths of my soul.

From the abyss surrounding me, a deep, thrumming call pulled at my senses.

It was like a tether—a vibrant connection that went deeper than the wounds on my back and the knife marks that sliced through my flesh. This call sang to my animal, and I could not ignore or turn away from the primal pull to answer. The melody healed me in places that I didn't even know were damaged. An icy-cold sensation coated my back and filled the holes under my skin with liquid fire, slowly bringing life back into my body. Magic flowed through me, repairing what was broken, giving me the strength to turn away from death's embrace and once again see the light.

I was jolted back into my body as my chest rose and fell with a full, steady breath.

"Spitfire!" The voice I had heard in my dreams spoke to me, using his unique nickname that I chose for myself when I was first brought here. And this time, he was real.

Cradled in a tender embrace, he wrapped me in a cocoon of safety I never wanted to leave. I felt soft lips leave my forehead as a trimmed beard brushed against my brow. Thankfully, he didn't pull away. Instead, he drew me closer to him, sitting on the ground and delicately moving me into his lap. He unlatched the clasp of his cloak and draped it over my naked, broken body. Carefully, he lifted my arms to tuck in the sides before returning me to the safety of his strong embrace, pulled in close to his chest. Without thinking, I nuzzled into the nape of his neck, sinking deeper into his hold that I never wanted to leave. The smell of fresh pine and mountain air filled my senses, and I knew without a doubt who had found me.

"I told you … I would find you," he whispered as his hand tenderly brushed my fallen hair from my face.

Did he know about my dreams? Did he somehow send them to me? Did he realize that he was my salvation in the darkness of my eternal damnation?

*Daxton.*

"*How* …" My throat was raw from my screams, and I barely even recognized the sound that came out of my mouth.

"Shh," Daxton hushed me as he pressed his cheek to my brow. "You're safe."

I believed him. There wasn't a single fiber of my being that doubted my safety when I was cradled in his arms. My animal seemed to sing inside of me. His protective presence both calmed and strengthened her as well.

I tilted my head to look upon the face I dreamed of in my dire moments of weakness. Did he know how he helped me when I was certain nothing else remained? Did he know that his face, his voice, had given me *hope?* To keep fighting to survive?

Daxton pulled his head back. His storm-gray eyes locked onto my face, and I saw him sigh in relief when he met my stare. "Skylar," he said my name like it was the only thing that mattered in this world.

I felt myself instinctively lean into him. There were no words that could convey the silent messages we were sending to each other, only feelings.

Gratitude.

Trust.

And most of all, hope.

I could see his caring and compassion shine in the light of the torch as he gently pulled me in closer. I shook with fatigue but still managed to reach up my hand and place it on his chest. He remained utterly still, allowing me to have complete control. I pressed my palm over his beating heart, feeling the rhythm of his courage thrum into my soul.

"I-I had to see if you were real." My voice cracked in a raspy reply. Hearing this, Daxton reached into his belt and unlatched a canteen of water.

Holy fuck. Real water.

He bit down on the cork and pulled out the tab before bringing it to my cracked lips. Water flowed into me as he slowly tilted the canteen until I consumed every last drop it held.

"Better?" he asked. I nodded and tried to sit up, but I failed and collapsed back into his chest. "Don't, Spitfire. Focus on breathing. That is all I want you to concentrate on. Breathing and living."

"Easy to say … harder to do sometimes."

I could have sworn he flashed me a pitiful smile before nuzzling his cheek against my brow. "Don't tell me you're backing down from a challenge now?" he teased.

"Not a chance," I whispered, almost in a laugh.

I felt my body begin to heal, or at least relax, as we fell into playful banter. I had become so numb that trying to feel anything felt foreign at first. But with Daxton, I didn't know how to explain it, I felt like a piece of myself returned or was stitched back together when he found me.

A shout erupted down the hall, and Daxton moved so fast that if I had blinked, I would have missed it. He clutched me with his right arm as he held out a large knife in front of me with the other. His soft expression vanished, and the Silver Shadow of legend returned. I hadn't noticed it before, but now, I recognized the stained black blood on his knife and clothes. He had slain hunters, and, by the looks of it, a lot of them.

Good. Fucking. Riddance.

Ice coated the floor beneath us as I shivered against his chest. He pulled me into him and positioned my body so I was protected by his own. Nothing was going to pass through his defenses. I knew he would protect me with his life and kill anyone who sought to take me from him.

A roar erupted in the cave, causing my heart to skip a beat. "Mag … Magnus!" My uncle came barreling into the doorway of the chamber, shifting into his human form the moment he saw me cradled in Daxton's arms.

"Skylar!" He reached out for me, but Daxton released a low growl, baring his sharp canines that I knew all too well.

My animal surged power through me, pushing me to reunite with my family. I tried to move my hand and reach out for Magnus, but I was too weak. I don't know how, but Daxton somehow sensed my fetal attempt to move and glanced down at me. Perhaps his warrior instincts made him more aware or alert to the world around him. Either way, he could read my desire to go to my uncle. I could tell he did not want to let me go, but, for my sake, he released me to Magnus.

My uncle scooped me up in his arms, tears streaming down his face with joy, relief, and sadness. "This should have never happened to you. I love you so much, Skylar … We never stopped searching."

"I know," I managed to say as his lift-me-off-my-feet hug stole my breath away, just like I remembered. Soon, another familiar face joined our party in my prison of despair. Even in the dark underground cave system, the flamboyant silver hair was unmistakable. "Glad you could join us, Castor."

The fae prince released a heavy sigh of relief, dropping his shoulder forward and smiling at me with a half-grin. "Why didn't you invite us to come along to the party? This place is so … charming."

"I left an invitation along the rocks to lead you here."

"Luckily, we found it," Daxton added.

Commotion from the stairway and above our heads cut our greeting short.

"We need to move out," Castor said to his brother. "Gilen and the others are rounding up the remaining hunters, but many managed to escape through hidden passages we didn't see from above."

"They're long gone by now," Daxton countered. "We could find them, but it would take time."

"We get her out first … That is our priority," Magnus said in a low growl. "Allow the shifters to handle our quarrel with the humans on our terms. This is not a matter for High Fae. Let shifters handle this. One of our own was taken from our lands. There will be blood spilled for this." I knew my pack would not allow this deed to go unchallenged. There would be blood. My people would eventually retaliate against the humans for this crime. "I'll shift and clear the way in case any hunters remain behind," Magnus said as he turned to Daxton. "Will you look after her?"

Daxton stared at Magnus with lightning in his storm-gray eyes. "I swear to protect her …" He said something else too, but my stupid brain was not functioning well from all the blood loss—and the almost dying part.

Magnus carefully handed me back to Daxton, who sheathed his knife and cradled me firmly against his chest like a newborn babe.

"Wow," I mumbled. "I'm not used to being carried or passed around like this."

"Why?" Daxton asked in a tease. "Are there no males strong enough for the task?"

I managed to crack a small smile … the first one since the full moon in the meadow.

Magnus shifted into his monstrous grizzly bear form and tore through the corridor. Daxton followed behind him, with Castor guarding our flank.

Fifty-five. An odd number, but one I memorized and counted as Daxton carried me back into the light. And one I counted to as Daxton ascended the staircase to my freedom.

The sun's rays were beginning to peek over the eastern mountains, piercing my eyes with stinging pain, but filling my body with the taste of freedom once more. The fresh smell of the clean air melted the final beat of strength I fought to carry. My animal stirred with happiness and joy. She was free, too.

*Thank you*, I prayed silently.

I turned and looked at another shifter who stood bloodied—yet strong and unbeaten. I didn't expect to see him here, but he still managed to join in my rescue—Shaw.

He looked at me with a depth of understanding and guilt that brought tears to my eyes. "I'm glad to see nothing could keep you down for long, Sky." He tried to give me a warm smile, but he knew, he knew the depth of the scars that lingered beneath the surface of my wounds. He knew the feelings of despair and anxiety I would need to overcome. He knew, and now, I did, too.

The scream of a bird rang through the clearing, and a second later, Gilen shouted my name, "Skylar!"

I glanced back up at Daxton as he supported my head against his chest. My world swirled and disappeared in the hazy cloud as I finally lost consciousness.

# Chapter Twelve

I was afraid that I had imagined my rescue and that it was all some cruel trickery or dream. Swallowing my fear, I dared to move my hand against the soft fabric of the bedding I was lying on, and to my surprise, it was *real.* My fingers gripped the sheet as I inhaled a deep breath to begin assessing my surroundings, realizing I was in the healing quarters of my pack that I knew all too well. My animal was surprisingly subdued, but I imagined it was because she was just as exhausted as I was.

The mage was now my mortal enemy.

*Blade.*

That was what I would call him, never knowing or truly caring to learn his real name. I would call him this … not for the various knives and iron weapons he used on me. No. Blade was his name because it would be *my blade* that would end him. My blade that would sever his sadistic existence of life from this world so he could never harm another soul again. My. Blade.

"She was just rescued from being tortured by hunters!" a loud voice exclaimed from outside the room. "Her mind is likely broken, and she cannot think clearly. She needs time to recover and come to her senses." Gilen's firm, assertive voice was unmistakable. I couldn't make out who he was speaking with, but it was very loud.

*Was this shitstorm really happening right now?* I asked myself.

The comments about being broken and unable to think clearly didn't settle well with me. I didn't fight to survive Blade's torture to wake up to *this.* I imagined that Gilen still disagreed with my decision to become the champion of the trials, and he wasn't letting his opinions about it remain quiet. I wouldn't stand for that. I would not allow my voice to be drowned out in the imaginary thunder that raged overhead, trying to silence my screams—to silence me.

"Nope. Not happening. Not today," I mumbled to myself with gritted teeth. No.

I decided to try and focus on moving my battered body. I started small to gain the little victories where I could. Twitching my toes and fingers seemed to work, so I gradually rolled my ankles and wrists.

*Well, those seem to be functioning properly, at least.*

I dared to move my right arm underneath me to push off the bed, which unfortunately activated the muscles along my back. A red-hot, searing pain sliced across me, making it difficult to breathe, let alone move. I refused to scream, though. I screamed so much during my capture that I doubted I had any more left in me.

I sucked in a breath that strained my still-broken ribs and clenched my teeth to try and move once more. No matter, I had become used to pain. Fighting through the searing agony of my ripping muscles, I forced myself upright onto my knees. The bed I was lying on sank with the shift of my weight, but I remained deathly still, focusing on my breathing and waiting for the throbbing pain to subside.

Opening my eyes, I recognized the familiar sweet scent of lavender that helped relax my aching muscles and allowed warmth to spread throughout my limbs. The stark white wood-paneled walls were clean and bright, reflecting the sun's rays through open windows and various mirrors that hung on the walls. I admired how Latte positioned them just right and how they were able to bounce the sunlight around the entire room. Despite the time of day, this room was always bright and warmed by the sun's natural beauty.

The other beds that lined the wall were empty, and I had a feeling I wouldn't have any visitors in here any time soon. Fresh flowers lay on the bedside next to me, lupine and fireweed intertwined in a beautiful purple bloom, giving a splash of color that made me smile. I turned my eyes upward and glanced at the ceiling, which, oddly enough, was one of my favorite details about this place. Various painted vines, trees, and plant designs decorated every corner. It was like being inside the forest itself instead of being trapped indoors and separated from the beauty of nature. It helped our patients feel connected to nature as they healed from various wounds and illnesses.

The incoherent bickering from outside the healers' quarters seemed to settle into a low rumble—thank the gods above. I swung my leg out from under me to sit on the edge of the bed with my feet resting on the floor.

*Not bad,* I told myself. *Now for the real test.*

I grabbed the bedpost and forced myself to stand. Every inch of my body screamed in protest at what I was struggling to achieve. Logically, I knew I needed the rest. I understood that only a day or two ago, I was inches from death's door, but I didn't care. I had to see it.

Luckily, the mirror positioned near the doorway was on my side of the room, but I still had to take five or maybe six steps to reach it. I shut my eyes and willed my legs to carry me across the floor. One step at a time, I picked up my aching limbs and slowly approached the mirror. When I reached the end of the bed, the pain was considerably less, still present and aching, but it was something I could easily manage.

Reaching out, I braced my hands against the sturdy wall with my shoulders hunched over. My palms landed on either side of the mirror as I raised my gaze and bravely looked at my reflection.

"Not the worst, but I have definitely seen better." I gave myself a pity chuckle and turned my face to the side to examine my sunken features.

I was not vain, but I did acknowledge that I was considered attractive among the female shifters in our village. However, my long brown hair, which always held a golden highlighted hue, now seemed dingy and dirty. The golden sun-streaked pieces that highlighted my face were almost gone. My cheeks were sunken in a little, and the exhaustion that clung to my eyes was expected—but still difficult to witness. The fire of my amber stare, however, was still there. My eyes burned with the reddish-golden blaze encased by a black ring around dancing flames. I smiled a full, happy grin as I dipped my head toward the floor.

"You couldn't break … *all* of me," I whispered to the empty room. "Thank you," I said with a heavy sigh to my animal. "You never left me alone."

There was no doubt that without her constant presence, I would have broken the first time Blade sliced into me. That, paired with the dreams and songs of the babbling creek, spirited my mind away when I couldn't face the reality I was forced to endure.

I glanced at my hands placed on either side of my reflection and cringed. I knew my recovery would never be that simple, but the thought of cleaning myself up in a warm bath helped.

*On to the next phase.*

I braced myself, readying for what I knew I had to face. Straightening my back, I untied the strap of the silk robe that crossed over in front of my torso and unveiled my naked flesh. The world around me turned to silence. You could hear a pin drop from across the room or a flutter of a bird's wings on the windowsill. Slowly, I lowered the robe beneath my shoulders, exposing pieces of my back, one section at a time. Holding the sides below my waist, I shut my eyes and rotated to my right. I brushed my hair over my shoulder and tilted my head to see what the mirror would reveal.

I gasped, quickly holding a hand to my mouth, trying to cover my mournful sob. The marks along my back were … There were no words for what they were, and I knew they would become scars that would *never* completely heal.

Visions of my last experiment with Blade flashed before my eyes. The sounds of his iron-tipped whip beating against me echoed in my ears. His ragged breaths and amused cackle twisted my stomach in knots. My legs trembled, and my breathing quickened at an almost uncontrollable pace. I could feel the fear rising in my throat, choking the life out of me where I stood. I was being pulled back into my memories, reliving my worst nightmare and feeling the guilt of my weakness and failure all over again.

Out of nowhere, I heard someone appear in the room, and I shot my eyes upward in the mirror to see who it was—Daxton.

"I-I didn't," he stammered, probably for the first time in his immortal life. "I didn't mean to invade your privacy. I heard you and …" He cast his eyes down and to the side. "I'm sorry. I'll go." He seemed embarrassed at his intrusion, but still, he didn't leave right away. Straightening his back, he sheathed his knife with an apologetic expression on his face.

"Daxton, wait!" I said in a panic.

I didn't want him to leave. It didn't make any logical sense, but I needed him to stay with me. Perhaps it was because, in my dreams, his voice comforted me and encouraged me to keep fighting. Or because he was the first to find me in my rescue. Regardless of my confusion, my animal seemed to understand this need and sent flickers of tingling sensations through my limbs. I wanted to be near him. I craved the protection and safety that he had proven he could give me. It was almost like a primal instinct that was guiding me to ask him to stay, and for once, I didn't fight against it.

Daxton froze at my plea for him to stay. In the reflection, I watched his eyes rise slowly from the floor, taking in every inch of me, carefully calculating every breath and movement. His gaze didn't linger on the scars across my back or the nakedness of my exposed breasts. No, instead, he focused his alluring gray eyes on the reflection of my stare with unflinching strength beaming from within. He boldly stepped toward me, crossing the distance that separated us as I remained fixed in his gaze.

I remained utterly still as he stepped behind me. I couldn't break away from the horror reflected in the mirror that bore the scars of my torture. In that moment, I was not strong enough to lift my robe and simply allow the memories to wash away like the rolling tide. I was locked in that iron cell again. Waiting for death, longing for anything to take away my suffering. I needed help.

"I'm here, Spitfire. You're never alone," Daxton said softly, caressing me with his whispered voice.

I could see his outreached hand begin to tremble as he finally allowed his eyeline to dip toward my exposed back. Fury burned in his stare. He clenched his hands into fists and pivoted away, trying to steady his building rage. With one glance in his direction, I could feel his anger mirroring my own, thrumming wildly through my middle.

"Can—" I stumbled for a moment, trying to find the courage to speak. Daxton tensed and turned his face toward me once again. "Can you help me? Please, Daxton?" I glanced down at my robe, silently gesturing for his aid in pulling it back over my shoulders.

His stormy eyes softened as he looked at me in the reflection. Daxton's hands delicately gripped the fabric as he slowly glided it up my shoulders and back into place. He was meticulous with each movement as his fingers brushed against my skin, analyzing every flinch and breath I took while he was near me. His touch was gentle against the healed skin on my flesh, creating a veil of safety that allowed me to breathe without a plaguing weight of fear.

I moved to close my robe as his hands reached out to grasp mine. I didn't realize I was shaking until Daxton tried to steady me. Despite his protection and comfort, the pressure of my terror built, and the world collapsed around me.

I started to hyperventilate. I couldn't catch my breath as the strength in my legs began to dwindle. Daxton was there in an instant and wrapped his arms securely around mine, lifting me off the ground and cradling me into his chest with ease. He held me tight to him, trying his best to comfort and calm me.

"What do you need? Ask and I will see it done," Daxton's deep voice whispered. I sobbed as I buried my face into his shirt. I balled my fists and slammed them down onto his chest and arms that didn't move or pull away. "I'm strong, Skylar," Daxton said with a commanding tone that was calm and steady. "Lash out all you want … Trust me, I have seen and been through my fair share of pains in this life. There is no need to feel ashamed or hide whatever you are feeling when you are with me. If you need a punching bag, I am here. If you need a shoulder to cry on, I will remember to bring a spare change of clothes and happily catch your tears." I shuddered with a suppressed laugh between my sobs, realizing my tears were drenching his shirt. "Anything you want or need, I will see it done. I'm here for you, Skylar. You are not alone."

The sincerity of his words and declaration had me crying for an entirely different reason than before. "Outside …" I shuddered as I closed my eyes and clenched the opening of his shirt in my balled fists, fighting the torturous onslaught of my memories from barreling through my mind. "I need to be outside, Daxton!"

There was a flash of silver, and the next second, we were both outside in the rich grass of the training fields. The feel of the fresh air kissing my skin awakened the inner strength of my animal spirit that sprang to life inside of me. Her heightened senses opened my eyes to the beauty surrounding me, helping to push aside the dark abyss of my mind.

The beauty of the dazzling fall colors on a warm autumn day was always my favorite. Orange and yellow specks of leaves on the birch trees danced in temperate winds that swirled around the tops of the trees. I looked upward at the vibrant blue open sky above my head. The deep sea of never-ending cerulean and sapphire was painted with whisps of white clouds that created images and figures of their own design. A change was coming, and the alteration of the season reminded me that nothing stayed the same for very long. The only constant in life was that each day was different, and we embraced it the best we could.

Thankfully, Daxton did not let go of me. His strong arms wrapped around my shaking torso as he intertwined our fingers, holding them tight against his chest as his brow dipped to meet mine. I leaned further into his embrace as we sank toward the ground. He cradled me between his legs and knelt with his knees spread apart on the grass, never once faltering in his hold on my trembling nerves.

Daxton slowly guided my right hand toward the ground to feel the brush of grass against my fingertips and the warmth of the dirt in my hand. "This is real. You are safe … You are free." I tried my best to settle my breathing, but it only quickened with my heart rate. I felt guilty for my lack of control, and I bit down on my bottom lip as it began to tremble. "Breathe with me," Daxton commanded. "In." He took a deep breath, placing one hand on my chest to help me fall into his rhythm. "And out."

One, two, three …

"Again." Daxton's command was firm but not harsh.

I didn't fear him. Something clicked inside my head that told me not to. Daxton was someone I could trust with my life. Someone that I knew would never hurt me and only wanted to help.

Eventually, I was able to follow his lead. Breathing and moving with him until I was able to stop the flow of tears and do it on my own. I glanced up at the open sky and held in a breath of air inside my lungs for a moment before slowly releasing it once more. The open air above calmed me, calling to my animal and reassuring us both we were no longer trapped in the underground prison.

"Skylar!"

I recognized the voice, followed by the sounds of others trailing in his wake. I turned my attention toward Gilen and my family as they ran toward me and Daxton. It didn't seem real—they were all here.

Gilen skidded to a stop. His honey gaze darkened, matching the bags under his eyes with concern, and his face was pinched with stress. It looked like he hadn't slept in weeks. His golden mangled hair flowed freely in the wind as he boldly straightened his stance and dared a step closer to me.

"Come with me, Sky," he demanded, holding out his hand.

I should have leaped into his arms. The Skylar before the meadow, before the hunters would have. But *I* couldn't move. I didn't want to. Gilen furrowed his brow and took another step toward me.

A deep, low growl came from behind me, paired with a snarl that made Gilen halt his approach. "Let *her* decide what she wants," Daxton said in a terrifying, threatening tone. "She needs to have the power of choice right now. She is in charge …"

I knew that all I had to do was ask or make the slightest move in Gilen's direction, and Daxton would let me go. But I didn't want to go to Gilen, not yet anyway. I didn't blame him for my capture … but the fact was that I was out alone searching for *him*. If he hadn't run off like that, maybe, just maybe, I would not have been captured by the hunters.

"Let her go, High Fae," Gilen spat, releasing his own wave of power through his command and stepping forward, challenging Daxton's warning.

As expected, the Silver Shadow persona reappeared, his eyes turning to stone. His lips pulled back from his sharp canine teeth as a predator's growl sounded from his chest. It was moments like this that reminded me our species were not as different as they appeared. To my surprise, though, I was still not afraid of Daxton—the opposite actually. In some strange turn of events, Daxton had become my protector, and I trusted beyond reason that he would do anything to keep me safe.

Gilen did not back down and began to take an aggressive stance with his shifter magic materializing around him. Talon was quickly at his side, preparing to shift if needed.

I glanced over at Magnus, who bent to whisper in Julia's ear, who then turned and spoke quietly to Neera. Whatever he told them made them calm down and take a few steps back from the gathering crowd. I watched them with a yearning that only my family could conjure. Love surpassed the distance between us as they wisely backed away from the tense commotion.

"Easy, Gilen," Talon said as he tried to steady his friend, but even I knew it was pointless. Nothing would be able to calm Gilen down in this state. His animal was on high alert, taking over his brain's logical, rational side. He was an alpha, and when confronted, he would refuse to back down to a challenge, even one from a High Fae prince.

I watched Rhea rush to Gilen's other side to try her hand, but it only made matters worse. When she glanced my way, I saw a wave of relief flash in her sad blue eyes. She mouthed, *Are you okay?* I nodded that I was—or at least for the moment. She pursed her lips and gave me a firm nod in return. I knew she would support whatever I needed. No questions asked.

The final person in my pack that I hoped to see at last stepped forward into my line of sight. I released my death grip on Daxton's hands, and he immediately turned his attention back toward me. I admired how he was able to listen to my silent gesture and helped me stand on my shaky feet.

I helplessly stared at Shaw, pushing myself to step away from Daxton's protection and standing on my own in the training field. Daxton didn't follow or hold me back, but I could sense his stare fixed on me, watching each step I pushed myself to take.

"Shaw." He didn't look at me at first. The moment he stepped forward at Rhea's side, he dropped his head down, refusing to meet my stare.

"Shaw …" I pleaded this time.

I pushed past Gilen without even a sideways glance. I knew it hurt him, and I hated myself a little because I caused him pain, but fuck it. I needed to speak to him, but right now, I could only focus on healing myself.

I finally staggered in front of the person who didn't need an explanation about the horrors of what I'd endured. I didn't have to describe the torment, the pain, the suffering … because he understood it all. And most of all, I knew he could help me heal from them.

I stumbled as I reached out for Shaw, and he caught me before I fell to the ground. His scarred hands clasped my arms, and I discovered he was shaking almost as badly as I was. My animal stirred beneath the surface, calling to his animal with a silent wave of power. Shaw felt her push of strength, and his dark, somber eyes finally turned to look at me. The shield that held back all his repressed memories and feelings shattered as our eyes met.

He knew.

I knew.

The same tortures I'd experienced at the hands of those monsters, were his as well. I felt our animal spirits reaching out to each other in the silence, giving unconditional love and support. I bent my head forward to meet Shaw's brow. I sighed as we both silently wept for ourselves and each other. I felt the scars on his arms as I held onto him tightly, like the ones on my back.

Rage boiled in my chest. Shaw was only a child when his parents were killed and he was taken. Yet somehow, he not only survived but thrived without his animal spirit to help guide him. I admired Shaw's survival and his strength. I could barely fathom how he was able to do it. He was a shifter worth more than all the jewels or gold in Valdor.

I could sense the others approaching as Shaw slowly released his grip on one of my arms. "Let us help you," he said with purpose. "That's how you will get through this. I know it might be the last thing you think you need right now, but trust me. We are here to help, and that is what you need right now. We love you, Skylar."

Rhea was the first one I allowed to wrap their arms around me, while Talon wisely stayed back with Shaw to give me some space. They didn't suffocate me but instead kept a steady hovering presence that made me feel safe. I watched Talon kneel and give Shaw an extra tight squeeze around his shoulders, understanding the pain he was reliving with me.

Finally, Gilen dared to approach me once more. I looked at him and saw the gut-wrenching agony in every breath of his being. I knew without asking that he regretted his actions from that night. I didn't need to blame him because I could see his own guilt eating him alive. Rhea released her arms from around my neck, remaining close by my side. I appreciated her silent support, but I couldn't hide from Gilen. He had also been there at my rescue. I remembered hearing him call my name as I blacked out in Daxton's arms.

I listened to see if my animal would give me any indication of what to do, but she remained surprisingly silent.

Gilen's eyes were haunting. His stare dug a hole into my soul. His sadness over what happened to me was clearly written across his face. He crumbled on his knees in front of me, dropping his head and sinking below my eyeline.

"I'm so … so sorry … Sky." He couldn't hold back his pain any longer. His hand covered his face as he openly broke down in tears.

I knew I should have immediately reached out and tried to comfort him. Maybe the old Skylar would have wept to see the male she cared for break down in such sorrow. She would have wrapped him in her arms and kissed the falling tears from his face, promising that he would be okay.

But I didn't. I hesitated.

I glanced back toward Daxton, who hadn't moved from where I left him on the grass. I tried to read the expression on his face, but I could not decipher what he was thinking. A deep pull in my chest tightened as Daxton looked at me from across the field. I was torn.

My eyes darted to the left as Castor crept to his brother's side, whispering a secret message that only they could hear. I could see Daxton nod in reply, but he still didn't avert his gaze from me.

Castor casually rubbed the back of his neck and shrugged. Before taking a step back from Daxton, he glanced at me and sent me a half-grin with a sly wink. I narrowed my eyes, trying to decipher the intent of his gesture, but I knew that it was pointless. Castor was a wildcard, but one that seemed to be extremely loyal to his brother.

I forced myself to turn my gaze away from Daxton and refocused my attention on Gilen. Taking his tear-soaked hand in my own, I reached out and grasped it tightly. I had never seen this side of him before. He was open and vulnerable, all because of how he must have felt for me. I grazed his knuckles against my cheek, and he moved to pull me into his embrace, careful not to brush against the wounds on my back.

His presence was warm and comforting. He was the same Gilen I had known my entire life and grown to care for.

He delicately lifted my chin with his fingers and bent to kiss my lips. He was gentle, but regardless of his intent, the overwhelming feeling of uneasiness churned my stomach. I pulled away from him, practically staggering backward, flinging my arms open and out to the side.

"I'm … I'm sorry." I shuddered as he tried to reach out and help calm me. He shifted to move closer, but it only seemed to make matters worse.

"Stop," I pleaded, and Gilen halted his approach. I saw Daxton rise to his feet, his expression hard as he searched my face for the cause of my panic.

Shaw came to my side as Rhea stroked my arms and grasped my hands. "It's the trauma from her capture," Shaw said with a deep, settling tone. "This is normal, Gilen. You can't overwhelm her like that."

I didn't bother correcting Shaw. I wasn't retreating because of what I went through. Part of me was still angry with Gilen. And as foolish as it seemed, I was putting some of the blame on him.

I watched Gilen's expression turn and crease with concern. "Tell me what to do, Sky."

"Just give me a second …" I muttered with shaking hands and a quivery voice.

I cared for Gilen. A part of me always would, I feared. His friendship was something I cherished and would never want to be taken away. But was this love? The mate bond was an unconditional sacred connection that bound two souls together as one. It was not something you could fight or deny. Even if one of the shifters didn't wish to recognize the bond, a piece of them would always belong to the other. But that was the problem. Nothing *more* was there. I listened for my animal, but there was no awakening, sense of longing, or pull toward him. True, I hadn't shifted yet, but Gilen had. Did he feel something I couldn't yet?

Then I felt the lick of ice magic caress the heating nape of my neck, cooling my shaking limbs. My breathing steadied, and my hands slowly stopped trembling. My mind was once again sane, and I felt a shift in the world around me begin to right itself. I didn't have time to turn and look in Daxton's direction before a new voice barreled through the training field.

"What in the gods' names do you think you are doing out here!" Latte's shrill yet terrifying voice broke my attention from Gilen. The short, stout, ill-tempered shifter healer marched across the training field with a menacing gleam in her eyes. "You!" she yelled, wagging her finger, poking Gilen in the chest. "Back up! She is not in any kind of state to be canoodling! The girl was … Well …" Her voice trailed off, realizing I didn't need a recap of what I went through.

Gilen might be a future alpha, but when Latte was in this kind of mood, not even Alistar dared to stand in her way. She was a big mama bear—in human and animal form. No one messed with Latte.

"I-I didn't bring her out here," Gilen stammered, trying to deflect the healer's mood.

"Oh, I know it wasn't you," she spat at Gilen. "It was that pesky High Fae who is constantly hovering! I had to threaten to snip off his pointy ears more than a few times to get him to leave the healers' quarters."

Gilen's hands clenched into fists of aggravation with this news as I frantically looked to where I had seen Daxton last. But he was gone.

"Where did Daxton go?" I asked.

"You don't need to worry about him," Gilen huffed with typical male posturing. "Not anymore."

"He wouldn't want to experience my wrath at removing my patient before I released her," Latte grumbled. "You … with the muscles," Latte said, pointing to Shaw, "help bring her inside. But be careful. Her wounds might look like they have healed, but she still has recovering to do from the damage done inside."

Gods be damned, I knew she was right. I could feel the fractures in my ribs each time I forced myself to breathe.

"Besides, the alpha wants to see you *now*, Gilen," Latte announced. "And you too, Beta!"

Shit … I had almost forgotten about my family lingering on the outskirts of the field. A pang of guilt hit me square in the chest. Luckily, it didn't last long as Neera sprinted through the field and latched onto me tightly.

Julia kissed my forehead and wrapped her arms around both of us. "I'm just so glad you're safe," she said through her sobs.

Magnus appeared next to Gilen after giving me a nod and a loving look. "We need to meet your father. The High Fae queen is waiting and has a proposal to counter your earlier argument."

"Good. Skylar needs to recuperate. And the humans need to be informed …"

Shaw offered me his shoulder as Gilen wore a reluctant

grimace that reflected his disappointment. I glanced down at my arm tattooed with evidence of my oath. My vow to compete in the trials and unlock the Heart of Valdor. I was relieved to see that the three eight-pointed stars created with my blood and magic hadn't been harmed during my capture.

Did Blade or the hunters know what this mark meant? They didn't mention it, or at least I didn't remember them talking about it.

"Stop asking questions in that mind of yours! You need to rest!" Latte scolded me before turning her mean stare to Shaw. "Bring her inside now." Shaw didn't hesitate, following Latte's orders and carrying me inside.

Neera, Julia, and Rhea followed, pleading with Latte to allow them to stay with me. I could hear the lies in their promises not to talk and let me sleep. I wanted them to come, but I also knew I needed to recover and have some time to myself. Latte gave a firm no and sent them away for now.

"I'll go, Sky," Shaw said, placing me back in bed. He handed me a cup of poppy tea that was waiting on the bedside table next to me. "Latte's orders. Drink up."

I looked at him with the most confused and complex expression I believe I had ever had in my entire life—and that was saying something. I downed the tea, feeling its magic work its way through my body, forcing me to relax.

"What do you mean?" I asked as I lay on my side.

He looked at me with shadows churning around the corners of his eyes, and I noticed he was physically bracing himself to answer my question. "I'll go in your place … for the trials."

"What!" I yelled as I practically shot upward out of my skin. Pain scorched my back, but I ignored it as I reached out and grabbed his arm. "What the actual fuck? No. No, Shaw. This is my burden to carry. Not yours!"

Shaw closed his eyes and sighed. "He asked, and I said I would go."

"Bullshit. Who asked you?"

"Gilen."

My eyes widened, and I physically shook with rage. "How dare he! I'm not some piece of property that he can make a claim to and speak for. I said I would go. I made the promise … I carry the mark of the champion of the trials. Me," I shouted, trying to get up, but then I staggered, falling forward.

Shaw calmly moved to help me back to the bed. He brushed

my hair aside and sat back on his stool. "They can remove the mark and choose another—"

"No!" I tried to scream, but it came out in a weak, pathetic whisper. Dammit, this poppy tea was working fast, and I cursed Shaw for his impeccable timing in this matter.

"You have been through literal death … torture. Let someone else go."

"No," I repeated. "You've been through this too, Shaw. How could I not go and expect you to do this? You've lived through the same thing."

It was then I realized something. He had kept a deep, dark secret hidden beneath the surface for far too long. I forced myself to fight against the pull of the poppy tea. "Shaw, look at me."

His sorrowful eyes carried so much pain, so much sadness that it made my own heart begin to break. Still, he could not lie to me. I was the one person who he didn't have to lie to about the horrors we both share that would forever leave a scar.

"We are stronger than this. I don't plan on dying when I get to the Inner Kingdom. As foolish as it may sound, I plan to win."

He stared at me for a long moment in silence and awe. "Sky … How the fuck are you this strong?" He slumped forward with his head buried in his hands.

"I was never truly alone," I answered. My thoughts went to my animal, but I also acknowledged the presence of another that I had comforting me in my dreams. "When those I love are threatened, I will stop at nothing to make sure they are safe. I will not allow you to take my place, Shaw. I love you, but this is not your burden to carry."

My eyes fluttered as I slumped helplessly against my pillow. I didn't say out loud what I knew he was thinking. Seeing my scars and knowing what torture I had been put through jolted Shaw back into his own nightmares. He was willing to go to the Inner Kingdom and compete, but not win. He was willing to go there to die.

Noble fucking cause, but I wouldn't allow it. He would get through this. We would survive this. If anything, we would rise above the incoming tide just to spite them all. My animal reached out to Shaw's, and I felt a wave of gratitude pass through me. She supported and agreed with my decision.

Finally, my eyes couldn't stay open any longer, and I drifted off into a poppy-induced sleep.

# Chapter Thirteen

When I awoke, my stomach rumbled so loudly that I swore the walls of the healers' quarters shook. I rolled onto my side, clutching my middle and groaning with an intense need to satisfy my hunger.

"Are all shifters this ravenous, or are you a unique exception?" My eyes snapped open to see Daxton, of all people, sitting in a chair at the foot of my bed with an ankle bent across his knee and a book open in his lap. "Your stomach was rumbling before you even opened your eyes."

I stared at him, unsure what to do or say. Looking around the room, I took note of where I was. Someone must have moved me in my sleep because these were not the stark white walls and forest ceiling to which I had fallen asleep. My stomach groaned loudly once more, causing me to blush and cover my face with embarrassment at my inability to control the noise.

"Gods, this is embarrassing," I muttered under my breath as a faint laugh of amusement caught my attention. I peeked through the slits of my fingers to try and sneak a glance at Daxton, and to my surprise, his gaze was still fixated on a book in his lap.

"I brought you some fruit, cheese, and bread," he said as he tilted his head to the side.

I followed his inclination and saw the tray of food waiting on the bedside table next to me. Without hesitating, I reached my hand out and grabbed a fresh piece of cheese from the silver tray. The sweet taste of the creamy textured goodness spread across my tongue in utter delight, causing me to release a moan of pleasure.

"Mmmmm," I said as I closed my eyes in utter bliss.

"Again, I must ask if all shifters have your special appetite—or reaction—when they get to enjoy a meal?"

I cracked open my eyes, noticing the smirk that crept up the right side of his face, revealing the dimple on the outside of his trimmed beard line. "It's just me," I said between cheese and bread bites. "The one and only. Aren't you the lucky one who gets to enjoy my company?"

"Lucky indeed," he teased as he returned his attention to the book in his lap.

I struggled but managed to stay upright as I placed the tray next to me, devouring my meal. I had been moved from the main healers' quarters to one of the recovery suites down the hall. Here, the wooden walls were painted with a hint of dark green, ideal for a healing atmosphere, with fresh plants on the floor and some sprouting inward from the open window. A large sliding screen stretched from ceiling to floor, allowing fresh air inside the room at all hours of the day. The luxurious bed was pushed up against the corner of the room with a lounging chase near the screen and a sitting chair at the other corner. A bedside table doubled as a small bookcase with various titles from the last inhabitant or patient to utilize this room. To my surprise, the door leading into the main hallway was closed and locked from the inside. Finally, a small yet cushioned armchair rested in the final corner near the foot of the bed, which currently held a very subdued, yet dare I admit, handsome High Fae prince.

"Did you move me in here?" I asked as I finished the loaf of bread and cheese.

Daxton held up a finger for a moment as his eyes scanned over a final passage of the page he was reading. "I did, yes." I glanced out the window, trying to determine what day, or even what time of day, it was. "Two days," Daxton said.

"What?"

"It has been two days since you were last awake. This is the morning of the third … well, almost morning. Dawn has just begun to peek through the window."

"Shit," I cursed, and Daxton gave me an amused yet puzzling glance. "Latte must have drugged me with the good stuff then."

"It seems she did. We have been given strict orders not to disturb you and allow you to rest in peace."

"And you seem to be following those to a *T*," I replied with a smirk, arching my brow and crisscrossing my legs in front of me.

"Clearly." He smiled as he glanced back down at his book.

I couldn't help returning his grin. I was not much of a rule follower either. "What are you reading?" I asked. Daxton placed a finger on the page, closed the book, and silently held it up for me to read the cover. "Ohh …" I answered, unable to help biting my lip, immediately recognizing the title. It was the book he had returned to me on the green sand beach, a very smutty yet action-packed romance story. "That's a fantasy novel," I said with an intrigued, questioning tone. "I didn't take you for a fiction reader."

"I would be lying if I said it was my favorite, but you were reading it, and I thought it would give us something to discuss when you awoke. I was told you loved to read, and I assumed this would be a good place to start."

"I do love to read," I said, touched by his genuine interest. "Who told you that?"

"Shaw," Daxton replied. "He and I have been taking turns watching over you while you recover. He visits when Latte allows, while I, well, I come in whenever I have a spare moment. We both agreed that we would work together to help you in these coming weeks."

"You and Shaw?" I asked, surprised to hear that they were working together.

"Yes. Is it all right with you if I help?" he asked with a genuine look of concern for a moment before it disappeared behind his veil of calm composure.

I clenched the blanket tightly with my fists, realizing he was asking for my permission. "I'm going to need some time to work through what happened to me. I don't want this to be a burden in my life and hinder me. Instead, I want to learn from it what I can and then move on." A look of pride swelled within Daxton's gaze as he gave me a firm nod. "I didn't do this alone. My animal was always with me, helping protect my sanity—keeping me from breaking." I left out the fact that I had heard *him* in my dreams. It didn't seem appropriate to bring that into the chaos of our lives at the moment.

"It's comforting to know that you were not alone." Dax said. I glanced at him with a questioning expression, secretly wondering if he had somehow magically reached out to me in my dreams to try and help me. "Shaw and I have an understanding about what you will need to try to overcome, and I promise you will have all the time you need to do this. The alpha's son was advocating for this on your behalf with our high queen the other day."

I sat up straight, surprised to hear Gilen fighting for me like that. What in the world was Gilen up to this time? "Okay. I am going to need you to explain that one a bit more."

"Shaw and I met with your alpha and his son. We both explained and justified that you need time to recover physically and mentally from what you have been through. With both of us supporting this, it was hard to refute. The beta, Magnus, agreed as well, but we needed to devise a plan to give you time while easing the queen's impatience."

"And what was this plan?" I asked with haste. "I don't like being kept in the dark."

He grinned. "I can tell …"

"Then spit it out, Daxton." I growled that last bit with some of my power intertwining with the words I spoke.

Daxton rolled his shoulders, feeling the brush of my magic but not backing down from it. "Queen Minaeve is traveling with your alpha and his son to speak to the human king about his hunters and how they are doing more than just patrolling the borders. They broke the treaty agreement from your previous alpha—"

"My father." My heart sank for a moment as I clenched my eyes shut. "Fuck. That could get very messy … very quickly."

"Colorful language for a lady."

I huffed a humorous laugh and crossed my arms with my knees tucked into my chest. "Lady? Seriously, Daxton, you're barking up the wrong tree there. I'm not your typical *lady* that I assume you have prancing around in the Inner Kingdom, wearing dresses and holding her tongue instead of speaking her mind. That's never been me."

"Don't forget colorful."

"Yes—and *colorful*," I replied with a skeptical feeling.

"Again … clearly. I believe your actions have spoken to this very point in my short time of knowing you, Spitfire," he answered with a sly grin. I narrowed my eyes and pinched my lips together to convey my opinion of his remark. "I sent Castor to accompany Alistar along with our queen to meet with the humans to try and avoid any explosiveness during their meeting. My brother's skillset with negotiations and politics is unmatched by any in all of Valdor."

"Good reason to keep him close by your side."

"Absolutely," Daxton said, nodding in agreement. "Your friends Talon and Rhea also accompanied the alpha."

"Makes sense." I knew Rhea wouldn't help tame any heated matters, but I assumed she would travel with her mate. Talon would be able to help Gilen stay calm. "How long do you expect them to be gone for?"

"A month, give or take a week but no more than two. We can't afford to be gone from the Inner Kingdom longer than that."

Silence drifted between us for a moment. I wondered if Shaw had mentioned my intent to be the champion. "I still …"

"You still wish to fulfill your oath to be the champion of the trials to unlock the Heart of Valdor."

"Yes," I confirmed with a straight nod.

He stared at me for a moment, lost in his thoughts, almost like he was mesmerized or shocked at how effortlessly I answered his question. "Brave. You are so brave, Skylar Cathal," Daxton murmured, leaning back in his chair and crossing a leg over his thigh. "I wonder if the gods themselves know how strong you truly are?"

"Strong? Or stubborn and slightly naive with a pinch of foolishness to drizzle on top?" I replied as I glanced at Daxton from the corner of my eye. He was remarkably still and silent, looking me over from head to toe in what appeared to be awe and perhaps admiration.

"You certainly are *more* than you appear to be, Spitfire. That much is clear."

"Just have to wait and see if this ends up being a good or a very bad thing," I answered.

Daxton shook his head and laced his fingers in front of his mouth, closing his eyes to pause for a moment. It was like he was calculating the different ways to approach the situation or possibly plotting various outcomes. I assumed this behavior stemmed from his practically immortal lifespan that had molded him in this way. With over five hundred years of living and surviving as high prince, I imagined he knew how to take a breath and think before he responded.

I took this time to glance over at the chaise and noticed a blanket stretched over the back, with the fresh imprint of a tall frame still embedded into the cushion. It dawned on me that Daxton had been in the room with me the whole night. His pine and mountain air scent was all over this place. Even though Shaw and others had visited, Daxton's was the strongest. He had been here the most.

"Do you enjoy reading, Daxton?" I asked, changing the subject.

"Immensely," he answered as he shifted, leaning forward and bracing his torso on his forearms. "When I have the time to read for pleasure, I enjoy historical fiction or books about different flora. Stories with a plethora of action with a hero and a villain or war reenactments tend to be my evening companions on calm quiet nights. I find the strategies in battle scenes enticing along with the depth of characters described alluring. But this," he said, flexing one of my favorite fiction romances in his hand, "this is a new genre I am beginning to open my eyes to."

"Our library is—" I stopped for a moment, realizing if he had that book in his hands, then he already knew where the library was. "Well, we don't have much, but it's at least something."

"Any knowledge that can be distributed and shared is not something to feel embarrassed about, Spitfire."

I shyly tucked a strand of dark blond hair behind my ear. "That was kind of you, but I can only imagine what your libraries must be like. You have had years, centuries even, to build and collect pieces of work. Our library has only recently become a staple in our community."

"From your previous alpha, correct?"

"Yes. You're a very observant creature, aren't you?"

"Or perhaps just nosy," he said with an all too familiar hint of sarcasm. "I have been asking questions to shifters I encounter, and they are typically happy to answer them. I'm always curious about changes that have occurred since the last time I was here. They, in turn, ask their own, and we both gain something. As I said, the exchange of knowledge is a gift."

"I believe I encountered a very different side of you the first time we met." My gaze dropped to his left shoulder.

"As did I," he answered, glancing down toward my right wrist, lingering on his bite mark.

"I imagine you learned a vital lesson the first time we met."

"Really?"

"Yep," I replied.

"Please, enlighten me," he said with a spark of light and amusement in his eyes.

"Don't lurk around in shifter lands without identifying yourself first. We assume intruders are threats and don't hesitate to protect our home and our pack."

"Indeed, lesson learned. Don't be a *stalker* …" he said with humor laced in his voice, and I couldn't help a hint of a smile appearing at the corner of my mouth. "If I may change the subject, I do have a proposition for you."

"Lay it on me, Princey," I teased as I leaned back against my pillow.

"You do realize that I have killed people for demeaning remarks made against me like that?" Daxton's stare bore into me as a wave of his power washed through the room, making the hair on my neck stand straight. However, instead of cowering against his magic, my animal and I saw this as a challenge and happily sent our own blistering spark of energy right back at him.

I gave him a coy smile as I taunted, "Yet here I still sit, unharmed and unafraid." I crossed my arms around my chest, analyzing his body language, trying to gauge if he was simply toying with me or if this was a real threat.

"You're correct," Daxton replied with a wicked grin. It seemed like he enjoyed the fact that I pushed back against him instead of sulking away in fear. If this was a test, I seemed to have passed. I was competitive by nature, and when Daxton challenged me like this, instinct drove me to push back. "*You* … never need to fear me, Spitfire."

"I know."

His eyes snapped to mine, and a deep, roaring fire began to build in my core. The thrill of a challenge excited me, and Daxton was by far the most intriguing opponent I had ever met. I could see a glimmer of excitement ignited in the center of his alluring gray eyes, paired with a mischievous grin at the corner of his mouth. I bit my lip, trying to fight back against my own playful grin.

"Returning to my previous inquiry," Daxton announced, clearing his throat and leaning back in his chair. "Since it seems I am here for a while longer … I would appreciate you giving me a list of book recommendations from your library."

"Really?" I asked in surprise.

"Of course. You sleep a lot, and I need something to pass the time."

"Sorry. Almost dying tends to have that side effect." He and I both physically tensed at my remark, and I felt a twinge of hollowed sorrow echo through my chest.

Fuck. I had almost died. That would have to be something I faced soon. I knew from Shaw's own experience that I would have to confront those memories and work through them, or else they would have a hold on me forever.

"Almost," Daxton said with a clenched jaw. He swallowed a heavy gulp and reached up to run his finger through his hair, tying part of it up and away from his face. His expression turned cold as he closed his eyes to try and settle his rising emotions. I was beginning to interpret the words he wasn't saying from his body language and the small gestures he made.

"Did … Was it your magic that brought me back?" I asked.

"I appreciate the compliment and trust in my abilities, but I am not powerful enough to bring someone back from the dead."

"Just the brink of it then," I added as I stared down into my lap.

I didn't hear his approach. I was so lost in my own thoughts that the world around me drifted into a haze. Daxton's hands were suddenly on top of mine as he knelt beside me on the floor. My breath stalled in my chest as the warmth of his touch spread across my skin, bringing me back to reality. He gently caressed my knuckles until our fingers were intertwined as one.

"You brought yourself back," Daxton stated with absolution. "I'm powerful, but alone … I'm not strong enough to accomplish such a feat. I simply created the bridge, and you decided to cross over. You did not give up, Spitfire. You are not weak. You are stronger than you know, and I thank the gods above that you were brave enough to make the choice to return." He tightened his grip on my hands, and I felt a strong pull at the center of my chest tighten.

"H-hand me a piece of parchment and a pen," I murmured, my insides melting at the sincerity and caring words he shared with me.

I almost felt unworthy of the compliments he gave me, especially when it came from a famed warrior like himself. Daxton nodded, released my hands, and stood up from the floor. He walked over to the bedside table, handing me what I needed.

"Is there any genre in particular you would like me to suggest?"

"Surprise me," he said softly with a change of demeanor, flashing me a kind smile. "In return, I'll select titles I deem favorites that you might enjoy. We could compare notes and discuss our various likes or dislikes of each other's choosing."

"I would like that," I answered as he stood patiently at my bedside. "I have read through almost every book in the library, but I would be happy to re-read and visit any story or book you would like to suggest." I scribbled the names of various titles as he waited, never impatiently tapping his foot or showing signs of annoyance.

"When we travel to the Inner Kingdom, I shall find new titles to entice your clever mind. I can compile a list of my own favorites, and when we travel to Silver Meadows, I will personally give you a tour of my private library," he added as he leaned his thick shoulders back against the wall.

"Wow," I exclaimed. "I can't tell you how much I would love that."

"Then I will make sure it is done."

I couldn't help my gaze from drifting over toward where Daxton stood. Heat rose in my core as I scanned over his muscular physique, admiring the handsome features of his face. His typical black tunic opened along his neckline, exposing a hint of his broad, firm chest. Silver swirls were etched into the fabric of his shirt, with an emblem outlining three mountain peaks on his shoulder. I bit my bottom lip, resisting the pull of desire that I felt washing over me.

"Here," I said, extending my hand with the parchment.

On a last-minute impulse, I decided to add something else next to the titles. I placed numbers along the sides, giving him a riddle to solve along with my suggestions. He reached out to accept the list as our fingers touched. I flinched, feeling a spark of enticing fire trickle along my skin with my animal's presence lingering near the surface.

"Your animal is strong," he said, accepting the list and looking it over. "It's not often a shifter is able to react to my magic like this."

"So, my animal is a treat for me, and for you. Oh, joy," I mumbled.

"It's a testament to how powerful you will become once you defeat the trials and are able to shift."

I stared up at him, partially in disbelief but also with a rush of gratitude for what he had said. "You … you believe I will be able to shift someday?"

"Of course," he stated. Daxton had answered the question so effortlessly and with such confidence that it was hard to form a rebuttal.

"But I will have to conquer the trials and unlock the Heart of Valdor in order to do so. This mark locks in my animal so I can't shift."

"And?" Daxton asked, tearing his eyes away from my list and locking his gaze with mine.

"You believe I will win?"

"I know you will." His confidence in my ability to defeat the trials was absolute and unwavering. "I know this because you have awakened something dormant inside my soul, Skylar Cathal. Something I never thought I would be able to feel …"

"What is it?" I asked, waiting on bated breath. My chest rose and fell as Daxton moved to sit next to me on the bed. His hand reached up to cup my face, and the same fiery spark of electricity passed through us.

"Hope."

I smiled at his response, remembering how he had given the same gift to me while I was alone in the hunters' underground cell. Of course, he didn't know any of this because I had dreamed all of it, but still, I believe it counted for something. He released his hold on my face and lifted the list in between the narrowed space separating us on the bed.

"There are numbers before the titles you gave me. Care to elaborate on the meaning?"

"Can't." I couldn't help the girlish grin spreading widely across my cheeks. "It's a riddle. Think you will be able to solve it?"

Daxton glanced down at the list again, tracing his fingers carefully over my writing. "I don't want to give you my response without further investigation. May I tell you my thoughts later?"

"You got it. Anything else you need?" I heard a soft chuckle escape his luscious lips, and he shifted as he leaned in. The space between us disappeared as his body moved closer to mine.

The handle of the door turned, and Shaw unexpectedly entered the room. He glanced between us, but Daxton didn't move.

"I should have expected to find you in here," he said to Daxton before glancing my way. "Skylar, how are you feeling today? Do you need anything?"

"I need to stretch my legs and get out of this bed," I answered, leaning backward against my headboard.

"I can arrange that," Daxton added with a devilish smirk as he shifted toward my feet. "In and out. No one would be the wiser if I teleported us."

Shaw stroked his chin, surprisingly contemplating Daxton's suggestion. "You sure you want to face Latte's wrath? She would be able to tell that you moved her by the change in her scent."

Daxton's face twisted as he contemplated Shaw's words. "Not many things in this life cause me unease, but that female is something else."

I couldn't help releasing a genuine laugh at his reply. Both of them turned and looked at me, relief washing over their expressions.

"What?" I asked.

"You laughed," Shaw answered. "It is good to hear your laughter, Skylar. We didn't know—"

"You didn't know what kind of shape or mental state I would be in after rescuing me." I could see the answer written on both their faces. I honestly didn't blame them. I still wasn't sure how I was feeling.

I was thankful for Gilen's quick thinking and taking the fae queen to speak with the humans. That at least gave me some time. I knew the act of kidnapping a member of our pack would push Alistar to confront the human king about his hunters.

Footsteps sounded in the hall. "That's Latte," Shaw taunted Daxton.

"Then that is my cue to disappear," Daxton answered as he arose from the bed. "Besides, I have some research to conduct in the library." He gave me a sly wink before he was gone in a flash of silver.

"I don't think I'll get used to that," I said.

"It's normal after a while," Shaw answered. "You ready to see everyone?"

"I mean … yeah. It was all I dreamed about or desperately wanted when I was taken. When I was in my cell, I thought about all of you and what I would give to see you again." I shuddered, feeling my chest tighten and my limbs begin to shake. My animal was there in an instant, comforting me like she had during my entire capture.

Shaw took Daxton's place on the bed and reached out to grasp my hands. "This is real, Skylar." I looked up at him with fear looming in my amber eyes. "I know this feels like a dream. That you will wake up and still be trapped underground … but trust me. This. Is. Real." He squeezed my hands tighter. "Use your senses. Scent is one of the most useful tools shifters have. Utilize that to help ground you to the reality of your freedom and safety."

Following his lead, I closed my eyes and inhaled deeply, collecting the different scents surrounding me. I could detect the familiar smell of pine from Daxton's distinct scent, but then I also smelled the fresh air drifting in from the screen doors, the flowers outside my window, and Shaw's earthy aroma. During my capture, I didn't have any of that. All I could see, feel, or smell was darkness, iron, and the stench of death.

"That's it," Shaw encouraged as my trembling hands calmed. I opened my eyes and looked at him, the grip of fear beginning to fade away. "Later, we will come back to this and work through these memories step by step. Daxton and I have a plan."

"All right," I said with a nod.

"Ready for your family?" I released a bright, beaming smile, and Shaw stood to open my door.

Neera nearly tackled me onto the bed while Julia and Magnus stood in the door frame, waiting for their daughter to release me from her death grip. I hugged her back just as fiercely, though, while captured, I was afraid I would never see them again. Neera moved to my side as Julia swooped in next, with Magnus encircling us both in his strong, robust arms. It surprised me that I didn't cringe or pull away from my family's embrace, and I attributed that to the comfort my animal gave me while captured. Without her, I knew this would have all been different.

"How are you feeling? Are your wounds healing?" Magnus asked.

"Strong enough," I said, shifting in my bed to accommodate all three of them in it with me. Shaw left as soon as the three of them piled in, wanting to give us some alone time together. "I'm stiff, but otherwise doing all right."

"And … what about otherwise?" Julia asked, and I understood that she was referring to how I was feeling emotionally.

"I-I don't know yet."

"It's okay that you don't." Julia reached up to gently tuck my hair behind my ear. "You look much better than you did two days ago, and you will only continue to do so. You are strong on the outside," she lowered her hand and placed it over my heart, "and on the inside, my brave daughter."

I smiled at her kindness. "Thank you for saying that." Neera snuggled in next to me as Julia and Magnus sat together at the foot of the bed. "So, what's new? I can't be the only exciting gossip happening around these parts." Magnus pursed his lips, and I knew he was debating how much to share with me. "Daxton already told me most of it."

"I knew I recognized that scent," Magnus said, shifting on the edge of the bed and glancing toward the chaise. "Was he here when you woke up?" I nodded my head yes. "Figures," he said with a heavy sigh.

I wanted to ask him about that, but for now, I held back my questions on that topic. "Will there be another war?" I asked, honestly a tad frightened of what he would say.

"No. Not yet," Magnus replied, but I couldn't say I 100 percent believed him. "With the wilt continuing to spread, Alistar always intended to meet with King Taran. Your capture added to Gilen's interest in securing our borders and protecting our people. The fact that they somehow convinced the fae queen to go with them is a miracle as much as a mystery."

"Daxton and Shaw had a hand in that."

"Doesn't surprise me," Neera muttered, looping her arm

through mine. "The prince … the one that can magically disappear."

"Daxton," I answered, letting his name roll off my tongue with a firmer sense of familiarity.

"Yeah …" Neera didn't miss anything. "He seems to be working with Shaw to help you recover, but you seem like the same old Skylar to me."

I curled my lips inward. "I mostly still am. But—"

"You don't need to explain," Julia said, narrowing her eyes at Neera. "I spoke with Shaw yesterday and then with Daxton. We know you are still planning to go to the Inner Kingdom and compete in the trials. The first trial … will not be an easy task."

I recalled the fae queen's words in the meadow. The trial would test my mind, body, and soul. Fuck. The mind, of course, was first, and if I was frozen in fear by the traumas of my past, there was no way I would survive.

"I will have to talk about it." The room went deathly silent. "About what they did to me. About the darkness that I can feel lingering like a stain on my soul." I unconsciously reached my hand across my chest to feel the crest of a scar below the collar of the back of my shirt.

"There's always a gift, even in the darkest experiences. You just need to figure out what it is. How you can use this to further strengthen and empower your transformation into the champion you were always meant to become." I looked at Magnus with a deep-seated feeling of respect and gratitude for his kind words.

"Each day is an opportunity to feel a little better," Julia added with a kind smile.

"Thank you," I said with a warm feeling of love wrapping around my heart. They were both wise beyond their years, and if I was going to survive the trials, I knew I had to start somewhere.

"All right," a voice boomed from a swinging door. Latte stepped into the room and eyed all of us from under her dark, long lashes. She put her hands on her hips with her sleeves rolled up, looking like she was prepared to brawl with someone. "What the? Where is he?"

The four of us looked at each other with confusion. "Who?" I asked.

"That pointy-eared fae with the silver and black hair! I know he was here."

"I just saw Daxton in the library," Shaw said, poking his head through the doorway. "I said you wouldn't have to scold him today for breaking your visiting rules."

"Lies," Latte cut in.

"We were just on our way out," Magnus added as he and Julia stood up from the bed. "We understand your rules, Latte, and we were not planning to stay long."

"Wise, Beta," Latte mumbled with a scowl. "Smarter than that high prince … I don't care what your rank is or who you are. When it comes to my patients and their healing, I am in charge. My word is final."

"Yes, yes, we know," Shaw whispered with a smirk, looking at me and circling his finger around his head in a funny gesture to make me laugh.

"You." Latte whipped her small, robust frame around and snarled at Shaw. "You are no better than the other one. Let the poor girl rest in peace! As I said, you two can begin your work tomorrow. No sooner. End of story."

"I know … I know." Shaw defensively held up his palms toward Latte.

"Now, all of you, out! I need to inspect Skylar's recovery." Latte's tone turned soft on that last note as she looked at Neera. "You will be able to visit again soon, I promise."

As my family left my recovery room, Latte took my vitals and inspected my overall health. She was meticulous in her efforts, checking my temperature, listening to my heartbeat, and assessing my breathing. I assured her I was fine, but she just told me to hush and allow her to work. Finally, the time came to inspect the scars along my back. I knew she would have to.

"It's all right," I said bravely.

This was the first step—confronting the marks left behind by Blade's whip and letting someone see the scars that left a mark on my soul. I didn't know why, but I felt ashamed of them. Even guilty. I slowly reached for the bottom of my loose-fitted shirt and brought it over my head. The muscles in my back ached with stiffness since I had been confined to a bed these past few days. But I also knew the tissue below the surface was still healing. Latte was so strict with limiting my movements because if I did too much too soon, I could bleed internally.

Latte paused as she took the shirt from me, but bless her heart, she didn't flinch or make any additional comments about what she saw.

"There were three tips on the whip," Latte said as she ran her fingers over my shoulder, touching the highest mark. "He struck you five, maybe six, times?"

"Five," I answered, as the memory of each lash burrowed its way into my mind. I felt my heart race as my breathing quickened. Fear was taking control.

"Call on your animal to help," Latte commanded. "I don't give a shit if you have not yet or cannot shift. You would not have been able to survive this if she was not with you the entire time. Tell her to get off her lazy ass perch and help calm your fears, girl!"

I followed her instructions, reached out, and she answered me without hesitation. Her calming presence and a fresh dose of power spread through my shaking limbs. We were now molding together as one being, not two separate souls inhabiting one body, but a united front that could never be torn apart.

"That's it. Keep that connection," Latte said with pride beaming from her expression. "That is a strong bond you have with your animal, Skylar. Use it. I don't know many shifters who are this in tune with their animal. It is a special gift. You are truly one of a kind."

"Can you feel her power?" I asked.

"Indeed, I can," Latte answered. "My bear is getting her own boost from it, and I am afraid I will need to excuse myself afterward so I can go shift and work off this excess energy." She reached for a salve from her pocket and spread it across my back before helping me put my shirt back on. "That should do it. Now, you need to rest. I have some more poppy tea to help knock you out so your body can heal."

"What if I don't want the tea?" I countered. I hated drifting off into a forced sleep. Shifters did fall into a natural sleeping state when our magic was drained, but this was different. I felt groggy and unlike myself.

Latte glared at me. "Well … how about a compromise?" She was twitching and fidgeting so much that I thought she would shift right here in the room.

"This is the last tea I will drink," I said in a firm tone.

"Deal." She disappeared for a moment, likely mixing the tea from her cart of supplies outside my room, and returned with a steaming brew. She handed me the cup and, like a good patient, I drank it all.

"Oh, and I have something else," Latte added, digging into her other pocket and retrieving a small oval-shaped rock. "Gilen … He asked me to give this to you. You were still asleep when he had to leave, but—"

I anxiously reached out to accept the stone and cradled it gently in my hands. "He … Did he visit me before he left with Alistar and the queen?"

"He did."

"Thank you, Latte," I said quietly, "I think I can feel the tea starting to work its magic." I wanted to be alone for the moment, and Latte's hovering was beginning to smother me. Thankfully, she took the hint and dismissed herself out the screen door, shedding her clothing as she ran off into the woods to shift. That was odd, but the tea was again taking hold of me.

Gods above. I hated this stuff.

I lay back against the pillows and pulled the sheet up to my chest. Slowly, I unclenched my fingers and looked at the small oval rock that Gilen had left me. As I expected, a beautiful painting was on one side of the smooth face. The deep blue and black colors swirled together with twinkling starlight dancing across the sky. He had painted me a magical starry night that looked like a dream. I turned it over in my hand and read the inscription on the back, *Until we can fly together.* Gilen's message touched and warmed my heart.

I turned on my side and held the oval stone near my chest, closing my eyes and dreaming about flying with Gilen. A part of me was still angry with him for leaving the night I was chosen and asking Shaw to take my place. But knowing he was in my rescue party, that he argued to give me extra time to recover, helped lessen the sting. Perhaps, I could forgive him.

# Chapter Fourteen

In the middle of the night, something tugged at my primal senses, telling me I was not alone in my room. I forced my subconscious to break through the veil of drugged sleep just enough to try and decipher what was happening. The smell of fresh pine and winter air tantalized my senses, indicating that it was none other than Daxton who had returned to watch over me while I slept. With my eyes unable to open, I allowed my hearing and sense of smell to paint me a picture of what he was doing in my room. For a while, Daxton seemed to stand utterly still in the corner. His breathing was low and steady, paired with little to no sound emanating from his person. I assumed he was reading or watching me sleep, but I had no idea why. Why was he watching over me like this?

Fuck this tea.

Daxton slowly meandered to the head of my bed, and I heard him drop something onto my bedside table. My heart leaped at wanting to know what it was, but I couldn't bring myself to break through the hold of the tea. I turned onto my side and felt the oval-shaped rock drop from my hand and trickle down onto the bed as my hair draped over my face. His scent grew stronger. I could have sworn he was about to reach out and brush the hair from my brow, but he stopped. I didn't even hear him breathing and thought he had teleported away, but the shuffling sound of folded parchment caught my attention. Next, I felt the weight of the oval-shaped rock from Gilen return to my palm, and then Daxton's scent disappeared.

When the tea wore off, I frantically glanced over at my nightstand to see a book with a piece of parchment sticking out from the top. I grinned and hurriedly reached out to hold the new treasure in my hands. I read the title and realized I had never heard of it before. I hastily opened the cover, and the fresh, intoxicating smell of an uncharted story sank into my soul as a stupid, girlish grin crossed my face.

By the grace of the gods … a new book? Was it my birthday

or something?

Carefully unfolding the piece of parchment stuck in the back, I began to read the letter attached to his wonderful gift:

*Dear Spitfire,*

*This book is from my personal library, and when I travel for long periods of time, it is a companion I often choose to carry with me. I trust you will take care of it while you enjoy, well, hopefully enjoy, losing yourself within the pages of this world. I often find myself doing the same, and this story is a favorite of mine to return to. Although there may not be a smutty romance series in these pages, I believe and perhaps challenge you to discover a different type of romance written by the author in this book. Love can manifest in a variety of different ways.*

*My notes from the novel I saved from the green sand beach are surprisingly delightful. I did enjoy the story. The theme of love surpassing the barriers of two distinct worlds holds a special meaning to me. I don't presume to know you very well—yet. But, if I may take a guess, one of your favorite scenes might be when the hero falls into the villain's (obvious) trap. And the heroine must turn the tables and rescue him. From that point on, the dynamic between the two characters shifts, and the male sees her as his equal. Even though, in my opinion, she had been that way from the start. He was simply an idiot until that point. As I stated previously, this is an assumption from my brief time knowing you, but I believe you personally identify with the strength and determination this character possesses. I weigh this from our encounters thus far and your ability to follow and make your own choices with unparalleled determination.*

I smiled. He was exactly right on both parts. I loved that the heroine could pull a complete turnaround and save the hero. I always admired a strong female lead in books. I also couldn't hide my glee at how he took notice of my personality. He was very observant, indeed.

*I also must add that the intimate scenes were very well written and … I may leave it at that for now. Perhaps my next read shall be your favorite from the list you have given me.*

*Oh, by the way, I believe I have discovered the answer to your riddle. The number next to the titles indicates how many times you have read each book.*

"Excellent!" I grinned. He figured it out.

*I will begin there and share my thoughts and notes when finished, but I must warn you, I am a fast reader. I hope you are as well. While confined under Latte's care, I would enjoy learning more about our champion of the trials. I hope we can continue exploring different worlds together through our shared interests.*

*Until the next adventure,*

*–Daxton*

The note, however, didn't end there. This last bit of writing was different from the rest. While the other parts of the letter were unhurried and elegantly written, the last paragraph seemed rushed.

*P.S.*

*I apologize that I didn't explain this earlier in my letter. You are now under my personal guard and protection as my ward, Skylar Cathal. I was given orders from the queen to ensure your safety, and I promise I won't become a burden. I will keep my distance while still overseeing your safety. You may not see me, but trust I am near.* ~~*Please know, I will*~~

*Always, your protector,*

*–Daxton, High Prince of Silver Meadows*

What did all this mean?

The next day, I was still confined to *solitude* under Latte's care. I was thankfully able to entertain myself with the book Daxton had left me. I finished reading it the day I opened the cover, and I had to admit, it quickly became one of my favorites. The story depicted a young warrior who lost everything and, despite the odds, managed to rise up to overturn the wicked king, saving his kingdom and his people. It was full of action and adventure. I couldn't put it down. I understood why Daxton dubbed it as one of his favorites.

That evening, I wrote a letter and placed it inside the book, leaving it next to my room's open window before going to sleep.

*Daxton—High Prince of Silver Meadows.* That was how he had ended his last letter, so I decided that was the route I would take.

*Your ward thanks you for your diligent care. I understand you take your duty very seriously, and I wouldn't want you to stray from your queen's command. I feel safe, knowing you are watching over me.*

All right, enough with the formality of it all. That wasn't me, and I didn't want to pretend to be anything other than myself with Daxton.

*Dear Daxton,*

*Couldn't help it. I've got to drop the formality. I'm neither good at that stuff nor that polished.*

*Returning to more enticing and exciting topics … your story of choice for me was amazing! I finished it today, not wanting to put it down and miss out on what was going to happen next. I enjoyed the action-packed chapters and the idea of the hero overcoming such turmoil and still never giving up. His resilience was remarkable, as was the hope he inspired in his people to fight with him and unite. Come to think of it. I can see why you chose this book for me to read. Thanks for that.*

*You know, since I'm traveling to the Inner Kingdom, perhaps it would be a good thing if I knew a little more about it. Did you bring any other books that describe the customs or history of your people? I would also love to take a gander at any books about the wildlife or the different plants that grow in your kingdom. I love romance, but any new book would be a treasure.*

*One time, I read a book about different types of land formations and the study of rocks. (Yes, rocks.) I imagine you are laughing to yourself right now at the fact that I found rocks interesting, but that was how I discovered the green sand beach. Sometimes, you have to look a little deeper to find the beauty in the world. Did you know that some stones are absolutely hideous on the surface, but when you crack them open, you reveal a hollowed center lined with beautiful crystals?*

*Well, I hope you find the top read from my list (nice job on figuring out the numbers, by the way) enjoyable. It's a trilogy, so I understand if it takes you a little longer to get through despite your superior reading skills. I'm looking forward to hearing your thoughts, and maybe you can even figure out which aspects of the story I hold above the others.*

*Regarding what you said at the end of your last letter, please understand that I don't find your presence a burden. While these letters are efficient for exchanging notes, I do prefer conversations face to face.*

I held back from saying anything more to that notion. I hadn't seen Daxton in a few days, but his scent still lingered in my room. I dared to admit that I missed him.

*But whatever you think is best. I will defer to your many … many … many years of wisdom. I look forward to reading your next book suggestions and notes. I believe Latte will release me soon, and I can't tell you how anxious I am to be free from the confines of this room. I long to see the green sand beach again and feel the wild nature forest engulf me instead of the four walls of this room.*

*Until next time,*

*–Skylar*

In the morning, the book on the window was gone, and the smell of fresh pine and cold winter air lingered in its place.

"You've got this, Skylar," Shaw said with encouragement. "We know what happens if you give up; that's dull and uneventful. So, why not try and find out what happens if you succeed."

As my healing continued, Shaw helped me work on different grounding techniques while discussing aspects of my capture that seemed to trigger my anxiety. Fear would be my enemy. I had to slowly work through the memories that gripped my heart in an iron cage and refused to relinquish their control. It was a bitch of a process to work through, but surprisingly, in each session I had with Shaw, I saw some improvement.

However, Shaw and I never discussed the final day of my torture. I felt he was cautious about that one, and I understood why. Nearly dying was something I knew I had to face, but I needed to walk before I could run. My animal helped as well. I knew if I didn't have her, the resilience I had built over the years would not have been able to withstand the torture from Blade.

Over the next few days, I had a lot of time to think. Books were left for me with a pine mountain scent lingering in the pages, but sadly, no letters accompanied them.

"Daxton's keeping his distance," Shaw told me. "But I'm reporting to him with your progress, and we are both amazed at how well you are doing. Be patient with yourself, Sky. Don't rush."

*Easy for Shaw to say.*

During this time of healing, I was beginning to realize everything I went through growing up had helped to prepare me for what I faced in that torture room and what I was about to confront in the Inner Kingdom.

Now, I was a member of the pack, but it didn't begin that way. I had to earn my place like everyone else, but as a half-breed, this journey was more difficult than most. Gilen and the others protected me when they could, but they weren't around all the time. I never whined about what happened to Magnus and bided my time until I could learn to defend myself. I would only earn my place and their respect if I did something different.

I had lost count of how many times I was cornered and bullied for things I couldn't control. For simply being born different, despite who my sire was, my blood was viewed by some as tainted. What I could control, however, was how to respond to my offenders. Eventually, I had had enough.

When I was thirteen years old, and my animal presence finally emerged, I did just that. I learned how to defend myself, growing in my physical strength and my animal's power. Determined to prove myself and no longer be a victim, I sought out the youth who had been my constant tormentors.

I foolishly singled out their strongest female, Sheila, ironically Xander's current girlfriend, for a challenge and lost—badly. I can still hear their laughs today as they stepped over me, taunted me, and kicked dirt on my face for my failure.

My nose was broken, my shoulder dislocated, and my eye

blackened, but what hurt most was my pride. I had challenged someone and lost. As the daughter of a former alpha, I thought my life was over. But when I came home, Magnus took one look at me and gave me a small smile and a curt nod of approval. I had lost this fight, but it didn't mean I would give up. Shifters didn't give up.

I realized he had known all along what was going on but allowed me to handle it on my own terms. If I was to survive in this pack and become a true shifter in my heart, I had to learn to stand firm on my own two feet.

The taunting didn't stop, but thankfully, they were lessened by my efforts. It became only whispers when I began utilizing my healing magic and training with Latte, and then practically silence when I proved skillful with a bow and joined Gilen's scouting party.

I never gave up. I couldn't.

Even though Daxton had kept his distance, I knew he was never far away. Whenever I felt the weight of my memories beginning to crash on top of me, I felt the whisper of his ice magic caress my skin. It calmed the raging fire inside my veins and simmered my boiling blood. I felt safe and protected. Nothing in the world could touch me as long as he was there. I knew I needed to be able to do this on my own, and I would get there, but baby steps first. It had only been a week, and according to Daxton, I had two, maybe three more.

The following week, Shaw, Neera, and Julia were frequent visitors when Latte would allow it. I could still detect Daxton's scent in my room. I knew he had checked in on me, but it always seemed to be when I was asleep. To my surprise, one morning, I awoke to the sight of two new books from our library with a note tucked in between the pages.

*Spitfire,*

*I'm happy to hear that your stamina is returning and catch glimpses of your smiling face from afar as you visit with your family. As I said before, I will keep my distance, but rest assured, nothing will harm you while you are under my protection. I will not allow it. Anyone who threatens or wishes to cause you harm will have to go through me … and trust me, that task is almost as daunting as the trials themselves.*

I turned my lips inward and cocked my brow. He clearly wasn't shy about broadcasting his power, but then again, he likely was not exaggerating. The stories of his fighting abilities were terrifying yet admirable. I recalled the tale of the human steward and Daxton's mercy, allowing him to flee. There was a balance to the high prince, and thankfully, his morality seemed to be in check.

*I appreciate your kind words and attempt to reassure me that my presence would not be a burden, but this is best for now. I want you to rest and recover, which is why I have held back writing you these past few book drop-offs. I have been working with Shaw and discussing your progress with him in great detail. When Latte releases you, I hope you venture to your green sand beach. I know how much it would mean to you.*

I smiled and closed my eyes, remembering the smell of the salty sea air paired with the sun's warmth that brushed my bare skin. I longed to return to the tranquility of that beach and feel like myself again. It was my favorite place in the world, and I knew it would be the first place I ventured to when I was released. Daxton was absolutely correct that returning there would mean the world to me.

*I hope you don't mind, but I identified some of the plant life I recognize here on the mainland that you can find in the Inner Kingdom. They have stars on the corner pages. There are some plants to be cautious of, and I have underlined those, hoping you read up on them for your safety. The other book I have for you is ironically about shifters. I added my own notes in the margin that describe the similarities and differences with High Fae. It was the best place to start regarding your request. Please rest assured, I promise you will learn about the Inner Kingdom when we begin our voyage overseas. Castor is the better instructor for this topic. I only want the best for you, so I will defer to him for this when he returns.*

*My notes from your trilogy, and yes, I did finish all three books.*

My brows arched with surprise and glee, happy that he was as fast a reader as he had suggested. For a second, I slightly panicked, wondering if he would taunt me for liking this trilogy or think poorly of me for reading it so many times.

*It is a very interesting story with various twists and turns, with a kingdom of ruin on the brink of death fighting to become whole once more. The brooding beast of a male, who is hurtful and hateful to all he meets, is actually a prince in disguise, and only his true mate can unlock his heart and help him save their kingdom from a deadly curse. The heroine, who we learn in the second book—even though we all guessed it from the start—is the prince's true mate. He tries to push her away to save her, and I must say that I understand the prince's decision. He knows he wouldn't be strong enough to let her leave to save herself and believes he will be her undoing, unworthy of her love.*

*When the heroine is forced to make a deal with the evil sorcerer to unlock pieces of the curse holding the kingdom hostage (that was a turn I did not expect), I can only imagine what torment this put the prince through. Letting his true mate leave in hopes she freed herself and never returning to his broken kingdom was difficult to swallow.*

*The ending was very satisfying to read, however. While the heroine was captured, the prince forced himself to become the true leader his mate knew he could be and rallied his people to unite. With pieces of the curse lifted from her deal with the sorcerer, they were strong enough to fight and overturn the evil horde. The heroine (a feisty spitfire, like someone I am getting to know), of course, escapes on her own and rallies an alliance to return and fight alongside her prince. Once they are reunited (in a very passionate chapter that I must admit I read more than once), the curse is broken, and they defeat the evil threat once and for all. I enjoy this book's ending. Sadly, reality doesn't always pan out this way. So it was pleasant to read.*

*I look forward to reading another of your suggestions, but I admit, I find myself reading through many of the shifter history books. I have not found any dated beyond the war, which is interesting. I am taking note of this and intend to show you the history books of your people before the divide.*

*Until next time, continue to heal, my Spitfire. Your strength is greater than you know.*

*Your ever-watchful protector,*

*–Daxton*

My mind was spinning, and I ended up reading his letter more than once that morning. I appreciated his openness and was glad he enjoyed the books, but that wasn't enough. I wanted to talk to him and see his expression when we discussed our various likes and dislikes—to feel his presence fill the room and swallow my attention without ever having to utter a single word. Reading his letters didn't fulfill my desire to see him again. I missed his calming demeanor and how we could speak to one another without constraint—which was a rarity for me. It was like I had known him all my life, and I could be myself. He made me feel like I was enough. Something treasured or even special.

I wanted to write a letter to tell him how I, Gods above. I didn't know what to write to express what I was feeling. My emotions were on a hiatus, and I didn't know what to think or do. The thought of Gilen flashed in my mind, and I felt confusion wrap around my thoughts, clouding my ability to make any type of decision. Perhaps the lack of a letter would raise suspicion enough to force Daxton to see me again. I had no idea why he had distanced himself. I was not too keen on his absence, nor was my animal. I would bide my time and wait for him to see me or perhaps I would find him once I was healed.

I had to see Daxton again. I had to try to make sense of this pull toward him and navigate the feelings I still knew I carried for Gilen.

Gods! *Damn you both for this madness.* Hadn't I already suffered enough without this drama?

Days passed with no sign or additional letters from Daxton. I was freed from the confines of the healing quarters and able to go home. Latte had given me the final go-ahead, and I was out of there faster than I thought possible with a promise that I would check in with her every few days. If I missed a check-in, I would be brought back to the healing room. I agreed, promising I would never miss one, and she was satisfied enough to let me go. Latte read me the riot act and gave me a long list of dos and don'ts, but then again, this was me. I wasn't going to hold back.

I knew exactly where I wanted to go.

Without hesitation, I headed toward the green sand beach, not knowing what I would find once I arrived. The cooling sea breeze kissed the skin on my face and neck, lifting my hair from across my shoulder and entangling it behind my back. I reached up to try and tame the mess of tangled hair with a braid that hung gently over my shoulder. Even though I was locked indoors these past weeks, the sunlight had been able to creep through the windows, and my golden highlights had returned. I was beginning to look and feel like myself again.

It was quiet as I climbed to the shoreline of my secret beach. A sanctuary that I knew would always be there for me. I didn't know what drew me to this place, but I knew it was something special. And for once, I didn't need to ask anything more.

Three weeks, almost four had passed since Alistar left with the fae queen to meet with the humans. I thought about all the what-ifs and all the different scenarios that could arise from this meeting, which I prayed was somewhat peaceful. I was glad that Talon had accompanied Gilen. Rhea was a hothead. Gilen tended to react to his emotions, but Talon was the calming mediator. He could ground them and help de-escalate a situation if it were to arise, and it was likely to. I was captured, tortured, and—

Fuck.

I almost died.

I did die?

My footsteps halted, and I clutched my arms around my chest, the memories flooding my fractured mind. Panic was settling into my chest, causing the breath in my throat to freeze like blocks of ice after a sub-zero winter chill. I couldn't force my chest to expand, locked in the spiraling darkness that captured me underground in that chamber.

I had stopped fighting. I gave up. Words I never dared to say aloud but knew them to be true in my heart. That was my greatest sin.

I fell to my knees as my hands reached out to grip the sand beneath my fingertips. I tried to ground myself as Shaw had taught me. Identify what was real and what was not. I was no longer trapped underground. I had survived … I had—

*But I hadn't.*

Tears streaked down my face as I crumbled. "I stopped fighting. I-I failed …" I said aloud to no one … to everyone. "I failed!" I screamed again. "I was not strong enough to keep fighting for my own life. How will I face and conquer the trials for all the others?"

The wind whipped across my back, filling my loose shirt and pulling me to sit upright. I followed nature's lead and tilted my head upward toward the sky, bracing myself for whatever would come next. There were endless possibilities, but I had to admit, I didn't expect to see *him* standing on the cliffs.

"Daxton?" His gray eyes illuminated with a spark of lightning as he looked at me with a firm, commanding expression. How was he here? Why was he here?

In a flash, he reappeared in front of me. "Stand up." He spoke the words as a command, not one he would expect to be ignored. "Stand up, Skylar."

On shaking limbs, I clung to the command, his dominating tone and posture guiding me. For perhaps the first time in my life, I found myself willingly submitting to another's power. I trusted that Daxton was trying to help me through this panic attack before I became lost to it again.

"Where … where have you been?" I shouted at him with a little more venom than I had anticipated.

He inhaled a ragged breath like my words had physically wounded him in some way. He instantly concealed the flash of pain, returning to the stoic warrior I met for the first time in the meadow. "I have not strayed from my duty to watch over and protect you," he answered.

"Right … your *duty*," I spat, clenching my fists. A twinge of anger worked through my spine, and I decided to cling to that rather than my fear. "I forgot. I am just your *ward*. Why even bother showing yourself then? Why write to me and share … share anything?" I rumbled with annoyance as I marched over to confront him. I glared upward at the fae warrior standing before me and extended my finger to poke him in the chest. "I didn't write you back on purpose, by the way."

Daxton stared down at my finger that was jamming into his firm chest before meeting my fiery gaze. A ridiculous, stupidly charming half-grin crossed his face, and that damn dimple on his right cheek appeared above his trimmed beard line. *Gods above*, I cursed to myself as a string of fire rippled across my skin, causing me to blush.

"I noticed," his deep baritone voice boomed. "Why didn't you write me? I've been …" He stopped himself from saying any more and shifted back a half step. His face twisted to the side as he ran a hand through his shoulder-length hair.

I cocked my hip and glared at him. "I didn't want to because …" Shit, I didn't want to because the letters weren't enough. Because. Gods be damned, why was I yelling at him? Why was I acting this way? Why did I even care this much?

"Because?" Daxton asked with narrowed eyes and a sly, confident expression that he didn't seem to try and hide.

"Well, clearly you know then," I scoffed as I brushed past him, approaching the shoreline. "I'm heading to the water. Are you going to continue to watch me like a stalker at an awkward distance?"

"*Stalker?*" He cocked his dark brow and curved his lip to the side.

"Take it or leave it. Watching over me from a distance these past weeks has earned you the title."

"And here I thought it was called being diligent in my duty to protect you."

"Right … as your *ward*." I elongated the final word, letting him know I wasn't fond of that title. I didn't want to be anyone's duty or forced responsibility. "Look, if you don't want to oversee my safety or whatever, you don't have to. I am not forcing you to do it, and I don't want it. I can take care of my—"

"Skylar," Daxton spoke, interrupting my rambling. My name escaped his lips with a soft caress that made my heart flutter rapidly inside my chest. What the actual fuck was this? Why and how could he make me so angry one second and then like this the next? "It is not a burden for me to be here with you. I asked to stay and protect you. I chose to stay behind and asked the queen to proclaim that I personally see to being your guard. The choice was mine, and I wouldn't hesitate to choose it again."

"Well, all right then." I shuddered, biting my bottom lip, not knowing what to do or say next. I gave him a sharp nod and turned my back to him to try and regain my composure.

I walked to the water's edge without turning around, trying my best to conceal my now crimson cheeks. I knew Daxton was standing behind me, carefully watching my every movement.

The large green crystalized sand was coarse against the palm of my hand as I crouched down to grasp a fistful in my fingers. I rocked backward onto my bum as I removed my boots and socks. I wanted to feel the sand between my toes and inhale the fresh breeze swirling along the crashing waves of the shoreline. This place was my sanctuary aside from the meadow I could only dream about.

"You coming down or what?" I called out as I tipped my head backward and up to the top of the beach. Daxton remained near the cliffs. His shoulder-length hair freely flowing in the light sea breeze, his dark pants fitting perfectly around his thick thighs, paired with a tightly fitted tunic that opened up just enough to glimpse the exquisite muscular physique beneath.

Gods, help me. This male was hands down one of the most handsome specimens I had ever seen. Even though I called him a stalker earlier, I never felt threatened or uncomfortable knowing he was around. It was actually the opposite. But I wouldn't dare admit that to him—not now, anyway.

A saccharine smile stretched across his comely square jawline, and I felt my insides turn into liquid fire. He closed his eyes as the breeze from the water's edge kicked up in his direction. Daxton tensed and clenched his right fist tightly while his left hand threaded through his free-flowing hair.

"In a moment," he called down to me.

"All right then," I said to no one as I glanced around the beach, releasing a heavy sigh of relief. It was empty, just as I had anticipated.

The evening air was warm even though the summer season would change soon, and I welcomed the cooling breeze that dried the sweat gathering along the nape of my neck. Untying the string on my pants, I let them fall to the sand as I approached the gently rolling waves in only my undergarments. The feel of the ocean waters encircling my feet and my toes in the sand was a therapeutic connection to the land that stole my breath away. As I waded past the breaking waves, I stepped farther into the green-tinted blue water that shifted into a unique turquoise before the deeper blue abyss of the open sea.

Closing my eyes, I allowed my mind to wander. Daring to brave the raging storm of my memories from my capture at the forefront of my mind. If there was any hope of facing them and conquering my fears, the time was now. It was here in this place that centered and grounded me most to Valdor. The remnants of an ancient volcano that now held a treasured piece of beauty unmatched by any other in this world. I could be brave here. I would not falter. I refused to.

I tilted my head back and extended my hands outward as I stepped farther into the water, encasing me in a natural caress that helped hold me upright. With one deep inhale, I bent my knees and submerged myself under the surface of the waves. Kneeling under the water, I opened myself to my memories, calling upon my animal to help fill me with a surge of her power and connect to everything around me.

Instantly, the horrors of my capture re-entered my mind.

The dark underground room of my torment, the bitter isolation between experimenting sessions, and memories of the pain inflicted by my captor's array of tools. The pain I could handle. That didn't trigger me as much now, but what I feared the most was facing the fact that I had given up. I had stopped fighting.

The overwhelming shame of that fact was suffocating. Knowing that in the end, Blade had ultimately broken me with his iron whip.

I screamed under the waves, releasing every ounce of fear, pain, and regret from that night. I screamed until bubbles no longer appeared around me, and the water returned to the tranquil nature from before. The air in my lungs was gone, nothing more remained inside me.

Motion in the water caught my attention as two strong hands clasped onto my shoulders under the waves and hauled me upward toward the surface.

"Skylar!" Daxton's touch and the sound of his voice were unmistakable.

The depth of concern in his tone awakened something locked deep inside my center, bringing me back from my swirling pool of anguish. I fluttered my eyes open to meet his gaze, and his saccharine smile from before had disappeared, replaced by wide eyes searching for a beacon in the darkness.

"Skylar …" He rasped. This time, his voice wavering with worry.

"Didn't know anything could make the Silver Shadow worry like this," I whispered. He didn't seem amused by my remark, tightly pursing his lips while shaking his head.

"What were you doing? You were under the water for far too long. You could have drowned."

"I was fine," I barked, straightening my back and bucking up my chin. "I can handle this. I can look after myself. I don't need you hovering over me like this and interfering. You stayed away this whole month, Daxton. Why are you suddenly here? Why have you decided to finally show up?"

His eyes narrowed, with his bearded square jaw clenching tightly as his grip on my shoulders loosened, dropping to my sides. I could have sworn a hint of pain or sorrow flashed in his expression, but it was gone the second I noticed it.

His head turned toward the swirling waters as he said in a low, hushed tone, "I never left you, Skylar. I—"

"You what?" I roared. "Daxton, you were there one day and gone the next. Promising me that I was never alone. You—" I didn't know how to say it or properly articulate my feelings.

My head was spinning with confusion as my animal flared in my chest, fueling me with a rush of fire that tickled my center. *Fuck it.*

"I wanted you to be there. I didn't write to you because I was hoping it would force you to come see me." I tensed as I shut my eyes, embarrassed by what I had just confessed. Daxton was the High Prince of Silver Meadows. A High Fae warrior … over five hundred years old, and I was merely a half-shifter human hybrid that he was bound to protect simply because I was the champion of the trials.

I felt the waters shift as Daxton waded to stand behind me. I kept my gaze forward as he stood only breaths away. Not touching me directly, but close enough for me to feel his presence.

"I never left you, Skylar. Just because you couldn't see me … didn't mean I wasn't there." I knew he was speaking the truth, a part of me always knew he was nearby, even if I wasn't able to see him. "I will always find you, Spitfire. We will always find each other."

The breath in my lungs stilled as he whispered those words to me. The same words I had dreamed of in the dark cell of the hunters' lair. Did his magic somehow send a message to me in my dreams?

How could he navigate through the mage wards protecting the lair and the irons I was locked in? How did he follow the hunters' trail?

"I was screaming under the waves …"

"Hence the bubbles," Daxton answered with a sarcastic tone, his deep voice vibrating along the nape of my neck. "What plagues you the most, Skylar? I know you've overcome the physical pain of your torture with Shaw, but something else is weighing you down. What is it?" Crap. Was it that obvious? "And before you begin questioning your lack of strength to hide that pain …"

My eyes widened with surprise, "How did you—"

"Like calls to like," he said with a heavy sigh.

I couldn't help turning my chin to glance back at him. "Daxton?"

"Like you … and Shaw, I have my own experience with capture and torture. I understand the shame … the guilt you feel at breaking under the hands of another. Regardless of the reasons, it is—"

"You don't need to explain, Daxton," I answered quickly. I could see the pain in his face reflect my own. His own past was torn and broken just like mine.

Instinctively, I reached out to grasp his arms floating in the water beside me. I gulped, slightly terrified at initiating contact with him, but to my surprise, he didn't fight me or pull away. We simply stood together in the water, allowing the memories of our pasts to float away with the churning waves. The rhythm of the waves crashing along the shoreline reminded me of the magical music from the trickling waters in Blade's torture chamber. The melody was simple, but it helped protect and transport me to a place of protection during my torture.

I began humming the soft tune aloud, the deep melody rising and then falling like the gentle rolling waves. The song held no words, only the ebb and flow of tranquility that wrapped around us like a comforting warm blanket. I was about to finish the song when Daxton's deep baritone voice fell in step with my own.

I was speechless. Falling silent to his beautiful, mesmerizing tune. He continued humming the song I heard from within my prison cell. He knew the song.

I tilted my head, and Daxton's eyes opened to meet mine. No words needed to be said between us. None could.

I turned to face him in the water, our bodies almost touching as our stares bore deep into each other's souls. I saw a world of beauty and strength lingering beneath his storm-gray eyes, coupled with unwavering courage and power. I felt myself lean toward him as I placed my left hand atop his firm chest. I felt him tense and close his eyes before his left hand drifted into the water to find mine.

"You."

Daxton nodded, his stare never leaving mine. "Skylar …I--" His voice unexpectedly trailed off as he tensed in pain. "Ahh," he groaned as he staggered backward from me, placing a hand on his head.

"Daxton, what's wrong?" I asked with concern. I could see that he was in pain, but I had no idea what it was from.

"I-I have to … go," Daxton said through gritted teeth. Regret radiated through his expression as a flash of silver appeared, and he teleported away.

A long wolf howl echoed off in the distance, followed by a voice hollering over the cliffs leading to the beach.

"Sky!" Shaw's voice bombed over the edge of the towering cliffs. "They're back!"

# Chapter Fifteen

Alistar and the High Fae queen had returned from their meeting with the human king Taran. Details, of course, were not shared with me and that really pissed me off.

"It's nothing you need to concern yourself with, Skylar," Magnus had told me. "War is not at our doorstep just yet. We were able to gain some ground through diplomacy for the time being."

*I highly doubted that.*

Much to my dismay though, my uncle didn't reveal anything more.

I was under strict orders to continue to rest at home for the next few days, even though my wounds were no longer on the mend and completely healed. The scars would remain, but everything else seemed to return to normal.

Since Rhea's return, she was my constant companion at home with Talon in tow. They were not allowed to attend the negotiations, but they did tell me that things were tense with Gilen, Alistar, and the fae queen. The High Fae were growing anxious, but Gilen constantly argued on my behalf that I still needed more time to recover. I could tell there was more they weren't telling me, but I decided to bide my time and wait. Regardless of their timeline, however, I knew I was still committed to the trials.

Shaw visited in the mornings, and he was glad to see progress in our sessions. I didn't tell him exactly what happened to cause this shift, only because I really didn't understand it myself. I told Shaw I went to the beach and screamed under the waves until I didn't have anything left in me. Resurfacing with a deeper connection to Valdor that helped ground me to the present and forget the past. Leaving out the details about Daxton.

Gilen was the only one I had not seen since they all returned. The rock he had painted for me sat on my bookshelf, reminding me of all the questions I had hanging between us. I was not fuming mad at him anymore. On the contrary, I had worked through the possibility of forgiving him. Whenever I heard footsteps outside my door, my heart skipped, wondering if Gilen would finally visit, but it never was.

Time had become our greatest enemy.

The wilt was progressing, and many of the coral reefs along the shores showed signs of decay, along with the trees near the meadows. Shifters were more in tune with nature due to our dual animal souls, and we could sense the looming doom encroaching on our lands. We could all feel the change.

Magnus was unhappy about me refusing Shaw's offer to take my place, but I knew he would respect my decision. I asked my uncle about the fae, but Magnus brushed it aside and refused to give me any details. Despite Daxton and Castor's aide in my rescue, he was still uneasy around them. However, throughout my month of recovery, I had formed a different opinion about them—especially Daxton.

On my final evening of isolation, Rhea planned a little celebration and some much-needed one-on-one best friend time. I was sitting quietly on my bed, reading one of the smutty romance novels Neera brought up that morning when Rhea burst into the room.

"Okay, time to put the book aside. I have some real-life shit to spill," she said with a mischievous gleam in her eye. Shutting the door, she pulled out a flask with a girlish kind of squeal. "I snuck it past Magnus! Can you believe it?"

I immediately closed my book and put it on the stack near the foot of my bed. "Fat chance," I teased. "I have no doubt he already smelled the sip you snuck before coming here and just rolled his eyes, knowing exactly what you had planned."

She frowned and pouted her lips. "Why are you trying to ruin my fun, Skylar?" I laughed, a good-hearted, honest, free laugh that had me clutching my stomach and rolling onto my side.

Rhea shrugged and eventually joined me. "Why …" She could barely breathe and laughed so hard. "Why is this so funny?" Rhea flopped on my bed beside me, and we laughed until we couldn't see straight. I hadn't laughed like this in what seemed like forever, and I was so happy that it was with Rhea.

"Okay, my turn." I opened my hand, and she gladly handed over her flask. I took a long, heavy gulp, downing the fiery liquid as quickly as possible.

"That'll put some hair on your chest." Rhea laughed.

"Eww … gross."

"What? The hair or the drink?"

"Both!" I exclaimed as we both laughed again.

"All right … all right." Rhea grabbed the flask once more and drained what was left. "Time for the good stuff. I need to talk to you."

My brows raised with surprise. "That's a little unnerving."

"Some of it will be." She twisted off the cap and stuffed the flask back into her pocket.

"Let's start with the less surprising. I want to hear about you and Talon."

A look of utter bliss crossed her face, and she smiled from ear to ear. "Oh, that stupid … wonderful," she paused for effect, "*mate* of mine."

"I knew it!" I slapped her shoulder playfully and hugged her tightly. "Are you happy?"

"More than I thought possible, Sky." And I could tell she meant every word. "Once the sun rose, I heard his wolf's call … and I knew. Every nerve in my body was alive, like liquid fire coursing through my veins. His song was a melody that carried me away on a cloud of happiness. The mate bond is real, and it's amazing. I love Talon, and I know he loves me." Her smile was contagious, never leaving her face as she continued to gush about her mate. "Before I shifted, I felt a strange yet present pull to him. In hindsight, it was why I always seemed to pick a fight or challenge him somehow. But it was our mate bond bringing us together. Now that we are mated, I feel whole. I can shift into my animal form, and I have my mate. My life is amazing, Sky."

"You sound love-sick," I teased her, concealing a tinge of jealousy. I longed to have what she did. It was the same with all shifters who were lucky enough to find their mates.

"Love-sick and proud of it, my friend," Rhea boasted.

"So …" I couldn't help it. I had to ask. "How's the sex?"

"Sky!" Rhea shoved me, her cheeks blushing to almost the same color as her hair.

"Ah, so it's the fur that gets in the way then." A pillow hit me square in the face, and I knew I deserved it.

"Of course, we consummated our mate bond that first morning, and it was the fucking best sex of my life. I'll tell you details another day," she boasted, showing me her claiming mark on the nook of her neck. She went still for a moment, her cheerful expression turning somber. "And then …" Rhea was suddenly uncharacteristically quiet.

"And then you learned that I was captured."

She nodded her head, fidgeting her fingers along the edge of my blanket. "Skylar, I'm so sorry. Talon and I should have gone with you to look for Gilen."

I held up my hand. "Rhea, stop. No one is at fault for that besides the hunters and their fucking mage. I don't mean to be cruel, but I am honestly sick of everyone's apologies and their pity. I can't stand hearing it anymore." The scars on my back would never heal, but the trauma I endured, I knew I would be able to conquer that.

Shaw and I often talked about it when he visited. I asked him about what he did to conquer the nightmares that would lurk in the quiet places of the mind and how he handled outbursts of panic or fear. He didn't have a solid answer, but he did tell me about how Talon helped him.

Shaw told me that if I was brave enough and let someone in, anyone that I trusted, they could help. With the trials looming, I decided to deal with this as much as I could here, but there were more important things on the horizon. I needed to be strong. Even if I was suffering underneath, I needed to swallow my fears and don my armor. I would not fail. I believed, I hoped, I would still be worthy enough to be the champion for my people.

"Yeah, about that." Rhea glanced out my window. "Has Gilen seen you yet?"

I brought my knees up to my chest and sighed. "No."

"Bastard," Rhea muttered under her breath. "He should be the one telling you this."

"Elaborate … Now, please."

Rhea brushed back her hair and rolled her eyes. "How much do you want? And how honest do you want me to be?"

"Go for it. I want it all, Rhea. There are too many questions in my life right now, so just give it to me straight."

"Alrighty then, I like this new shift in you. Not backing down and standing up for yourself. It looks good on ya." She reached down into her boot and pulled out a second hidden flask. "I knew we would need this other one." She took a long gulp and tossed it over to me. "The day after the full moon gathering, when we realized what happened to you, Gilen completely broke down. He shifted into his roc and immediately started searching for you. Not even Alistar could force him to shift into his human form. He was locked inside his animal, refusing to communicate with anyone."

"I-I didn't know …"

"It's okay. We honestly couldn't make sense of it either. Luckily, the High Fae brothers jumped into action and gathered a group of us together to search for you. Daxton was the one who first found the wagon trail."

"So it wasn't Gilen who led the search party?"

"No. No one could talk to him, but I believe when he realized what we were planning to do, his animal began to loosen its grip on him. Once that happened, the tracking accelerated, and we followed as best we could, but those fucking hunters are crafty."

I knew exactly what kept them from finding my scent. "The iron."

"Exactly."

"Then how did you find me?"

Rhea rubbed the back of her neck. "I still have no idea how Daxton tracked you, Sky. And I didn't bother to ask. I was just so relieved we were able to find you. We had been searching for a little over a week with no trail to follow once the dirt turned into rock. Until …"

"My blood! So it did work?"

"Smart thinking there, you clever fox. The silver and black-haired fae was already leading us in that direction when Gilen confirmed his route, finding your trail."

"Wait … wait, hold on a second. Daxton was leading the search parties?" This was news to me. I put it together that he joined with Castor, but I had no idea he led them.

"Yeah, I don't know how, but his instincts were spot on. They saw things I would have missed and even picked up on the hunters' magic. Once they pointed out the difference to Magnus, he shifted into his bear and could follow it until we hit the mountains. Once we reached the eastern range, we separated into two different parties. That was why I wasn't there when you were found. Magnus and the two princes went one way while Gilen, Talon, and I took another group. The horn you must have heard was a signal to the others when their lair was found."

"The horn. I definitely heard the horn bellow twice. That was why they were so panicked when they came to get me." It all made sense now. "When I was carried to the surface, I remember Gilen screaming my name."

"That was the first time since you were taken that he shifted out of his roc."

"Why?"

"Great question!" Rhea threw her arms up in the air. "The bastard should be here to answer that one."

My mind raced with questions, but the one I needed an answer to most was the first to come out of my mouth. "Rhea, why did Gilen ask Shaw to take my place?" My friend turned to me. She didn't say anything in reply, so I asked again, "Why would Gilen ask Shaw to take my place?"

Rhea crossed her arms in front of her chest and mumbled, "Fucking. Bastard."

I was now completely confused. "Rhea. Do you want to tell me, but you can't?" A firm nod was all I could get. "You are under an alpha command." Her deep blue eyes shone with agony as she nodded once more.

"As I said … bastard." Rhea's second flask was now officially empty, following a few more colorful curses.

"Why would Alistar command you not to speak on this?"

"Not Alistar," Rhea grumbled as she screwed on the cap.

"Gilen?"

Another nod, yes. "Gilen is powerful, Sky. His magic has steadily grown since he shifted, and he will soon be stronger than his father. We can all sense the change … even Alistar. He is going to abdicate the role of alpha to Gilen soon."

My eyes widened, and my jaw fell to the ground. "That is insane!"

"Call it crazy … but it's the shifter way. It would be stupid for Alistar to claim his position when there is another ready to surpass him. You know that just as much as I do."

"Yes, but still …"

"Hard to wrap your head around? Join the club. Talon is nervous even if he won't openly admit it to anyone but me."

"Talon would be Gilen's beta, right?" I asked, already knowing the answer.

"Without a doubt. He would need guidance from Magnus, but since our mating, both our powers have also increased."

Ahh, the second perk to a mate bond. When shifters consummated the bond and claimed each other, they shared their powers, combining their magic and making them stronger. Their shared power stemmed from their unity and grew with their commitment to one another. The claiming mark made the power-sharing possible, and even if a pair did not have a mating bond, they could claim each other and still share their combined magic. In a way, it ensured that the pair would always be able to protect the other, even if separated.

"One could argue … that you could be the beta, Rhea." I could see her smirk and roll her eyes at me, laughing.

"We would be a stronger pack if Talon and I worked as a team. We could both fill the role, providing additional support to our new alpha."

That response from her shocked the hell out of me. Talon was clearly having an effect on her.

"Really? Aw, Rhea. Look at how good you have become at sharing," I teased.

"Yes, well, enough about all this drama. Tell me about what you have been reading recently. Anything I should be trying with my new mate that you have read about while locked up in solitude?"

Rhea and I stayed up until dusk lingered outside my window. A long, deep howl sounded outside in the woods, and I could see the glee of excitement ignite in Rhea's expression.

"Talon?"

"Yes," Rhea answered with a euphoric smile.

"Go," I said, nudging her out of the room.

"You sure? I mean, Sky … Shaw told me what you said about his offer, and I …"

"Go," I said once more to reassure her. "I'm not leaving tomorrow, so go to Talon tonight."

I couldn't do this now. I wasn't sure I could ever really say goodbye to Rhea. But right now, her mate was calling to her, and she deserved happiness. I would not stand in the way of my friend experiencing the unconditional love of her mate. She gave me a bone-crushing hug and kissed my cheek before skipping out my door.

# Chapter Sixteen

Alone in my room, I returned to reading my smutty romantic story. I was just getting to the good part when Rhea came to surprise me earlier, and I was eager to return to the unfolding budding love story. The characters confessed their feelings for each other were more than just friendship. It was true love, and they were beginning to explore the physical aspects of their new relationship.

The reading was beginning to fire up my libido, which, I had to admit, had been somewhat silent during this past month of recovery.

It could have been the whiskey—okay, the whiskey definitely helped, paired with erotic nighttime reading—but either way, I was extremely aroused. I needed to find relief from this building tension.

I lay back on my bed, untied the string of my pants, and moved my fingers below my waistband. Slowly, I circled the top of my opening as I continued to read. I imagined myself in the place of the female in the story. The build-up was intense. My muscles flexed with tension as I plunged my fingers inside myself and moaned with pleasure.

I was so close—

"That is, hands down, the most sensual sound I have ever heard in my life."

My eyes snapped open, and I jerked myself upright in bed, quickly righting myself and removing my finger from below my waistband. I looked around the room, utterly embarrassed at the thought of anyone seeing, let alone hearing, me.

"Please, don't stop on my account." I hadn't heard his voice in some time, but I knew exactly who it was.

"Gilen Warrick!" I screamed in a hushed tone. "What the hell are you doing here?"

My window, which was cracked open, moved aside as Gilen filled the frame. His golden hair was longer than I remembered, gently falling in front of his face as his high cheekbones shifted, his smile widening upon seeing me.

"Hi, Sky," he purred.

With my cheeks flushed, I curled my knees into my chest. "Again … what are you doing here?"

"I planned on coming to see you tonight."

"That's news to me. You haven't even bothered or thought to stop by before now," I said, glaring at him. "There are things we need to talk about, Gilen."

"There are." His head tilted over toward my bookstand that held the rock he had painted for me on top. "I see you received my gift."

"And?"

"And … I know we need to talk about a lot of things, Skylar, but does that really matter?" He said moving through the frame of the window. "Can't we just be here … right now, with each other? You have no idea how much I've missed you."

His confession made me pause, retracting my claws and softening a bit. "Regardless, it doesn't explain why you were lurking outside my bedroom." I didn't sound as hard as I wanted, but I couldn't fight against the rush of feelings I had for Gilen that were returning to the forefront of my heart.

"I didn't mean to startle you," he replied as he pushed his hair back and away from his face. A sly grin curled at the corner of his mouth that he could not hide from me or simply didn't bother to. "But as I approached your house, I heard the most entrancing moan of pl—"

"No … no, stop." I shuddered, interrupting him. I held up my hands to cover my crimson face, begging him not to continue. "I was having a *private* moment. Not meant for you or anyone else."

"A shame," Gilen replied, a devilish grin on his face as he crept toward me, casually leaning over the foot of my bed.

"A shame?" I asked, cocking an eyebrow in his direction.

"I would give anything for your private moment to include me," Gilen answered in a deep, low voice laced with passion, his hooded eyes holding me in a heated stare.

Okay, I was mad, confused, and so many other things at him … but damn.

My stomach fluttered, and I could feel the faint thrumming between my legs now begin to throb with ache. I swallowed a gasp as I bit my bottom lip to turn away. A low growl emanated from Gilen's chest that sent the hairs on my neck standing straight. It wasn't aggressive or predatory—instead it was like a purr of delight.

"That should be mine," Gilen said as he sat on the end of my bed, grasping my chin between his fingers and running his thumb along my bottom lip. "That and so much more."

Without a second to think or say anything in reply, Gilen leaned in and kissed me. His tongue parted my lips, and I moaned in response to the taste of his kiss. He quickly moved to pull me into his lap. I wrapped my legs around his hips and raised up on my knees to kiss him deeper. My tongue dipped into his mouth as I looped my arms possessively around his neck, tugging on the back of his hair to hold him exactly where I needed him to be.

Gilen moaned against my lips, encouraging me to continue exploring his mouth with my own. He possessively groped my ass as his hips began to buck upward, running his hardened length between my aching thighs. I pushed my breasts against his firm chest, feeling his rapid breaths match mine as the friction between our writhing bodies erected my nipples into hardened points. Pleasure radiated through my core as Gilen moved his hands under my shirt, ravaging my body with his heated touch.

Gods, he felt amazing. I had been pushing back my pain and suffering for so long that giving into this erotic escape of my senses felt like a dream.

To my extreme dismay, Gilen released his hold on me and broke our kiss. His breathing was heavy, and when he opened his eyes, I could see the depths of his desire raging behind a whisper of control.

He wanted me.

I wanted him.

Gilen bit his bottom lip, moving his hands to cup my face, delicately stroking my hair aside. "Want to come flying with me?"

Sitting on his lap, I could feel his erection pushing up against my apex as I slowly began to circle my hips. "You sure you want to go flying right now?" I asked in a hushed whisper against his ear.

"Fuck, Skylar," Gilen cursed through clenched teeth, his eyes rolling to the back of his head. "You're sure you're still a virgin? Not complaining, as I am clearly enjoying every second of this."

"I never said I wasn't experienced in … other things," I answered as I lowered my lips to the base of his ear.

Nibbling on his earlobe, I felt him stiffen and shudder between my thighs. All my confusion from before had been brushed aside, and all I wanted to do was forget the pain I had endured—to live in this moment and the heated passion that Gilen was feeding me.

The erotic sensations shooting through my body were so intense I didn't know if I could break away. Gilen grabbed my hip with one hand and pulled at the base of my neck with the other. His teeth nipped at the skin on the crook of my neck, causing my mind to become a haze of lust and ecstasy.

His breath was ragged as he fought against his own desires, his voice quivering and laced with heat. "Not here, Sky … Come fly with me." He shifted my weight off his lap and stood from the bed.

My hooded eyes were heavy with lust as they drifted down to his fully hardened length, visible through his loose pants.

"I believe he has other ideas," I said, gesturing to his hardened shaft.

"Fly with me first?" he asked again. "I promise it'll be worth it."

"Fine," I grunted, not bothering to hide my disappointment. "I'll fly with you."

"Don't sound too excited," he answered with a deep chuckle in his chest. "Trust me … it'll be worth it."

"You've said that."

I knew there were so many other things we should be discussing, but right now, none of them mattered to me. I just wanted to continue what we started.

Together, we climbed out my window and leaped onto the ground, rolling to catch our momentum so we would go unnoticed. Gilen gestured toward the woods, where a small clearing was on the other side of the trees. He grabbed my hand, and I felt sparks dance through my skin as I happily followed his lead. Once we dashed through the trees and were a safe enough distance from my house, Gilen stopped.

His chest heaved heavily, and I could see a slight nervousness creep into his confident exterior. He turned to face me and slowly began to remove his clothing.

I couldn't help gawking at Gilen as he pulled his shirt over his head, his eyes never leaving mine as he watched me carefully. Broad shoulders filled his muscular frame with sculpted abdominals leading down to a deep V shape at the top of his narrowed hips. He slowly, almost too slowly, pulled at the drawstring of his pants, and I felt my heart rate accelerate out through my chest.

A heated grin turned at the corner of his mouth, and I realized he was enjoying this slow reveal almost as much as I was. With one swift pull of the tie on his waist, his pants began to fall, but he shifted too damn quickly to reveal anything below his hips.

"Tease," I murmured as I scowled and furrowed my brow. The majestic roc squawked in amusement and rolled its large golden head in my direction. "So, I just climb on up?"

Gilen bobbed his tan and gold feathered head, holding my stare with the same honey-colored eyes he held in his human form. He bent his legs and lowered himself to the ground. A massive wing extended outward so I could easily ascend onto his back.

I climbed up and awkwardly wrapped my arms around the base of his neck, clenching his feathers tightly with my hands and thighs. He cooed to me and, in a flash, leaped off the ground, wildly soaring through the air. I kept my eyes shut and clutched onto his golden, black-tipped feathers near his neck for dear life.

Once in the air, Gilen squealed at me, and I finally swallowed my fear and opened my eyes.

The breathtaking beauty of flying in the sky was unlike anything I ever hoped I would experience. My animal was alive inside my chest. She rattled against the confines of my human skin, power rushing through my limbs with a sense of joy and euphoria. I spread my arms wide, letting the air circle around me, and drifted into this feeling of freedom. Flying felt so natural, so peaceful. I always had a difficult time guessing what form my animal would take one day, but this experience confirmed one thing. We were made for the open sky.

Gilen glided over our pack's territory, soaring high into the clouds before diving back to earth. I laughed with pure bliss, enjoying every second of this experience with him.

The meadow from our full moon gathering came into view, and Gilen gracefully swooped down to land in the tall grass. He lowered his wing, allowing me to slide from his back and onto the ground. I twirled around in circles and squealed with pure joy like a small child. The thrill of flying cleared away my sadness and gave me a rush unlike anything else I had ever felt.

"I knew you would love flying," Gilen said, shifting back into his human form.

I turned to look at him and saw … all of him. He had carried his clothes in his clutched talons, but he hadn't put any of them back on. The desire in my center sizzled as my breath quickened with each step he took in my direction. I swallowed heavily as his heated gaze bore into me, making the world around us disappear.

He pushed back his dark, wavy blond hair and coyly smiled at me. "You … you did like it, right?"

"Correction … I loved flying," I answered.

Ignoring any lingering reservations I might have had, I crossed the distance between us, throwing caution to the wind, and launched myself into Gilen's arms. I kissed him, hungry for the passion and heat I thought only he could give me. Gilen groaned as he eagerly returned my kiss, thoroughly running his hands over the curves of my body. His breath quickened as our kiss deepened as we laid down together in the meadow.

I boldly reached down and caressed his muscular body until I found his hardened length with my fingers. I traced my hands along the V-shaped muscles of his lower stomach before gripping his manhood firmly with the palm of my hand. Gilen inhaled a sharp breath and pulled back in surprise, a sensual moan escaping the corners of his decadent mouth.

"You like this?" I asked as I began stroking him. I moved slowly at first, beginning at the base of his erection and caressing him until I reached the soft tip. I paused, bringing my fingers to my lips to lick them before returning to his hard cock.

His eyes were heavy as his head fell back. "Fuck, yes. Gods, Sky … That feels amazing."

A surge of pride filled my chest as I pumped him faster, using the beads of liquid that dripped from the tip to help lubricate my hand. His hips rocked in rhythm with me. It thrilled me to know he was this responsive to my touch. I moved my free hand beneath the waistline of my own pants and began to play with myself while I worked him.

"Allow me," Gilen growled as he cracked open his eyes, realizing what I was doing. I felt an explosion of pleasure rocket across my flesh as his fingers found mine and replaced them. "Like this?" he asked in a gravelly voice. "Is this how you like to touch yourself when you think no one is watching?" His fingers vibrated against my apex, circling my clit with the same rhythm as my hand on his cock.

"Yes," I moaned as the build-up of pleasure continued to rise. Fuck, I needed this. I needed him.

"Take off your shirt," Gilen demanded.

I released him and quickly pulled my shirt over my head. Immediately, Gilen latched onto my exposed breasts, meticulously sucking my nipples until they were firm to a point. His fingers, now soaked from my arousal, easily slipped between my folds. His kiss deepened, rolling my hardened nub in his mouth and around his teeth as he plunged his fingers inside of me.

"Oh … Gods, Gilen!" I screamed, unable to silence my moan of pleasure.

"These next," he added, taking the lead and stripping my pants free from my body.

My legs began to tremble as he continued right where he left off, thrusting fingers into my opening while he swirled his thumb across my clit. There was a slight sting of pain that caused me to flinch, and Gilen immediately slowed, sensing my shift.

"I'm sorry … I forgot," he said with a heavy, heated breath. "Wow. You really haven't been with anyone before, have you?" Gilen retracted his fingers and gently began working my clit again. "Don't worry. I will make sure you are ready for me."

Moving me beneath him on the long grass, he kissed me again. Slowly, this time, Gilen began vibrating his fingers against me in an intoxicating rhythm that gradually filled me with pleasure without the sting of pain from before. I threw my head back, relishing in the pleasure that danced wildly through me. My pulse quickened as he nibbled on my bottom lip before migrating his kiss down toward the base of my neck. He turned his delicious mouth onto my nipple again, teasing it with licks and pinches from his teeth. The wind-up began to spin in my center, swallowing me as a deep thrumming need throbbed between my legs.

"You are so wet, Sky …" Gilen growled as his magic began to flood out from him in intense waves. "I want you," he demanded as he continued fucking me with his hand.

I ground my clit against his palm, the intensity becoming almost too much to bare. Gilen released a deep, amused chuckle as he slowly released my nipple from his mouth.

"Why are you stopping?" I asked, almost breathless.

"You are very responsive for a female who has yet to lay with another male," Gilen teased with a cocky grin.

"I've had boyfriends in the past," I countered, barely able to catch my breath. "I'm not a naive prude."

"I can see … and taste that," he answered as he sucked on his fingers before kissing me. I ran my hands along the thick cords of muscle that framed his body, desperate to explore every inch of his sculpted frame. "But … has anyone ever kissed you *here*?" His finger returned to dance along my entrance, stilling my breath in anticipation of what he intended to do.

My stunned silence was all he needed to hear. Gilen's hooded eyes sparked with lust as he lay me on my back in the grass. His fingers traced along the sensual curves of my hips as he slowly began to worship my naked flesh. His fingers gently slid over my skin, causing me to shake with anticipation.

Licking his lips, Gilen parted my knees and greedily dove into my center. I arched my back as a heightened wave of intense pleasure rocketed through me. His tongue played with the bundle of nerves at the top of my opening. He teased me, rapidly moving his tongue and flicking my clit before devouring me whole. He stayed here until I was thrusting against his face, reaching the edge, on the verge of shattering in climax.

"Not yet," he said with a taunting purr as he pulled away, wiping his face before moving to kiss my lips again. "I want you to come *with* me … while my cock is buried deep inside of you."

Holy Gods—Mother and Father. This was it.

Gilen positioned himself between my dripping entrance that throbbed with desire. "I want you, Gilen," I rasped. "I want this."

Gilen softened his lustful gaze on me, and a deep sense of longing flooded through my middle. He bent down to lightly kiss my lips, slowly moving his kisses across my chin toward my ear and then down to the base of my neck.

He reached down to shift the head of his cock, so it was lingering just outside my entrance. "I want to claim you as my mate, Skylar."

Time itself stopped.

I grabbed his face between my hands, my heart pounding inside my chest with every mixed, crazy emotion someone could feel.

"What did you just say?" I felt my animal spark to life in my center, highly aware and alert. Instinct was driving me to push back and fight against his confession to claim me.

"I want to claim you as my mate. I can feel your animal's power, Skylar. She is there, right below the surface. Tonight, when I claim you, we will be able to combine our powers, and my mark will save you from the trials. I will claim you as mine."

"Am I your *mate*, Gilen?" I asked the question even though I didn't need it. My animal answered for me.

When Gilen had said he wanted to claim me, she exploded with chaos. She did not want to be claimed by his roc. If she could speak to me with words, I could only imagine what type of colorful language would come out of her mouth.

Confused by my hesitation, Gilen pushed himself up onto his

forearms and shifted backward. "Skylar, it doesn't matter if you are or not. I want *you* as my female. You will carry my children and help me create a dynasty that will be unchallenged for centuries. That fire of yours will finally be tamed, helping secure my station as alpha and protect our pack."

*Like hell it didn't matter.* I shoved at his shoulders, pushing him farther backward.

"Why?" I roared, my rage bubbling just below the surface.

"What do you mean, why? How can you even ask that? After all we have been through? Since we were kids, this pairing was made for us."

"By whom?" I demanded. I knew Magnus would never agree to something like this.

"Since my father learned of your healing magic. As the daughter of a former alpha, you were already a desired match as a mate regardless of your mother's blood … But once your healing powers emerged, it was decided."

"But not by me!" I screamed, utterly outraged at the thought of this.

"Why are you getting so upset?" Gilen asked. "You care for me, Skylar. Our animals might not be a mated pair, but that doesn't matter. When we kissed for the first time under the willow tree, I knew you had feelings for me. You can't deny it."

"But we are *not* a mated pair."

I couldn't believe what he was saying. I shook my head, trying to make sense of this, but nothing was coming to light. I did know, however, that my animal did not want him to claim us. There was something else he was not telling me.

"My parents don't share a true mate bond …" Gilen answered, his eyes narrowing with a look of hurt flashing across his face.

Everyone knew Alistar and Helen were not a mated pair, but still, they chose each other and bore Gilen. They took a risk, joining themselves together while knowing they were not mates, but there was also a difference …

"I can't let you claim me, Gilen," I said slowly, trying to make him understand. "I'm the champion of the trials, and I'm going to the Inner Kingdom."

"Not if I claim you," Gilen shot back. I didn't know what to say or how to respond to that. "That's why I asked Shaw if he would take your place. If the champion is mated or claimed, the High Fae will not take you. Especially if it's the alpha's claim."

"You are not the alpha, Gilen."

Gilen's frustration was building, and I could see his rage was on the verge of exploding. "That was why I left that night, Skylar. I needed a moment to calm down, and then my father pulled me aside and explained everything to me. He is willing to pass the leadership of the Solace pack to me without a challenge. He would have done it that night … but I refused. I needed to see you first."

"But I left the meadow to find you."

Gilen lowered his gaze to the ground, guilt and shame crossing the features on his face. "I didn't find you in time."

My head was spinning. Was this an option I could take? *Do I say fuck off to my animal and accept Gilen's claim on me? Do I allow Shaw to take my place? Or do I honor my commitment and go?*

"Gilen, am I your mate?" I asked again, realizing he never answered me the first time.

Gilen sucked in a deep breath and sagged his shoulders. "No."

My animal sent a smug *I told you so* feeling through our bond. *Shut it,* I would scream if we could actually speak to one another.

"I still want to claim you, Skylar." Gilen moved closer and reached out to try and kiss me. For a second, I allowed myself to imagine what it would be like to say yes. To give into what I thought my heart wanted. But then, a different feeling flooded my senses. Instinct told me to fight back and run away.

"No!" I screamed with a push of power in my command. Gilen staggered back, the look of dismay etched into the lines of his face. "I will not allow you to claim me." I rose from the ground and gave him a cold stare. "I thought I cared for you, Gilen. I even imagined that we could be mates, but you just want to use me." This wasn't enough for me.

"How … how could you say that?" he demanded, standing to meet my challenge.

"I will not be used as a pawn and placed on the mantel of a male who only sees me as a trophy." He hadn't realized it yet, but I had figured out *why* he wanted to claim me. The truth of that betrayal cut just as deep as the scars on my back. "You said it yourself, Gilen. Once my powers emerged, your father made this pairing. If you claim me, we share a bond that allows us to exchange our power. You want me … just because I can increase your strength as alpha. To share my magic in a claiming mark."

Gilen balled his fists, his patience disappearing and expression turning to pure rage. "You will *not* deny me, Skylar." The lack of denial only sealed in the pain of the truth.

"I already have," I answered back.

He started to move forward, and I could tell his instincts were driven wild by a push from his animal. The need to claim what he believed was his had taken over. I stepped back and held up my hands.

"Stop, Gilen. I said no!"

He ignored my warning and continued to move toward me. Shit—I didn't want this life. Gods, Rhea and Shaw were right. I didn't want to merely be a breeding tool for a male who only wanted to use me for my gifts and not respect me as their equal. I needed more than that. *I* was worth more than that.

"I said no!" I commanded this time, sending a pulse of my power through my words. "Stop."

Gilen froze, unable to take another step forward.

Panic rushed through me, and before I could think or say anything else, I grabbed my discarded clothes and took off at a run through the woods.

I ran until my feet were numb and my chest burned with fire. I ran until I was certain no one was following me. Until I knew without a shadow of a doubt that I was alone. I gasped for air as I leaned up against a tree trunk, pulling my clothes back over my naked body as the night closed in around me.

Somehow, I had overpowered Gilen with some kind of magic. An alpha command? I melted to the ground and looked down at my trembling hands.

What the hell kind of power was that? *What did I do?*

Instead of breaking down and crumbling to pieces, I pushed the fear aside and latched onto my rage. I clenched my fists and beat them hard against the dirt, screaming with frustration into the emptiness of the night. Exhausted, my head slumped onto the cold ground, and I curled up into a ball on the forest floor. I rocked back and forth, trying to steady myself, repeating a mantra over and over again:

*I will not break. I will be strong. I will not break. I will be strong. I will not break. I will be strong.* I told myself this repeatedly until I believed the words I was saying. That night, I stayed in the woods, alone with my thoughts until I eventually watched the sun peek along the horizon, bringing forth the hope of a new day.

# Chapter Seventeen

Dawn danced along the treetops, urging me to rise from the floor and embrace what was to come. I pushed myself up and brushed the dirt off my clothes. Latte expected me to report to her this morning, and I knew better than to disobey her orders. I was filthy, exhausted, and confused, but there was no way I was going to go back home last night. I didn't want to see or speak to anyone about what happened. I still wasn't ready to even think about it.

*Betrayal.* That was what hurt me the most.

I'd uncovered Gilen's intentions for wanting to claim me, but it still didn't lessen the pain. Physical torture, yeah, sure, bring it on. But this—this was different.

My heart ached. I thought I was in love with Gilen. Gods above, I thought he could have been my *mate.* I cursed myself for not being able to detect his true intentions sooner. I was warned time and time again not to pursue these feelings. I was just too naive to see the truth behind Gilen's actions until he was seconds away from claiming me.

A part of me was relieved to learn the truth, even though it hurt like hell to discover it. I was a stupid, idiotic, foolish sack of potatoes.

*Yes, potatoes.*

I knew Latte would lose her mind if she saw me in this state, and a scolding was not something I was particular in the mood for today. I rubbed the sleep out of my eyes and got a strong whiff of what I smelled like.

"Gods above … I need a bath."

I didn't have the overwhelming desire to jump in the cold river, though. Sure, any other day this would have been a fine option, but I wanted to soak in a deep, hot bath. And lucky for me, I knew exactly where to find one.

In the training grounds of the alpha's estate near the river, there were recovery areas that would cater perfectly to my needs.

There was a large bathhouse that gathered fresh water from the nearby streams, which allowed for a luxurious soak in a tub and hot steams to refresh your spirits.

Traveling silently through the early hours of the morning, I was able to reach the estate without running into anyone along the way. I ducked around toward the riverside and waited to see if the coast was clear of any early risers. Satisfied that no one else was here, I got to work prepping the bathhouse, starting a fire to heat river rocks with the hopes of fitting in a quick steam while my bath water heated up. A good steam would help wash away any trace of scent from last night.

I cringed and froze for a moment, my mind flashing back to the memories of Gilen.

*No, Sky*, I told myself. *Screw Gilen.*

I wasn't meant to be caged or used as a breeding tool to help secure an alpha's rule. My magic was special. I knew that, but I also deserved more than this. If I never found my mate, at the very least, I deserved to be respected and loved for who I was and not just because of my abilities.

I opened the rickety wooden door of the bathhouse and quickly slipped inside. The slitted bottom floor allowed for water to drain back into the river, while the fortified ceiling above trapped hot air for the sauna. I pulled down on the lever in the corner to begin filling the enormous tub that could easily house more than three people and went outside to start working on stoking the fire.

The hearth of the bathhouse burned outside in a submerged pit that allowed air in to fuel the flames but kept it contained so it wouldn't burn everything down. I tended the fire with logs from the nearby stack, and while I waited, I decided to split a few more. It would take the rocks a minute to heat up enough before I could move them toward the sauna opening.

I picked up the axe and began to split firewood and kindling for the next group to use the facility. Keeping my hands busy also helped keep my mind occupied. I was so focused on preparing everything that I almost missed hearing the commotion in the training yard.

"Who is training this early in the morning?" I wondered aloud.

Curiosity, of course, got the best of me. I checked on my fire and bath water, making sure they were where I needed them, and scurried off in the direction of the sound. Crouching down in the tree line, so I didn't disturb anything, I saw them … *him*. My heart began to race as a warmth in my core simmered, transforming into a flush of heat. I hadn't seen him since he left me alone on the green sand beach, and—curse the gods—I missed him.

Daxton and Castor were sparring against each other in the open field of the training area. I could see the same patterns and movements repeating over and over again, realizing they were working through a training exercise. Daxton seemed to have the upper hand against his brother, besting him at each go-around they attempted. The movements were fluid and unbroken; Daxton was so fast and light on his feet that it almost seemed like he was dancing. Castor moved with a similar grace, but it still fell short of matching Daxton's finesse.

A solid thud sounded as Daxton's fist collided with Castor's jaw. He stumbled back and cursed loudly. "Fuck, Dax! We have been at this for hours!" Castor roared as he wiped the blood from a cut on his lip.

"And you still haven't managed to counter the final attack. Your weeks away have lowered your guard, and you have been slacking on training." Daxton rolled his broad shoulders and reached down to pull his shirt over his head. "Again."

I inhaled a sharp breath at the sight of Daxton shirtless on the training field.

"Why am *I* landing on the opposing side of your lovely mood today?" Castor asked, following his brother's lead and removing his sweat-soaked shirt, but Daxton didn't move or even acknowledge his question.

Castor was leaner than Daxton, and on his inner forearms, I could make out the designs of two unique tattoos that decorated his skin. They were moving so damn fast though I wasn't able to get a good look at what they were.

From this distance, I could see evidence of deep scar marks that ran along Daxton's exposed torso. Twin jagged cuts spanned over his firm chest muscles, with one long line that began at the deep V of his abdomen and curled around his back toward his ribs. This male held the scars of a battle-hardened warrior, and I couldn't turn my eyes away from him.

For a second, as he pivoted toward me, I noticed a tattoo marking his left shoulder, expanding across his left chest and down his arm. *That was definitely new.* I didn't remember it being there the night I healed him. The black markings were bold and fierce, creating a pattern that centered around a scar on his left chest—my scar.

Daxton dodged Castor's kick and dropped his guard, opening his right side for attack. I assumed he did this on purpose because after watching them repeat these eight movements in a continuous loop, I was beginning to catch onto the pattern. He was trying to see if Castor would see it, too, and he did.

Castor lunged forward and managed to tackle Daxton onto the ground. The males exchanged blows, wrestling on the grass, neither yielding to give the other one the upper hand. Castor gave a combo knee to the inner groin and elbow to the face to force Daxton to release his death grip around his neck.

Daxton grunted and folded over. "Low blow."

"Quite literally, no?" Castor raised to his hands and knees, panting with exhaustion. "You have a death wish today or something, Dax?" he rasped as he spat blood onto the grass. "Again, I must ask … What the fuck has gotten into you today?"

Daxton stood, readying himself to begin again. "Don't tell me you're scared to go another round?"

"With how you are acting right now? Yes. Absolutely, I am. You have a look of death in your eyes that has been there since last night and hasn't gone away despite me kicking your ass all morning."

"I believe I am the one still standing … So *I* am the one who has successfully completed the ass-kicking," Daxton countered.

*Hmm, clever, and also, from the looks of it, very accurate.*

The breeze shifted, changing directions in the field, and the males suddenly tensed and stopped. That was definitely my cue to leave. I quietly sank back into the brush and dashed through the trees back toward the bathhouse.

The smoke was rising from the outdoor hearth, and steam began to steadily build. I grabbed the long poker to move the heated river rocks to the sauna and dripped cold water onto the hot stones. Steam jetted upward, and I sealed off the opening.

I was so looking forward to this, hoping it would be just what I needed to wash away the memories from last night.

Standing up, I turned around and walked toward the entrance. Rounding the corner, I was suddenly stopped as I ran into a solid wall of muscle that appeared out of nowhere.

"Ugghh," I grunted as I bounced off the firm bare chest of none other than Daxton himself. "What are you doing here?" I asked as I awkwardly staggered back, trying to recover my footing. I couldn't help the heat rising in my cheeks and boldly stared at the High Fae. I was taller than most females and some of the males in my pack, but he still had a good head of height over me.

Daxton was utterly silent.

I cocked my hip and rested a hand on my side while I furrowed my brow. "Okay, look, I don't have time to figure out what you are doing. Trust me. I'm not in the mood for games."

"Are you all right?" Daxton asked.

"I-I've had better nights," I admitted, giving him a perplexed look, crossing my arms around my middle.

He took note of my posture, and his expression altered into one of concern. "What happened?" His stare bore into me after he quickly scanned me from head to toe, looking for any sign of injury.

I shifted, hugging myself as I fidgeted with my feet. "I … I don't feel like talking about it."

"It looks like you have been out in the woods all night." Daxton's eyes hardened as his nostrils flared. The muscles in his shoulders and chest tensed as he turned away from me. If I didn't know any better, it looked like he was revving up for another fight.

I cautiously took a step back. "I was—" I began as he snapped his cold eyes up to meet mine. For a moment, my words froze on the tip of my lips, swallowed whole by the intensity of his stare. "A night sleeping alone on the forest floor doesn't always lead to the best mornings. I came here to clean up before meeting with Latte for my last check-up."

Daxton relaxed his clenched fists, softening the muscles along his square jawline, and reached up to scratch the corner of his trimmed bearded chin. "You were alone?" He seemed genuinely surprised, perhaps even, dare I say, grateful?

"Yes." That was a strange question for him to ask, I thought. "Why does that matter?"

"Because … I can smell another male's scent on you."

Shit. I didn't anticipate running into anyone before I had a chance to clean up. If Daxton could smell Gilen's scent on me, I knew the others would, too.

"Like I said … I don't want to talk about it." I tilted my head at him, confused by his reaction. Daxton seemed conflicted but also somewhat relieved to hear I had spent the night alone in the woods. What was he getting at? Why did it matter to him that I was alone or with someone else?

I rolled my eyes and lightly shook my head. "Look, I need to clean up, so if you would kindly move aside?"

To my surprise, Daxton smiled. An honest, truthful smile that shone like the rays of dawn, sporting twin dimples below the ridge of his high cheekbones. I fought the urge to reach up and cup his face in my hands to trace my fingertips over those marks I knew rarely saw the light of day.

My stomach dropped as he dipped his chin and pivoted off his foot to turn away from me. I suddenly regretted asking him to move, but that regret quickly changed to outrage.

Daxton marched right up to the bathhouse door, grabbed the handle, and went inside.

"Excuse me, *Princey*!" I yelled, pounding my fist on the door. "What the hell do you think you are doing?"

"Bathing. This *is* a bathhouse, isn't it?" I heard a deep chuckle of amusement, which only infuriated me more.

"That is *my* bath! You can't just stroll in and steal it from me!"

Silence.

"Daxton!" I roared.

"I won't steal your bath. I promise."

I didn't believe him. "You're damn right. You're not stealing it!" There was no way I was going to let all my hard work go to waste and give up that deliciously soothing tub for anyone.

I removed my dirty clothes and quickly rinsed them off in the river before hanging them to dry near the heat of the hearth. I splashed the heated river rocks with a douse of fresh water to create a plume of steam inside, grabbing a towel to drape myself with. I was comfortable with my body and nudity, but this male wasn't going to get a free show today. Opening the door, I hurried inside, closing it quickly behind me to eliminate any excess steam from escaping the bathhouse.

I could barely see anything through the thick clouds as his voice drifted through the space. "As promised, your bath is untouched, Spitfire."

I could just make out the outline of his body through the fog. He was reclining on the wooden bench on the opposite side of the bathhouse. His head was tilted against the wall while his thick, muscular legs were casually stretched out in front of him.

Wait … His *naked* legs.

I quickly spun my head to the side and saw his black and silver training leathers hanging on the hook by the door. Gods. Above … Daxton was naked. My cheeks flushed as I hurried over toward the bath that was filled to the brim with hot steaming water.

"I hope you don't mind," Daxton murmured. "I added oils

from the corner shelf to your bath. They should help you relax."

I approached the tub and smelled the sweet scent of lavender infused into the water. "Thank you," I answered with a bite to my voice. I was about to drop my towel, but an unnatural shyness forced me to freeze.

Shifters were used to nudity. Half the time, our people walked around naked, either from just shifting or preparing to shift. We wore loose clothing that could easily be taken off or repaired if they ripped from our animal shifts. But right now, I was very, very aware that Daxton was sprawled out naked across the room from me.

"No peeking," I shouted, clutching the towel around me.

Glancing over my shoulder, I noticed Daxton move to rest his forearms on his strong thighs that carried the weight of his sculpted physique. I gulped a very loud and noticeable breath. My animal seemed to perk up, her curiosity spinning like a top in my chest. The steam was thick enough, combined with the dim lighting, to conceal certain areas I was taught not to stare at from a very young age. I didn't dare allow my gaze to linger, but I couldn't curb my wildly inappropriate imagination from picturing what lay beneath the obscure layer of steam.

Fucking hell. I couldn't let myself imagine or even think about going down this road. No matter how riled up I still was from last night, *he* was simply not an option for me. *This* was one of those horrible ideas that I never should or would get to play out.

*Daxton was off limits*, I told myself. However, I wasn't sure if I believed it.

"From my studies … I understood that shifters were comfortable with nudity. Was I wrong?" Daxton asked as he shifted forward and tilted his head to the side to give me a playful, narrowed glance. "But even through this steam … I can see you blushing, Spitfire." His deep voice had a kind of sing-song tease to it, adding to my already rising embarrassment.

"*You* … are not a shifter," I scolded him. "And this is *not* a normal situation." I paused for a second to purse my lips in frustration as I watched his grin widen. "Just close your eyes until I get into the tub, please. No peeking!"

Daxton leaned back with a mischievous gleam in his expression as he spread his toned muscular arms across the back of the bench. A devilish grin spread across his firm jawline as he closed his eyes and covered his face with one hand. "Not peeking."

I didn't want to wait and test him, so I dropped my cover and quickly slid into the depths of the bath. The warm waters washed over my skin, relieving me of the dirt and grime I had accumulated during the night. Choosing to ignore Daxton's presence for the moment, I grabbed the bar of soap and scrubbed every inch of myself clean. I wanted to wash away the memories. I wanted to scrub each of them away in the steaming waters of this tub. Once I was satisfied with my cleanliness, I sank below the surface to disappear from the world. Hitting the bottom of the tub, the silence of the water calmed my mind. I drifted into a peaceful bliss, forgetting everything around me aside from the steady beating of my heart. Unable to hold my breath any longer, I sprang up from below the surface.

I held back a startled yelp as I faced a very naked Daxton hovering over the lip of the tub. "Refreshing dip?" he casually asked as he stood at the edge of the bathing pool, the rim hitting just below his lower abdomen.

"I said no peeking!" I exclaimed as I splashed him with a wave of water. He laughed and took a step back, unfazed by my reaction. "Move back over to your side!"

He held up his hands and stepped back toward his bench, steam swallowing his figure once more. "Sorry, I was only checking to make sure you would bob back up to the surface."

"It *was* relaxing," I shot back at him.

He sat closer to the tub this time, reclining the bench directly adjacent to me. "I'm still relaxed …" he answered. "Does my mere presence upset you or cause you distress?"

"No," I answered quickly. "No … you don't bother me."

Daxton flashed me a half-smile, satisfied, it seemed, with my response. The truth of the matter was that I was relaxed when I was with him. I felt safe when Daxton was around, and most of all, I believe I trusted him.

"I wanted to ask you something," Daxton said.

Intrigued, I turned in the water to face him. "Okay. Go ahead. What do you want to ask me?"

"Will you still compete in the trials of the Inner Kingdom? I'm aware of an alternative offer that may allow you to abdicate to another." His gray eyes hardened to stone, transforming from the carefree mood he was in only a moment before.

"Yes," I answered with unwavering confidence. I didn't bother to elaborate beyond that one simple answer, witnessing a mixed sparkle of hope gleaming in Daxton's expression.

"Even with the knowledge that you could stay. You still

willingly choose to go?"

"Yes. I will not push away my responsibility to another. This is my task, and I still willingly accept that this is my fate." I didn't know how he knew about the claiming rule Gilen had told me, but then again, Daxton knew a lot of things I didn't.

Daxton stroked his trimmed black beard and ran his finger up toward his hair. He released the tie at the top, allowing his thick locks of silver and ebony to fall freely around his face. I watched him inhale a deep breath as his arms flexed behind his head. Even in this stillness, he projected power and strength. He was a marvel of a male, the epitome of what a warrior should be. Terrifying but also remarkably beautiful.

Slitting one eye open, he smugly asked, "Enjoying the view?"

My eyes widened, but I refused to give him the satisfaction of catching me off guard. "Please," I huffed, "I'm a shifter. There are naked males running around everywhere. There's nothing below that layer of steam I haven't seen before."

His dark chuckle filled the space between us. "Really?" he asked, his deep voice dropping an octave lower. "Care to test your theory?"

I raised half out of the tub, pushing my breasts forward and up on the edge while still lingering under the surface. I searched his expression as his half-slitted eyes widened, now keenly alert and fixated solely on me. His breathing began to quicken as the taut muscles that encased his body flexed and popped with tension. Daxton watched me as I scanned my gaze over his body, and I somehow managed not to blush. It was now my turn to grin, realizing that I was able to entice this kind of reaction out of him and loving this feeling of control.

"Really," I replied, playfully sticking my tongue out before slipping back under the water.

Daxton's barreling laughter was like music to my ears. He folded forward, his hands on his forehead as his body vibrated with his laugh. I couldn't help but join him, quietly chuckling behind the fold of my arm.

"You," Daxton said as he angled his head toward me. "You are most certainly *more* than anything I could have ever dreamed, Spitfire."

My breath stilled as his glossed-over eyes looked at me like they were peering into the depths of my soul. Tearing off layers of my being until he found the center of who I was buried deep beneath.

"When did you get that?" I asked, motioning to the new tattoo on his left side.

His gaze dipped down for a moment, following the outline of the black ink before returning to find me. "A few days ago when Castor returned."

"What made you decide to mark your skin? What does the design represent?"

"Always with the questions …"

"You get used to it, promise." I smiled softly.

"They represent a warrior's journey. Overcoming defeat, developing strength, and above all, never losing hope."

"It's drawn over the scar I gave you," I added. "Why there?"

Daxton traced his fingers over the scar that seemed to be the center of Castor's design. I bit my lip, trying to push aside the idea of my finger tracing over the lines of his flesh.

"Believe it or not … no other scar I carry or wound I have received in all my battles throughout my long life have ever brought me to death's doorstep. I thought it fitting to highlight the wound I thought would kill me, as none have ever come so close before."

My breath stilled. He didn't seem angry or upset, but I was definitely shocked by his confession. I knew he was in jeopardy of dying that night, but I had no idea it was that severe.

"When will we leave for the Inner Kingdom?" I asked, tactfully trying to change the subject. I didn't know if I was going with him, Queen Minaeve, or Castor. But I hoped that when the time came to say goodbye to my home, Daxton would be there with me.

"We …" Daxton was careful to emphasize the word, and a piece of me glowed in delight. "We … will need to leave soon. The queen will depart once we meet with your alpha and you have formally confirmed your decision."

"Sounds like a plan. Why is Queen Minaeve leaving before us?" Not that I minded, I was just simply curious.

Daxton mulled over my question for a minute before answering. "With her absence, the decay … or the *wilt*," he corrected for my benefit, "has likely spread. Minaeve's magic is the only weapon that is able to keep it at bay. To add to the misery and destruction, vile creatures are born from this death, Spitfire. Creatures that threaten the lives of my people every day. I worry about their safety in my absence. While my magic is not as effective as Minaeve's against the spread of the wilt, I am able to kill the creatures that dwell within it."

I could see the lines of distress form in the crevices of his hard yet handsome face. "You mean aside from nature literally dying … creatures are born from it?" Talk about adding salt to the wound.

"Yes." Daxton sighed heavily as he continued, "The wilt was magically created. We don't exactly know why or how, but we are left with the aftermath and side effects of its evil."

"I see," I answered. "So the *wilt* has a magical presence that destroys and possibly absorbs the life energy of Valdor. It is taking the life of our world and making it into something new."

Daxton's brows shot upward. "Impressive. Yes, that is exactly right."

I gave him a smug grin over my shoulder. "Not too shabby for a shifter-human half-breed, eh?"

Daxton genuinely smiled once more, making my insides flutter. "Not at all." He waved his hand, and a sheet of ice appeared over the heated rocks, creating an even thicker layer of steam.

"So, in addition to magically being in one place and then another, you have ice magic?"

"A gift from our father," Daxton answered as the steam rolled over his body, releasing the tension of his thick muscles. "Castor is able to manipulate it, but he cannot create it like I can."

"Your parents must be very proud."

"I-I imagine … or hope they would be."

I immediately recognized the hesitation in his voice. It was the same tone I used when I spoke about my parents. High Fae were an immortal species, but from how he answered me, I imagined his parents had made the crossing to the afterlife—just like mine.

"Have you read any more of the books from the list I made for you?" I asked. "I was glad to see you enjoyed the trilogy I recommended. It truly is my favorite, and I must admit you were correct about my favorite parts. I like a strong heroine who is able to step in and save the hero from time to time."

"I'm glad to hear that," Daxton replied, his thick shoulders relaxing. "I admit I haven't been able to tear myself away from my recent project of studying your people's history, however."

"What have you been learning or researching?" I asked.

"Customs mostly. I'm trying to learn all I can about shifters and humans to help train you for the trials to come. I haven't done this in the past, and I wondered if there was any advantage or disadvantage to the trials we simply missed with the other champions. The first you must face alone, but we don't know how we could help, or if we can with the others."

I was touched that Daxton not only acknowledged my dual lineage but also the fact that he was researching them both. Sometimes, I felt that my human heritage was often forgotten or ignored.

"But none of our older texts even mention the trials or are older than the war of races."

"Correct, which is odd to me," Daxton said.

"It must have been an alpha command to not write or speak of the trials, but my question is, why?" I asked running my hands in the water. "Also, why is it the same for the human records?"

"A very good question," Daxton added. "I assume it was to protect the pack, or the humans might not have kept much of a record when they traveled to Valdor. Worry and fear can spread faster than a disease. Imagine if you lived in fear your whole life anticipating our arrival."

"Or we could have been preparing for it," I countered.

I allowed my mind to drift into a different reality where we knew of the trials, the wilt … if all of this was common knowledge. Would another have volunteered if they trained for this? Would I be more prepared if I knew this was my fate?

"Indeed. That's a positive way to look at it." Daxton stood up from the bench and walked across toward the doorway. "I'm afraid I need to return to check on Castor. This has been enjoyable, though. Thank you for the company."

"I wasn't the one initiating an absence between us," I murmured as I spun to look at the wall, splashing water outside the tub. At first, he didn't say anything, but I could tell my words had landed a subconscious blow.

"It was needed," was all he said in response. I could hear him grab his pants, but he didn't seem in a hurry to put them on. "No peeking," Daxton taunted in a deep sing-song voice.

Oh. My. Gods. With utter embarrassment, I buried my face in my hands, sinking into the water. I could hear his amused chuckle as he turned the handle to open the door.

"Wait!" I yelled.

Daxton stopped, and I could feel his gaze burning into the back of my head. "Yes, Spitfire?"

"Will you help train me?" I asked. "Will you teach me to be strong enough to survive the trials and win?" He didn't say anything at first. The male was so damn quiet and still I thought he might have left.

"You already have all the strength you will need to win, Skylar." His voice was firm, unwavering. "But yes. Of course I will help train you. I will teach you how to become a weapon so you no longer have to live in fear of one being used against you ever again."

"And strong enough to never let anyone use me either," I added. The memory of what Gilen said to me last night flashed into my mind.

"Or used as one," Daxton repeated. "I promise I will teach you all I know."

"Thank you." I hugged my knees tightly to my chest. I knew he was still in the doorway, watching over me to ensure I was all right. "I'll find you later, Daxton," I called out.

To which he replied, "We will always find each other."

# Chapter Eighteen

When I entered the healers' quarters, Latte was just as grumpy as ever. "You're late," she snapped as I walked in.

"I'm really sorry, Latte," I apologized.

I hated being late. I really did. It always made me anxious and nervous. I guess there was no real explanation as to why. *Just one of my quirks, I guess.* Ever since I was little, I was always first in line, first to arrive, and being on time meant I was late.

"Go sit over there and wait. Since you were late, I saw another patient first."

"This early in the morning? Who?"

"None of your business if they don't want you to know," she snapped. Gods, she was in a mood this morning. Feistier than her normal self. I wondered what upset her. It couldn't have just been me.

"Hello, Skylar." His sing-song voice echoed like a taunting melody, and his overly confident, borderline cocky, demeanor was almost too much for me before breakfast.

"Castor," I muttered, throwing an unimpressed look in his direction. I crossed my arms at my chest and turned toward him. "What brings *you* in here?" I sneered with a sarcastic tone with my brow cocked upward. I knew exactly why he was here. Daxton had been kicking his royal ass all over the training fields that morning, and I was fortunate enough to witness the end of it.

"Refreshing smell in the air," Castor countered. "Do I detect a hint of fresh lavender?" He narrowed his eyes and flashed a playful grin.

*Oh, all right then. Let's play.*

"Why yes, thank you. I was in the bathhouse this morning. Shifters don't always smell like the dirt and the woods, you know."

"Apparently not, and in case you were wondering, I do … know. Some of your females have been very open with me during our stay on the mainland." He watched Latte mumble to herself as she left the main room to retrieve supplies in the pantry. "Quite steamy inside those bathhouses, isn't it?" he added, and I scowled at him.

"Why are you here, Castor?" I asked. "Can't your healing fix whatever injuries Daxton gave you this morning? I thought High Fae were tougher than that, but perhaps not?"

"I assumed it was you watching us. Hard to keep your eyes away from perfection," Castor replied in a sing-song taunt without flinching. "Your cheeks are flushed, my dear. Care to elaborate on how your bath went?" He dipped his head back, flashing me a sly grin and leaning back against the wall while crossing a leg over his knee.

My tone dropped into a low, flat sound. "What?" I barked with a scrutinizing glare.

"When you mention my brother's name, your cheeks flush." His dark brown eyes sparkled with a hint of a scheme brewing. "Anything you would like to share?"

"Castor … you—" I was about to grab a pillow and throw it at his beautifully smug face, but lucky for him, Latte returned with a tray of herbs and healing supplies.

"You two males sure got into a scuffle this morning," Latte murmured as she set the tray next to Castor's bed. "Now, off with your shirt so that I can examine your bruising. I can shoo Sky away if you like. She *knows* how important patient privacy is." If looks could kill, Latte would have the highest kill count in all of Valdor by now.

"She's fine." Castor winced as he leaned forward and removed his tunic. "She deserves to see what a real male form looks like."

"Oh, Gods … Please." I rolled my eyes and sighed as loudly as I could. "Trust me. I've seen better. And besides, you're not my type."

"Pity," Castor snickered as he shifted under Latte's care. "It's the silver, isn't it?" he asked, pushing back his hair. "Too much?" I scowled at him, but it only seemed to encourage him to continue. "Ahh, I see now … You favor the darker-haired males, then."

Okay, I had officially had enough of Castor's antics for the morning. "Latte, respectfully, please move aside … I've got this."

"Oh no you don't!" Latte tried to stop me, but I was already calling my healing powers to my hands.

I dashed toward Castor and placed my palm on his clean-shaven, narrowed jawline, repairing the cut on his lip and quickly moving down toward his bruised collarbone. He was not as strong as Daxton, but there was no doubt that he was an extremely powerful being in his own right. His lean body was exquisitely toned with a firm muscular build. Glancing down toward his chest, I noticed a rib out of place that was causing discomfort and likely difficulty breathing. I moved my fingers over his stomach, which held a very defined six-pack like his brother's. Unlike Daxton, however, the close proximity with Castor did nothing to spike my desire or cause heat to rise in my center.

"There, that should do it. How do you feel?" I asked.

"Annoyed!" Latte cursed at me as she stomped away to return her tray of supplies to the pantry. "Manners of the youth are dooming us all!"

Castor sat up and took in a deep breath, feeling for the cut that was no longer visible on his lip. "Impressive. I can see why Dax is so intrigued by you … Your beauty is more than skin deep."

"Thank you," I answered with a heavy dose of sarcasm, "is sometimes the best response. Then I say you're welcome, and we can both be on our way."

Castor's lips curled upward in amusement. "Already tired of my company?" he taunted, trying to toy with me like I was his sole source of entertainment.

"As you said before, I prefer darker-haired males." I tossed his shirt at his face and promptly seated myself on the bed across the room. Castor chuckled to himself, and my eyes darted to the tattoos on his arms while he lazily continued to dress. His right inner forearm had a large crescent moon with an iced snowflake in the center. The edges were sharp and beautifully blended together to create a mesmerizing design that was hard to tear my eyes from. His other arm held a blazing sun, with an open eye staring out from the center. They were both extremely detailed and elegantly designed.

"Hopefully, you are healed enough to attend the fae queen's meeting this morning." Latte sighed heavily at Castor before glancing at me. "Witnessing what Skylar just did, I can't lie and say she needs more time to recuperate."

Castor seemed indifferent at the mention of his queen as he finished dressing. "I appreciate your willingness to help, Latte," he said as he tucked in his shirt, readying himself to leave. "And, Skylar, thank you."

"Look at that," I teased lightly. "The saying is wrong … Old dogs *can* learn new tricks."

Castor winked at me, giving a nod to Latte, and took his leave from the healers' quarters without any additional quips in reply. I smiled, satisfied with a small victory against the cunning silver-haired and tongued fae.

Latte returned her attention to me and began her exam.

"Those High Fae males are impressive … And between you and me—"

"Latte!" I exclaimed.

"I am old … not dead, Sky."

I was flabbergasted and had to grip the edges of the exam table to keep from falling to the floor with laughter. She was mumbling and cursing under her breath because *she* wasn't able to attend to her patient personally.

"Castor has an air of arrogance that sways between charming and me wanting to punch him square in the face. He knows he's attractive and doesn't shy away from flaunting that knowledge."

"Isn't that some of the fun?" Latte chuckled. "Then there's the other one … with the silver midnight-streaked hair."

"Daxton." Fucking Castor. I immediately put my hand to my face, trying to hide the flush I felt on my cheeks.

"Now … that is a male. Wherever he wanted me to go, I would happily follow."

"Latte," I stammered, raising my brows in shock.

"At first, he terrified me, but once he relaxed and dropped his stone-cold demeanor, I could see a shift that made me want to grab a blanket and brave his frigid tempers. He has a rugged beauty to him with the longer hair and trimmed beard …"

I think my mouth dropped to the floor.

"Don't gawk at me like that, Skylar. Many of the other females and I have talked about this. Many of the males whisper and say similar things about their queen. I don't know if all High Fae are blessed with such magical, ethereal beauty, but these three certainly are."

"Okay, new topic," I interjected as I bit my lip. "Do I finally have a clean bill of health?"

I didn't need to talk about how handsome or beautiful the High Fae were. It was hard enough to forget. Castor had an alluring facade coupled with more self-confidence than a rose in full bloom. I hadn't had much interaction with Queen Minaeve, but she carried herself with a high brow of arrogance that seemed reserved for royalty. She knew how breathtakingly beautiful she was and didn't shy away from flaunting it.

Daxton was … He was something else entirely. A fearsome, powerful protector with a hidden softer side underneath a stone-armored exterior. All our shifter animals reacted to the pulses of magic we felt emanating from him, but he didn't boast or flaunt it like

Castor or even the queen. I understood why Latte, and apparently other females in the pack, were drawn to him. If Daxton were a shifter, he would undoubtedly be an alpha.

"Oh yes, yes. Get up. You're fine." Latte swatted me away. "You need to get ready for the meeting anyway."

"What meeting?"

"The one I would have told you about if you had been at home in bed this morning."

*Shit.*

"Where were you, Skylar?" Magnus's robust frame filled the doorway, and I was slightly terrified to turn around and face him.

"Whatever do you mean, Uncle?" Maybe if I played dumb--

"Don't even think about trying that with me."

Shit, shit … shit. I was most definitely in trouble.

"I will save you from my scolding because it looks like the beta has one already planned for you. Good luck." Latte patted my shoulder and returned to organizing her pantry of supplies. "She's all yours, Magnus."

*Thanks for nothing, Latte.*

Magnus turned in the doorway just enough to allow me to pass, and I could tell he was not happy. "Let's go, Skylar Cathal."

Crap, he used my full name. "Magnus, I'm sorry if I worried you." I truly was sorry if I had caused distress to any member of my family. I knew they had been through hell worrying about me while I was captured.

Magnus didn't say anything as he motioned for me to follow him, and I happily obeyed his silent command. Guilt was eating me alive as we walked toward the main entrance to the alpha's home. We stopped at the main double set of doors, and he finally turned around to face me. Fear lurked in my uncle's eyes as he placed his strong hands on my shoulders and pulled me tightly into his chest.

"I don't know how to feel about this … About any of this, Sky. It terrifies me."

I latched on tightly to my uncle. "I'm scared, too," I admitted.

"You are more than just my niece. You understand you are as much my daughter as Neera is, and Julia feels the same, right?"

"Of course I do." I turned to kiss his bearded cheek and slowly released my grip around him. "But this is something I have to do," I said, seeing the fear in his eyes despite his efforts to try and hold it back. "Trust that you raised me to be brave enough to do this. And strong enough to return home."

Magnus held his breath and looked at me with the unconditional love a father could only give his daughter. "I love you."

"I love you, too," I replied as he clutched my hands between large, calloused palms, bending his brow to meet mine.

Memories from when I was young flashed through my mind as we stayed frozen in place, admiring the life we shared together. From day one, Magnus was there to support me and take care of me when no one else would. His strength held our family together, never letting us fall apart. I knew I was his daughter in every way that mattered.

"And because I love you, I will support you in whatever you decide, Skylar. You will have your family here, always and forever."

I squeezed his hands tighter. "Thank you." His words spread across my skin like a blanket of warmth on a cold winter night, wrapping me in a cocoon of strength and confidence, knowing he not only respected my decision but also supported me in making it.

"You ready? The High Fae are waiting inside with Alistar. We are meeting to discuss your decision and the timeline for departure to the Inner Kingdom."

"It's not going to be a very long meeting. They know that, right?"

Magnus huffed a laugh. "When *your* mind is set on something, nothing can sway you. Just like Emery." My heart softened at the mention of my father. Magnus didn't do it often, but it always comforted me and made me smile each time he did.

"Let's go get this meeting over with." I motioned for him to lead the way into Alistar's estate.

We walked down the long hallway to the stairs that led to Alistar's meeting room on the second floor. Paintings of former alphas of the Solace pack adorned the halls, watching over us, even after their crossings into the afterlife with the great Mother and Father. Most were in their animal forms, but a few decided to have their human faces painted. As we approached Alistar's private quarters, I paused to look at the one alpha I longed to see the most.

My father, Emery.

He stood in an open grassy meadow under the light of the full moon, which shone brightly over his head. Fireflies danced around him as he clutched a deadly yet decorative dagger in his left hand. The blade was a treasured heirloom of our pack that was passed down and carried by each alpha. It was magically made and could cut down anything it pierced and, conveniently, never needed to be sharpened.

My father died with this weapon clutched in his hand, never letting it go—even in death.

My father's long golden-brown hair, which I shared with him, flowed over his thick shoulder as his piercing forest-green eyes, that lived on in Neera and my uncle, seemed to come alive through the canvas. The shapes of our eyes and brow line were identical, and there wasn't a soul alive that could doubt I was his daughter. In this painting, he wore simple brown training clothes that Magnus said were almost always torn to shreds when he shifted into his bear form. Whenever I looked at this picture of him, I felt safe and protected. Emery Cathal was a true alpha, one that I was honored to call my sire.

"Sky?" Magnus called to me softly. He knew exactly what I was doing and waited patiently for me to join him before entering the meeting room. I was never able to meet my father, but I hoped he would be proud of what I was doing. I hoped that I was a daughter worthy to be his heir.

Magnus turned the handle of the carved wooden door, and together, we entered the meeting room. Queen Minaeve wore an elegant but simple-looking black dress with a plunging neckline and high slit against her bare thigh. She sat near a roaring fire inside the alpha's private quarters with other armchairs across from her in a gathered circle.

Daxton and Castor stood behind her, dressed in fitted dark-colored shirts with the three-peaked emblem on their shoulders paired with grey dark pants and boots. No weapons were visible, but that didn't mean none were hidden. They had stone-cold expressions plastered on their faces, hardly turning to acknowledge me as we entered.

Alistar arose from his plush cushioned seat upon our entrance and lowered his head in a respectful half-bow to his beta and then a nod to me. Alistar never looked down on me for my mixed blood, and I knew it was out of respect for my sire and my uncle. He sat across from Queen Minaeve with Helen at his side closest to me, and to my shock and dismay … *Gilen* was seated on his other side.

My animal's power stirred within me, and I knew my anger blazed inside my amber stare. Gilen refused to look at or even acknowledge me as we took our place within the small circle, which infuriated me even more.

"I'm glad to see you have fully recovered, Skylar," Alistar said with a calm, even voice.

I faked a kind smile toward Alistar and his mate, sitting in a chair near the door while pure rage simmered inside me. I was so angry at *all* of them. Gilen intended to claim me, and Alistar had not only agreed but possibly encouraged it. I would make it clear to these males once and for all that I was not something they could command and push around. I was going to the Inner Kingdom.

"Thankfully, your recovery didn't take as long as the future alpha anticipated," Queen Minaeve said without a hint of empathy in her voice. In fact, she seemed almost annoyed. "But we cannot wait any longer. Our world is dying, and I can feel that the decay has spread since my absence. The people of the Inner Kingdom are … suffering."

"We understand all of this, Queen Minaeve," Alistar answered. "Skylar needed time to recover, and with the alternative selection presented to us the other night"—he looked to his right at Gilen—"other options needed to be explored."

Like claiming me against my will so they could use my power for themselves and force someone else to go in my place. *Sure, let's call that new information.* It had a nicer ring than … *betrayal.*

"I have been informed that Skylar Cathal still intends to be named champion." Minaeve gave Alistar a smug look of distaste and defiance.

"She will be claimed and marked as my mate," Gilen growled.

*Over my dead body!*

I jolted upright to my feet, and Magnus was immediately at my side, grabbing my arm so I didn't lunge across the room and try to strangle Gilen with my bare hands. "I rejected your claim, Gilen," I growled loudly. "Nothing has changed. I am going to enter the trials."

"You cannot go if the alpha of the Solace pack intends to claim you as a mate. And that's what I still intend to do," Gilen countered, and I could feel the room grow tense … beginning to freeze.

Actually freeze.

My skin felt the kiss of ice as my breath created a fog when I exhaled into the room. Daxton stepped forward, his gray eyes blazing like a winter storm on the frozen ice-packed mountains.

His stare bore into Gilen as his deep, thunderous voice echoed across the room. "The queen has a chosen champion, and the selected has voiced their desire to go. Your opinion does not have any stake in this decision. I advise that you step down. Now." Daxton's commanding presence was terrifying, the room shaking with the pulses of the magic emanating from him. It sent chills up my spine and even caused Alistar to stagger, shifting toward his mate, Helen.

"Daxton." The queen reached out a hand and tenderly stroked his arm. "I believe the alpha's son is aware of all this … Calm your magic or else the shifters will turn into blocks of ice and become more useless than they already are."

My insides twisted at her insult and the sight of the queen touching Daxton with such familiarity. I watched him meet her gaze and slowly regain control of his power in the room. The ice-cold grip no longer chilled my skin and bones. Alistar uneasily twitched, and I knew he wanted to support his son, but he also understood his responsibility to help uphold my promise. The promise sworn by magic etched into *my* skin with *my* blood.

"Would you accept another?" Alistar dared to ask, and I about lost my mind.

"No!" I screamed as Magnus grabbed my other arm, pulling me flat to his chest. "I am going. No one else."

"Silence, young one." Minaeve waved her hand, and the room went unnaturally still. My voice was somehow siphoned away from my throat. "I believe we have been too soft with you shifters on this visit. You have mistaken our patience as weakness, but I assure you this is not the case."

Suddenly, a violent blast of power jolted through the room, attacking each shifter and bringing us all down to our knees. I gripped the carpet, trying to muffle a scream as the queen's psychic blast twisted and crushed my mind. I could feel the pressure build inside my skull, but I couldn't do anything to relieve the pain. It was excruciating.

"I believe you have made your point, Queen Minaeve," Daxton's voice broke through the tortuous blinding pressure, and I realized he was trying to convince her to stop.

"You don't want to kill the champion before she can compete, now, do you?" Castor chimed in with his brother.

Minaeve wasn't in the mood to listen, however. A deeply wicked smile crossed her scarlet-painted lips as she increased her attack on everyone else—except me. Magnus screamed, and my heart sank into my middle.

"Magnus!" I gritted my teeth, trying to break through the pain and crawl to him. To somehow heal him and take away his pain. "Stop. Please," I begged, looking up at the fae queen. "I am coming with you. I am volunteering to go with you. Hurting them is not helping anything. I will go, I swear it!"

I could see the fear in Daxton's eyes, and I quickly glanced at Castor only to see the same fear reflected in his. They both knew she wouldn't stop. She planned to kill them all to make a point and show her strength.

"What do you want from me?" I shouted in pain and confusion. The screams from the others intensified, and I knew they were only seconds away from death. Her magic somehow draining, siphoning the life from them.

Before Queen Minaeve could send a final pulse of magic to end their existence, Daxton took her face in his hands and quickly pressed his lips to hers. Minaeve dropped her magical assault immediately and encircled one arm around Daxton's neck while the other wrapped around his waist. I helplessly watched as she pulled him toward her, increasing the intensity of their kiss, claiming his mouth for her own pleasure. Daxton remained utterly still, allowing the queen to mold herself against his body.

The sight of Minaeve with her hands and lips on Daxton made me want to vomit. I began shaking on my hands and knees despite the slow release of the queen's hold on my mind. I clenched my eyes shut, refusing to open them. A soft moan of pleasure escaped from Minaeve, and it was enough to make me double over and collapse on the floor. Magnus reached out to steady me, hoisting me up off the ground.

I dared to look at them, seeing Minaeve finally pull her lips away from Daxton but keeping a possessive arm draped around his waist. She turned to face us. "Do you wish to question the shifter's choice again, son of the alpha? I'm not sure Daxton will be able to persuade me to stop if I have to show you how important our departure is again."

Silence filled the room. Gilen couldn't manage to bring himself off the floor just yet.

"I will leave for Aelius today to begin preparations in the capital for the first trial," the queen said as she glided across the room toward the door with Daxton close behind. "Daxton and Castor will take the second ship and escort the champion to the Inner Kingdom in no more than two days' time." The room was silent, with only nods of understanding as a reply.

"Good," Minaeve sneered. She turned to Daxton, running her fingers across his chest before they migrated along his neck and into his hair. "Come to my chambers before I leave for my ship. I will need to take your offering before I sail through the veil."

"Of course," Daxton answered without hesitation as all the High Fae took their leave.

*Offering?* What did that mean? How did the queen hold so much power over them? More and more questions were spiraling through my head.

"This is not happening!" Gilen grunted, breaking my train of thought. I could feel Gilen's rage as his power surged to encompass the room. He pounded his fist against the chair and started storming across the room toward me. I was not afraid to face him again. He was steps away from me when another person stood up in my defense.

"Back down, Gilen." Magnus bore into him with a cold, hard stare I had never seen before. "The female has rejected your claim. You will not pursue her any further. There is no mate bond … Therefore, you have no claim to my daughter."

"I will …"

"Gilen!" Helen interjected, reaching her son's side. "Let her go."

"But—"

"Let. Her. Go … son." Helen gently placed a hand on Gilen's shoulder to try and calm him. Alistar came to his other side and did the same.

"Skylar, go back to the house. I will meet you there. Julia and Neera need to see you before you leave," Magnus said in a low, hushed tone.

"Aren't you coming with me?"

"Not just yet." Magnus continued to stand in between me and Gilen, blocking his access and view of me. "Go now, please. I need to speak with Alistar and Gilen—alone." I didn't hesitate and ran for the door. I wanted to get as far away from Gilen as I could. The betrayal still lingered in my heavy heart.

Turning toward the staircase, I saw Queen Minaeve and Daxton walking together down the guest wing hallway. My heart leaped inside my throat as she pulled Daxton inside a room and latched the door shut.

There was no clear reason why I did it, but I turned away from the stairs and took a step down the hall toward them. My animal awakened inside me, her instincts telling me something was wrong, that I needed to help Daxton. I was halfway down the corridor when a firm arm grabbed me and spun me in the opposite direction.

"Skylar," Castor exclaimed as he pinned me against the wall.

His eyes were transitioning from pitch black back to their dark brown color, and they were wide with fear. "What in the gods' names are you doing here?"

"I-I don't know," I answered in a panic. Why was I down here? This was by far one of the stupidest decisions I had made in a long time. What was I planning to accomplish?

"Is Daxton …" Castor gave me a hard look that made me pause. "I-is Daxton all right?" I stammered, genuinely worried. It didn't matter if Castor believed I was sincere or not. I realized at that moment that I was starting to care about Daxton, and I didn't like the idea of anyone I cared for being harmed.

Castor cautiously glanced around the hallway, his eyes darting and his head tilting like he was listening for anyone lurking nearby. "Not here. You need to leave." He grabbed my hand and guided me back down the hall, the stairs, and finally out to the woods.

"Go home, Skylar."

"No! Not until I know that he's all right," I snapped back at him. "Castor, what's going on?"

His scrunched forehead told me he was debating what to do or what to tell me. He pursed his lips but ultimately hung his head in defeat. "The queen is leaving without us. Daxton is doing what he has to in order for her to return to the Inner Kingdom safely."

"And what does that mean exactly?" Minaeve seemed powerful enough in the other room when she almost killed us with a blast of her psychic magic. Why did she need Daxton?

"Nothing you want to hear or know the details of—"

"Tell me, please," I almost begged. "Can I help him?" I wouldn't hide the fact that I was worried about the brave fae who led the charge into the lair of the hunters to rescue me from death's doorstep.

"I can't," Castor answered, and I could see concern etched on the lines of his face. His hand ran through his bright silver hair. "Dax will be fine … He … he … knows what he's doing."

"Then why are *you* so worried?" I could see through Castor's lie from a mile away. He might be a master of illusion and persuasion, but he could not hide this. Not when it really mattered.

"It is not my story to tell, Skylar." He stepped back and turned to leave.

"Castor!" I yelled, jumping in his path.

"What will it take to get you to listen to me and go home?"

I pressed my lips into a firm line. *Nothing*, I wanted to spit back at him. But I knew he was not going to allow that to happen, so I would compromised, hoping he would do the same.

"Promise me … that you will come find me if he needs my help. Promise me this, and I will turn around and go home."

"Right now?"

"Now."

Castor silently mulled over my offer, and after seven silent seconds, he gave a firm nod of *yes* in return. Understanding our agreement, I honored my word, turning on my heels and running home.

# Chapter Nineteen

It was just past midday by the time I made my way home. Neera and Julia were working in the kitchen, anxiously waiting for me to return. I slid through the doorway, and they both turned to greet me with open arms. One look at their faces had me balling like a newborn babe. I couldn't hide anything from them. A big part of me was dying just to let everything out. I had bottled up Gilen's betrayal and tried to stay strong, but this was all just too much. I confessed everything to my family as Julia worked in the kitchen, and Neera sat patiently by my side, listening to each horrific detail I shared. I told them why Gilen wanted to claim me, about how he wanted to use the claiming mark to access my powers, and his plans to sacrifice another shifter to take my place in the trials.

A part of me still couldn't believe this was all real.

I couldn't believe I thought he could have been my mate … my fucking mate! My animal churned inside me at the thought of him biting me with a claiming mark. I could tell she was just as angry and upset as I was.

"He's not worthy of you, Sky," Neera said as she shifted to glance out the window. "He only wanted to trap you and keep you for himself. It is a blessing from the Mother and Father that he was not your mate."

"I can't believe he tried to stake a claim on you *again* in the meeting with the High Fae queen," Julia chimed in as she pounded a pile of dough in the center of the kitchen.

"Magnus stepped in and stood against him," I added.

"Good," Julia grunted as she punched the dough with her fist. "If I had heard otherwise … Magnus would be permanently sleeping in a den outside."

And I didn't doubt it.

"Does that help?" I asked, tilting my head at the very tender ball of dough.

"Yes," Julia answered as she wiped her brow, now covered in flour. "Care to join in?"

"Absolutely." I stood near the island corner, and she pushed over another dough ball for me to tenderize.

Neera decided not to join but remained with us in the kitchen to keep me company. She was uncharacteristically quiet, and it was beginning to make me nervous. We could always talk to each other, and Neera was eternally open with me regardless of what was going on in our world. We were not born as sisters, but our bond was no different. I loved her. I loved all my family, and knew I would miss them terribly.

"What has you troubled, Neera?" I couldn't ignore her silence any longer.

She sighed and leaned forward on her elbows. "I don't know how I feel about this, Sky."

"Well, telling me exactly what *this* is would help."

She rolled her eyes to the side and glared at me with her adorable scrunched-up, freckled face. Neera couldn't pull off mean or angry if her life depended on it. She was as gentle and precious as a butterfly—someone I would do anything to protect. I couldn't help but laugh to myself. I didn't know how many more of her *angry* faces I would get to see.

"Everything!" Neera yelled, her outburst practically slapping the smirk right off my face.

Wow, she actually yelled at me. This made Julia stop hammering her fists into the dough and look at her daughter with surprise. Neera pushed away from the table, stormed outside the kitchen door, and disappeared into her garden.

Julia released a heavy sigh. "Go to her, Skylar."

"Shouldn't I just give her some time to calm down before I go out there? I have never seen her act like this. It's … unnerving."

Julia refused to look at me as she began to roll the dough into small, rounded biscuits. "We don't …" I could hear her sniffle, trying to hold back her tears, and I sucked in a pained breath. They were trying to keep themselves together for my benefit. "You don't have time, Skylar. That's the whole point."

I dropped the dough on the island and gazed at my surrogate mother. "I plan on returning, Julia."

"I know you do," she answered. "But the unknown is too much for her. When you were captured, Neera didn't stop crying for three days. She drifted into a numb existence that we barely brought her out of."

My chest tightened with guilt, not knowing how to help.

"What do I say to her? How do I say goodbye to Neera … to all of you, Julia?" I bit my lip to try and keep myself together. "I hadn't thought about how difficult this part would be."

Julia wrapped her arms around me and held me tight. "We don't know either, honey. Maybe … it's not a goodbye. As you said, you intend to win the trials and return. Take that approach. This is not a goodbye. *It is a see you later.* Talk to her and help her understand your reason for going."

I pulled my short but feisty aunt in close and soaked up every little bit of her I could. She was so strong and steady—the heart and soul of this family.

"Thank you," I murmured, "for everything. For taking me in when Magnus found me. For accepting me for who I was and embracing me as your own. My life was blessed by the gods when they tied my fate to you."

Julia released me and grabbed my face with her hands. "No, my dear. Fate brought you to us, and we are the ones who are blessed by having this time with you. Thank you for enriching our lives and for giving up everything to save Neera without a second thought. You have *more* power and strength than you realize, Skylar." She kissed my brow and hugged me tightly.

*More.*

Someone else had said that exact same thing about me not too long ago—*Daxton.* My mind carried my thoughts away to the male fae that had somehow worked his way into my head, and for the life of me, I couldn't seem to shake him. It wasn't just his strikingly attractive features that enticed me, but it was also how he carried himself. I was beginning to catch glimpses of his humor, which only made me like him that much more. Daxton made me feel strong, protected, and most of all, that my voice had merit. I could honestly say that I trusted him.

I left Julia in the kitchen and wandered into the gardens to find Neera. The sunflowers were beginning to bloom. Their stalks hovered just below my shoulders as I walked through an endless sea of greenery. Neera loved her garden. It was her place of peace, and I imagined that when she had her own place someday, her entire house would be surrounded by one. She was tending to some overgrown raspberry bushes, and I knelt next to her to help prune them away from the lilies.

"Do anything different to the raspberries this season?" I asked as I popped a fresh golden raspberry into my mouth. "They taste amazing as always. Should we gather some to make a pie or tart tonight?"

"Will you be here long enough to even enjoy it with us?"

Ouch. Nice punch to the gut there, Neera.

"Might be. Depends on when you open up and start talking to me. Or the other option is that we can just sit here in the weeds until the fae come to take me away." Neera stopped trimming the raspberry bushes but still refused to look at me. "Come on, Neera, talk to me, please. I can't do this without you."

"That's just the problem, Sky." Neera turned her beautifully sweet freckled face toward me, and all her bottled-up feelings poured out. "It should have been me," she screamed with tears soaking her eyes.

I remained silent. She needed to let this out. Neera had to scream and allow all the feelings she had bottled up to come to the surface. If I had learned anything this past month with Shaw, it was that denying how we are feeling only does more harm than good. We needed to face our fears head-on if we were ever going to conquer them.

"It should have been me! The queen chose me … Me! Not you!" Tears were flowing down her cheeks now. "How am I supposed to live with myself knowing my sister took my place? That I was not strong enough to say yes! That I let you jump blindly into the unknown … and possibly death."

I reached out and clutched Neera to my chest, wiping the tears from her face as I whispered to her, "This was my fate. Never yours, dear sister."

"How was this *your* fate, Skylar?" she asked me as I slowly stroked her hair.

"Do you remember that night when I didn't shift?" I asked her, steadying my nerves. "Do you remember that the fae queen stopped and looked at me and Shaw in the meadow first?"

Neera turned her head to look at me. "I-I—"

"Well, I do." I knew I had to tell her everything about that night. She would not be able to accept anything less. "My animal presence surged inside me that night, Neera. I felt my power rise when the queen stopped and looked at me in that meadow. It was a silent question, but one that I knew I had to answer. When I did not shift, I understood I would be the one traveling to the Inner Kingdom." Only a shifter would understand the gravity of what it meant to have our animal spirits present themselves in such a way.

"Your animal agrees with your choice?"

I nodded without hesitation. "Yes." The fae queen might not have spoken to me in the meadow, but when she looked at me, I understood why I didn't shift. My animal did as well. We resisted the alpha's call because fate had other plans for us. "When I was taken …" Neera tensed as I cleared my throat to continue. "When I was taken, I asked myself … why continue? Why don't I just break and give up?"

"Why didn't you? How did you fight against all of it and never give up hope?"

Her questions had complex answers, and I wasn't ready to dive into all the layers with her right now, but I was confident in my progress working through them. Even though I failed, it didn't mean I would give up.

"I made a vow … I promised to represent our people and do everything in my power to heal our world. My responsibility. My fate."

That answer seemed to resonate with Neera. If she knew some good came of this seemingly impossible mission, I knew she would be able to understand.

"So … you really believe you will succeed?"

"I believe I have no other choice," I said with a sad smile. "I have a pack counting on me and a family I need to come home to."

"Da-damn right you do." Neera tried, but cursing just didn't fit her.

I slung my arm around her shoulder when we heard footsteps behind us. "Julia told me I could find you two out here." Magnus came into the clearing and knelt beside us. "Sort everything out?"

Magnus and I didn't need more time to address my decision. One thing I admired about my uncle was that he handled everything in a calm and decisive manner. If I told him right now that I was running away and had changed my mind, he would not ask questions. He would find supplies, help me pack a bag, and create a distraction so I could escape. When someone he loved needed anything, there were no questions for him. He would do everything and anything to help.

Neera nodded, wiping tears from her face. "Skylar and I talked."

"Well, you *yelled*," I added. "And … somehow, I was the rational, reasonable one, and *I* talked." Neera rolled her eyes and chuckled. I directed my questioning nature to Magnus. "Everything settled at the alpha's home?"

"The fae queen was escorted by the silver prince to her ship and sailed away just before I left. Apparently, there were two ships waiting along the beach that were cloaked by another High Fae's abilities on board. Very impressive magic. She can create illusions …"

"Wait," Neera interrupted. "So, she's just gone?"

Magnus nodded.

"You only said one of the princes escorted her?" I asked. "That's strange."

"I thought so, too," Magnus added as he rubbed his bearded chin. "Daxton was nowhere to be seen." I didn't miss the peculiar look Magnus was giving me as he mentioned his name. "Castor was the only one with her when she was escorted to her ship."

"Where was Daxton?" I asked. I could see Neera's mind spinning at my reaction. "He seemed quite eager to be at her beck and call during the meeting earlier. It's surprising he didn't personally see her off."

"That was a bit unnecessary, in my opinion," Magnus rumbled, never a fan of public displays of affection.

Me, on the other hand? I loved it. If I ever managed to find my mate, there would never be a question of desire or passion in the union. A big part of me longed for that physical attention and connection with my partner. I could tell that my animal needed that type of attention as well, which was fine. A little affection never hurt anyone, and I knew I would happily return the favor.

"I was under the impression neither of the males held a liking for or even freely followed Queen Minaeve," Magnus added.

"Really?" I asked with a little too much spark, which caught Neera's attention again. "What made you think that?"

"It's in the minuscule mannerisms in her presence, how they address her as 'the queen' instead of 'my queen', and how they are summoned almost forcefully … perhaps even against their will to her side. I believed they tended to her out of obligation, not affection or devotion."

I beheld my uncle with a peculiar look, recalling how Daxton and Castor both tensed with pain the night I went to heal Daxton's shoulder. It looked like they were being attacked, but nothing was touching them. And then again, the same reaction when we were on the beach together.

"But he kissed her?" I blurted.

"Who?" Neera asked with increased curiosity.

"Daxton kissed Queen Minaeve while meeting to discuss

Skylar's decision to travel to the Inner Kingdom for the trials," Magnus answered, annoyedly closing his eyes and rubbing his temples with his fingers. This was treading too close to gossip for his liking.

"That's not the entire truth," I countered. "He kissed her while she attacked every shifter in the room with her strange siphoning magic."

"Well … that was rude," Neera huffed, crossing her arms.

"And exceptionally painful." I shook my head.

Magnus mulled over his thoughts before speaking. "I have faced death more than once in my life, and I must admit … I had the feeling of death looming while Minaeve used her magic. It was very powerful and dangerous."

Neera covered her mouth with her hands, gasping in surprise. "Oh, Father!"

"We are fine, my daughter. Nothing to fear."

"Besides, she is gone now, Neera."

"Well, good riddance!" Neera stuck her tongue out to emphasize her point.

*Join the club, Neera.* "I can't say I disagree with you there." I sighed heavily. "Too bad I will have to see her again sooner rather than later."

"But … won't both the princes be escorting you to the trials? Daxton told us he swore to protect you as his ward. That means you'll be safe, right?" The innocence of Neera's question touched my heart. She was searching for someone, anyone, to look after me.

"Daxton told me I would be leaving with him."

"When was this?" Magnus asked with a skeptical expression. Gods be damned, he never missed a thing.

"Before my check-up with Latte." I was going to have to dance carefully around my answer to this question. "I saw him in the training fields with Castor. I spoke with them before I met Latte and told them I intended to still go. That was how the queen knew."

Magnus nodded, and I internally gave myself a pat on the back for my quick thinking. I did not want to inform my uncle that I shared this decision with Daxton while bathing naked in the bathhouse.

"That makes more sense now," Magnus answered as he shifted and sat closer to Neera.

He bought it. *Thank the gods.* "What did Gilen and Alistar have to say?"

"Nothing you want to hear. Trust me on this, Sky, and don't ask any more about it."

*Good luck.*

"Where are they now?"

Magnus rolled his eyes and grunted with annoyance before answering me. "Alistar wisely took my advice and immediately left with Gilen to visit the eastern region shifters. If Gilen is going to be our next alpha, he needs to be presented to the Satellite regions and sub-alpha leaders."

"Do you agree with that decision?" I asked my uncle.

"It was my advice that they leave."

"No, no. Not that." I shook my head. "About Gilen being Solace pack's next alpha."

"I'm more curious to know what *you* think about this decision, Skylar?" Magnus countered.

To which I very bluntly replied, "I think that's a bullshit question to ask me right now."

"But I'm still asking it." Magnus looked at me sternly, making me curl my toes.

"Are you seriously asking me to be the bigger person right now? Really, Magnus?" I could feel my amber eyes ignite with a red-tinted glow. Magnus crossed his thick arms in front of his chest and patiently waited. I knew he was not going to let this one go. "Ugh!" I groaned as I stood up and paced back and forth. "Can I decline to answer?"

"No," he stated plainly, never once changing his expression.

"Then I say screw Gilen. He can go jump off the cliffs and smash his brains on the rocks for all I care." Magnus glared at me, but I didn't budge.

"Come on, Father, that is a lot to ask of Sky."

"It's really not," he answered. "If Skylar is willing to test herself in the Inner Kingdom to determine whether she is worthy of unlocking a magical heart stone that can heal our land, then, no. This is not too much to ask her."

*Curse you, Magnus, and your logic.*

"The dynamic of our people is delicate yet strong at its core. The alpha is our leader—our protector. We respect power and the ability to use that power for the good of our people." I was stating the obvious, but sometimes it helped to begin with what you already knew as fact.

"So, you believe Gilen should be our alpha?" Magnus asked again.

"Does he not possess all the necessary attributes of an alpha?"

I countered. "His father, Alistar, trained him since he was born to take this role. He is the heir … And his animal is a mythical roc. No one can dispute Gilen's power, which is why Alistar is abdicating to avoid a challenge to the death and passing the role to him. He sees and recognizes Gilen as the strongest among us. He is the best person to lead our pack and keep us all safe."

"You believe these traits are enough?"

"Gods, enough with the questions, Magnus," I yelled with frustration. Didn't my uncle realize what kind of internal torment this was putting me through? I hated Gilen for what he had done to me. His betrayal of our friendship and my feelings hurt almost more than Blade's whip. I trusted Gilen like a naive fool and fell for his bait, hook, line, and sinker.

"Do you know all the details about what Gilen did to Skylar yesterday, Father?" Neera asked as I turned my back on them both.

"Your mother told me, and I assumed the rest from the meeting … But Skylar is a grown female, and she can handle herself. I raised you both to be strong and independent. Always learn from your mistakes so you become wiser from them. Sky doesn't need someone rushing in to fight her battles for her. She needs someone to stand beside her."

I internalized what Magnus was saying, and as much as I hated this situation, I was also grateful for the freedom he was giving me. "Gilen will be a strong alpha for Solace." The words fell like stones from my mouth. *Sometimes, I hated being the better person.*

"Is that what you truly believe?"

"Yes. I don't like to admit it for my own personal reasons … but yes." I shifted uneasily, playing with a nearby flower. "Even though his betrayal of my feelings was hurtful, he wanted to keep my powers to help protect the pack. His intentions for me were shit, and his execution was far below acceptable. But he could successfully fill the role as alpha for our people."

Magnus stood up, and I felt his hand on my shoulder. "Not many could have spoken so honestly about this as you just did, Skylar. I will honor your decision."

"Would you not accept Gilen as the alpha if I had said otherwise?"

"No, I would not."

My brows raised, and I felt my jaw drop as I swiveled to face him. "What the fuck, Magnus? Why would you … What?" Confusion would not accurately describe the state of mind I was in.

My uncle casually smirked and gazed off into the garden with a soft, glossed-over expression. "You will understand someday."

"Umm, I highly doubt that one. But sure, okay, let's go with *someday*." I gave up trying to figure this one out. I had officially run out of logic to make sense of all the crazy things that were going on in my life. "Remember when things were simple? And you were just trying to get me to attend combat training with the others?"

"Never overlook the quiet moments." Magnus laughed.

"Dinner is ready if you three are!" Julia's voice echoed through the garden from the kitchen.

All three of us ventured back into the house and sat down together as a family to feast on Julia's rendition of beans and meat with special biscuits that melted in your mouth. I didn't know how many more of these moments I would have with my family, and I wasn't about to waste what little time I had left.

"So, when do you leave?" Neera asked.

"Tomorrow is my last full day here," I answered before biting into a delicious biscuit with a hint of honey and rosemary. "We set sail the following morning."

"Well, what do you want to do?"

*How did I want to spend my final day here?* There was no guarantee I would ever return. I believed I would, but still, there was a great chance I wouldn't. I looked around at my family's home and knew I wanted to be there.

"I want to cook one final goodbye meal to share with everyone I care about." Julia sighed with sentimental joy, until I added, "And then … get piss drunk, forget for a moment that I am leaving on a ridiculously dangerous endeavor, and have an evening full of fun and laughter with no regrets."

Magnus nearly spit out his water as he tried to hold in his laughter. "I was worried for a moment after your first comment."

I winked at him. "Had to give you one last wildcard."

"Who would you like to invite?" Julia asked. "Just to get a head count to help prepare."

"Anyone is welcome to come," I answered. "Tell the whole pack to come for drinks, but for the dinner, I would like only you three, Rhea, Talon, and Shaw."

"I'll start to make preparations then." Julia smiled and patted my hand. "What are you going to make for us?"

"My famous pasta dish." I grinned. "What else?"

"The one with the layers of meat and cheese and sauce!" I

could hear the excitement in Neera's voice. She loved my pasta meal … They all did. It was my favorite to make because they all enjoyed it so much.

"I might be able to stumble upon the wine cellar at the alpha's house and roll out a barrel or two," Magnus added with a sly, smug grin.

"Get Rhea to help you. I bet she will grab one full of whiskey."

Magnus took the final bite of his buttered biscuit, saying, "I have no doubt, especially after she snuck her flasks up to your room the other night."

"Flasks?" I grinned. "So, you knew she had not only one but two?"

"I knew," Magnus answered as he stuffed a spoonful of his soup into his mouth.

*Knock. Knock. Knock.*

"Skylar!" a voice yelled my name from the other side of the main door.

*Knock. Knock. Knock.*

"Skylar! I need you!"

I sprang up from the table and sprinted toward the front of the house. As I turned the handle to the front door, I could detect the scent of who was on the other side. Opening the door, I readied myself for whatever was to come next.

"Castor? What are you doing—"

"I'm holding up my end of our promise!" His eyes were heavy, and his breathing was ragged. "I need you to come with me."

"Now?" I asked.

"No … tomorrow morning after a long, restful night of sleep and maybe a breakfast buffet," he said sarcastically with a long sigh and a melodramatic eye roll. "Yes, now!"

I glared at him. "That sarcasm is not going to get you anywhere, mister."

"It's Daxton—"

My heart skipped a beat as I froze, unable to move in the doorway. My stomach dropped, and I couldn't seem to find my voice to speak.

"He needs a healer … Skylar. He needs you."

"Latte lives just on the other side of the alpha's home. Why not find her?" Magnus asked as he stepped behind me.

We both ignored my uncle. I knew why Castor had sought me

out. My gut had told me something was wrong when I tried to walk down that hallway toward Daxton. My instincts were guiding me to help him, and I cursed myself, knowing I should have listened to them.

I reached for my cloak hanging by the door and stepped outside into the cold, damp night. "Lead the way."

# Chapter Twenty

"This way," Castor said as he turned and sprinted into the darkness of the night.

Without hesitation, I sped off after him. If he was here, that meant Daxton needed me. Castor swore that if I returned home, he would find me if I could help. I had no idea what I was walking into, but if Daxton needed me, I would be there. I owed him that much, at least.

Castor and I raced past the main village center, staying on the outskirts so we were not slowed down or distracted. If my people saw me racing off after him, it might cause them to worry, and I didn't want that hanging over my head.

Castor sped up, and I forced my feet to follow. Shifters were fast, but it was clear that Castor was in a league of his own. We reached the training fields, and he dashed to the stairwell leading up to their room. He leaped up the steps, taking two at a time, with me matching each stride he took. Racing down the hallway, Castor stopped at the door leading to their shared room.

"I can't exactly explain *why* he's hurt, Skylar," the silver-haired prince whispered, his normal sing-song voice disappearing behind a veil of concern. "But … I'm worried."

"Was it the queen?" It was the only thing I could think to ask.

Castor nodded as he turned the knob and opened the door to step inside. The room was clearly divided. On what had to be Castor's portion of the room were dozens of drawings, sketches, and an empty bottle of wine on the bedside.

The opposite side of the room had a large desk with dozens of books spread out and pages marked for later review. I could see the titles of shifter and human histories open with scrolls and notes etched into parchment. Daxton had not exaggerated his fondness for reading. The window near the desk was cracked open, and I knew from this vantage point that it looked out onto the same area that my room did when I was still recuperating. Daxton had been watching over me this whole time.

"You blasted fool!" Castor cursed as he dashed to the far side of the room.

I gasped when I saw Daxton lying face-down, practically lifeless on the floor. He was sprawled out near his bed in the corner, and my heart sank at the state of him. His eyes were darkened, and his fair skin, which always glowed in the sunlight, appeared dim and sunken around his cheeks. Daxton's head fell back. He was unable to do much more than grunt with discomfort as Castor wrestled to hoist him back onto the mattress.

"You were supposed to remain in the damn bed, Dax," Castor cursed as he picked his brother up and managed to lay him on his back. "Stubborn fool!"

Daxton didn't answer or even open his eyes. Dear gods, what happened to him?

"Any time you want to come in and help?" Castor snapped at me from across the room.

I still hadn't entered their chambers, and I forced myself to take a step forward. I approached Daxton's bedside and carefully examined him from head to toe.

"What did this, Castor?" I demanded.

As soon as I spoke, Daxton groaned and tried to turn his head even though his eyes remained shut. His body began to shake uncontrollably, and we both reached out to try and steady him. "He is as cold as ice!"

"I know," he grunted. "Why do you think I came to find you?"

"What the hell is going on here? You need to tell me everything right now," I yelled while I began removing my shirt and pants. With Daxton's body heat plummeting, I knew from my experience with the healers that he needed skin-to-skin contact to try to re-warm him. "I don't care if it makes sense or not. Tell me what you know."

"First, tell me what in the gods' names *you* are doing?" To my surprise, Castor averted his eyes when I finished undressing down to my undergarments.

"He needs body heat," I scolded as I climbed into Daxton's bed, propped his back up against my chest, and wrapped myself around his middle. "Help me remove his shirt." I didn't see any open wounds or obvious injury, so I assumed he was suffering from something internally. Hypothermia? Or some kind of malfunction with his magic?

"I need skin-to-skin contact to work my healing magic

regardless, and this is also the quickest way to raise his core temperature."

Castor didn't ask questions and immediately followed my command. "I'll grab another blanket and stoke the fire."

"Good. While warming him, and I can start trying to heal him with my magic." I wrapped my arms under Daxton's and cradled his body against mine. He was larger than me, so positioning him between my legs from behind was not easy. My legs wrapped around him to keep him in place as I carefully supported his head against my shoulder, pressing my cheek to his brow.

I could feel Daxton try and turn his head to see who was holding him. "Stay still," I commanded in a whisper. He immediately stopped moving, and I could feel his heart begin beating faster against my grip on his firm chest. "I've got you, Daxton. I'm here—"

"You found me …" His words were a whisper on an exhale of breath that I could scarcely hear.

"We will always find each other," I answered back. "Isn't that what you told me?" I could have sworn I felt his body relax against mine as a hint of a smile turned at the corner of his mouth. The room heated quickly, thanks to Castor tending to the already crackling fire in the hearth. I was beginning to work up a sweat, but Daxton's skin was still cold to my touch. "Another blanket, Castor. Wrap it around us like a cocoon."

He took the bedding from his own side and wrapped it around us, pulling tightly at the edges and tucking them in so no heat could escape. Daxton moaned as the blanket tightened against him, and I tried my best not to move.

"I have never seen it this bad, Skylar." Castor's face was pale. His dark eyes refused to leave his brother's face, watching over him like a hawk. "Can you start healing him now?"

"What exactly am I healing, Castor? It feels like nothing is physically wrong with him, but he is fading …" Castor remained still, and when he refused to answer me again, I lashed out at him with a pulse of my magic. "Dammit, Castor. Tell me now! What happened to Daxton?" My animal pushed power into my command. Just like the other night with Gilen, I felt a rush of magic as I spoke to Castor, and I could see him flinch against it.

"Queen Minaeve," Castor answered through gritted teeth. It seemed like he was trying to fight against answering my question, but he could not. "She took an offering of Daxton's power."

"And what does that do? What does she take in an offering?"

I felt my power thrashing through me.

"She absorbed his power, taking it for herself so she could pass through the veil without us."

"Is that the type of offering Daxton mentioned before? The sacrifice other royal High Fae gave to her so she was strong enough to fight off the wilt?"

"Yes." Castor nodded with his dark eyes set firmly on me.

"So, let me make sure I have this right. She literally sucked the life out of him? What the actual fuck, Castor!"

"They … We have no other option," he answered again. "She siphons and suppresses their powers, cementing her authority and reign over our kind." Castor was silent for a moment before beginning again. "Skylar … Daxton is one of the most powerful High Fae born in the Inner Kingdom. After our father died, his powers and reign passed on to Dax. That, combined with his combat skill, killing capacity, and our mother's gifts … well, no one should be able to stand against him. If he hadn't …" He paused, his face twisting with rage. "If he didn't offer so damn much to Queen Minaeve—" Castor stopped, and for once, I thought it best not to press the matter further.

I returned my attention to the male cradled in my arms. Anger and rage roared inside me. How could a queen selfishly take from her people like this? A true ruler would never intentionally harm their subjects. To me, it seemed like Queen Minaeve was using the other royals for her own selfish greed and power.

"How often does this happen?" I snapped.

"Too often, but more is required during the trials and when her own magic is depleted." Castor dipped his head low. "Dax never allows her to siphon from me. He should have this time, though … because she will publicly ask this of him again the evening before the first trial is unveiled."

"You've got to be kidding me," I exclaimed.

"No, it's her own wicked way of keeping Dax, along with the Crimson City's High Prince Adohan, in line. Seamus of Aelius willingly falls into her bed and freely gives her anything she asks, but he is nothing more than a mind-reading puppet."

"That's … a lot to take in," I confessed.

"You asked," Castor said defensively, and I very badly wanted to stick my tongue out at him in defiance.

Instead, I allowed myself an eye roll and turned my attention back to Daxton. I moved my hands over his taut chest muscles and called upon my healing magic. I didn't know where to begin or direct my powers, so I took a chance and focused on the strong heart beating inside his chest. Maybe If I healed him here, it would naturally spread throughout his whole body. It was the best chance we had, so I closed my eyes and focused all the magic I could on healing Daxton's essence, giving back the energy of life stolen from him by the queen.

Healing Daxton drained the wells of my magic, taxing me more than I had anticipated. I ignored my own shaking limbs and continued pumping my magic into his center. The coloring returned to Daxton's face, and I could feel his arms and legs begin to shift without a grimace of pain on his face.

"It's working!" I breathed heavily. Gods, it felt like I had run the span of our mountain trails or fought my way through the front line of the human king's royal guard.

Castor knelt next to the bedside, holding his breath with anticipation. "How did you do that?" Castor timidly asked.

"You brought me here to heal him. What do you mean how did I do that?" Through my haze of exhaustion, I still managed to gave Castor a dumbfounded glare.

He sighed as he rolled his eyes. "No. Not that. You made me tell you about what the queen did to Dax. I couldn't fight back against your command. Against telling you everything you asked."

Oh, well, shit. That was a new twist. I hadn't realized my command had that effect on him. I figured my yelling, combined with his brother's distress, made him fess up to what Minaeve had done.

"I don't know what you mean," I answered, trying my best to lie.

"Yes, you do." Castor narrowed his eyes into slits. "This wasn't the first time you have commanded someone to obey your will, was it?"

On cue, saving me from answering, Daxton groaned and tried to turn his head. Lucky for me, this was enough of a distraction for Castor to drop the topic for now.

"Daxton?"

His gray eyes fluttered open, and he scanned the room once before turning his sight on me. "Skylar?"

"Welcome back," I said with a heartfelt grin. He wasn't fully healed yet, but I could feel the temperature of his body steadily rising.

"Dax?" Castor gripped the bed tightly, waiting for his brother to answer him.

"Why did you bring her here? I didn't want her here, Castor,"

Daxton said in an angered voice.

"Minaeve is gone, Dax," Castor quickly rebutted, but it didn't seem to make a difference.

Well, that wasn't the welcome or thanks I was hoping to receive.

Castor pursed his lips and glanced away. "I didn't know what else to do. I thought you were dying, Daxton."

"Even after what I told you in the fields?" Dax quickly snapped at him, trying to push himself up.

I had no clue what Daxton meant by that question, but it was clear Castor did.

"No." Castor sighed. "But I knew you needed her. There was no way we could get through the veil with you in that state. I am not strong enough to pass through alone, and you know it."

I felt Daxton shift and try to break my hold. "Hold off on that right now, big guy," I said firmly, moving my hands along his chest. Gods be damned, this male was built like a statue.

Daxton stilled, thankfully following my instruction. I didn't have a very strong hold on him, but regardless, his willingness to listen was appreciated. Healing Daxton had weakened me to the brink of my magical limitations, essentially replacing his energy with my own. This was different from any other healing I had tried.

"This is going to take more time than a normal wound to heal. If I go slowly … the side effects for me will be less severe. With how much the queen took from you, I agree with Castor. You are lucky to be alive."

"Why did this offering affect you so much, Dax?" It was Castor's turn to ask the questions. "You have never been drained like this before."

"She asked for it." It was all Daxton was going to tell him—well, at least for now, with me in the room. Maybe after I left, he would be more willing to tell his brother exactly why he was knocking on death's door.

"Makes sense," I added. "I imagine your devotion to her outweighed your own personal needs. You made that quite clear during our meeting this morning."

The room was suddenly deathly silent. Castor looked at me with the most shocked and horrified expression I had ever seen from him. He gulped loudly and slowly removed his hand from the bedside, backing away from Daxton and me.

"What?" Daxton's voice was venomous and cold. Even when

I shot him with the iron arrow, he hadn't spoken to me like that. I didn't know how to respond.

"What … what did I say?"

Castor shook his head at me as he backed away until he was safely on the opposite side of the room.

Daxton's breathing intensified, becoming ragged and animated. His fingers untucked the blanket's fold, and he pushed himself out of my grasp to turn and face me. "What did you say?" Despite his weakened state, Daxton planted his arms on either side of my head, pinning me up against the wall with his heavy body.

"I said it made sense why you would give Queen Minaeve anything she asked for," I replied, unsure of why this was such an issue.

"Why?" Daxton growled, flashing his canines at me. "How…could you ever think-"

"Because you kissed her," I exclaimed. Wasn't that obvious? I watched how he embraced the queen and followed her seductive touch into her private quarters. Even a blind man could see what she intended to do with him behind closed doors. "You obviously are romantically tied to her in some capacity. I don't know customs of marriage or mate bonds with your kind … but how you kissed her and followed her into her rooms left little to the imagination."

Pure silver fire seemed to glow in Daxton's eyes. The room turned ice-cold around me as his power pulsed in uncontrollable waves. His magic was threaded into his emotions, and right now, both seemed to be out of control. His rage was bubbling over the surface, and for the life of me, I still didn't understand why.

"What?" I thrust my hands forward into Daxton's chest, colliding against a firm wall of muscle that didn't seem to budge. I pitifully tried again to push him away, but Daxton refused to move.

"I *despise* her," he growled with hooded eyes. "With every breath I take and with every beat of my heart, my hatred for her only grows. Do not *ever* insinuate I have any kind of affection for Queen Minaeve." Daxton was deathly calm as he spoke. I could feel the fluctuations of his power butt against my own as he tried to control his rage.

I was taken aback, but I refused to cower in front of him. So, I leaned forward to meet his deathly terrifying stare with one of my own. "Don't get bent out of shape because I called out what I saw. I didn't know any better. You and Castor never even hinted about hating Minaeve."

My animal's power rose to the surface of my itching skin, and I knew my eyes were blazing with fire. I would not back down. I was not afraid of his power or a dance for dominance. After what I had been through, I was not afraid to meet his challenge—not one fucking bit.

A deep growl emanated from Daxton's chest, and I didn't tremble with fear like others in my situation would. Instead, a steady pulse of excitement and arousal stirred in my center. The challenge thrilled my animal, giving way to my shifter instincts to fight, and I was secretly loving every second of this.

"Don't add insult to my injuries, Spitfire." Daxton dropped his arms and moved to give me space, keeping his stone-cold eyes locked with mine. He wasn't backing down, either.

"Speaking of injuries," I added, tilting my head to the side with a whisper of a grin. "Get back into our cocoon. I'm not done healing you yet." Daxton's stormy stare didn't even flinch, outright refusing me.

"Come on … get over here," I protested, opening the blanket and inviting him back in.

Daxton didn't utter a word as he stilled, not moving one inch. He glared at me like a kid who had just gotten picked on by a no-good-rotten bully.

Had I hurt his feelings by assuming he had a romantic relationship with the fae queen? What kind of fucked-up world were they living in? And why the hell had I volunteered to be thrown into this chaos? It was clear that life in the Inner Kingdoms was worse than I had ever imagined.

I softened my expression in an attempt to make amends and understand what he was feeling. "Did what I said … about—" Daxton tensed, and I only assumed it was in anticipation of hearing her name escape my lips. I suddenly realized that I had deeply wounded him with my assumption. *Well, fuck.* I felt like the lowest dung beetle in the hole.

"I'm sorry, Daxton," I said softly, trying my best to empathize with the pain he was clearly feeling. "I misread the situation entirely. I realize you don't owe any further explanation than you've already given me, but please know I am truly sorry for offending you."

The room was deathly quiet for a long while. The fire crackled loudly in the hearth as time seemed to stand still. Without speaking, Daxton moved toward me, wrapped the blankets around us both, and relaxed his bare back against my chest. Once again, I encircled him with my body and allowed my healing powers to flow into his chest.

The three of us sat in silence over the next few hours. I continued slowly healing Daxton, and to my relief, he was regaining his stamina and vigor.

"Can I get you anything, Skylar?" Castor asked from the opposite side of the room, smirking at the sound of my roaring stomach.

"I need to eat," I answered. "It's taking a lot of my energy to replace what was lost, and shifters have a naturally high metabolism."

"Say no more. What would you like?"

"Anything … Everything you can find in the kitchens, please. But don't trouble the staff if it can be helped."

"How much longer will it take to heal my brother?"

"I don't know." I could feel Daxton getting stronger, but he was not out of the woods yet. I was trying to take my time and ensure I didn't deplete my energy too quickly. This was a steady marathon and not a sprint.

"I'll return soon then." Castor casually slipped out of the room, leaving Daxton and me alone.

I wasn't going to be the first one to speak. I had already apologized for unknowingly offending him … and I truly felt awful for what I had insinuated. But in my defense, he made that kiss look pretty damn realistic. I remember the sickening feeling when I looked up and saw them together. It felt wrong, like the world was turning upside down and the sky was now under my feet kind of wrong. I wanted to stand up and scream at the top of my lungs for them to stop.

"What's the matter?" Daxton casually asked.

"What do you mean?" I unintentionally snapped at him. Reliving their kiss had made my tone harsher than I had intended.

Daxton curled his right hand around my knee, lightly tracing over the back of my leg before migrating down to my ankle. "I can feel your muscles clenching. You're tense."

*Well, now I am tense for an entirely different reason.*

"Something *was* on my mind, that's all." I hugged him a little tighter and pressed my cheek to the side of his head so he couldn't turn his temple to look at me. I inhaled a deep breath to try and settle my frustrations, and Daxton's scent of pine and cold mountain air tantalized my senses, calming and centering my thoughts back to this moment with him.

"Care to elaborate?"

"Do you care to elaborate?" I countered.

"I will if you do."

Interesting idea. It only took me a second to agree, but I waited a few moments before answering him. "You got yourself a bargain, Princey."

I felt him huff a single laugh. "I've warned you about that," he growled, but I knew this one was all bark and no bite. "Very well, ladies first."

"I'm not your typical lady," I reminded him.

"No, you're not," he replied, tilting his head a little to peek at me. "We are both naked aside from our undergarments, and you have your body wrapped around mine. I would say this is very unladylike behavior."

"Hard to accomplish a devilish act in this position, though," I added, blushing.

He chuckled, closing his eyes and leaning back against me a little more. "You'd be surprised what can be accomplished in positions such as this."

I was sure my heart skipped a beat as a low pulsing sensation began to throb in my middle, very aware of every area I was touching Daxton.

"Why didn't you want me here tonight?" I asked.

Daxton shifted against my hold, adjusting himself so he could turn his body to face me. "I didn't want you to see *me* like this. After what I had to do in the meeting, I was … ashamed."

"You were ashamed of kissing Minaeve?"

"Not too fast," he interjected, with the dimple on his right cheek making an appearance above his trimmed beard. "It's my turn." I squeezed him tightly around the waist with my thighs to ensure he knew I didn't appreciate him cutting me off. But I would play by the rules for now. "Why were you tense a moment ago? Is healing me straining you?"

"Ah, ah, one question."

"Fine," he said with a hint of a smirk. "What were you thinking a moment ago?"

A strange, comforting feeling came over me, and I knew that he was genuinely asking out of concern for my well-being. "I was reliving your kiss with Queen Minaeve, and it infuriated me all over again." I had no reason to lie to Daxton. A big part of me wanted to be honest and open with him.

"Interesting," he replied, giving no further insight into what he was thinking. "All right, your turn."

"To follow up on my previous attempt … What were you ashamed of?"

Daxton braced himself as he prepared to answer. "I have deep scars on my body and soul, Skylar. They are from various battles of defeat and victory as a warrior, but others run deeper than just the surface of my skin. Minaeve is the high queen, but I do not willingly follow her rule. She has done things to me that I won't burden you with right now … but understand I was ashamed to willingly give in to her carnal desires and to kiss her … in front of you."

"I see." I honestly had no clue what that all meant, so I donned the best poker face I could manage.

"Is healing me straining you?" he quickly asked.

"A bit, yes. You are very powerful, and it's obvious the queen siphoned too much from you. I'm managing at this slow rate, but when the food arrives, I won't apologize for a lack of manners and scarf down every last morsel."

"I wouldn't expect anything less." Daxton seemed amused, and it put me at ease. "I did it for you."

I stilled for a moment before asking, "Kissing Minaeve?"

"Yes." Daxton nodded.

"Why?"

"Because she was hurting you, and she was seconds away from killing those you loved. I knew there was no other way to distract her."

Before I could ask another question, Castor entered with a tray full of food. My eyes widened, and I swear my stomach rumbled loud enough to be heard across the entire pack lands.

"Seems like I came back at just the right time," Castor said as he approached Daxton's bedside. "Everything simmer down?" The question was directed at his brother.

"Yes, and I believe you have used enough energy to heal me for the night, Spitfire." Daxton moved to unlatch the blanket and sit up on his own.

I felt myself lean in toward him, and he stopped. His hand lingered on my bare leg, sending goosebumps across my entire body. He glanced over his shoulder, giving me a longing look that made me regret healing him so quickly. My heart rate sped up as he looked at me with that special spark in his eye. I didn't know what to do, so I shifted the blankets to cover me, pretending the goosebumps were from a cold draft in the room.

"I forgive you for earlier, Skylar. You didn't know …" Daxton said quietly. "Thank you for apologizing. I appreciate it."

I was speechless, probably for the first time in my entire life. I knew asking about it again would only upset him, so I let it be. I hoped he knew that if he wanted to talk, I would listen. I might not have known then how he felt toward her, but I did now.

Castor placed the tray of food in front of me, and my attention turned to the delectable treats that would soon fill my belly. I devoured a small loaf of bread with meats and cheese while Daxton walked around the room. He rolled his thick shoulders, one now sporting a new decorative tattoo, flexing cords of muscles along his back and twisting to bend over to reach his toes. He performed slow, methodical movements to test his mobility, and I couldn't tear my eyes off him, awe-struck by how aroused I was by just watching him move around the room. Denying that I was attracted to him was no longer a fight I could win.

Daxton paused in the middle of his exercises and slowly turned toward me, lightly sniffing the air.

"Castor. Out. Now!" Daxton commanded, and without arguing, his brother was gone in an instant.

I watched Daxton closely as he stalked across the room and slid onto the bed next to me. I gulped as he moved closer, his body only breaths away from mine, my heart racing a million miles per second inside my chest as my throat dried and heat flushed the cheeks on my face.

"May I?" he asked, pointing to the half-devoured tray of food, his eyes showing a hint of fiery passion burning in the depths of his storm-gray eyes.

"H-help yourself," I answered, blushing at the intensity in his eyes that boarded on desire. "I don't think I can manage another bite."

Daxton brought a bite of bread and cheese to his mouth, and I felt myself practically swooning as I watched the food pass over his delectable lips. "We don't have the sense of smell shifters do, but we can detect changes, Spitfire. And—" He stopped. "Spitfire?"

Swaying a little, I grabbed my throbbing head as my vision started to become foggy. *Oh no*, I thought, unable to sit upright. Suddenly, a wave of exhaustion overtook me as I slumped forward, catching myself on the edge of the frame.

"Skylar, are you all right?" Daxton was there in an instant. His strong hands supported my shoulders, helping me lean back against the wall. He looked worried; the hunger I swore I saw moments before was quickly replaced with concern.

"Just tired," I whispered. I couldn't believe how quickly things had turned. "With my basic needs met and the nerves gone, my body is finally forcing me to rest. This is normal for us, by the way."

"Normal?"

"When shifters exert too much energy or are severely wounded, our bodies naturally shut down once we feel safe. So we can heal, and survive."

"I see." In a silver flash, Daxton fastened the latch on the door and then teleported back to my side. "I'll take over for now, Spitfire," he said softly as he pulled the blanket from the floor. He slid in behind me on his bed and tucked me securely into his chest. I was too exhausted to protest, and to be honest, I didn't want to. I nuzzled into his embrace as he wrapped his strong arms around me, keeping me safe and protected from the world.

Before closing my eyes, I asked my final question for the night, "Can I trust you, Daxton?"

I knew I didn't have long before my shifter instincts pulled me into a deep sleep. Whenever we were past the point of magical exhaustion or needed to heal a massive wound, we slept until we regained our strength. Shifters couldn't fight it once the sleep began to set in.

"Yes, you can trust me," he whispered softly against my brow just before I drifted to sleep. "I trust you."

# Chapter Twenty-One

I swear to the gods, I have never slept so soundly in my entire life.

True, it was partially due to my shifter instincts shutting my body down, but it was also because of the male who held me tight against his chest the entire night. I didn't want to move. Wrapped in Daxton's arms, I felt comfortable and protected. I had succumbed to the shifter's sleep once before, ironically with Gilen. But he was never able to comfort me like this—no one had. Daxton stayed with me throughout the entire night, never once leaving my side or letting me go.

Trust … *I trusted him.*

I could depend on Daxton, and with so much unknown in my future competing in the trials, I was glad to have him in my corner. At least, I hoped he was. I took in a deep breath and smelled the familiar scent of the cold mountain air with the fresh hint of pine. My animal practically rolled over with delight and contentment.

"Welcome back … again," Daxton said in a soft voice as he adjusted his arms around me.

I shifted my body, testing the mobility and strength of my limbs, before tilting my head up toward his face. He was so damn handsome it almost took my breath away. I quickly tried to douse the spark of desire from catching, but he wasn't making it easy. Daxton held a look of pure bliss, resting his right hand behind his head as he turned toward me.

"I hope I wasn't too much dead weight on your chest all night," I said, almost immediately regretting it.

*Really … Okay, really, Sky? That was the first thing to pop into your head this morning? Not "Thank you for looking after me"?* I buried my face into the side of his tattooed chest, praying he was still groggy from being asleep and didn't catch what I had just said.

"You don't need to worry," Daxton huffed, stroking my head to encourage me to unbury my face. His smile was relaxed, just like his gentle touch that continued migrating down my arms as he pulled me closer toward him. "I'm strong enough to hold you through the night."

When I was brave enough to look at him, I noticed an openness and vulnerability that hadn't been there before. It was hard to explain the mesmerized look he was giving me that I couldn't bear to break away from. I felt drawn to him. Like a rope had tied itself to my chest and was tugging at my center toward Daxton's.

"What's that look for?" I asked, tilting my head with a smirk.

His smile widened. "Oh … there is a reason."

"And that is?" I flipped onto my stomach and propped myself on my elbows. "Care to elaborate or enlighten me?"

Daxton released me and placed his arm that was underneath me behind his head, giving me a playful wink. "Later, if you're lucky."

"Great. Now, I will never know. I am one of the most unlucky shifters in this pack. I swear I always get caught in the middle of something." I flung my hands up as I flopped my head into the sheets.

Daxton laughed a deep, wonderful sound that sent a happy fluttering sensation throughout my body. The room's mood had changed drastically since last night, ranging from fear to aggression, desire, openness, and now laughter. *Talk about your whirlwind of emotions.*

"You're full of surprises, Spitfire."

*Knock. Knock. Knock.*

"As much fun as it is being locked outside and sleeping on the floor, I would prefer what little comfort the accommodations here can bring me," Castor's muffled voice snuck in through the bottom slit of the doorway. "The morning has passed, and the other shifters that wander by are beginning to snicker at me. I knew I should have found a maid to keep me company last night."

"It's what time?" I exclaimed as I jumped out of the bed. "No! I can't believe I slept that long. Oh my Gods … I have to get back home and get ready. We are leaving soon, and … and I-I …" I stammered, frantically spinning in place. Daxton sat up and reached down to hand me my clothes that were tucked away under the bed.

"Oh, right." I shuddered, realizing I was still only in my undergarments. "I'll, um, need those."

He lifted a brow and gave me a half-smirk. "I should hope so."

I quickly got dressed and raced to the door, unlatching the lock. Castor leaned against the doorway, with one knee bent and his arms crossed in front of his chest. He looked annoyed, but thankfully, his frustration was not at me.

"Happy now?" Castor asked with a heavy dose of sarcasm

targeted toward Daxton.

"For now." Daxton didn't look at his brother. Instead, his soft gray eyes were locked solely onto me.

"Right, um." I shifted awkwardly as Castor pushed past me to sprawl out on his bed. "So … I was going to ask, when are we leaving for the Inner Kingdom?"

Castor's head, which was buried in pillows, didn't move, but still, he managed to mumble loud enough for us to hear him. "It has to be *soon*, Dax."

Daxton nodded, still leaning against the wall and sitting upright in his bed with only our shared blanket covering his bottom half. His smooth, bare chest, where I had slept all night, was surprisingly comfortable for being so firm. My eyes danced across the fresh ink, admiring the eloquent markings that balanced power and finesse, fighting the urge to curl up in his arms again.

"We need to leave tomorrow morning, Skylar. Cas and I will prepare the ship and inform the crew. Does this give you enough time to say your goodbyes?"

"Yes, absolutely. I was afraid you were going to say we had to leave tonight. Tomorrow is just fine." I assumed Daxton needed another day to regain his strength, and I was glad I was still able to spend tonight with my pack. I was about to leave but stopped and turned back toward their shared room. "Oh, I also wanted to ask. Would you both like to come tonight?"

"Come … to what?" Castor answered with his muffled voice buried back inside a pile of pillows. "I always enjoy …"

"Cas," Daxton warned, and I could hear Castor laughing through the endless layers of feathers.

Castor popped his head up from beneath his pillows. "What, Dax? We have been away from home for a while now, and sharing this room has limited my normal routine."

*Males.* I shook my head and sighed loudly. "I am preparing a meal for my family and friends tonight, and then the rest of the pack is invited to come for drinks and other festivities at my family home. Would you two like to join?"

"It would be an honor. Would you like us to attend after the dinner?" Daxton answered for them both as he offered me a kind smile and sat forward on the bed.

"I would love to have you both there for the dinner, actually." I wanted Daxton and Castor there with my family. I thought it would help them come to terms with my departure if they could trust them as I did.

"Really?" Castor cocked his head to the side, looking at Daxton and then back at me.

"Yes," I said with amusement. "You two have sort of become my friends in this strange turn of events. And I would like you there. I'm saying goodbye to one part of my life and embracing another. Shifters and High Fae should be allies, not enemies. I think having you two there will help the others come to terms with my decision and give them a sense of peace, knowing who I am traveling with."

"Friends." Daxton bowed his head and looked to Castor. "Well, what do you say, brother?"

"Food and wine?"

"The best pasta dish you will ever eat and barrels of liquor, plural, from the alpha's private cellar." I said.

Castor grinned wildly. "Perfection. Now, this is the type of amusement I have been missing."

"And whiskey," I added.

"Even better."

Daxton chuckled lightly at his brother's remark and rose from his bed in nothing more than briefs that barely covered anything. Crossing the room, he ignored Castor with his focus singled in on me. "We will see you tonight, then."

Before I could even manage a stray thought, Daxton delicately reached out for my hand and kissed it gently. The feeling of his lips against my skin tingled and danced with sparks of fire. "Thank you for helping me last night, Spitfire. I'm truly in your debt—even more than before."

"Y-you can call me Sky," I stuttered nervously. The emotions stirring inside me were wild and unpredictable. "Normally, I'm only called Skylar if I am in trouble or when someone wants to make a point with me."

He tilted his head and gave me a relaxed grin that showed a hint of his sparkling white smile. "Very well. But on occasion, I believe I will still call you Spitfire. Since we are considered friends now, you may call me Dax if you wish."

"That is way easier than High Prince Daxton Aegaeon of the Silver Meadows … or Silver Shadow. Those are a mouthful." Again, his lips turned with a mischievous grin encroaching on his face.

He cleared his throat. "Indeed, it is a mouthful."

I narrowed my eyes with crimson flooding my cheeks, realizing the suggestive meaning behind my choice of words.

"Seriously, Dax!" I playfully slapped his shoulder and took a step from the door. "That is *not* an appropriate conversation between friends."

"You … are the one who said it." His grin now widened to a full smile.

I rolled my eyes and scoffed as I walked away, but I couldn't help turning around one final time to look at him. I paused for a second, unable to move my feet in the other direction. My instincts and my animal were telling me to stay.

"Everything all right?" Dax asked.

"Yes, all good," I mumbled, fidgeting with my hair and tucking it back behind my ear as I tried to regain my composure. *Oh … Great job, Skylar. You look like an idiot when you are supposed to be the one shifter who can conquer the trials and unlock the Heart of Valdor. You are off to a fine start getting your feelings all riled up with Daxton. There is no way that would ever happen.*

"See you both this evening?" I hollered with only a half-shaken voice.

"Yes, we will see you then," Daxton replied as I forced my feet toward the stairs and in the direction of home.

"You were gone all night!" Neera stated, following in my shadow. She hadn't left my side since I had gotten home. I couldn't even lock her out of my room when I went to change. "What happened? Why did Castor come for you? What was happening? And why do you smell like a pine tree?"

"I thought *I* was the one who liked to ask the questions," I taunted Neera.

"Ugh, Sky!" she growled at me. "Just tell me!"

"Not a chance." I laughed with my own twisted amusement. I knew I would eventually tell her, but it was just too much fun dragging it on like this.

"Well … you better tell *me*." Rhea entered the kitchen with a barrel of whiskey propped under each arm. Outside, I could hear Magnus and Talon rolling the other larger barrels into the front of the house.

"Rhea!" I smiled and leaped over to give her a hug. "Perfect timing. I'm just about to put the dish over the fire in the oven. It's just about at the right temperature."

"Good," she said, taking out the cork with her teeth. "That

means it's time to start drinking … and to start talking."

"Yes!" Neera agreed, giving me a triumphant glare.

I grinned. Neera thought I was going to spill all the juicy details she had been hounding me for all day. Ha, yeah right. It was not going to be that easy.

"Talon," Rhea called out, "get a big glass of wine for Sky when you come in here. She apparently has some storytelling for us while the pasta dish is cooking." Damn you, Rhea. She knew how to get me to talk, and she didn't hide her triumphant smile about it either.

"Fantastic," Talon said as he entered the kitchen with two very large, very tall glasses of wine in each hand.

"Those both for you, Talon?" I teased.

"On the contrary … both are yours." He grinned sideways, the crooked bridge of his nose shifting with his smile as he slid both glasses toward me and snuggled in behind his mate. Rhea kissed him lightly before returning her attention back to me. My heart warmed to see them together like that. The mate bond was a sacred union that brought happiness and joy to the partners' lives. I was very thankful that my best friend was able to find that in Talon—and vice versa.

"You two need to go get a room," I teased as I picked up one of the glasses and took a heavy sip. "The PDA is getting a bit much, and I have hardly seen you two together since you have been back."

"We have one." Rhea winked. "And it's used often as well. Talon had a small cabin built near the river, and a few days ago, we moved into it together. It's perfect."

"We are enjoying every inch of our *small* … cabin," Talon growled as he nibbled on Rhea's neck.

"I did say perfect. Did you miss that?" Talon silenced Rhea with a swift, passionate kiss.

I could detect the scent of their arousal and knew if we didn't stop them now … we never would. "Okay, enough for now, Talon. Don't make me kick you out of here on my last night. If you can't behave for a few hours, then we're going to have to give you a time-out."

"All right, all right." He laughed, holding up his hands and placing them into his pockets. "I'll give you two hours. But I can't promise more than that."

"I'll take it." I grinned.

"Here, this will help keep your hands busy." Rhea handed her mate a tall glass of whiskey.

"Is that wise?" Neera asked. "Adding alcohol to a newly mated couple on the verge of the female being in heat will lead to them …" Neera blushed.

"Fucking?" Rhea stated bluntly with amusement. She knew Neera couldn't bring herself to say what we all knew she was thinking.

"And it will likely be in my garden!" Neera exclaimed.

"That sounds intriguing," Talon answered with his pale blue eyes locked onto his mate.

"Neera," I scolded. "Don't give them any ideas." And then I turned to Rhea. "Is she right? Are you on the verge of being in heat?"

Rhea only smiled and not-so-slyly interlaced her free hand into her mate's pocket. "Weren't we supposed to be talking about *your* recent nighttime adventures?"

"Seems I have arrived at just the right time to leave," Shaw announced as he entered the kitchen, his scars along his arms shimmering against his skin as he rolled up his sleeve. "Are Rhea and Talon at it yet?"

I ran to Shaw and gave him one of the biggest hugs I could manage. "Which *yet* are you referring to? Fighting or fucking?"

Shaw turned his dark eyes around the room to assess the mood. "Pre-fucking then. Got it. So, we maybe have them for a few hours before they disappear."

"Exactly." I winked and hugged him once more. I clung to him tightly, sinking into his arms with ease and an unhindered understanding.

I was going to miss Rhea, Talon, and my family like crazy, but I couldn't deny that I was going to miss him the most. Shaw and I always shared a love of knowledge and wonder of the world. He was quiet and patient while I sometimes tended to be loud and impulsive. We also shared an understanding of what we experienced at the hands of the hunters and their mage.

"You all right?" Shaw asked. "You're shaking, Sky."

I pulled back and realized I was crying. "Shoot, I-I …"

Rhea crossed the kitchen to me with Talon and Neera close behind. They all wrapped me in a giant hug that almost squeezed the air out of my lungs, but it was totally worth it.

"You get this one," Rhea said as they released me.

"We all agree," Shaw said with a soft smile.

"Just this one for the night … That's the only one. We are celebrating, and there are no tears at a party," Talon added as he flipped back his shaggy black hair and slung his arms over Rhea's shoulders.

"Fine," I said as Neera looped her arm through mine and handed me *one* of my very large glasses of wine.

"Drink up." She laughed.

"Are you joining me?" I asked.

"If you want me to, I definitely can." Neera didn't typically indulge in drinking. She had one terrible hangover the first time she tried wine and had sworn off it ever since.

"Don't sweat," I answered as I kissed the top of her head. "You can be the voice of reason tonight when everyone else is acting foolish."

"Great." Neera sighed. "I'm going to bed long before that happens."

"Old lady." I laughed.

"Hey, Neera," Shaw began. "Can we steal time alone with Sky before her delicious dinner is ready? Would you mind helping Julia and Magnus outside with the seating?" Neera didn't want to leave, but she could never turn down a request from Shaw. I think a big part of her had a secret crush on him.

"On one condition," she said.

"Name it." Shaw flashed her a grin that spanned from one ear to the other. Hmm, maybe it was a two-sided attraction? That would be an interesting pairing.

"You have to tell me everything later."

"Deal." Shaw held out his hand, and Neera shook it before giving me a tight squeeze and venturing outside.

Talon slid a smaller glass of wine over to Shaw while we all sat around the kitchen island together. They were happy to sit with me, knowing I couldn't leave my dish unattended. I had to turn it every so often to make sure the edges of the pasta and cheese didn't burn to a crisp.

"So," Shaw said, "you were with the two High Fae all night? How did that go? And … what were you doing exactly?"

I bit my lip and took another long sip from my glass. "How did you know?"

"We all knew that part, Sky," Rhea answered. "You smell like them. Daxton … in particular. Is something going on between you two?" I blushed and finished half of my tall glass. "All right. What's going on?" Rhea pushed.

"I healed him last night."

Talon shifted, and his interest immediately piqued. "You *healed* him?" This earned a firm elbow from his mate.

"Yes." I went to the oven to turn my pasta dish and returned to my three very confused friends on the edge of their seats, waiting for my answer. "Do you remember how Dax said that the queen's power was the only magic that could combat the wilt?" They all nodded. "And the part where he said the fae have been sacrificing and trying to battle against it this whole time?"

"Yes," all three said in unison. I knew we didn't have much time, so I was just going to have to get to the main points.

"Queen Minaeve." I even tensed a little when I spoke her name. Gods, it was going to be hard when I had to see her again. "It's hard to describe, but she drained Daxton's magic. The fae queen siphoned his life's energy and took it for herself. That is the sacrifice Daxton was talking about. All royal High Fae offer her their own power so she can combat and contain the wilt."

They were silently mulling over the information I had just shared. I allowed them some time to process all of this, casually drinking more of my very large glass of wine.

"You were able to heal him?" Shaw asked.

"Yeah, it put me in a shifter's sleep … but I was able to help."

"If healing him put you into a shifter's sleep, Sky, that must have taken a fuck-ton of energy from you," Talon added as he pulled Rhea closer to him.

He was worried or possibly feeling Rhea's concern through their mate bond.

"He was suffering. After what he did to rescue me, I-I don't see a problem with what I did."

"She's got this under control, Talon." Rhea patted her mate's arm to ease his nerves. "So … *Dax*."

*Dang it*, I cursed inside my head. Rhea had caught onto that one.

"I invited them both to eat with us tonight." All three of them gave me a surprised look before turning to each other.

Shaw emptied his glass of wine, sliding it over to Talon for a refill. "You trust them, don't you?"

I took another sip and nodded. "Yes … Yes, I do. I mean, you worked with Daxton to help me get through the trauma of my capture, Shaw."

"I did," was all he said to my comment.

"It makes sense." Rhea fidgeted with her glass as Talon pushed back her auburn hair, placing a kiss lightly on her cheek. "I can see what Skylar is doing."

"Then help *me* understand, my love."

Rhea sipped her drink and looked at me with her crystal-clear blue stare. A giant weight lifted off my shoulders at the understanding that shone in her eyes. She had accepted my decision to go with them. She understood they were not our enemies. That I was going to the Inner Kingdom for our pack, for all of Valdor.

*Thank the gods for you, Rhea.*

"We are not at war with each other. They came here to ask for help because they could no longer fight the wilt on their own. We have all seen what this death magic is doing to our home. If we don't do anything, our world will die, and there is no hope for any kind of future. Sky is volunteering to go … And I know she will win. She will unlock the Heart, and she will set us all free, once and for all. We are upset because she has to leave, but our anger does not need to be placed with the High Fae."

Shaw raised his brow with a sense of clarity. "Wow, Rhea. I have to admit I'm impressed."

"You can't always be the enlightened one of the group, Shaw," Rhea snapped, taking another long sip.

I laughed. "Touché, my friend."

"So, they are joining us for dinner tonight?" Talon asked.

"Yes, they should be here soon, actually."

I could see Talon shift with uneasiness. Rhea turned her head and began stroking his back, sensing his weariness through their mate bond. "What is it, babe?"

"Sky," Talon hesitated, and I could only guess what this was about. I mentally braced myself for what I knew he would ask. "I'm sorry, but I don't want you to have regrets when you leave. Have you seen or talked to Gilen since the other night?"

"Talon!" Rhea shouted, giving him a firm smack in his chest. Apparently, my refusal of his claim was already a well-known fact within the pack.

"No, it's okay, Rhea." I checked on the pasta dish one last time, bringing it out to cool on the island. "I don't want to see him tonight, Talon, but I know I will see him before tomorrow morning."

"The morning?" Shaw asked.

"That's when we are leaving. Castor and Daxton were preparing the ship today in order to leave in the morning."

"This is our last night with you." Shaw's hazel eyes were heavy with a deep sorrow that pulled at my core.

"Not the last one," I answered with a steady voice as I nudged his shoulder. "I promise I will return. I refuse to believe anything different. This is my fate."

I didn't survive the caves and the torture of the hunters and Blade only to travel to the Inner Kingdom and fail. I refused to believe I would fail. Every fiber of my being came to life the moment I made my promise to the queen of the High Fae that night in the meadow. I was born for this. I would not—could not—fail. Everyone I loved depended on me, and I refused to let them down.

My animal sent a soft wave of acknowledgment and power through me, reminding me that I was far from alone in this fight.

"Skylar," Julia called from outside. "I believe your *other* guests have arrived."

# Chapter Twenty-Two

All four of us scurried to the window to see none other than the two High Fae princes walking toward my family home through the woods. Castor wore a decorative black jacket trimmed with silver that opened around his collar, exposing the deep V of his lean, muscular chest. His tousled hair was messy and swept to the side as he meandered through the open woods. His normal swagger of arrogance matched his witty, playful personality perfectly.

Daxton, to my surprise, donned relaxed yet tailored apparel. He wore a dark, long-sleeved tailored shirt that wrapped comfortably around his broad shoulders. The crisscross on the front of his shirt exposed the top of his smooth chest, which I remembered all too well. The shirt was outlined with silver thread that matched the three-peaked mountain designs that decorated his shoulder. His mostly silver hair was pulled back, highlighting his strong jaw framed by a trimmed midnight-colored beard. Which I knew from recent experience was surprisingly soft to the touch. He walked with authoritative grace, holding his shoulders back and down as he marched through the woods.

I glanced down at my own clothes, stained with flour, sauce, and various specks of food from working in the kitchen all day. I looked horrible, and I didn't think I had time to change or make myself presentable for anyone.

Rhea noticed me and pushed me out of the kitchen toward my room. "You two go play nice," she called out to Talon and Shaw. "I need to help Skylar clean up before everyone gets here. Tell them we will be five minutes."

"So, you mean ten?" Talon teased.

She scowled at her mate. "Watch it, wolf."

I could see a twinkle in Talon's eye as he grinned. "We will play nice. Go help Skylar. She has so much food on her we could eat a meal on what she's wearing."

Shaw laughed. "Here, you will need this." He handed me my almost finished first glass of wine.

"How thoughtful of all of you …" I couldn't finish my

thought as Rhea shoved me out of the room to the stairs.

"Go get undressed. I will get you a washcloth and a wash bowl."

"Thank you." Rhea was the best.

I quickly undressed and began rummaging through my drawers for anything suitable to wear. Adult shifters tore through clothes if we didn't remove them in time when we transformed into our animal forms, so much of our clothing was free-flowing and loose—something we could easily discard if we needed to shift quickly. We didn't focus on or prioritize fashion or fancy clothing. Well, some did, but that was definitely not me. I scratched my head, wondering if I even owned a dress or anything half-decent to wear.

"All right, here we go," Rhea said as she entered. "Oh no," she said, placing the wash bowl down. "Don't tell me you have *nothing*? Really, Sky, we've talked about this. You should have something nice stashed away for a special occasion."

Rhea marched over to my dresser and tore through my clothing options as I washed my face. She wore a long maroon skirt with a very high slit that rode against her upper thigh. The waist was held together with a single knot at her hip that draped over her curves. Her top was black with different interlocking lacings tied in the back, the front lowering in a deep v-cut. She loved the color red, and she was dressed to impress tonight. I knew Talon wouldn't want to or be able to keep his eyes off her.

"Where is that one dress at?" She glared at me, putting a hand on her hip. "You didn't get rid of it, did you?"

"The dark one," I exclaimed. "No. I could never give that one up, even though I still don't know how you convinced me to buy it. I've never even worn it …" I shyly admitted. "It's hanging on the back of my closet door."

"Perfect!" Rhea raced over and found it tucked safely away under a long cloak. "You're wearing this. And don't even try arguing."

"What? No, I …"

"Why not, *Skylar*?" Rhea smiled, holding the midnight-black dress. "Put it on."

"Fine." I rolled my eyes. Dual slits ended at my thighs, and it managed to hug my high hips at just the right place. The high-waisted dress had a plunging neckline that almost reached down to my navel. I could count on one hand the number of times I had worn anything close to this. Come to think of it, I had no idea when I had last worn a dress. I bent to attach a dagger to my upper thigh but struggled with the tie on the back of the dress.

"Can you help me finish dressing, please, Rhea?

"Sure thing? Why—" Rhea stopped as I turned my back to her. "Oh gods … Sky."

"Don't," I said firmly. "I can't right now, Rhea." I realized she had not seen the fifteen scars on my back from Blade's whip. I knew what they looked like, but I was healing. A little bit more each day, I realized that instead of being afraid of these marks, I should find strength in them. Strength in knowing that I survived and did not give in.

"Just tie the back for me, please." Rhea silently nodded and overlapped the shoulder straps so my scars were covered. "Thank you."

She smiled at me, but I could still see the pain in her eyes. "There. Now give us a spin." I twirled, allowing the slits on each leg to fan out the long flowing gown. "Now that's a dress for a special occasion. I believe you are presentable now."

"Well, good, 'cause it's all I've got."

Rhea laughed, looping her arm through mine. "That and a dagger, apparently."

"Never go anywhere without it nowadays. Shaw's advice."

Rhea nodded in understanding. "Well, let's go. I can't wait to see Talon's face when we come down with time to spare."

I could hear everyone gathering outside, and I wouldn't have thought twice if they started eating without us. I wanted them to have a carefree evening full of laughter and good memories. And to be honest, I needed it, too. Magnus and Julia arranged a long rectangular table near the edge of Neera's garden, with various oil lanterns strung between the trees. A large grass clearing along the back of the house would later be filled with music and other members of our pack joining the party. The house looked absolutely perfect. It was everything I had hoped for and more.

Rhea made us stop by the kitchen to retrieve my second glass of wine before joining the others outside. "Here … you're gonna need this."

"Damn right I will." I was already feeling the effects of the first glass, so I knew I needed to take this one a little slower. However, something told me I would need a touch of liquid courage this evening.

Stepping out into the yard, I took in the sight of everyone casually seated at the outdoor dining table. Magnus and Julia sat together, talking with Talon, who had an empty seat next to him reserved for his mate. On the other side of the empty chair, Castor casually lounged back with an already half-empty glass of wine, conversing with Shaw. Neera sat across from Magnus with an empty chair that I knew was reserved for me, and on the other side was none other than Daxton.

The second Rhea and I stepped into view, I watched as Daxton turned, his attention centered solely on me. His focus was unwavering, similar to being unable to look away from a beautiful sunrise or the wildflowers in full bloom. He held the same awe-struck look on his face that he did earlier this morning, and I couldn't help but tilt my head and give him an inquisitive curve of my lips. He blinked, smiled, and moved his chair back to stand at the table. The others stopped their own conversations as their heads turned to Rhea and me.

"It took you long enough," Neera chirped. "We're all starving!" Everyone laughed and took their seats once Rhea and I joined the group in our respective places.

"Don't wait for us," I answered, gesturing to the meal sprawled out in front of them. "The food will get cold, and I won't be responsible for anything less than delicious." It didn't take much convincing for my family to happily oblige to my request. Immediately, Talon dug into the platter with Shaw anxiously following suit. I helped myself to a serving as well and enjoyed every single morsel.

"This … This is truly something," Daxton complimented, turning to me. "It rivals any meal I have had in over five hundred years."

"Thank you. It's fun cooking and preparing meals for special occasions like this. Baking tends to be my go-to when I am mad or frustrated, though. Something sweet always seems to help make the day better."

"Wait. Wait … Five hundred … years?" Talon's jaw practically dropped onto the table.

"Yes," Daxton answered.

"Okay, I have to ask … how old *are* you two?"

"Talon," I seethed, giving him a weary look.

"It's fine," Daxton answered, wiping his mouth with a napkin. "Castor was very young when the great war divided our people. He wasn't old enough to take up arms to defend our lands, but I was old enough to lead a section of our warriors in battle."

"Ya, we read about it," Neera added. I cast her a glare, warning her not to embarrass us.

"Really?" Daxton asked as he glanced my way with a coy grin. "Did you discover anything interesting?"

"Interesting? Well, I will have to see for myself if the legends are true," I replied as I slowly sipped my second glass of wine.

"Good to know for when we begin your training," Daxton added, taking a drink.

"What training?" Magnus asked, his deep voice rivaling Daxton's as it boomed across the table.

"Skylar has asked me to help her prepare for the trials. I promised I would teach her everything I could. I think it is important she is well-rounded and prepared for anything once we are in the Inner Kingdom."

"But she is your ward, right? You told us you swore to look after her." Neera's words were meant to be comforting, but they did the opposite.

His *ward.*

"I did. And I will do all I can to protect her."

"What will Sky face once she enters the trials?" Shaw asked, changing the subject.

Daxton paused and gave Shaw a thoughtful expression, perhaps trying to decipher or analyze any hidden intent behind it. Shaw was crafty, and after spending time together, Daxton was beginning to catch on to Shaw's complexity.

"Castor is the better storyteller," he replied.

Castor lightly dabbed his face with his napkin before lounging against the back of his chair. "It involves three distinct parts or sections one must pass, assessing the chosen shifter's—"

"Mind, body, and soul," I spoke the words I had heard Queen Minaeve say inside my mind that night in the meadow.

"Exactly." Castor arched an eyebrow at me and leaned forward on the table.

"Where did you hear that, Spitfire?" Dax asked.

"Spitfire?" Rhea interjected with a curious look.

"Daxton's nickname for her," Castor answered shortly with a wave of his hand, keeping his stare locked on me.

"Did the queen tell you?" Dax inquired.

"Yes. She said the trials would challenge my mind, body, and soul. Testing the strength and the worthiness of my own heart. *You must be willing to sacrifice everything you have and everything you are.* That is what she told me … before she approached Neera."

"I see." Daxton stroked his bearded chin, deep in his own thoughts. I wanted to ask what he was thinking, but Castor started before I had a chance.

Rolling up his sleeves to expose his dual sun and moon tattoos on his forearms, Castor began again. "The first trial will be of the mind; it is the same each century … and it is the queen's favorite. Well … the only one we have seen thus far."

"So, the queen creates the trials, then?" Magnus asked.

"No … no … no," Castor replied, sipping his drink. "The Heart of Valdor is locked away, and for every lock, one must find a …" He paused for effect.

"A key!" Neera exclaimed.

"Correct. The gods knew how powerful the Heart was, so they designed three tests. Each giving a worthy shifter a key to the next trial. With something as powerful as the Heart, more than one key to access it makes sense."

"How do you know that?" Shaw asked. "Where is all this documented? There is nothing written about this in Solace." And Shaw would know … He somehow noticed details the rest of us missed.

"Our libraries in Aelius stretch back to the beginning of time itself. One ancient scroll in particular is magically bound to the trials and the Heart of Valdor," Daxton added.

"And the first task is a doozy," Castor said, finishing his glass and looking around to fill another. "None have succeeded in mastering it."

"What is the first task?" I almost didn't want to know, but I couldn't help asking. I knew it involved the mind, but that was it.

Daxton looked to Castor, who shrugged his shoulders and twirled his wrist, gesturing for Dax to answer my question. "A labyrinth."

"A labyrinth!" The wheels in my mind began swirling. "How big is it? What will I face in there? Where is it located?" I spat out questions without even pausing to take a breath between them.

"Always with the questions." Daxton shook his head, trying to hide a half-smile at the corner of his mouth.

"A labyrinth is a deadly task that not only challenges your mind with all the twists and turns but challenges you physically as well. Labyrinths have a single continuous path that leads to the center, and as long as you keep going forward, you eventually will reach the end … if nothing kills you in the process. Only the shifter champion can enter this trial, so we have no idea what to expect inside. Only that you should expect the unexpected," Castor explained.

"I will help you in any way I can, Spitfire." Daxton delicately placed a hand on my shoulder to comfort me. I watched as Magnus and the others took notice of his familiarity with me, but I chose to ignore their glances and focus solely on Dax. "I made a promise to you, and I intend to keep it."

I nodded. "I trust you will." We stared at each other, and for a moment, I forgot about the seven other people gathered around the table with us.

"I believe this is the opposite of what you intended to focus on this evening, however," Daxton said, looking around at my family and friends. "I know I ask too much, but trust me when I tell you I will do everything in my power to ensure Skylar passes each and every trial. And that she will return home to you all."

Magnus cleared his throat, drawing all our attention to him. "You both risked your lives to save Sky from the hunters. I have never seen such lethal skill in combat paired with deductive and tactical intelligence. You have already proved to me that you will look out for her. If Sky trusts you, then that is enough for me."

"And me," Julia added.

"You tore those hunters to shreds," Talon added. "If you can do that, I don't believe there's much you can't do. And that includes teaching Skylar something new." Rhea nodded in agreement with her mate.

Shaw cleared his throat to speak next. "I was with your scouting party from the start, and I still don't know how, but you managed to find Skylar when no one else could. Clearly, she is important to you both for her role in these trials, but understand that Sky is one of my closest friends and …" He paused, looking at me the only way a true friend could. "And I believe she is the strongest person I know." *Dammit, Shaw. I already had my one cry allotted for the evening.* "I would follow her bravery anywhere. If she trusts you, then I do as well."

I glanced around, not at my friends but at my *family*. Their confidence in me gave me a flood of strength that I knew would help carry me through these trials.

"All right, now that we all have stuffed ourselves with Sky's delicious food and had that sentimental moment … let's have some fun and set up the rest of the party for the pack," Julia announced.

"I'll set up the bag toss." Talon jumped from his seat to organize some of the games we loved as kids.

"Just a second, love." Rhea reached down below the table and retrieved nine small glasses, filled to the brim with a strong-smelling clear liquid. "A final cheers, just us. To commemorate the night."

My stomach turned. "What's in there?"

"It's best if you don't ask questions you really don't want the answers to right now, Sky. And just let the night take you where it will." Shit. This was her own special brew of moonshine.

"Magnus?" I turned to him.

He laughed and grabbed one of the glasses. "I expect you to do it if I am."

"Neera?"

"This is my one … and only," she said, eyeing the clear liquid with a dreadful expression.

"Come on," Shaw said to Neera as he reached for his own. "It won't bite that much. I promise."

Castor already had his own in his hand as Daxton grabbed one for himself and me. "What do we cheer to?" I asked awkwardly.

"To you … you idiot." Rhea rolled her eyes. "To Skylar!" she yelled as she held her glass high in the center of the table.

"To Skylar," everyone echoed.

The glasses clinked, and we each swallowed our drinks in one quick gulp.

"That was amazing!" Castor exclaimed.

I barely kept mine down as I reached for a cup of water on the table. I was glad I wasn't the only one to do so, with Shaw and Talon following my lead. To my surprise, both Julia and Magnus took theirs like champs, hardly flinching as they drained their glasses.

"What kind of trouble did you two get into before having me and Neera?" I asked my aunt and uncle.

"That is not a story to tell tonight." Julia laughed as she leaned into Magnus, who kissed her forehead.

"All right … Castor." Talon stood up and pointed to the silver fae. "You're on my team. I have seen how good you are at throwing knives. This game will be a piece of cake for you, and I am picking *you* as my partner."

"Not fair." Neera pouted.

"Ah, the little sister wants to play?" Talon taunted. "Well … pick a partner."

"Who said I was playing this shifter game of bag … toss?"

Castor asked with a skeptical look on his face.

Rhea turned to him and said, "The females always give a kiss to the winners … And there will be plenty of those here tonight."

"Well, why didn't you lead with that?" Castor sprang to his feet. "Let's set this up."

Other pack members were beginning to arrive at our home, and I happily greeted each and every one of them. Some gave me grateful thanks while others gave me warnings. In my heart, I knew that each one of them tried in their own way to wish me luck.

The cold, hard fact was that the wilt was beginning to spread. A month ago, it was only visible in the coral reefs and along the shoreline, but now it was moving onto the mainland. Trees were turning brown and withering to dust, along with flowers and some of our recent crops. We didn't have any magic to stop it. The only thing my people had was me.

As the night continued, musicians gathered along the tree line and lively songs filled the evening festivities. My friends and family all danced with glee, and we took turns enjoying the freedom of the music and electricity of the night. I danced with Rhea, Neera, and Julia for as long as my feet could muster. To my relief, a slower-paced song flowed with a softer melody that pulled you into a tranquil, swaying rhythm.

"Would you dance with me, Spitfire?" Daxton appeared at my side with his hand held out to me.

"I'm not sure I can walk, let alone dance and keep up with your gracefulness, Dax."

"Then I shall help carry you," he answered with a playful grin I could not turn down. "Please?"

"All right, just one more, and then I'll have no choice but to sit down." I placed my hand in his and followed him onto the grass-filled dance floor.

"Whatever you need." And I knew he meant it.

Stars danced above our heads, twinkling with starlight that sparkled against the blackened sky and a bright beaming moon. There was a distinct shift in the evening—turning from dusk to the later hours belonging to the nocturnal creatures that lived their days concealed by the mysterious darkness. Cool wisps of air tickled the base of my neck as my hair flowed across my shoulder and fell across the front of my face. Daxton took notice and reached up to brush it aside for me, delicately tucking a strand behind my ear. His knuckles brushed against the curve of my cheek, sending bursts of electricity through his lingering touch. Heat rose in my center as he locked his gaze with mine. Taking my hand, he led us toward the musicians.

Couples flocked to either side of us as the melody softly flowed in a tranquil rhythm, our bodies swaying in beat with the song as our feet glided over the worn grass. Daxton held my left hand as he placed my right atop his broad shoulder. His eyes lingered on the mark he had made on my wrist, his finger gently tracing over the scar. It sent waves of sensation surging through my body with my animal's presence keenly piqued and on high alert. He pulled me in close to his frame, placing his free hand on the small of my back as he effortlessly guided me through the steps to an unknown dance.

His ease and ability to step in perfect rhythm with the music surprised me. I felt weightless, with Daxton leading me through a new world created solely by the entrancing melody that echoed through the night. We swayed to the rhythm of the music, never once taking our eyes off each other. I bent my head to rest on his shoulder as I breathed in deeply, sinking further into a peaceful rhythm that made the world stop. The feeling of being carried in his arms to the harmony of the music was magical.

There was no definite answer, but I could see a difference in him that I hadn't noticed before. He was open, honest, and above all … genuine with me. Showing me a vulnerable side that I felt no one was ever really able to see, and it made me want to do the same.

But, what was I thinking?

Gods help me. What was I doing?

I came to a stop. My heart fluttered in my chest as my breathing became rapid and uneven. Fuck. I was about to leave Solace and travel to the Inner Kingdom to enter trials that no one had survived. Gods, no one had survived the first one, and yet I was supposed to win all three? Every shifter before me had failed and died.

I dropped Daxton's hand and tried to steady my shaking limbs.

"Skylar, what is it?" Daxton immediately sensed my distress. He reached out to try and pull me back toward him, desperate to help in any way he could.

I knew he meant well, but I couldn't allow this. No … that wasn't the whole truth. I could not allow myself to even imagine this, whatever this was.

I put my hand on his chest to push him away. "I … I just need some air. I need to be alone for a moment. This is all just—"

"Take all the time you need," he answered in a flat tone, sincere concern flooding his expression. I could tell he wanted to reach out and close the distance between us, and I would be lying if I didn't want that, too. But … I couldn't. We couldn't.

I turned away, shutting my eyes, unable to look at him without confessing my selfish desires that I knew were foolish to even imagine.

I ran.

Sprinting through the woods, I lost myself to the wilderness that swallowed me whole. I was a fucking fool. Trying to distract myself with the thought of or imagining feelings for Daxton was naive. I was no more than a hopeful cure for Daxton and Castor. Yes, I trusted them to keep me alive, but I also knew they *had* to. If I died before competing in the trials, then it would be another century of offerings to the queen and the potential destruction of their world before they could find another to replace me.

That was it, right?

It was foolish to hope or even imagine anything different. My head was spinning from the dancing, the wine, and every raw, complex emotion I was feeling. I cursed myself for allowing a romantic emotion like this to creep into my mind. Besides , I had already fallen for that once before. I had almost given myself to a male who only wanted me for my magic, and I was never going to allow myself to be used like that again.

My animal stirred, and I could feel her try to influence me to turn around and head back toward my home. However, I was not in the mood to listen. Instead, I picked up the hem of my dress and ran until the melody of the music faded away to the sounds of nature. Crashing through the trees and various brush, I found a small clearing to calm my nerves.

Collapsing onto my knees, I fell forward, trying to catch my breath.

I was alone with no one else around, so I figured this was a loophole for my one and only breakdown for the night. So, I wept. I cried and wrapped my arms around myself as tears streaked down my face. I looked up to the moon, the Father, sending a prayer for strength and guidance. And then, I prayed to the sleeping Mother for her comfort and warmth.

With long, deep breaths, I braced my hands on my knees and stood in the clearing. "No more," I announced to no one and everyone. "I am Skylar Cathal of the Solace Shifter Pack. I am strong enough to face this challenge and stubborn enough not to lose. I promise, Valdor … I will free you. I swear I will give all that I am to unleash the Heart of Valdor and heal our world."

I reached for the knife I had strapped on my upper leg and sliced my hand. Blood flowed from my palm, dripping onto the stained earth below my feet. This task was not just for my people, the fae, or humans … It was for our entire world. A breeze flew toward me, encircling my body and twirling my dress and my hair up into the air. The birds of the night sang a tune as the trees seemed to sway.

My offering was accepted. Valdor was pleased.

"A promise sworn in blood … freely given and sworn with purity in your words and heart. A vow like that is near unbreakable." I knew that voice.

"What do you want?" I barked as I kept my back toward him. I didn't know if I would be able to control the rage inside me if I turned to look at him.

"Will you turn around so I'm not having a conversation with your backside, Sky?"

"I don't know if you deserve more than that," I answered, crossing my arms at my chest.

"You're right." Well, that reply caught me off guard. "Please, Sky … Just look at me." There was sorrow and regret in his words, which pulled at my heartstrings, which I once thought belonged to him. A breeze kicked his scent toward me, and I could tell he came here by himself. We were alone together in this clearing—just the two of us.

Reluctantly, I half turned toward him, cocking my hip out and giving him a pitiful, disdained look. "Why are you out here, Gilen?"

"Why are you?" Gilen countered as he stepped closer, his dark pants and tunic blending into the trees that surrounded him.

I took a step back, and it made him pause. "I needed some space, *alone*."

"Even though the party I was asked *not* to attend … is all for you?"

I made a mental note to thank Talon for obviously informing Gilen that I didn't want to see him tonight.

"What do you want?" I was cold and indifferent, and I didn't want him here.

"I was on patrol when I heard someone running. I came to investigate, and to my surprise, it was the female of the hour. Alone and crying. Why were you crying, Sky?"

"I was having a private moment, *alone*."

"Were you regretting your decision?" The spark of hope in his voice made my skin crawl. Would he ever stop with this?

"No, Gilen. I am leaving," I snapped. "Stop trying to force this and keep me locked away on your mantel like a prized possession. I refuse your claim and any other feelings you pretended to have for me."

"Feelings that I … *pretended*?" Gilen growled and grunted in frustration. Fisting his hair in his hands and pacing along the invisible divide between us. I could sense his magic curling around him. His roc was right near the surface, ready to leap into action and shift. "Gods, Mother and Father, help me get through to this female," he roared as he stopped and stared at me.

I held out my hand to halt his advance, but he disregarded my warning and lunged forward to grab it, pulling me in close to his chest.

"Gilen, stop," I yelled. "I don't want—"

"I am in love with you, Skylar!" Gilen didn't move a muscle as he stared at me with his deep, somber, honey-colored eyes. Holy. Gods. What did he just say to me? I couldn't believe it. "I didn't say it before. I was a coward that night, and I thought you already knew. Wasn't it obvious that I was in love with you? That I have been for a long time now?"

"How can I know something if you've never told me?" I countered, still trying to push him away. I didn't care what he wanted to say to me. This felt … wrong. It was the only way to describe it. My animal was the driving force behind me denying his claim the night in the meadow … and now it was my turn.

"Stop fighting it, Sky. I love you. I know you love me too."

"No, Gilen," I roared, startling him. He released his grip on me enough so I could move away. "If you loved me … If what you are saying is true and not some lie to convince me to stay here, then you would let me go! You would support me in this decision."

"Gods above, Skylar! You are meant to be my alpha female. You know that. Never before have our bloodlines been able to form a union like this. We will create a dynasty together … A strong pack that will no longer have to cower in fear of the humans or the High Fae. Don't you want that?"

"The war is over. High Fae are not our enemies anymore, Gilen … and not all the humans are evil."

"Bullshit."

I glared at him, my power pulsing. "*I* am half-human, Gilen!"

"A fact I am aware of and will generously overlook."

That final remark struck a hole in my center, and I knew I would never look at him the same way ever again.

"I will *never* be your mate, Gilen." A sense of tranquility washed over me as questions about us all came to an end. "I see now that even if this twist of fate did not fall to me, I would *never* let you claim me. If you really loved me, you would accept all of me and let me choose my own path. My true mate would never force me to do something I didn't want to or place me on the sideline like some prize."

"I will have you, Skylar," Gilen growled and stepped forward, fury now burning in his eyes as he tried to reach for me again. "A *half-breed* … will not deny my claim." His hands grabbed me, and as much as I hated myself for not reacting fast enough, I had to keep my wits about me.

Gilen was stronger, faster, and a superior predator now that he had shifted and unlocked his animal's true power. I didn't know if I could fight him off.

Suddenly, out of nowhere, a large hand reached out and grabbed Gilen by the throat, throwing him aside like he was nothing more than a pebble. I stared, dumbfounded at the tall, fearsome warrior that appeared out of thin air—Daxton.

His cold storm-cloud eyes were locked onto Gilen, death barreling through his gaze. He bared his teeth, releasing a low growl from the back of his throat that had the hairs on my neck stand straight. The ground began to freeze underneath me as sharp shards of ice sprang from the earth, surrounding me and encasing Gilen on the ground. A long silver sword magically appeared strapped to Daxton's back. He grabbed the pommel and unsheathed the mighty weapon, pointing it directly at Gilen's throat.

He spoke slowly, his voice like cold death. "Approach Skylar again and touch her without her permission … I will freeze your beating heart inside your chest and cut you down where you stand." It wasn't a threat. Daxton said it like a promise. "You are only still breathing because I know it will hurt her more if I kill you."

Gilen stood from the ground, breaking through shards of ice with green shimmers of his own magic beginning to float around him.

"This does not involve you," he roared, rising to meet Daxton's challenge. Was Gilen on some kind of imaginary high? Why the fuck would he ever think he could answer Daxton's challenge?

Against a normal High Fae, yes, sure. But not Daxton.

"When it comes to her safety, I will do everything to make sure she is protected."

"Again, it doesn't concern you," Gilen growled, and Daxton answered with his own. These two males were on the verge of killing each other. This duel would only end with death, and I was not going to let that happen.

"Enough! Daxton, I don't need you to step in." I stormed out between them, placing myself in front of his sword, forcing him to lower his weapon. I could feel hatred and rage emanating from every facet of his being. He was willing to kill for me, and I knew Gilen's blood would have stained the grass beneath our feet if I hadn't stepped in when I did. "Daxton," I said again, looking into his eyes and searching for the person I knew hiding underneath the facade of Silver Shadow.

"I never doubted that," Dax replied. His eyes narrowed with annoyance as he sheathed his sword, and I took that as my cue to turn my attention back to Gilen.

"H-him?" Gilen stammered. "You are siding with *him* and turning your back on your own people?"

"I am siding with Valdor, Gilen! That is what you don't understand. Daxton is on my side because we are both fighting for the same thing. We both want to heal our world and free it from the wilt."

"Oh, really?" Gilen huffed a laugh. "That's all? And if you decide not to go … how would the high prince react? Would he simply just let you go if you decided to be my mate?"

"That's not even—"

"You are one of the most dim-witted, narrow-minded alphas I have ever met," Daxton spat with an ice-cold tone. He looked at Gilen with a look of pure disgust. "I would honor Skylar's choice. No matter what she decides, I will support her decision."

"Why?" Gilen pressed. I could tell he was trying to get at something, but I just didn't know what.

"Because, unlike you … I *respect* her."

Well, damn. If that wasn't the base for a strong foundation, then I didn't know what was.

Gilen narrowed his eyes and mumbled something under his breath. With my focus on Daxton, I missed what he said, but apparently, Daxton didn't.

Silver flashed, and Dax reappeared on my other side, punching Gilen square in the face and knocking him backward into the ground.

"Speak that way about her again, and I will end your pathetic excuse of a life. I don't care what position you hold or what treaties still stand."

I rushed over to Daxton's side and desperately tried pulling him back. "Dax—"

He was shaking with rage. I wasn't sure what Gilen had said, but I knew from the look in Daxton's eyes that if I didn't get him out of there, he would kill Gilen. Our soon-to-be alpha wouldn't be an easy victory, but I didn't want this bloodshed on my conscience. Either way it turned out.

"Take me back home, please, Dax. I am done here, and I want to go back." Gilen rolled over and sprang to his feet. Blood poured down his face as his breathing became rapid and uneven. He was about to shift. "Please. Now, Dax!"

Daxton snapped his head toward me and looped an arm around my waist, possessively pulling me close to him. I molded into his frame as his arms tightened around me, holding me up and supporting me, just like he always did. I opened my eyes toward Gilen and prepared to speak to him for what could be the last time.

"I hope you find balance and happiness, Gilen. Become the alpha our people need to not only survive but thrive. I know … you can do this."

"Skylar—"

In a flash, we were standing in the clearing, and the next, I was alone with Daxton at the front entrance to my family home. Daxton didn't say anything, and I didn't feel the need to explain anything either. Neither of us moved away from the other as I leaned my heavy head onto his shoulder. To my surprise, he didn't turn me away. Instead, he wrapped his other arm around me, holding me up just in case I wasn't able to stand any longer on my own. We remained on the front steps for a long time, leaning into one another and embracing each other's comfort. My animal was calm in Daxton's presence, granting me waves of confidence and strength that I didn't feel with anyone else.

Daxton shifted his hold on me, and I tilted my head upward to meet his gaze. His hand gently stroked my face, cupping my chin in his rough, calloused hand. "Are you all right, Spitfire?"

"That is a multilayered question." I grinned, trying to lighten the mood. "But yes. For now, I'm all right."

"Would you like to return to the festivities? I believe there are some still dancing."

"Did anyone notice I was gone?" I asked.

"Of course," he answered, never once taking his eyes off me. "But with the amount of wine drained from the barrels this evening, it was assumed you just went to sleep."

"You didn't think that."

"No."

"How did you know where to find me, Daxton? How did you know I was in trouble?"

He smiled at me, and the butterflies in my stomach began doing backflips while flying. "Because … I will always find you."

I narrowed my eyes at him before rolling them and sighing a huff of a laugh, wrapping my arms securely around his waist. I didn't want him to leave. "Because we will always find each other?" And it was then that I knew—Gods be damned, even against my better judgment—I knew I was beginning to have feelings for him beyond just friendship.

"Glad you are starting to catch on," Daxton answered with a saccharine smile, exposing the dimple on the side of his face.

What I wouldn't give to kiss those dimples. To stroke my hands over his body and taste every inch of him. Desire pooled in my middle, with a deep-seated hunger to reach up and bring his lips crashing down against mine. My chest felt heavy, and my inhibitions began to waver from all the wine. Daxton's eyes softened, and he reached up to brush back the hair along my shoulder. His touch lingered against the nape of my neck, and I could have sworn I felt him begin to lean down toward me. Opening his mouth, he was about to whisper something when a sound cut through the silence of the night.

"Ssskyyyllar," Rhea's drunken voice boomed across the way.

I released my grasp around Dax's middle and backed away shyly. He gave me a toothless grin, mouthing the word, *Tomorrow*. There was a silver flash, and he was gone.

Rhea stumbled, turning the corner of the house, but Talon caught her before she crashed to the ground. I could tell she had enjoyed herself a bit more than usual.

"You got her?" I asked Talon. "Need a wagon or a wheelbarrow for a ride?"

"That wasss … meant for me, right?" Rhea countered. "Because I'm going to take my mate home and ride …"

Talon quickly covered Rhea's mouth with a kiss to stop her from continuing. "Okay, my love. That's enough for tonight. I'm taking *you* home."

"Yesss!" Rhea exclaimed as Talon scooped her up into his arms. "Take *me* home while Skylar takes home that fucking terrifying six-foot-four High Fae with a body that was made for her to s—" Her words trailed off as her head relaxed against Talon's chest. I immediately covered my face in embarrassment, hearing her snores already booming.

"Oh. My. Gods!" I cursed, my palm covering my face, utterly mortified. "She's *lucky* she's already asleep, and Daxton is gone."

"When do you leave?" Talon asked, shaking his head and kissing Rhea's brow.

"Dawn, which I know is only a few hours away. Please promise to meet me before I leave?"

"If we missed you leaving, Rhea would never let me hear the end of it. I intend to live a long life with her, and I would prefer it to be a happy one."

"I agree. See you then." I winked and waved good night.

Magnus, Julia, and Neera were already fast asleep, and much to my surprise, Shaw was sleeping soundly on the chair in the corner of our living room. I imagine Daxton grabbed Castor and magically whisked him back to their ship or wherever they were staying for the next few hours. I stumbled up to my room, exhausted and longing for a few moments of sleep before I stepped onto a ship and sailed away.

# Chapter Twenty-Three

*The darkness was overwhelming.*

*I was bound and gagged with no other soul in sight. I couldn't move my limbs. The weight of iron chains dug into my flesh, blocking any magic from aiding my escape. But that wasn't the worst part about being locked in this dark prison. It was the mind-numbing, deafening silence. How did I get here again? Who was coming for me this time?*

*The faint sound of footsteps began to build as torchlight lingered down a long, dark corridor. Panic started to set in with the scraping sounds of an iron-tipped whip dragged along the stone floor.*

*"No, no," I mumbled, trying to free myself.*

*"My pet …"*

*My heart stopped in my chest. Blade.*

*It was the unmistakable voice of my own personal damnation. The mage who sliced through my flesh bit by bit, conducting experiments on me with a twisted, sadistic enjoyment.*

*"We didn't get to finish our experiments. You were taken away from me too quickly." His voice was growing louder as the torchlight burned brighter. "We have more to explore together, my pet."*

*No. Not again. Please. Gods, not again.*

*The beaming light from the torch appeared behind the locked cell door, and I knew what awaited me on the other side. "Hello, my precious pet. We have more work to do today." As the handle turned, I screamed as torchlight blinded me …*

"No!" I screamed, jolting upward with my hand clutching at my chest. I panted with pure terror, sweat coating my shaking hands and pale white face. I curled up into a tight ball and rocked myself back and forth on my bed, roaring with a deep-seated fear that tore my throat raw. *It was a dream … It was not real. It was just a dream. It. Was. Not. Real.* But each time I closed my eyes, I saw Blade's face behind the cell door.

Shaw came charging into my room, took one look at me, and knew exactly what was happening. He raced over to my bed, grabbed my hands, and pressed his forehead to mine. "Breathe with me, Sky,"

Shaw instructed calmly. I wanted to follow his lead. I *wanted* to catch my breath and steady myself, but I just couldn't. The darkness of my nightmare was folding in on all sides.

Shaw released my hands and threw back the curtain, revealing the morning sun's rays. "Look, Skylar," Shaw demanded. "Open your eyes and see the sunlight. You are not underground. It was a dream; it was not real. You are safe." He returned to my bed and grabbed my hands again. "Focus on this feeling. Ground yourself in what you know is real. Feel the bed underneath you. Focus on the morning sun's warmth and the sound of my voice."

My voice trembled. "It was so real, Shaw."

"I know," he whispered.

Shaw knew all too well what I was experiencing. During this past month, Shaw shared with me that he had these night terrors, too. This was the type of grounding technique that Talon showed him, and it helped bring him back from night terrors.

"Dammit, Blade," I cursed his name … cursed his existence. I would someday end his sorry excuse of a life if it was the last thing I did in this world.

"Skylar!" Daxton appeared in the doorway. His face was tight with concern as he raced over to my bedside. Shaw wisely moved aside so Dax could slide in front of me. "What's wrong? Are you hurt?"

"I'm … I'm … all right," I said with a less-than-steady voice. It was not enough to convince him as he continued to look me over for any sign of injury. "It was a nightmare, Dax. That's all."

He stopped and cupped my face with his hands. "I was already on my way to wake you when I heard your scream."

"It was a dream, nothing more."

"Dreams have more power than you realize, Spitfire."

I bit my lip as the intensity of his stare locked onto mine. A part of me felt a wash of relief to have him here. I knew I could handle myself, but Daxton wouldn't hesitate to cut down any threat that dared harm me. As he proved last night, Daxton was willing to kill for me if needed. He rubbed my cheek with this thumb as I reached up to hold his hand. When our hands intertwined, the spark returned across my skin, and I wondered if he felt it as well.

"I'm all right. I promise."

"Is this the first one you've had since your release?" Daxton asked. He turned to look at Shaw.

"It's not," Shaw admitted on my behalf. Daxton inhaled a

sharp breath, and the look of disappointment crossed his face. I knew it wasn't directed at me. He was displeased with himself for not knowing about my nightmares. "But she is getting better at grounding herself when she wakes up."

"Hey," I interjected, leaning to the side to look at Shaw, "I can answer that too, you know." Daxton sat very still, his hands clutching mine, but I could tell his mind was racing elsewhere.

Shaw fidgeted with his feet. "Yes, but he's a little more intimidating than you, Sky. You have met your match with him around."

*We'll see about that.* I glared at Shaw, who wisely averted his eyes and shifted toward the open door. "I'll give you two a moment and go see what Julia has prepared in the kitchen."

Daxton gave Shaw a quick nod, and he returned the gesture as he moved toward the doorway. It seemed like they were getting along or at least had a basic level of respect for each other.

"Julia is already awake?" I asked before he snuck away.

"We all are," Shaw replied. "There was no way we were going to miss sending you off."

I was touched that even though we were all awake only a few hours ago, they all returned to ensure we had one final farewell. Shit. This was not going to be easy.

"Thank you, Shaw," Daxton said with his eyes still meticulously scanning me from head to toe. He stood up from his kneeling position on the ground, rising to his towering six-foot-four stature.

Shaw remained in the doorway and looked to Daxton. "Look after her for me?"

"On my life," Daxton replied, and I knew without a shadow of a doubt that he meant it.

With that, Shaw took his leave and closed the door behind him.

"What do I need to bring with me?" I asked, trying to forget about the heart-wrenching task I still had waiting for me downstairs. "I realize that I never even thought to ask about what to bring …"

"I'll make sure you are provided for, but I would suggest you bring a small bag, one spare change of clothes for travel until we reach the Inner Kingdom, and perhaps a trinket that reminds you of your home."

"Good idea," I said, looking around my room. "Small … right?"

Dax followed my eyeline to my bookshelf at the corner of my

room. "Small," he repeated. "There are vast libraries in Aelius, where your first trial will take place, and I promise you will have unlimited access to this and my own personal library when we travel to Silver Meadows." Daxton leaned against the door, casually crossing his arms in front of his chest.

"I-I'm going to travel to Silver Meadows?" I asked with surprise. He just said that the first task was in Aelius. Did this mean he believed I would actually win the first trial? I smiled as I waded through the stacks of books on my shelf.

"Something amusing?" Dax asked, and I could feel his gaze following me as I walked to the opposite corner of the room.

"You said *when* we travel to Silver Meadows. Does that mean my persistence is wearing off, and you believe there is hope? Do you think I might actually win the trials and unlock the Heart of Valdor?"

There was a silver flash as Dax teleported across the room to stand at my back. I whipped around to face him, looking up into stormy gray eyes that filled me with a rush of desire I could no longer ignore. He placed a hand on the wall behind my head and leaned his body over mine. The look he gave me left me breathless, erasing all sense of logic and reason from my mind. His scent enthralled me. The wildness of the mountain air mixed with pine set my heart racing, and my animal's power thrummed in my chest.

Daxton was a terrifyingly powerful High Fae warrior, and any other being in this world would be cowering in the corner with him standing over them like this. But for me, it was the opposite. His dominating presence was a challenge, not a threat. When he cornered me like this, or when his magic lashed out and pounded into my flesh, I was always eager to answer his call.

"I never doubted your power, Skylar Cathal. And yes, I am saying your full name to make a point with you." I huffed a laugh as he reached up with his other hand and lightly grasped my chin in his fingers. "You are stronger than you know, Spitfire. You have power burning inside of you that I have waited centuries to find. You have awakened a feeling inside of me that I thought was long gone—never to surface again."

I swallowed a gulp of air as Daxton's hips shifted, his body only breaths away from mine. "And … what *feeling* is that?" I bravely reached up and placed my right hand on his chest, where my arrow had almost killed him. I could see the bold, swirling design of his tattoo peeking out of his shirt near his collarbone, which centered around my mark and decorated the left side of his shoulder.

"Hope," Daxton replied with a half-grin, tilting his head down so his cheek brushed against mine as he pushed away from the wall. My chest was heaving, and I knew by the smug look on his face that he could smell the change in my scent.

Fucking. High Fae.

I never did get the chance to find a release that evening when Gilen appeared at my window. If I was fortunate enough to have some privacy on this trip, I could release all the pent-up sexual tension that Daxton annoyingly triggered.

I glared at his smug yet devilishly handsome smile. "Oh, you know exactly what you are *doing*, don't you?"

"I have no idea what you are talking about." He was a damn good liar, but his taunting, sultry grin gave him away. Bastard. He was enjoying the fact that he could make my body respond to him in this way. He clearly found it humorous to toy with me.

"How long will this voyage be?" I tried to change the subject as I picked out two books from my shelf and stuffed them into my bag.

"It will take us three, maybe four days to sail through the veil and into the Inner Kingdom. We will dock in Niamh Bay and travel on foot to Crimson City. It is there that you will get your first taste of court life amongst my people, but I must warn you that High Fae courts are different from how things are conducted here with your pack."

"Wait, I thought Aelius was where the first task was located?"

"It is," Daxton answered, returning to his carefree lounging posture against the wall. "We need to meet with High Prince Adohan in Crimson City first, and together, we will travel to the capital of Aelius to rendezvous with Queen Minaeve and Seamus, High Prince of Aelius, before your first trial officially begins."

"Oh great …" I didn't try to hide my discontentment at the mention of the fae queen.

"Careful," Daxton warned. "It's clear you will need lessons from Castor before you meet with Minaeve again. That look that you just expressed would earn you a quick trip to the dungeons, champion or not."

"I don't see why my opinion would even matter that much."

Daxton pushed from the wall and stepped toward me, leaning over the edge of my bed and flexing the strong muscles in his arms. Tension began to build in my center as my mind got away from me, consumed by thoughts of those arms holding me like they had last night on the doorstep. Would I ever stop gawking at him? I cursed myself for not having a better grip on my wandering eyes. You would think a shifter who had grown up seeing and being around nude males and females, all my life would be better at this.

"Never underestimate your worth in my presence, Skylar Cathal." He winked, making a point to use my full name. "The queen is powerful, yes, but the dynamics of the courts and realms of the Inner Kingdom are flawed."

"Flawed? How? Is there an uneven balance of power or tension?"

His lip curled up with amusement. "More questions," he said with a spark lighting his gray eyes.

I bucked up my chin and gave him a look. "Does it really surprise you?"

"On the contrary, I look forward to them," Dax answered, trying to hold back the grin that held the secret dimples on his cheek. "Not everyone favors her. It is only her magic that keeps her seat of power—not the love of her people."

"Ya don't say," I exclaimed, cocking my hip to the side and shrugging. "I would have *never* guessed."

"Careful, Spitfire." Daxton's mood morphed, his darker, more serious demeanor coming to light.

"I'll be careful, I promise … I promise. It's just you and me in here, so I'm not holding back my opinions."

Dax crossed his arms in front of his brooding chest and mumbled to himself. "While I am pleased that you are open and honest with me, it seems your lessons with Castor will need to start sooner rather than later."

"What do you mean by that?"

"My brother is unlike any other when it comes to understanding and, at times, manipulating the different fae courts within the realms. He is my second because while I command and lead the armies of Silver Meadows, he is an expert at interpreting motives and can adapt to any situation thrown at him. Castor is the reason I was able to begin forming allies, and he understands the workings of the three different realms of the Inner Kingdom better than anyone I know."

"That is … impressive."

"He is a spectacle, however. I wouldn't dare tell him you think so highly of his skillset or else it will go to his head."

"Very well," I said with a tittering laugh. "But what exactly will he teach me?"

"Cas will teach you the art of deception and give you a brief but vital history lesson of the various royal houses. He will teach you about those you can trust and those that you need to approach with caution."

"What about my training with you?"

"Don't worry." Daxton grinned, and it struck a spark through me that both terrified and intrigued me at the same time. *Calm down …* I scolded myself. "Our training will take place each day before your session with Castor."

"Good."

I opened my dresser, realizing I was still in the same dress from last night. There was no way sailing in open waters would be comfortable in this outfit. I found my brown leather pants and decided to pair them with a matching quarter-sleeved brown jacket layered over a white tunic that laced around my middle. It was lightweight and comfortable—perfect for long days of travel.

"Would you mind?" I lifted my hands, pointing toward the door. "I need to change. I won't be wearing this dress on our voyage."

"No, I don't mind," Daxton answered as he raised his brows and chuckled, appearing to make himself comfortable.

"Out."

"Oh. You should be more specific with your requests, Spitfire." His deep laughter followed him as he turned around on his heels in the direction of the doorway. "I'll be downstairs. I hate to rush you. But the ship is ready to sail, and we need to leave promptly."

"I understand." I sighed. "But the longer you linger, the longer this is going to take."

"No peeking?" Daxton asked, stalling in the doorway.

"No. Peeking." I marched over and promptly shut the door in his handsome, complacent face.

I dressed quickly and made my way down to the living area, where all of them were waiting for me. I noticed Daxton step aside, excusing himself out toward the front porch so I could say goodbye to my family.

"We wanted to send you off here," Julia said, holding back her tears. "It would just be …"

I rushed up to hug her tightly. "I know." If they followed me to the boat, I didn't know if I would have the strength to board.

I turned to Neera next, lifting her off her dainty feet and squeezing her as tight as I could. "I love you, sis." She hugged me back, kissing my cheeks before rushing to Julia's open arms.

Talon and Rhea surprised me by sandwiching me between them. "Don't crack a rib," I joked.

"Shut up and accept it," Talon teased.

"No such thing as too much love," Rhea added, and damn them, they were right. I could have held onto them for another hour, but I knew time was slipping away. "Until we see you again." Rhea braved a smile as Talon held onto her tightly.

I was so thankful that they had found each other. A true mate bond was never something Rhea really wanted, but by the look on her face, she could never live without it now. Their bond was something I envied, and I hoped to feel even a fraction of that someday.

Finally, it was Shaw's turn. "I won't say goodbye to you," I said.

He was confused for a second, but then he beamed a cunning smile through his sorrow. "Because this is not a goodbye. It's a see you later."

"Knew you were the smart one of the group. Make sure to keep them all in line while I'm gone, would you?"

"Absolutely. It's a full-time job with this lot, and I'll miss my partner in crime." I leaped into his arms as he pulled me in tight. We never had the romantic kind of connection like the one I foolishly dabbled in with Gilen, but there was a strong sense of companionship with Shaw. I knew I could count on him, and it was the best thing I could ask for in times like this. Shaw released his hold on me so I could say farewell to the final person in my family—Uncle Magnus.

I stepped out to face the shifter who raised me. My uncle … who found me as an infant and took me in without ever asking why. He recognized my father in me and loved me unconditionally like his own daughter. Never once did I feel the agonizing pang of losing a parent because of the love given to me by Magnus and Julia. I even got to experience what it was like to have a sibling when Neera was born. There was never enough I could give back to him—never enough time to thank him for all he had done for me.

"Magnus … I-I …" He lifted me off my feet, and I could feel his teardrops falling on my shoulder. It took everything I had not to break down in the doorway. I knew if I was ever going to turn back and renounce my vow, it would be here. But I also knew Magnus would never let me do it.

"You can do this, Skylar. We will see each other again … And not in the next life, but in this one." There was no holding back my tears now. "My daughter, you are a true blessing. We simply have to share you with the rest of the world now." Magnus released me and kissed my brow, deeply inhaling my scent before stepping back to Julia's other side.

My family. They were the reason I was risking it all, and I took a moment to memorize each one of their faces so that when I closed my eyes, I would remember them.

"I love you all." I boldly turned to face the unchartered fate that lay before me. I closed my eyes, breathing in the scent of my home, and putting it all to memory so that when I was scared or felt alone, I knew I had this waiting for me to return to.

Daxton waited patiently on the bottom steps of the porch. His dark tailored shirt and pants framed his strong shoulders, which I wanted to bury my face into and cry, but I held back. I kept my chin up high and dared to take the first steps away from home.

As I found the last step, he reached out his hand to grasp mine. "Let me take it from here, Spitfire."

He moved behind me, placing his chest against my back as he encircled me and held onto my hands. The world flashed silver, and in one single breath, I was standing on the green sand beach, looking out onto the ship anchored in the sea that would carry me away from home.

"Ready?" Dax asked.

I knew Dax could teleport us directly onto the ship's deck, but he stopped here—just for me. This was a special pit stop for me to say my final farewell to my home. I didn't know how he knew, but this beach was a very special place for me. I reached down to scoop a handful of olivine-crystalized grains of sand, reliving all the memories I had of this place.

My homeland held so much love and happiness. But it also held betrayal, and horrors I knew I would forever be fighting to escape. But how can we admire and treasure the joys without knowing the darkness?

I bravely stood and faced the stoic fae warrior at my side. "I'm ready."

There was no hint of fear or a whisper of regret when I spoke to Daxton because I truly was ready. I said my goodbyes and was at peace with what fate had in store for me. I was ready to leave my home and discover an entirely new world full of danger, uncertainty, but perhaps most of all, *hope.*

I extended my hand, and Daxton latched onto me once again,

teleporting us in a flash of silver onto the deck of the ship awaiting us in the harbor. I took a step to steady my wobbly sea legs as I glanced around at the beautiful vessel that would carry us across the sea.

The boat looked to be about one hundred feet long, with a double mast carrying three white sails apiece. The mainmast held a crow's nest at the top, and I could make out a sailor pulling at the rope to help secure the sails. The rest of the fae crew quickly followed silent commands, readying the ship for departure on the parting sea that divided the Inner Kingdom from the rest of Valdor.

I watched them all with a sense of awe. Each one of them was unmistakably High Fae. It was one thing to know I was traveling to the Inner Kingdom, but experiencing it was different. I would be the only shifter and/or human, submerged into a culture I did not understand or really fit into. Yes, shifters originated from High Fae with the magic of the Heart of Valdor and the creation magic of the gods, but that was a very long time ago.

But perhaps we weren't as different as it seemed.

A slender male wearing a long sea-green coat with a sword strapped to his waist approached me and Daxton. "Silver Shadow, we are ready to set sail for Niamh."

"Very good, Captain Fjorda," Daxton replied, hovering close to my side.

The captain had tanned skin with deep, unsettling seafoam-green eyes that churned like the sea. His long light-brown hair was pulled back in a ponytail that fluttered with the sea breeze, highlighting his pointed fae ears and high cheekbones. Like Daxton, he had a neatly trimmed beard, speckled with blond and brown, that outlined his firm jawline. Apparently, beauty was a common trait among the High Fae.

"Is this … *her*?" the captain asked, and it seemed like the entire crew stopped and fell silent.

I glanced around at all the new faces, their attention collectively set on me. Each sailor on this ship had weathered expressions, but they were not worn from exhaustion. Instead, it looked like they were sun-kissed by the Mother herself and molded by the love of the sea. The salty air clung to their scents like it was seawater that flowed through their veins instead of blood. The lines along their eyes told stories of happiness and pangs of joy and sorrow, and they all looked intently at me.

"Yes. This is the female shifter that *volunteered* for the trials." Daxton remained by my side, his hand discreetly brushing against my back.

Captain Fjorda surprised me when he knelt in front of me and bowed his head. "Thank the gods, Mother and Father, for bringing us their child to save us all."

The other High Fae on the deck all did the same thing, and the ones hanging from the mast or along the sides lowered their heads, each of them repeating, "Thank you, Great Mother … Thank you, Great Father."

Fjorda arose and reached to secure his sword at his hip. "Welcome aboard my ship, fair shifter. You may choose any lodgings you wish. The *Opal* and its crew are honored to ferry you into the Inner Kingdom."

"The *Opal*?" I asked, glancing around.

"The name of my ship, of course. A beauty such as this must have a name to honor her, and pray tell, what is your name, beautiful champion?" Fjorda stepped closer, his gaze looking me over in an inquisitive way. His eyes lingered a little too long, in my opinion, and it made me feel uneasy. Daxton's power pulsed around us in response, almost like a warning, his gaze turning hard as it bore into the captain.

Did Daxton not trust the captain? Was he a steward of the queen, and someone I needed to be on guard around?

"Skylar Cathal," I answered, with my attention darting toward Daxton's touch that remained on my back.

"Cathal?" Fjorda repeated my last name, looked to Daxton, and then again to me. He halted his approach, and the intensity of his lingering gaze began to diminish. "That is an old name … I have not heard it in some time, but still."

"Or you can call her Spitfire," a familiar voice added, waltzing into our circle of conversation. "That one seems to fit her best."

"Castor," I answered with a beaming grin, turning toward his approach. I couldn't help but giggle at how he carried himself once he joined us. "Don't tell me you tried to go head to head with Rhea last night."

"That shifter …" Castor managed to find a barrel to sit on and hung his head in his hands. "That is not a normal female."

"You let a female best you at drinking, Cas?" Daxton asked, clearly taunting him with a low booming voice. "That's very unlike you."

"If I had the energy to argue right now, I would." Castor glared at Daxton with a fiery stare. "But the world is spinning, and we are about to sail out into the unstable sea. Can you make fun of me later when I have two sturdy legs to stand on?"

"Where is the fun in that, Cas?"

"I mean it, Dax. Back off for now, would you?"

I left Daxton's side and went to where Castor was sitting on top of a barrel. Without asking, I gently placed my hands on either side of the temples of his forehead. "Do not throw up on my boots. These are the only ones I packed for the voyage," I warned.

Castor's eyes widened as he looked behind me at Dax. "What are you—"

"Shh," I silenced Castor as I called upon my healing powers to untie the knots of pain in his mind from divulging in too many spirits in one evening. "There. That better?" I smiled as I stepped back to examine my handiwork.

"You're a gods send, Sky!" Castor boasted. "Dax, we need to keep her around—always!"

"She is not a tool or a toy for *you* to play with, Cas," Dax scolded. "Spitfire, I advise next time you let him suffer a little longer, so he learns his lesson. But I do agree with the latter part of his statement."

"It can be handy," I said with a sarcastic wink and salute to Daxton. He smirked at me and rolled his eyes with an amused huff of a laugh. "I do this all the time for Rhea."

"You have magic? You can heal sickness?" Fjorda's jaw was hanging open—about to fall and hit the deck of his ship. "How?"

"I am not *just* a shifter." I felt like I was announcing it to the whole crew, and it turned out I was. All eyes were on me again. Each High Fae within hearing distance stopped what they were doing to listen to my explanation. "My mother was human … Well, a mage, I believe. I inherited my magical gift of healing from her."

"This is intriguing." Fjorda stroked his blond speckled beard, glancing at Dax and Cas. "She might be the hope we have all been waiting for." Whispering erupted all around us, and I couldn't hide the wave of nervousness from my expression. The captain noticed and quickly ordered everyone to return to their stations immediately. "The winds are calling. Back to your stations."

"Let's have a look around the ship," Daxton suggested. "I will take you to the stern, where there are different quarters you can choose from for our trip."

"Choose any you fancy," Fjorda added. "I am at the bow of the ship, but other than that, take any you wish. Unless you would prefer my company, then I would be happy …"

A low, almost menacing growl escaped from Daxton as Fjorda's eyes snapped up to meet his. No longer was Dax standing behind me, Silver Shadow had taken his place.

I watched Fjorda swallow a trickle of fear and straighten his shoulders, one hand slowly creeping toward the pommel of his sword at his hip. A twinge of excitement tingled along my spine to see Daxton's reaction. I relished in his protectiveness. This violent side of him didn't scare me; in fact, it seemed to do the opposite.

"Thank you, but I will find my own quarters," I answered, placing my hand discreetly on Daxton's side. He responded to my touch, tilting his shoulder toward me and softening his gaze as he looked in my direction. Fjorda nodded, darting his eyes between the two of us as he wisely took his leave.

"This way," Daxton said in a low, hushed tone, never once taking his eyes off me.

I followed Daxton as we carefully walked around the busy sailors preparing the ship to launch out to sea. Each High Fae had remarkably gorgeous features. Their sun-kissed skin from a life on the open sea showed signs of weathering, but it only added to a layer of their beauty. They glanced at Daxton as he passed them by, giving him a wide berth like a shark approaching a group of minnows, but it wasn't fear shining in their eyes. They looked at him with a deep sense of awe and respect that nearly took my breath away. Respect and honor. These were the qualities I knew these people saw when they looked at Daxton. He acknowledged a number of sailors and thanked them for their service in ferrying us across the sea passage. Many thanked him in return, and he humbly accepted their gratitude, trying his best not to interfere with their work and being mindful to stay out of the way when he could.

"It never stops," Castor whispered as he came to my side.

"What never stops?"

"Daxton is revered nearly everywhere we go in the Inner Kingdom. They know that he sacrifices his life and power to the queen to protect us. And no …" Castor paused and gave me a sideways glance. "He does not broadcast or boast about it. Trust me, that's the most annoying part."

"Opposite of what you would do, I imagine," I commented back, snickering and rolling my eyes.

"Are you kidding me? Of course I would! If I had the fawning attention my brother does, I would definitely use it to my advantage. And the advantage of being welcomed in every city, in every house, in every bed …" Castor winked, flashing me a sinfully dangerous grin.

"Castor!" I yipped as I smacked his shoulder, but he didn't even seem to flinch.

"Dax really needs to start your training soon," Castor teased. "If that is the best punch you can throw, we may need to rethink you being a 'hope' for us all."

I balled my fist and stepped into my swing this time, hitting him straight in the center of his chest. "Ohh." Castor flinched as he stepped back. "Well, that's a little better anyway."

"Her training will start this evening, Castor," Daxton called from up ahead. "That also gives you time to plan what you will be teaching her on this journey."

"You have your work cut out for you, Dax. I don't envy your role in this one bit."

"I am not hopeless," I argued back at Castor's latest comment. "You want me to prove it?"

"Cas," Daxton grumbled.

I looked at both of them and noticed a silent exchange between the two brothers.

"All right … I'm backing down." Castor raised his hands and stepped back. "You're getting touchy in your older years, Dax. Why not relax and have some fun?"

"Inviting me to have fun landed you with a busted nose last time, brother." I could see the hint of humor light up on Daxton's face as I happily leaned back to watch the show. "Skylar could use a demonstration before we begin our training—care to oblige?"

"Not one fucking bit. I remember the last time I was your demonstrator with Zola, and that did not go well."

"You also need to train, Castor."

"And I will—don't worry. I can't give up on this gorgeous physique. What would my adoring companions say?"

"That fate smiled on them because they no longer held a desire to bed you," I mumbled, but they both heard me loud and clear. Daxton was struggling to hold back a laugh.

Castor scowled at me. "Clever, *shifter*."

"Come on, Sky. Let's find you a place to rest." Daxton stepped to my side and escorted me to the back of the ship.

"I'll go meet with Fjorda. I doubt, after that fun pissing contest a few moments ago, he would be comfortable meeting with only you, Daxton."

"He should have known better," Daxton answered plainly. I

looked at them both, confusion etched into every fold of my face. What were they getting at?

"I have little doubt he will be testing that line again." Castor and Daxton looked at each other for a long moment, not saying anything aloud, but there it was again. "I will make sure he understands."

"It would make the trip more tolerable. I'll meet with you soon after I show Skylar to her room." Daxton gave a nod of dismissal to Castor before he turned around toward the front of the ship.

"See you later, Castor." I waved, cocking my brows skyward.

"Oh, joy …" he answered, rolling his eyes with a heavy sigh. Castor shook his head and turned away to meet with Captain Fjorda at the stern of the ship.

"I didn't overstep, did I?" I asked Daxton once Castor was out of earshot.

"He will be fine. Since our absence from Silver Meadows, I imagine he misses the banter. Zola never lets him get away with anything, while Gunnar only encourages him. It is an interesting dynamic back at home, but never dull. It will be nice to have another sane mind around to help keep them all in check."

I stopped tilting my brows upward and turned my head to the side. So many emotions were rolling through me that I didn't know what to make of this. "You sound so certain that I will get to meet them."

"I'm convinced that you will make it through the trials, Skylar. You are different from every other champion selected, and you have given all of us a reason to hope for a better life."

"Explain *how* I am different exactly." I crossed my arms, still skeptical. "That part is not making much sense to me."

Daxton smiled a large, toothless grin. "Because … no one has ever volunteered."

"Is that why Fjorda and the other fae on the ship were—"

"Yes." Daxton nodded, and it was like a switch in my mind clicked. No one had volunteered to go. Everyone else must have been forced. A deep sadness for the former champions lurked in my heart. "Come on, let's find you a suitable cabin on this ship," Daxton said, reaching up to place a hand on my shoulder.

"I'm interested to hear more about Gunnar and Zola," I added as I stepped to his side once more. We walked to the back of the ship, where an intricate wooden railing designed with crashing waves created a peaceful overlook. "Along with anything you want to share about your home."

"I would be happy to tell you—" Daxton stopped mid-sentence, his gaze shooting upward into the sky.

"What is it?" My line of sight followed his, and I was able to see why he froze on the back deck of the ship's bow. A large roc was soaring over the ship, its golden wings with black-tipped feathers blocking out the sun as it soared through the clouds and down toward the water.

Gilen.

I stood my ground, prepared to fight him off in his beast form if I had to. There was no way he was going to pull me off this ship.

"Get behind me, Skylar." Daxton pushed himself in front of me as a silver sword materialized along his back. He wrapped a protective arm around my middle, but I sidestepped him and dove to the railing.

"No, Dax. I won't hide behind you." I was not a cowering damsel in distress who would fall to the side while a male stepped in to handle my business for me.

The majestic roc swooped down, hovering behind the ship in mid-air, staring straight at me, with Daxton close behind. His massive wings flapped to keep him hovering as he squawked and turned his head. I didn't understand him. Gilen was not yet the alpha, and he couldn't speak into our minds yet as his father could. What I could see in his eyes, however, were tears. The mighty animal flew closer before soaring back up into the open sky. A loud, sorrowful call sang from his chest as he released his clutched talon. A small rock tied with a string and parchment fell through the sky, landing in my outstretched hand over the railing.

Gilen took one final swoop past the ship and flew back toward the direction of the green sand beach. My heart was bursting as I saw members of my pack lined up along the shore. A long, beautiful howl sang across the water, and I knew it was Rhea saying her final farewell.

"I'll see you all again," I promised, clutching the rock to my chest.

"I know you will," Daxton answered.

# Chapter Twenty-Four

I blindly picked the first room Daxton showed me. Still trying to unpack all that had just happened, I walked into the small private quarters to sit on the rickety bed that stretched along the edge of the room. I clutched the stone Gilen dropped for me against my chest as I stared off into the small space.

I knew Daxton was still with me in the room as the door latched closed. He didn't leave me alone, and I was actually thankful for his company. I didn't know if I wanted to talk to Daxton about Gilen, but his presence was still comforting.

"Do you want me to leave?" Dax finally asked after I continued to stare at the wooden planks of my wall in silence. Gods, I must have looked like a mess.

"Stay, please," I asked with a shaky voice. "It's nice having you around. But I don't know if I can talk about this—"

"There is no need to explain or rationalize how you feel, Spitfire. You asked me to stay … and I will remain with you until you say otherwise," he answered as he slid onto the opposite side of the bedding I was resting on.

With the size of the room, there was nowhere else for him to sit, that was what I told myself anyway. I felt a rush of tension melt from my shoulders as I dropped my clutched hands into my lap. Daxton's calming presence helped settle my shaking nerves, and even if I didn't want to talk to him, I couldn't stomach the thought of him leaving just yet. I appreciated his understanding and the absence of pressure he was placing on me to discuss what had happened. I knew he would sit here with me all day without me even having to ask him.

Slowly, I opened my hands and turned over the rock that Gilen dropped from the sky. A delicate portrait of a fireweed flower was painted on the backside, and attached was a piece of parchment with my name written on it in Gilen's handwriting.

"What flower is that?" Daxton asked, looking down at the stone.

"Fireweed. It's a wildflower that grows near the mountain

ranges of our pack lands."

"Is it your favorite?"

I paused for a moment, wanting to be honest with him, even if I wasn't always honest with myself. "It's one of my favorites, but it's not the one I love the most."

"I see … The coloring is beautiful. I don't believe we have this flower growing in the Inner Kingdom."

"Gilen is a talented painter." The silence following my compliment overtook the room. Daxton didn't leave, but I sensed him shift away from me, putting more than just space between us. He was uneasy when I mentioned Gilen, cautious even.

I untied the parchment and read the small bit of writing inside:

*I am sorry I was scared and acted so foolish, Sky. Please be safe … you truly are the best of all of us. Yours Always, Gilen.*

Well, that was not what I was expecting. Daxton didn't look to read the parchment. Instead, he tried his best to interpret my reactions, carefully monitoring the smallest shifts or expressions for any indication of how I was feeling.

"I accept his apology." Daxton tensed as I started speaking. The tension between us in this small room was so thick that you could slice it with a knife. "But it doesn't change how I feel about him."

"How do you feel about him, Skylar?" There was a change in Daxton's tone that caught me by surprise. He always spoke so confidently, but this time, his voice wavered with uncertainty.

"I thought I truly loved Gilen, but we were never meant to be." Gods, I finally admitted it—I even said it out loud. I thought for the longest time I had loved him, but after his betrayal and relentless attempts to force his claim on me … I realized it wasn't love. It couldn't be. Perhaps I was simply in love with the idea of him. "I will care for him as my friend, always, but I realize now that I never truly loved him. I couldn't give my heart to someone who would seek to control me like that." Daxton tilted his head my way, listening intently as I continued. "Before you and Castor even arrived … I felt like I was missing something. I was always daydreaming, wrapped up in the lives and places the characters in my books would get to travel and experience. I was wandering in my old life until …"

Here was my moment. I could jump off the cliff and hope there was someone there to catch me—even if I was terrified to take the leap. "I don't know," I mumbled, turning away from Daxton. "I … I guess I changed. Fate had a different path for me to find."

"I see," Dax answered again. Glancing back, I couldn't read

anything from his expression as he kept his gaze cast to the floor. "Did you change? Or did you simply become who you were always meant to be?"

My animal's awareness piqued, and it surprised me to sense this staggering presence from her. "Fair question," I answered. "I guess we will have to wait and see." I stretched my arms out wide and accidentally brushed my fingers against his hand. The moment I touched Daxton's skin, my animal seemed to sing a soft, quiet melody in my head. I immediately recoiled and jumped up from the bed.

Daxton didn't move. "Everything all right?" He stared at his own hand before slowly looking up at me.

"Hmm? Oh, yes, I'm just hungry or something or tired. Probably both … I missed out on Julia's breakfast because I was distracted by my goodbyes."

"I'm beginning to wonder when you are not hungry," he teased. "Well, you are in luck," Daxton added as he pointed to my bag. "Take a look inside.

I scurried toward my bag near the door and hurried to loosen the top. "Oh Julia, you beautiful killer mountain kitty." I smelled the buttery biscuits and fresh ham without even opening the wrapping. I took out a biscuit and opened it, placing a slice of cheese and meat inside. "Okay, you've got to have one." I handed one to Daxton and made another one for myself. "Well?" I asked in between bites of deliciousness, waiting for his reaction.

"I have to say, this is delightful. Am I to assume that as long as I have your company, there will be more meals that rival the pasta dish and this breakfast?"

"I don't come any other way. What can I say? I like to enjoy the food I eat." Daxton almost choked on his breakfast and punched himself in the chest to get his bite down. "You, okay?"

"Yes, it's nothing …" he coughed. "Just swallowed wrong, is all."

"Uh-huh." I didn't buy it for a second. He was trying not to burst out laughing and almost choked on his breakfast. It was very un-high-princely of him, showing me a softer side to the terrifying Silver Shadow facade and letting me see the true Dax he was inside. "*Friends* … should not lie to each other," I bantered.

"Friends." Daxton's soft smile of amusement made his hard features soften, making him even more handsome, if that was possible. "I hope you know I only have the best intentions for you, Spitfire."

"I told you that you could call me Sky … Remember?"

"I know." There it was again. That knee weakening saccharine grin I only saw when it was just the two of us. The one that could make my insides melt, even if I was frustrated or upset. "But I enjoy the nickname I have for you. And I'll use Skylar when I really need to get your attention."

"And your point is?" I could feel my animal spinning like a top inside me.

"There is a reason …" he answered in a sing-song voice that teased me with a secret. Seriously, ugh, was he ever going to give me a straight answer?

Suddenly, a rogue wave crashed against the ship and rocked me forward into the bed—directly on top of Daxton. I was utterly speechless as I sprawled on top of him. Daxton caught me from crashing into his face, his hands bracing my hips as my arm braced the wall next to us. I was just inches from his face, looking straight into his luminous gray eyes that drew me in like a moth to a flame. My animal pushed her power through me, and I knew my eyes were flashing an amber, fiery glow. I moved my knees to straddle Daxton's waist, the weight of my body pressing up against his.

I shifted and placed my forearm on the bed next to his head, admiring how the beautiful streaks of black highlighted his hard yet comely features. I felt the soft touch of his hair on my fingertips as his pine scent flooded my senses, kindling a burning hunger in my center. His hands released their hold on my hips, and I held my breath, waiting to see what he would do.

He didn't move to push me away. Daxton's fingers slowly traced up the length of my torso, caressing me with his gentle touch that seemed to be reserved only for me. Goosebumps trickled over my skin as my nerves seemed to twitch like sparks of an open flame. His hooded eyes flickered with heat as my hips pressed against his. I couldn't detect a change of his scent in the air, but I was beginning to feel a very convincing response building between my thighs. Daxton's expression might have remained unchanged, but I could feel the tension intensifying between us. Feel the desire building … This was not a one-sided attraction.

*Oh Gods. What the fuck was I doing?*

I shook myself and quickly pushed backward off Dax, dismounting from his lap and trying my best to calm my flushed cheeks. "Um, thanks for catching me. I clearly don't have my sea legs yet." I rubbed the center of my chest, where I felt a strong thrumming pulse that matched my quickening breath. My limbs trembled as I waited for him to do or say *anything*. My glazed-over eyes studied him intently as I waited in antagonizing silence. One … three … seven seconds … I never thought time could move this slowly.

Dax sat up and bent over onto his forearms. I didn't know what he was doing, but he closed his eyes for a moment and took a few deep breaths. "I believe balance is a great place to start your training."

"Perfect, sounds good," I said all too quickly. Hell, I was so scattered I would probably have agreed to anything he said without even thinking about it.

"The ship will add another layer of difficulty."

"Outstanding!" I gave him an awkward thumbs-up, and I immediately wanted to retreat inside myself from sheer embarrassment. For crying out loud. One second, I was literally straddling him, and the next, I give him a thumbs-up like a child? I was a complete and utter mess.

Lucky for me, Daxton found my unique charm humorous. That or he took pity on me, which I agreed would be a valid choice. "Rest for now, Spitfire. I will come for you in a few hours. How does that sound?"

"Like a shifter's paradise. I have food and a soft place to sleep. I'm all set."

"Good," Dax said as he rose to leave, closing the door behind him.

I flopped down, curled up in the soft blankets, and turned over onto my side. Before I even heard the door latch, my eyes were drifting shut.

Thankfully, I didn't dream.

After the nightmare from last night, I was worried my dreams would follow me to the Inner Kingdom. But that was a battle for another day. Right now, I needed to focus on mastering everything Dax and Cas were willing to teach me. If I was going to succeed in the trials, I needed to learn how to survive—and fast.

I opened the door to the back of the ship and looked around to see how far we had ventured out into the open sea. Valdor was quickly fading behind us as we sailed southeast. I could barely make out the landmass that contained everything I knew and cared for. Dax said it would be a little less than a week's journey, but we still had to pass through the veil.

The veil was a massive magical barrier that divided Valdor from the Inner Kingdom territory of the High Fae. It was believed that no one could pass through, but apparently, every century, they did so to find a shifter for the trials. According to Daxton and Castor, the fae queen's magic weakened despite her siphoning ability, and unlocking the Heart became their only avenue for helping combat the wilt. That, or the magic absorbed from the life sacrificed from the shifter in the trials.

I still had no idea what the veil looked like or how we would sail through it on this massive ship. It was an impenetrable wall of magic that was erected after the war between the races. Shifters and humans divided the mainland of Valdor, while the High Fae were secluded in their territory. However, we had no idea that they were suffering.

I turned around the corner of the stern to face the open deck space on the other side of our sleeping quarters. I noticed adjacent doors on either side of my own room and assumed they belonged to Daxton and Castor. As I passed by the door to my right, I smelled the fresh, crisp mountain air with a hint of pine, and I knew it was Daxton's. The one to the left had Castor written all over it, exuding his rich wine scent. I marched along the deck until I found my travel companions, Daxton busy building something.

"What is that for?"

Daxton looked up and casually flashed me a half-smile, and I swear my insides fluttered. "Your balance training," he replied.

I didn't know how he managed to do this to me. I knew I was attracted to him. *I mean, who wouldn't be?* He had become someone who not only trusted but respected me, and that was a rarity in this world worth paying special attention to. But the question was, did he see me the same way? Was it even allowed? A shifter-human and high prince of the fae? Ha, right. Fat chance.

Daxton was working on securing curved pieces of wood to a small, circular, flat surface. He ran his hand over the top, and magically, the pieces fused together.

"Wow! What just happened?"

"Hello … It's magic, Sky," Castor taunted from behind me.

"Yes, but … Wait. You can access magic to perform smaller tasks like fusing wood? What else can you do? Does it wane your strength like my healing magic does? What are your limitations? Can all High Fae do that?"

"Dear Gods, female," Castor exclaimed as he waved his hands over his ears. "Silence her incessant questions, would you, Dax? Some of us are trying to work here."

Dax rolled his eyes and placed his balancing apparatus on the deck of the ship. "It's normal to have questions, Castor. You are the one giving her the history lesson, and I can only imagine she will have more."

"Hello … Still in utter shock and disbelief over here," I announced, placing my hands on my hips and pursing my lips. I stared Dax down, trying my best to give a menacing look and force him to answer me.

"That's cute," he teased.

"It won't be cute in a hot minute if I don't get some answers."

"Challenging me? Is that wise?"

"For you? No." I crossed my arms and continued to stare him down. "I don't back down easily … Haven't you figured that out yet?"

"Learning something new each and every day with you, Spitfire." He grinned.

"You are very … very lucky I don't have my bow right now."

"Threats of violence already? How lovely. But tell me, how would killing me get you your answers?"

"Come on, Dax!" I threw my hand up in the air, at my wit's end with his playful banter.

"All right, all right. I'll play nice—for now." He positioned his balance platform on the deck and motioned for me to step onto the flat surface. "But it comes with a price. Get on."

"I don't usually mount things just for fun."

Daxton bit his lip, holding back his laughter. "Clearly. But if you want your answers … you will *mount* my contraption."

I gave him an unimpressed glare. I couldn't believe I walked into that one. I was cautious but stepped onto the weirdly shaped stool. The curved bottom made me sway, and I nearly fell flat on my face. Luckily, Dax was there and caught me before I tumbled over.

"This is going to be tougher than I thought." I grimaced.

"Afraid to rise to the occasion?" Dax arched his brows, giving me a sultry stare.

"No," I answered in a breathy voice.

"Widen your stance and focus on tightening your core. That is the point of concentration when you are in battle. Everything stems from and begins here." He placed a hand on my stomach, and immediately, I tensed every muscle in my body. "Good," he answered, letting his hand linger against my heated flesh. He let go of me and took a tentative step back.

My legs wobbled for a moment, trying to balance the curved pieces underneath my level platform. "Like this?"

"Yes, that's it."

A wave hit the ship, sending me sideways, and my feet slipped out from under me. I tumbled and collided hard with the deck of the ship. "Ouch." I grimaced as I tenderly rubbed my backside.

"Get back up and try again," Dax said in encouragement. "For each minute you manage to last, I'll answer one of your questions."

"Deal!" I sprang up from the deck and stepped onto the balance platform. I focused on my core and found my balance faster the second time around. Shifters, like the High Fae, had heightened physical strengths and senses compared to humans. I was half-human, but I was still able to catch on quickly.

Dax waved his hand, and a small hourglass appeared beside him. "One minute."

I watched the sand drain from the top, each grain slowly trickling down, forcing me to stay balanced for one second longer than I thought I could. When the top was empty, I grinned and threw my hands up into the air. "Done!" Naturally, I relaxed my center and wobbled, crashing face-first back onto the deck. "Ouch."

Daxton tried his best not to laugh. "Indeed, you did. All right, get back up there, and you get one question."

"Restart the time. I bet I'll get two more out of you before I lose my balance this next round."

He gave me an intriguing look and happily turned the hourglass over once I had my balance set on the platform. "Tell me about your magic."

"That question has a variety of different answers, Skylar."

"I plan on being up here until I get them all." I gave him a confident grin, and he nodded his head, acknowledging my slight, although subtle, improvement.

"Magic is different in the Inner Kingdom than on the mainland of Valdor. We believe it has something to do with the veil, but regardless of that fact, yes. I can utilize my magic to complete other tasks when I need to. For example, Castor can manipulate ice, while I can create objects from ice and command them to my needs. Not everyone has the same abilities."

"Do you need to expel your magic in order to keep it balanced?"

Dax looked at the hourglass, and to his surprise, it was already empty. He turned it over. "Yes. Even though the queen siphons my power in her offerings, I need to balance my magic. Using it in spurts helps take the edge off the pressure that builds within our bodies over time."

"Kind of like a gateway or a dam?" I asked.

"Precisely. Castor and other descendants of royal bloodlines can access their unique magic in similar ways, but the less power you have, the less you need to release it. Others simply have abilities to access a well of power, regardless of their bloodline, but they are rare." He glanced to his side again and raised his brows, noticing that he needed to overturn the glass a second time.

"All right. Have you ever used your magic on me?"

Daxton seemed taken aback by this question, but I had my reasons for asking him. "Yes. I admit that I have."

"When?"

"I believe you have to earn another minute before we dive into that." I pursed my lips, determined to get my answer from him. This was important to me, and there was no way I was backing down. I didn't care how hard my legs were shaking or how difficult it was to concentrate. I was going to hold out for one more answer.

The sand completed its cycle, and Daxton turned it over once more. "When you were in the cell of the hunters' lair, I used my magic to help you."

I was so surprised by his answer that I lost focus, tumbling again onto the deck. I remembered every agonizing second of my time in that prison—the pain of each slice of my flesh, the twisted amusement of Blade, who healed and tortured me. The shined-out eyes of my captors didn't hold a single ounce of remorse about what was being done to me.

But most of all, I remembered the pull of death … It promised no more pain, no more suffering, an end to everything I was forced to endure. But then, I remembered a different melody that called out to me. It pulled me back into my body, urging me to keep fighting and begging me not to give up. It was a promise that this would not be my end. That there was something better for me—that there was *more.*

"You can heal wounds?" I asked, already knowing the answer.

"Some, yes. But not like your magic." His voice was heavy like he was fighting some kind of internal struggle to retain his composure and keep him from revealing the whole truth to me.

"You healed me. It was your magic I felt that brought me back from death's door. It drained you. Even after a month, it still …" I couldn't believe how much he had given to help save me. "When you offered yourself to the queen—"

"Yes."

"Why?" The entire ship disappeared from my conscious mind—all that remained was me and Daxton. We were locked into each other's gaze, unable to break away as the invisible tension between us continued to build.

"There's a reason," he whispered with a breathy voice that I could barely hear.

"Care to enlighten me if I earn another minute on the balance platform?"

Dax walked over to me, reached down to grasp my right hand, and pulled me upright so our bodies were pressed together. "Soon."

"Soon?" I asked.

He nodded as he moved to reposition the balance platform. "Again. We need to continue your training. I admit I enjoyed our playful banter, but it is time to refocus our efforts. I won't be responsible for poor instruction when it concerns your success in the trials."

Our training session continued for the next three hours. Dax increased the difficulty each time I managed to balance on the platform for more than three-minute increments. He had me balance on one foot and then the other. Closing my eyes, and then eyes closed again with only the right, then the left foot down. I didn't know perfecting my balance would be so taxing. The smaller muscles in my ankles, feet, and legs were screaming for relief. Near the end of our training, I didn't know how much longer I could stand on the deck, let alone his makeshift platform.

"Good, now stand on the deck and hold a high plank. We need to strengthen your core muscles so your balance improves."

"What?" I asked, slouching over my aching ankles and shaking legs.

"Come on. I'll join you." Daxton lowered himself onto the deck and placed his hands under his shoulders, readying to push up into a high plank position. I groaned in displeasure but inevitably joined him.

"Good. And up," Daxton commanded, pushing upward in one smooth motion.

I lifted myself off the deck and focused all my dwindling

energy on tightening my stomach, remaining steady in a plank position. The ship's casual rocking added a degree of difficulty, just like the balance platform, but I didn't let my disdain show. I looked up in front of me to see Dax looking relaxed and easygoing while my arms and legs were beginning to shake.

*How long is he going to last?*

The seconds, seemed like hours. I couldn't control my convulsing body any longer and collapsed onto the deck. I glanced up at Dax, who continued to hold his plank. "Okay, you won," I grunted. "You don't need to show off anymore …"

His deep chuckle vibrated along the boards of the ship. "This is only my warm-up, Spitfire. While you study with Cas, I will be doing my own training."

"Warm-up? Right …"

Castor joined us with rolls of parchment tucked under his arm. "He can hold that for a solid five minutes, without ever trembling, Sky."

"Five minutes! Yep, I'm out." That was impressive, and a part of me was beginning to wonder what Daxton couldn't do.

"Go study, Spitfire. I'll see you both later."

Castor reached to pull me to standing while Daxton remained where he was on the planks under my feet.

"All right, see you later then, Dax."

"Lucky for you, our lessons will only be an hour," Castor added.

"That's it?" I asked Castor as I followed him toward the cabins located in the stern of the ship.

"That's how long I anticipate being able to stomach your insistent questions," Castor answered with humor in his tone. But a big part of me also knew he was dead serious. I would have to filter them or maybe even write them down and ask Dax later.

I smiled to myself, satisfied with my plan. "That's understandable." I shrugged as we entered his private quarters.

"All right." Castor secured a detailed map of the Inner Kingdom onto the wall of his room. "Let the real lessons begin."

# Chapter Twenty-Five

One hour, my ass.

I managed to keep my questions to a minimum, and Castor ended up lecturing me for an additional two hours. My plan might have backfired, but I was genuinely intrigued by everything he was willing to teach me. The dynamic of the High Fae courts was complex, reminding me of a delicate, deadly spider's web. You would be caught and killed if you stepped the wrong way. However, with a keen eye and sharp mind, you could manage to navigate through the pitfalls and traps.

Castor's quarters were, very fortunately, much larger than mine. He arranged a table near the far wall where he displayed a newly constructed map of the Inner Kingdom. The map was extremely detailed, and judging by the fresh black stains on the palms of Castor's hands, he drew this from memory while I was training with Daxton.

"What are the three main seats of power in the Inner Kingdom, Skylar?" the teacher asked his pupil. Castor was testing me to see if all the information he was spewing was sinking in. Lucky for him, I was not just a pretty face.

"Trick question because technically, there are four."

He grinned and swooped his silver hair from his face. "Very clever—and correct. Please describe the four."

I always prided myself on excelling in my studies. Growing up, we learned to read and write at a young age, and I devoured every scrap of reading I could find. I wanted to know absolutely everything. Maybe it was because my own beginnings had so many secrets that I just had to uncover all the rest.

"High Queen Minaeve is the first." I cringed a little as I said her name and watched Castor notice my obvious discontentment.

"Mastering the art of deception and disguising your true feelings … will be lesson number two." He waved his hand in a flickering gesture. "Go on, and don't forget the details we discussed."

"Minaeve is the high queen of the fae, and she has held her seat of power for well over five hundred years. She holds psychic siphoning magic that can combat and drain the wilt, but her stamina depletes quickly."

"And …?"

"She overcomes this flaw by accepting offerings from the other royal bloodline of the High Fae."

"Which kingdom and ruler is she closest with?"

"Aelius and High Prince Seamus." Castor smiled with a proud gleam in his eyes, so I continued. "Seamus and his family's bloodline hold gifts of the mind, comparable to Queen Minaeve and her siphoning magic. Prince Seamus can read minds, but he must first come into contact with you in order to do so."

"Very good. Aelius will be the most difficult for you to navigate, but we will prepare you by visiting Crimson City first. Which others with gifts of the mind are in his family's bloodline?"

"Anjani, Seamus's cousin and his second, can create illusions. She was the one concealing the ships that traveled to Solace and left with the queen. Rhett is not a direct descendant of their royal bloodline, but he has the powerful gift to see past events through contact with an object. If a murder occurs with a blade, for example, he can pick up the weapon and see what happened."

"Dax and I will also train you to shield your mind to protect itself with your shifter magic to combat these powers. Shifters don't necessarily utilize it, but the magic that is used to shift into your animal forms can be used to form a shield or a barrier. It is not as strong as ours, but when trained, you can learn to protect yourself. Now let's continue." Castor sat in the corner and pointed to the northern area of the map. "Crimson City. That is where we will take you first. What do you recall about the royals there?"

Out of nowhere, a loud, obnoxious rumble echoed across the room. I threw my hands around my stomach and blushed, embarrassed at how much my stomach was voicing its unpleasant emptiness.

"What in the gods' names was that?"

I slumped forward onto the table, letting my forehead fall flat onto the surface. "Look, I don't know how often your people need to eat, but shifters need food … often. Our metabolisms naturally run high, and our stomachs tend to voice their opinions when empty."

He convulsed as he struggled to hold back his laughter. "That … That was your stomach?"

I lifted my forehead from the table and glared at him. My stomach answered with its own empty rebuttal, and that was enough to send my teacher into a gut-wrenching laugh.

"It's not *that* funny," I snapped at Castor.

"Oh … yes, it is," he said, wiping a tear from his eye.

"Castor, we have been at this for almost three hours … And you only said you would last for one!"

"Complaining already? I thought you were enjoying learning about all this. Dax informed me you are a reader like he is."

"No, no. I am!" I waved my hands at him in defense. "It's just that …" My stomach growled again. "After Daxton's three-hour session … and then yours. This is all interesting, but my mind is melting. I'm seeing double, and I can't seem to focus on anything but—" The growling sounded once more.

Castor shook his head, palming his face with his hand. "Shifters are an intriguing specimen. Finish with the Crimson City, and then we can go find that stomach of yours something to eat."

I sat up so quickly that I got a head rush, but it was worth it if it meant I would be eating soon. "Adohan is the high prince of the Crimson City, with his wife Idris and their twin sons Astro and Finn."

"*Mate*," Castor corrected.

"Mate, wife … Is there a difference with your kind?" I asked with genuine interest. This unveiled aspects about the fae culture, piquing my interest far beyond figureheads and territories on a map.

Castor shifted in his seat and leaned forward on his thighs. "There is a very significant difference. Idris is not merely Adohan's wife … she is his *mate*."

"Is it similar to shifters' customs then? We have recognized mate bonds among our kind, and I guess a claim is comparable to a marriage. Some pairings and claims are not from a mate bond but instead are chosen. Is this the same for your people?"

"In a way." Castor stroked his bare chin and leaned farther onto his forearm, deep in thought. "Our mate bonds are more rare compared to shifters. And I don't mean to sound insensitive or an ass when discussing your mate bonds, but there is nothing more sacred than a mate to a High Fae."

"Fat fucking chance it means more," I spat back at him with a simmer of anger laced into my words. "Perhaps they are not as rare compared to your people's, but shifter mates would die for each other, and the pair become possessive while the bond is made. I recall more than a few males and females that would beat the living shit out of any shifter who so much as glanced sideways at their mate. When the claim is made, and the bond sealed for eternity, magic and power are shared between the pair. Not just this life … but for all eternity. It is also common knowledge that the other is not far along when a mate dies. We never take another partner."

Castor mulled over my comment for a moment, likely reading my expression for any sign of lies. Once satisfied, he nodded in firm, brief acknowledgment before continuing. "It seems you have answered your previous question then. Yes, mated High Fae and shifters have nearly identical responses when it comes to their partners. However, ours only occur at a fraction of the rate as yours. Perhaps it was a special adaptation your race was granted when the gods created your kind or a balance to our immortality."

"Good assumption," I added.

"Oh, Spitfire, I never assume. I always clarify." I rolled my eyes at him as he snickered at me. "When a High Fae feels the call of the mate bond, nothing will keep them from their mate's side. The pull to be near them, see them, talk to them, touch them. It is *everything*. I have witnessed the world being torn apart all for the love felt through the bond. No, excuse me, it is more than that. Our mate bond goes deeper than mere devotion. It is a connection—"

"Of the soul," I finished for Castor.

"Exactly."

I had so many other questions about this mate bond, but I thought it best to ask them another time. My stomach was burning a hole in my center, and right now, I needed to eat more than I needed to wonder. A rarity, yes. But desperate times called for desperate measures.

"All right, Idris is the *mate* of Adohan." Castor nodded with a satisfied grin. "They live in the high desert kingdom of Crimson City. Their bloodline has the gift to command and manipulate fire with Adohan and his mate having this ability."

"Be careful where you step and whose bed you end up in there. A spiteful lover can set fire to that beautiful hair of yours if you're not careful."

"This from personal experience?"

"Possibly," Castor replied as he ran his hand through the longer silver hair on the top of his head. "Most important question now … can you trust them?"

Castor mentioned that Adohan was an ally of Daxton's, but for me to personally trust someone? That was a trick question. I was warned never to fall victim to the unknown. Castor constantly reiterated that my intuition would always be my best adviser. Shifters had a unique sense about them with the shared bond with their animals. Even though I hadn't shifted and couldn't until the end of the trials, my animal was still a constant presence for me. Cas encouraged me to listen, to heed her warnings and follow every instinct. In the Inner Kingdom, Castor said my animal would be my closest ally aside from Daxton and himself.

"Not until I meet them for myself."

"Excellent response." Castor stood up from his seat and opened the door. "Now, let us go find some food before you pass out on my table. I didn't plan on hosting just *your* company this—"

I didn't even give him a chance to finish his final thought, not needing to hear the intimate details of his sexual endeavors. I sprinted past the door and eagerly searched for any sign of a meal on the ship. I could smell food cooking and let my nose lead the way. Fish wasn't one of my favorites, but I was too damn hungry to care. I stepped around to our training area and nearly salivated as the reality of a full belly was slowly inching closer.

"I was wondering when Castor would finally release you." Like usual, Daxton appeared out of nowhere, nearly scaring the pants right off me.

I jumped and turned to face him. "Would you stop doing that …" My words trailed off into nothing as my mind turned to mush, right along with my body. Daxton stood mere inches in front of me, holding a plate of steaming rice and fish in one hand while casually flinging his shirt over his shoulder with the other.

My eyes widened as I took in the sight of his taut chest glistening with beads of sweat from his vigorous training session. I felt my animal stir inside me as I allowed my eyes to linger over the spectacle of his body. The muscles in his bulging biceps flexed, connected to broad shoulders that housed a core stronger than the gates of the human king's palace. His rippling muscles along his abdomen flexed as my eyes followed it down to the deep V cut into his lower waist.

Gods … so many emotions were running through me I couldn't seem to get a grip on my control.

"I knew you'd be hungry." Daxton's voice was heavy with a hint of exhaustion. He must have been training the entire time I was studying with Castor.

"In more ways than one, apparently," I answered back, unable to move from where I stood.

Dax raised his brows with a surprised boyish grin as he stepped closer to me. I could feel the heat from his body radiating off his fevered skin. His eyes were watching me closely as he said, "Let me know how I can help … satisfy your needs. All you need to do is ask."

Dammit, that was smooth. Why couldn't I come up with a line like that? Also, what game was Daxton playing? For the longest time, I swore this attraction was one-sided—something I had built up in my crazed, sexually deprived mind. But now, I wasn't so sure. Well, two could play that game. I bit my bottom lip and watched as his gaze lingered there for a second longer than it should. His throat bobbed, and I knew he was interested despite being unable to detect a change in his scent.

"Your hand," I answered.

"And what about my hand?" His hooded eyes sparked with a hint of lust as he shifted closer, setting the plate of food down to his side so our bodies were practically touching.

"You have my food." I grinned and sidestepped him to snatch my plate, skipping over to a barrel to sit on, and began happily eating the fish and rice. I didn't dare glance up, even though I knew he was watching me.

"Didn't get any for me, did you?" Castor sighed. "Typical."

"Don't even start, Cas," Daxton groaned as he waved his hand, and two additional full plates appeared. "I was just *handing* Sky hers." Oh yes, I definitely didn't miss that one. I hid my smirk behind my fork as best I could, peeking my hooded eyes over toward Dax, who was wearing an equally mischievous expression.

"What did you learn about today with Castor?" Dax asked as he sat near the base of the barrel I had perched on.

"The dynamics of the royal bloodlines and different regions of the Inner Kingdoms," I managed to say between shoveling food in my mouth. I know it was not the most ladylike behavior, but they had seen me at my worst.

"Quite a place to begin. How'd she do?" he asked his brother, who delicately chipped away at his meal.

Castor glanced my way, and I gave him a wide grin full of food. "Table manners, I imagine, will follow soon."

I winked at him as I gulped down the bite of fish and rice.

"She's hungry."

"Starving," I corrected Dax. "Starving."

"Yes, her stomach was why we cut our lesson short."

"You had her for three hours," Daxton countered in my defense as he took some of his food. I looked down at him with a soft smile, happy to see I wasn't the only one surprised by the length of my lesson.

"And yet there is still so much more to teach her," Castor added as he conjured a glass out of thin air. He walked over to the barrel next to me, glanced around to see if anyone was watching him, and tapped the cork. "Now, this is a fine wine. Care to try some, you two?"

"Sure." I shrugged while Dax nodded, and Castor conjured two more glasses. "So, did you create these glasses, or just summon them from below deck?"

"Clever question," Castor answered. "It takes more magic to create, so oftentimes, we simply summon items that we know are nearby."

"Isn't that just being lazy?" I asked as Dax fought back a laugh.

"Using and honing your craft is not lazy," Cas countered, sipping his wine. "It is to our advantage to grow in strength." He eyed Daxton. "Just the same as magic."

I pressed my lips together with a thoughtful expression. "I have to give it to you. I agree. I didn't think about it like that."

"No rebuttal or question?" Castor's eyes widened. "I would bow and say my task is complete, but I fear this was a simple stroke of luck."

"All right, that's enough bickering for the moment," Daxton said lightly with amusement. "What did you learn about the royal families, Spitfire?"

"High Queen Minaeve is allied with Prince Seamus in Aelius. He and his family are highly gifted with powers of the mind, telekinesis, illusion, mind-reading, and the ability to see the past through objects—that one seems the most bizarre to me."

"Rhett's talents are indeed unique. What about Crimson City?"

"Adohan, his *mate*," I began, careful to articulate for Castor's benefit, "Idris, along with their sons Finn and Astro, can manipulate fire. Crimson City, unlike Aelius, is allied with you." Dax raised his eyebrows with a suspicious glance at Castor.

"I didn't teach her that," Castor said in defense, holding up his hands.

"Call it my shifter intuition." I smiled as I finished my plate of food and moved on to my glass of wine.

"Shifter intuition, hmm." Daxton swirled his own glass before taking a heavy gulp. "Well, it is right so far."

"Cheers." I bent over and clinked my glass with Dax's, and I could see that spark of amusement twinkle in his gray eyes.

"You have improved today, Skylar, but I assure you that you have a long way to go." Castor finished his meal and downed his glass of wine. "All right, I am off to find my company for the evening if there is nothing else you need from me tonight, Dax?"

"No, brother. You are fine. I'll see Sky off tonight."

*Shit. Alone with Daxton? Calm down … Calm down*, I told myself.

"Who is this *company*?" I asked with a tone I had heard Neera use more than a few times in my life. It was fun toying with Castor. It reminded me of what I had with my cousin. I was beginning to see him in a brotherly role, and for once, I was not the oldest. I now understood the fun of poking fun at your elder sibling.

Castor strutted to the opposite side of the deck as a gorgeous female High Fae appeared at his side. Her beautiful long braided blond hair swung down to her hip, and her deep brown eyes were mesmerizing in the darkening evening light. The female wore a practically see-through night slip that left little to the imagination of what lay beneath. She had it all out on display and rightfully so. Every High Fae I had met held an angelic beauty that made me feel a twinge of inadequacy.

Castor snaked an arm around her waist and pulled her lips to his. She moaned as she melted into his arms. "Good night," he said to us with a playful wink as he led her away to his quarters.

"Cas is never shy about his promiscuous sexuality," Dax murmured. "You get used to it."

"It doesn't bother me. I just enjoy teasing him." I fidgeted with my wine glass as the sun finally set, welcoming the cool evening air. "So … what about you?" Yes, it was an extremely personal question, but I was feeling bold tonight. What was in this wine anyway? I was already feeling the effects of it, and I had barely finished my small glass.

Dax narrowed his eyes and glanced back over his shoulder toward me. "Why do you ask?"

"Curiosity. Have you ever known me to hold back and *not* ask?"

Dax shrugged and took another sip from his glass. "No, in this short time that I have known you … I can't say that I have. I am more private about my personal endeavors."

I uncrossed my legs and dangled them over the barrel, leaning over to get a better look at the high prince sitting at my feet. He seemed relaxed and confident, stretched out and reclining with one leg bent and his arm resting over his knee with his shirt still casually tossed to the side. I imagined the breeze from the open sea helped cool his heated flesh. The cold pine scent that followed him wherever he went was stronger than ever right now, surrounding the two of us on the deck of the ship.

The final rays of the sun kissed his high cheekbones, outlining the concrete jawline and his trimmed ebony beard. I wanted to reach out my hand to caress his face and lace my fingers into his flowing silver-black hair. I wanted to … fuck. This would *never* end well. My animal wasn't helping as she kicked up the intensity of ever-building hunger. I crossed my legs to try and curb the pressure building between my thighs. My gaze wandered to Daxton's lips that I secretly fantasized about tasting for myself.

Shit. I needed to leave. This was not good. I shouldn't be fawning over Dax like this. It was foolish to expect this male, who likely had a plethora of breathtakingly gorgeous females to indulge himself with, to want anything more than an alliance with me. If only I could force my body to listen to my head, this would all be fixed. But it seemed I was unable to do that at the moment.

"What is on your mind?" Dax casually asked as he reached to lightly brush his fingertips against my knee. His touch only spun me up more. Gods, I wanted him to trace his fingers upward along my thighs to my now throbbing center. I wanted those fingers … I wanted those hands on my body again. Liquid heat spread through me, my desire for him rising despite knowing that this could only end badly for me.

"Nothing," I answered, curling my toes and clenching my thighs tighter together.

Daxton's voice dropped into a deeper sweltering tone. "Skylar, it's not polite to lie to your friend."

"Then allow me to correct myself." I folded over, moving closer to his eye level. "Nothing I want to *talk* about."

"But there is something you want to do? Can I lend a *hand*, perhaps? Or another form of aid?"

*Smug* … *Arrogant* … *Handsome* … Dammit, I was royally fucked.

"Nope! Not tonight!" I announced as I pushed myself off the barrel, putting some much-needed space between myself and Dax. "I'm going to bed. Good night."

"Whatever you say." He didn't leap up to chase after me.

Instead, Dax remained seated on the ship's deck, leaning against the barrel and casually sipping his glass. "Until tomorrow, then, Spitfire." His half-grin exposed the dimple on his cheek, and I felt my knees wobble as I began to wind up like a spinning top.

*Get moving*, I told myself. Lust threatened to overtake the rational side of my brain as I practically ran away from Daxton across the deck. I didn't care what my body was feeling or how turned on I was, I couldn't act on these feelings. I wouldn't allow myself to tumble down that hole yet again. I slammed the door shut and crumbled against the frame, melting to the floor with my heart pounding inside my chest.

My animal was insistent on trying to lure me back outside, but I refused to give in. *I know … I know. But that is not going to happen*, I scolded myself. Determined to remain in my room, I sought out one of the books I brought with me. I decided I would read one of my favorite novels to try to escape into another world or spark a new wave of inspiration and quiet my animal from her insistent nagging. Everything would return to normal tomorrow, and I would stop fawning over Daxton.

I turned the dial of the oil lamp, igniting a spark that illuminated the center inside a glass casing. The room was dark after the sun finally set along the western side of the ship. I stripped down into my bindings and underwear before climbing into the surprisingly soft and delectably comfortable bed. Turning down the brightness of the lamp, I settled into my covers and began reading one of my favorite adventures that, of course, had a little dose of romance. I had read this story probably a dozen times in my life. My favorite part was when the two characters destined for each other finally realized what was there all along—love. It was no mate bond, but it was beautiful and pure.

True love, followed by a wild and crazy, world-turning-upside-down kind of passionate sex. I read the descriptions of the characters' enthralled lovemaking, and I would be lying if I said it wasn't turning me on. Laying back, the images sprang to life inside my mind's eye, and I slowly began to touch myself. I imagined what it would feel like to have a male caress me, kiss me, and make love to me with the uninhibited passion described in this story.

I didn't want to just have sex.

Over the years, I could have accomplished that task with a handful of willing males in my pack. No. I needed something more. I wanted a deep personal connection to make the experience special and honor what was being shared. I blamed Neera for her romanticized viewpoint rubbing off on me. Until then, however, I was able to see to my own needs just fine.

I adjusted my bindings, loosening them from my chest, and reached down toward the apex between my legs. My fingers moved across the top of my undergarments, diving beneath the surface, desperate now to release the pent-up tension rising within. The build-up over the past few days was almost unbearable now. I lightly circled myself with my two fingers before pressing down harder and moving them forward and back over just the right spot. Pleasure began to flood my body, and heat pooled in my center as I fell into the euphoric feeling I was giving myself until a very noticeable moan crept through the wall near my head.

*Castor?*

The next sound was clearly from a female, followed by a prominent grunt and some loud, meticulous thumping that could only mean one thing. *Gods help me. I could hear Castor fucking through the wall.*

At first, I was embarrassed … But then I thought, *screw it*, and decided to embrace the situation I was in. It was wrong—so wrong—but also arousing to hear them. I continued to stroke my clit, allowing my fingers to dip inside my folds that were dripping with anticipation as I pictured the scene unfolding on the other side of the wall, hearing Castor tell his female to turn over on her hands and knees as he began pounding her from behind. She screamed for him to fuck her harder as the rhythm of their pace increased.

I grabbed my breast and twisted one of my nipples, imagining someone was here with me, giving me just the right amount of pain to add to my pleasure. I was just about to plunge my slickened fingers inside my opening when a large thud landed right next to my head, jolting me out of my trance. The slapping and rapid erratic sounds changed, and they were now throwing off my mood. *To each their own* … I was not one to judge, but I also wasn't in the mood for something quick and dirty. I wanted something more sensual and slow. So I grabbed my pillow, spun around, and relocated the head of my bed to the other side.

The moaning and bangs of their coitus were reduced to background noise as I continued right where I left off. I fondled myself with my fingers again, followed by slow pulsing circles that got me right back on track. I released my own moan of pleasure as my mind drifted off into a cloud of ecstasy.

"Oh. Gods …" I couldn't help what happened next, and

honestly, I didn't want to. I was no longer imagining Castor and his female or the character in my book. It was Daxton.

It was Daxton's hands that were cupping my breast, and Daxton's fingers that were slowly circling my dripping entrance before diving inside of me. I imagined how his long fingers would feel inside my opening, bringing new sensations and pleasure to life that I had never dreamed of being real. And then I dared to dream what it would feel like to have him fill me with his cock. For him to be my first and bury his hard length deep inside of me, feeding my need for him and satisfying me like no one else could. My thumb—well, in my mind, his thumb—massaged the bundle of nerves at my apex as his fingers danced inside of me, curling them just right.

*I was in trouble now.*

I was in the deep end of the pool, sinking into the daydreams I'd denied myself for far too long. Rational thought was long gone. Tonight, when I saw Daxton shirtless after his training session, I imagined what it would be like to bite down on the base of his neck just below his collarbone as he thrust himself deep inside my aching center. Regardless of the fact that I had no logical claim to him, I wanted to leave a mark on his flesh so no other female would think to take him for themselves. The thought of a powerful male like Daxton being mine drove me higher into a field of pleasurable ecstasy.

His neck, of all things. Gods, there were too many options for how I wanted to kiss and caress just his fucking neck. I pictured Daxton's hands possessively caressing my curves, holding me with a relentless grip that never broke, while his delicious lips crashed into my own—devouring me, mind, body, and soul. Our kiss deepened as Daxton's tongue explored my mouth with a feverish hunger that would never be satisfied. Gods alive, I wanted to taste those lips.

"Yes. Gods, yes!" I moaned as I pumped myself harder, releasing cries of pleasure a bit louder than I had intended.

"Mmmm," a deeper-sounding moan laced with heated pleasure drifted through the wall behind me.

*Daxton?*

I froze. I knew my room was sandwiched between Dax and Cas, and I knew he was on the other side, but … Oh. Gods. Was he alone? Or had he found another female to bed for the night? The thought of him even touching someone else was beginning to send me into a blind rage. So, I stopped and listened carefully.

Silence.

And then there it was again—a deep, sensual moan that

caught my breath in my chest and melted my core. He was alone, and he was doing the exact same thing *I* was. I grinned a wicked, sultry smile and happily continued pleasuring myself, throwing all caution to the wind now. Letting my mind freely wander and picturing Daxton on the other side of the wall.

I slid my fingers in and out of my dripping-wet center, thumbing my clit with the other hand flat against the wall, picturing Daxton's strong hands stroking his own hardened length. I could hear his ragged breath through the thin slits, and it only spurred me on more.

Gods, please excuse me, but I'd bet the fate of these trials that his cock was amazing.

The wall behind me began to freeze. Daxton's magic was spreading through the barrier between us, slowly caressing every inch of my skin. I welcomed the cold touch of his presence, and my animal responded by pumping a surge of power through me to send back to him. The touch of his ice trickled along my neck, slowly outlining my breasts before piercing my already hard nipples. The pleasure was wickedly delicious. The feeling of pain was only there for a second before pleasure took its place. It was almost like he was here with me, our magic intertwining and dancing between the barrier that separated us.

I arched my back as I pumped myself faster. I was so close, on the verge of exploding with an intense wave of pleasure that continued to build and build. The final touch that sent me over the edge was hearing Dax on the other side of the wall moan as a strong blast of his magic hit me. It sent tingles and pricks of sensation across every inch of my flesh. We both shattered, coming together with loud moans of utter satisfaction. Waves of intense pleasure rolled through me as the icy-cold touch of my skin slowly melted away.

Throwing both hands over my head, I felt completely relaxed and satisfied after having one of the most intense orgasms of my life. I moved my bindings back over my breasts and curled onto my side. I was able to find my release, but the thoughts of *him* lingered in the confines of my mind. *I mean, how could they not?* Gods above. I had just masturbated to completion with Daxton. And as odd as that idea might have been to others, I found it incredibly arousing.

I drifted to sleep, picturing Daxton's face.

Was it logical? Nope, definitely not.

But sometimes, I had to ignore the logic and bask in the glory of the moment. In the morning, I planned to deny this ever happened, but for now, this was our dirty little secret.

# Chapter Twenty-Six

In the early hours of dawn, the deck of the ship was practically vacant as most of the crew on board continued to sleep soundly. Only a handful of sailors manned the wheel and various posts, and they didn't even seem to notice my presence. Venturing to the front of the ship, I leaned over the railing to look out into a vast ocean with no landmasses in sight.

"I didn't anticipate this lovely sight as I awoke this fine morning," Fjorda said as his cabin door opened and closed behind him.

"I'm an early riser, and I was able to sleep really well last night." Due to factors I was *not* going to share, but I do admit I hadn't slept so soundly in a long while.

"There is nothing that rivals being rocked to sleep by the waves aboard the *Opal.* I will agree with you there, fair champion." Fjorda turned to one of his crew members overseeing the ship during the night. "Go get some sleep. I will take over for now."

"Yes, Captain." The fae gave a short nod to Fjorda and made his way toward his bunk below deck for some much-needed rest. The sailor paused for a moment as he passed me and tilted his head downward, dipping his shoulder forward as well. It took me a second to recognize the gesture as a bow of respect, but when I did, I gave him one in return. His smile was kind and genuine, giving me yet another reminder of why I volunteered for the trials in the first place. It was not just my home I was trying to save.

"It won't be long now," Fjorda said as he stepped beside me along the railing. "Perhaps another few days. The winds seem to be in our favor, speeding this trip along."

"Long until what?" I asked as the winds suddenly changed. I glanced upward at the flag flying on the mainmast as it twisted and turned around on itself.

"The crisscrossing winds will be the first sign we are nearing the veil." Fjorda looked out onto the sea with his piercing seafoam eyes. I had no idea what the veil looked like or even where it was located in the vast, endless sea. The elders told us that it surrounded the Inner Kingdom on all sides, locking all the fae kind in and keeping all others out. "Prince Daxton is the reason we can safely pass through," Fjorda added, pulling me from my train of thought.

"Why him?" I knew my cheeks were blushing at the thought of Daxton, and I shifted off the railing to try and catch the morning sea breeze.

"He or any of the other royals with enough power can manage to pass through. Each century, we have ferried passengers aboard my ship to find a shifter to unlock the Heart, and each time, the Silver Shadow is always on board. It is practically tradition now."

"Again … why Daxton?"

"Because it strains the magic of my kin," a voice bellowed. Out of nowhere. "I'm strong enough, they are not. It's simple, so don't tax yourself trying to read between any invisible lines." Dax muttered as he came beside me. "Also, I don't like the idea of causing anyone pain or suffering if I can help it."

I jerked and playfully smacked his arm. "Quit doing that! You startled me so badly that I nearly fell overboard. How did you know I was up here anyway?"

He leaned over the side of the railing, lightly brushing up against my arm and sending goosebumps across my bare skin. *When would I stop reacting to him like this?*

"When will you realize, Spitfire … I will always find you."

I rolled my eyes with a heavy sigh. "We will always find each other?" I asked with a heavy dose of sarcasm in my voice. He winked at me with a wide, unencumbered smile, and my insides began smoldering once again.

"I knew Spitfire was a perfect name for you."

The gods be damned, I needed to stop looking at him like that. But when he smiled like that, it made the world around us disappear. It was like nothing else mattered, and that was the most terrifying thought of all. Because there *were* important, world-altering twists of fate that mattered. There were responsibilities that Daxton and I both needed to prioritize. However, these moments of quiet bliss I shared with him were getting harder and harder to turn away from.

I noticed Fjorda looking at us, glancing first at me and then toward Daxton, who hadn't taken his eyes off me since the moment he materialized at my side. "I'll give you two the stern. I need to check on the ship and man the wheel," Fjorda said, giving both Daxton and me bows of respect as he tended to the morning duties of the ship.

And then it was just us.

I didn't know what to say, and I doubted he did either. Should we just move on and ignore everything that happened last night? Should I just casually ask him about our next training sessions or where we could find some breakfast? What was the right thing to do in this situation? It was times like this that I wished Rhea had come with me. She would know what to do and how to navigate this mess.

My chest tightened as I dared to turn my head toward him. "So …" His thick hair was loose, flowing effortlessly in the winds that circled around the ship. I fought back every instinct I had to reach my hand out and run my fingers through it, pulling him closer to me like I imagined last night.

*Yup, I was just asking for trouble now.*

Daxton raised his brows and tilted his head, leaning toward me. "Yes?" Curse that debonair smile of his. Anyone would guess that, right now, he didn't have a single care in the world.

"Last night, I, umm …"

Dax silently reached for my hand, gently turning it over in his rough, calloused palms. He watched how our fingers seemed to dance together in a silent song that only we could hear. "What do you want, Skylar Cathal?"

"Going full name on me, huh?"

His eyes softened as his toothless grin grew wider. "Because I am asking you a serious question. How do you feel about this? What do you want?" His other hand reached up to cup my cheek, his touch clouding my head even more than it had before.

"I-I …" I was speechless. Unable to string together a single coherent thought, but Daxton still didn't pressure me to answer. He patiently waited as I fumbled to articulate what I was feeling. Shit. What did I want? I had no fucking idea … or maybe I did? Maybe I was just afraid to admit it. Afraid to be vulnerable and possibly get hurt.

"I will always respect your choice, Spitfire. I know my focus should be on preparing you for the trials, but …" Dax pursed his lips, leaving his thoughts unfinished. I could see he was struggling with a decision, and I desperately wanted to know what it was.

"I'm not sure," I answered honestly. "This is—"

"It's all right." He gently released my cheek and gave me a reassuring smile as he took a step away. Why did the distance between us seem farther than it actually was? "Are you ready for another round of training this morning?"

His sudden change of subject caught me off guard. "Wait … before breakfast?"

"It won't be as long this morning, I promise. I want to run through the basic set of exercises we will use for hand-to-hand combat, and then we will find you some food."

"I don't like this plan." I scowled, two lines forming between my brows.

"I'm aware." Dax straightened and placed his hands on my shoulders, turning me toward the back of the ship where we trained yesterday. "Come on."

I grunted and groaned the whole way there. I was happy to train, but I was hungry—no, correction, I was starving. I wasn't sure I would have complied for anyone but him at that point.

Dax placed the balance platform aside, moving next to me so we stood shoulder to shoulder. "Today, I'm going to teach you five basic movements that you will practice each day before we train. Once you master the flow of these, then we can advance your training." I nodded and watched him carefully, keenly aware of the proximity of our bodies and his mountain pine scent as it danced against the sea breeze. "Now, I understand you have basic instruction in fighting techniques—"

"All shifters are trained to fight and taught basic self-defense when we are younger," I interrupted.

"Yes, but … *you* were also off balance. Hence, the reason I started with the platform." I scoffed at Daxton but allowed him to continue without interrupting further. He was a deadly weapon in the flesh, so it would not be wise of me to ignore what he was trying to teach me. "Focus on these movements and understand what areas of your body you are leaving vulnerable so you can anticipate your opponent and attack."

"Okay, got it."

Daxton led me through the five different exercises, ensuring my form was perfect in each one before I moved on to the next. He watched me carefully, and if I was even a breath out of balance, he was there correcting and encouraging me to try again. I mastered the first step, but I struggled to navigate to the second and third, which played off each other with a defensive block followed by another counterstrike.

"Don't get frustrated. You're doing great. Keep trying," Dax told me countless times, never getting upset or impatient with me.

Not wanting to disappoint him, I gritted my teeth and tried once more. I stepped forward with a punch and then followed it through with a spin and a block to my blind side.

"Perfect, Spitfire! Now, the third movement, and we can get some breakfast."

Hearing that pushed me harder, and I flowed into the third exercise, a side kick following a balanced landing on both my feet. "Did I do it right?" I hesitated to ask.

"Let's eat," Dax proclaimed, and I practically squealed with joy.

The grits and eggs were already handed out to most of the crew, and I wondered if Dax knew this and wanted them to eat first. I appreciated his consideration for the hard-working crew and agreed it was only fair for us to eat after they had their fill. We were merely passengers on this ship.

"Are Castor and his companion going to join us anytime soon?" I asked after finishing my plate.

"Not likely," Dax grunted with a deep chuckle. "I believe I heard them again this morning after you left."

"I'm glad I awoke before they did then."

"Oh really?" I saw the mischievous gleam in Dax's eye, and I slumped my back against the side of the ship. "You didn't enjoy their boisterous company last night?"

"Really?" I asked with as straight of a face as I could muster.

"It didn't entice you? I could have sworn you enjoyed listening in." My cheeks burned bright red. "What kind of kinks do *you* have, Spitfire?"

"That is none of your business!" I threw my empty plate at Daxton's head, but he was too fast. He caught it in mid-air and gave me a smug grin of amusement. "I could ask the same of you," I sneered, crossing my arms at my chest with a scowl. I stuck my tongue at him to just seal in my displeasure.

"I wouldn't deny or feel embarrassed by what I desire. Nor how I satisfy my certain needs." His smoky gray eyes flicked up at me, and an intense wave of hunger simmered from his stare. My cheeks flushed for an entirely different reason.

"And what do you desire, Dax?" I asked as I dared to lean in closer to him. What the hell was this feeling in my chest? It was like an invisible tether was tugging me toward him, appearing and then disappearing in the next second. Was it his magic somehow affecting me like this?

"You first, Spitfire." He set the plates down and shifted his body toward me.

And the game continues … "I want to win the trials."

"Excellent." Dax smirked and jumped to his feet, extending his hand to me. "Then get your ass up and let's continue your training." His voice was rougher now, more serious as the glimmer from before disappeared behind the commanding presence of the Silver Shadow.

Determined to prove that I was unafraid of him, I accepted his hand and pulled myself to my feet "Lead the way … *Princey*."

We continued right where we left off, and I managed to master the other two movements. I trained with my dominant hand and foot leading the exercises, and then he had me change to my opposite side. This proved more challenging, but I refused to give up. Dax patiently walked me through each step, never once snapping at my failures—only encouraging me to keep going.

"It's important to highlight our strengths, but also be aware of our weaknesses and try our best to make sure they are balanced. You are right-handed, with a dominant right foot as well. Practice these five movements with your left side until they feel as natural as your right. In battle, it is never a guarantee that you can attack and defend with your right. Enemies are everywhere, so it is important to defend yourself from all sides."

"How long did this take you to master?" I asked as we took a break to drink some water.

"I have been trained in combat since I was able to walk," he answered, taking a sip from the canteen.

"Wow, your parents allowed you to train that early on?" I was shocked. "They must have grown up in a similar manner then, or is this just a custom of the High Fae to train for battle so early in life?" I asked without thinking as I moved through the different stretches to ease the ache in my body.

"My parents …"

There was that pause again, and I knew the pain that lingered in those silent moments. "I'm sorry, Dax. You don't have to talk about them if you don't want to. Trust me, I understand. You don't have to explain anything to me."

"With you … I honestly don't mind." His reply caught me off guard. I stopped what I was doing and sat silently beside him, trying to give him strength and support in any way I could.

"I'm here to listen." I reached out and gently touched his

knee. His eyes opened to find mine, and I could see the depths of the sorrow of lost love that could only come from true grief.

"My parents were mates." I suddenly understood Castor's emphasis on the term from our lessons the other day. "They loved each other so deeply and passionately that it inspired divided kingdoms to unite. Long before the veil or the wilt and before we were forced to follow the rule under the high queen, our lands and people were divided. My parents were both warriors from neighboring realms. My father Khalon was the ruler of Silver Meadows, while my mother Arabella was a warrior of Aelius. There was disagreement about resources and trade, so war naturally followed between Silver Meadows and Aelius. Believe it or not, it was on the battlefield that my parents first met each other."

"Did they try to kill each other?" I asked intently, listening to his story.

"They did, actually." Dax laughed lightly. "Castor tells this story better than I do from asking our mother countless times when he was younger."

"I want to hear it from you." I shifted to squeeze his hand gently, and in return, Dax smiled at me.

"The mate bond can be instantaneous for some, and this was undeniably the case for my father. He saw my mother, Arabella, from across the battlefield, and in a single breath, he knew that his entire world would change. She was a fearsome sight to behold, with a silver bow in one hand and an endless supply of daggers strapped to her chest and belt."

"A female after my own heart," I said with a soft smile.

"My father retold that moment to us countless times, but he always said it was hard to describe accurately. One day, he would always tell us, if we were lucky enough to find our mate, we would know without a shadow of a doubt who they were." Daxton's gaze drifted away, like he was traveling through time. "My father also told us to do everything in our power to never lose them. To fight for their happiness, for that is where true love and a deeper meaning in life can be found." Daxton held his breath, and I knew other memories were flashing through his mind.

"What happened next? What did the Silver Meadows and Aelius warriors do when they saw each other?

"My father felt his mate's soul tether with his, and he immediately called for his people to stand down. Arabella, my mother, was not a direct descendant, but she was still a beloved member of the royal bloodline. She saw my father, Khalon, command a ceasefire, and she did the same with the warriors she led. My father removed his helmet in the middle of the battlefield and walked across the bloodied dirt and earth to place it at her feet. He knelt before her, took her hand in his own, and announced the mate bond. Vowing then and there to unite the kingdoms and stop the fighting if she would have him."

"Since you and Castor exist, I'm guessing she accepted?"

"Not without complications along the way." Dax sighed. "But for the purpose of time, yes. She recognized the bond as well and accepted his hand."

"Wow, a love powerful enough to unite the two kingdoms. That's remarkable."

"Yes, Crimson City also agreed to a united alliance, and all three seats of power worked together to govern our people as a whole. For a long time, there was peace with not just High Fae but shifters as well. As you can recall, some of your people lived in the Inner Kingdom."

"Did shifters have a seat of power when your parents united the High Fae kingdoms?"

"No, not to my recollection. I believe a stronghold of shifters did reside in the Inner Kingdom, but they governed themselves."

"Maybe they lived most of their lives in animal forms and didn't comply with the rules of the High Fae. I have read about some shifters becoming lost to their animal souls."

"Is that common?" Daxton asked.

"No, but some do prefer their animal forms."

"Interesting. Perhaps they had their own governance, but I don't recall there being much interaction between the two species in any official stance."

"Hmm, interesting indeed," I answered, narrowing my eyes and thinking to myself. "But there are four seats of power now with a high queen. How did that come to be?" Dax gripped my hand, and I knew this was where everything unraveled in his world.

"I was young and naive."

"Preaching to the choir." I nudged his shoulder, trying to ease his distress. "Trust me, Dax. I won't judge you for anything that happened in your past."

"It all began to fall apart when my mother died." The air stilled in my lungs as the sorrow in Daxton's expression consumed the lines on his furrowed brow. "My mother was one of the first victims of the wilt. She went on a scouting mission with her trusted guard near Crimson City borders to investigate a disturbance rumored to be infected with some form of dark magic. At thirty-six, I was already a commanding officer in our army. So, I stayed with my father to lead the battle on the front lines against the humans and shifters when she—"

"It's all right, Dax. I'm here." His grip tightened on my hand as he began to shake. I did my best to steady him, making sure he knew I was there to support him.

"He knew," Dax began, his hands trembling. "The moment my mother died … he could feel their mate bond sever. His connection to her fell silent and numb, leaving him utterly alone. I had never in all my years witnessed such heartbreak. His roaring screams were heard throughout the Inner Kingdom—even across this narrow sea to the mainland. I was broken by her passing, as was Cas since he was so young, but my father … he was completely shattered."

"How old was Castor when this happened?"

"Far too young, only ten. He wasn't old enough to compete in the gauntlet, which all males and females who want to become Silver Meadows Warriors must pass in order to be worthy to carry our silver mountain emblem."

"What happened next? This was leading to the final standoff that divided shifters and humans from the fae, wasn't it?"

"Yes, and it was an absolute bloodbath." Daxton's eyes glossed over, and I could see him falling back through time. "As high prince, my father was supposed to lead the front, but his grief hindered him. He practically lost his mind over our mother's death. There was no other option—I had to step in and lead in his place. Our enemies were everywhere, and worst of all, the wilt was beginning to spread against our backs. We had been fighting for nearly a week straight. The strength of our forces and magic were non-existent at that point, and my powers were nothing but a mere memory. But still, we continued fighting. We had to." Dax released my hand and closed his eyes, trying to focus.

"What is it, Dax?" I asked with concern as I knelt before him.

"It's … I can't remember the details."

"I imagine you must have blocked it out or were too exhausted."

"No, it's not that." He stood up and began pacing. "I can't remember. Why? Why can I not remember?" His brows furrowed, with two lines of frustration pinched between them.

Hell, I was confused for him. "Dax?" He didn't respond, so I tried again. "Daxton." I fronted him and grabbed onto his shoulder. "Breathe." He followed my command and took in a deep breath. "Good, now just try and focus on what you *can* remember."

"Right, okay." Dax pushed past his frustrations and began his story again. "I don't know exactly how because we were separated when it happened, but my father fell on the battlefield." I noticed how his fingers flexed into fists, his shoulders tensing as he recalled this difficult memory from his past. "I can close my eyes and picture him on the ground in front of me. My hand clutched in his, and with his final breath, he passed his power and reign to me." The agonizing sadness in Daxton's expression left me breathless, with tears threatening to stream down my cheek. "Losing my mother wounded us all … but at least we still had *him*." I could see his eyes narrow as a single tear dared to trickled down his face. "Not a single day passes that I don't miss them both."

I reached up and brushed it away before it hit the ground. "His last gift was to give you the strength he had left so you could keep going," I said in a soft tone as I held his face in my hand. "Your bravery honors their memories, Daxton. If I can see it … believe that they can, too."

Dax leaned into the palm of my hand and nodded a silent gesture of gratitude. "I took full command of Silver Meadows forces, and we drove the human and shifter soldiers into a momentary retreat. With them gone from our shores, we refocused our efforts on the threat within. Then … I remember Minaeve." His tone and demeanor changed at the mention of her name. He spoke in a deathly calm voice that was anything but comforting. "She appeared out of nowhere, placing herself along the border, facing off against the wilt and using her magic to weaken it and push it back." Dax closed his eyes again, trying to recall the details that seemed to be alluding him. "Then … there was a flash, and suddenly … the veil appeared."

"So, the divide of our races was not an agreed treaty?" The truth of that had my head spinning. We all thought the veil was constructed by the High Fae because of the treaty, but Daxton remembered it differently. "If shifters are descendants of the High Fae, why were we fighting against each other? What was the reason for any of us to be fighting in the first place?"

"Differences are easier to identify and use for reasons to isolate or hate one another, Spitfire. If I learned anything from my parents, it's that diversity can make you stronger. They showed me that a person's character matters most, not where they came from."

I mulled over everything that Dax told me and tried to take it all in. "We were told the division of power and land was an agreed treaty, and we left the Inner Kingdom because of the High Fae. That your people created the veil to keep us all out."

"It couldn't be further from the truth."

"How so?"

"The veil keeps the wilt contained … somewhat. It doesn't prevent the spread entirely, but it does slow the progression. We don't know exactly how it was made, but it was probably some kind of divine intervention from the gods combined with an immense power source."

"You think it's connected to the Heart of Valdor, don't you?"

"That's my theory. And when you unlock its power to destroy the wilt, I believe it might also tear down the veil as well."

I sighed and leaned back. "Just add it to my list of things to accomplish."

"No problem. Anything else you wish for me to add to this growing list?" Dax asked with a playful wink. "Tree climbing, perhaps?"

"I'm already excellent at climbing trees, so no need."

"Different type of tree … Spitfire." I smacked his shoulder, and he rolled with laughter.

Choosing to ignore his blatant remark, I allowed my mind to drift over everything Daxton had shared with me. His parents were victims of the wilt and the war, and it seemed like all the power and responsibility of his people, along with his brother, were thrown onto his shoulders all at once. My respect and admiration for all he had to do and continued to do each day only grew. It was hard to remember that while Dax and Castor only seemed to be my age, they were actually well over five hundred years old. High Fae were immortal, which had advantages but also carried heavy burdens. During these past five centuries, they lived through so much torment, time after time, on a never-ending journey that was shrouded in darkness. The wilt was a shadow of death lingering behind them their entire lives.

"I'm sorry," I said, and he looked at me with a questioning stare. "I'm sorry you had to live so long in a constant battle to save our world. I'm sorry you have lost so much …"

"You don't need to apologize, Skylar." Daxton grasped my hands, and the world shifted around me. His eyes swirled with such depth of emotion that I didn't know I would ever understand.

"You—" His glazed-over eyes sparked with a swell of emotion, making my heart warm with a smile. "You have given me a reason to *hope* again." His hand moved to grasp my chin as he gently stroked my bottom lip with his thumb. "Skylar, I—"

"Well … good morning, everyone!" Castor announced loudly, and I quickly retreated away from Daxton's touch. "Ahh, what did I miss this morning? Anything interesting?"

"You missed breakfast," I murmured.

"Oh, I ate." Castor grinned, and I threw him one of my aggravated scowls of disgust. "Ahh, perfect. The morning is now complete with an eye roll from the shifter." Daxton didn't say a word as he turned to walk away.

"Where you off to?" Castor casually asked.

"We are approaching the veil sooner than we thought," Dax answered as silver flashed around him, and he was gone.

"What's going on with him?" Castor asked. I was staring at the last place I saw Daxton, unaware that Castor was even there or asking me a question. What was he going to tell me before Castor interrupted us? "Hello? Skylar? Hello?"

"Oh, hey," I swatted Castor's hand away from my face.

"I asked you a question. What is going on with my brother?"

I debated not telling Castor what we talked about, but seeing as it was also a piece of his past as well, he deserved to know I was aware of it. "Dax told me the story about your parents."

Castor's eyes widened. "He did what?"

"He told me about how they met on the battlefield, about their mate bond, and about …"

"No." Castor waved his hand and took a seat, steadying himself. "He talked to you about it? Actually in detail? With words?"

"Yes," I answered with a peculiar stare.

"There are not many things that surprise me anymore, Skylar, but you have just given me the shock of a lifetime." What was he getting at? Castor was acting strange. He was a character, to begin with, but this was out of the ordinary even for him. "Daxton has not spoken about our parents since that final day on that battlefield when our father died in his arms and the responsibility of our kingdom … passed to him."

My eyes widened. I didn't know what to say or how to respond. Daxton trusted me enough to share it with me. "Wow."

"For once, we are in the same state of shock. You seem to have achieved the impossible and somehow managed to get him to open up and talk to you."

I had no idea how or why Daxton shared that with me, but I was glad that he did. "Well, I'm glad that impossible tasks are in my favor before I enter the trials."

"Indeed." Castor's gaze drifted over the side of the ship, and I could see he was deep in thought. "Let's find me some food, and then we can continue our lessons from yesterday. In a few days, we should reach the veil, and then we will enter the Inner Kingdom. There is too much to teach you and little time to do it."

I nodded and showed Castor to the gally. We didn't have much time before I would be thrown into the world of the High Fae. I would not only be challenged with the trials but would also have to survive the mind games of the fae courts, and from what I could tell, they were just as deadly.

# Chapter Twenty-Seven

Two more days passed, and the ship's crew were readying themselves to pass through the veil, but I still did not know what to expect. The days on the ship passed by like the first, but for the life of me, I couldn't seem to get Daxton alone. He continued to train me in the mornings, with Castor's lessons following in the evening, and by the time night fell, I was exhausted.

I kept wondering what else he was going to tell me before Cas interrupted us. I desperately wanted to know what he was going to say, but unfortunately, I hadn't had the chance to ask him.

"What will happen once we cross the veil?" I asked Castor after we reviewed various strategic players of each kingdom of the High Fae.

"The veil is pure magic. When we cross through, your body will be flushed with its power—unlike anything you have felt before. Dax will be able to create an opening, but everyone on the ship will still come into contact with the veil's magic."

"What will it feel like?" I wondered if it would affect me differently than it did the fae due to my hybrid shifter-human blood.

"For every shifter before you … the effects have been the same as us. It's a wild, intoxicating rush. Imagine being drunk on your finest wine … while also feeling the slam of adrenaline from battle. Everything is heightened. The world feels raw against your fingertips, and the magic that dances across your skin ignites every nerve ending in your body."

"Is it painful?"

Castor shook his head. "No, not painful. More bothersome or annoying if you don't enjoy indulging in the side effects."

I wondered what side effects he was referring to, but I decided to keep that question to myself for once. With my feelings for Daxton running amok in my head, I didn't want to touch that subject with a ten-foot pole. And judging by the distance he was putting between us—yet again—he was in the same boat as me.

"How many times have you crossed?" I asked.

"This is my third time traveling to the mainland to find a

shifter. Dax would not allow me to go the first two trips, but I have insisted on coming on the final three."

"I imagine he didn't want you coming until he knew it was safe."

"Ha," Castor blurted with a short humorous laugh. "Sure, that's the reason."

Oddly enough, the dynamics of the Inner Kingdom were beginning to make sense, especially with the details Dax shared with me about his parents. And he was right about it being drastically different from my pack. Shifters worked together for a greater cause to support one another. The combined efforts of the pack benefited everyone's safety, security, happiness, and well-being. It seemed the High Fae had some of these qualities, but they were divided. Their people had advantages, but their lack of unity was their downfall. Even with a high queen ruling over all of them, it was apparent they were still struggling to unite. Five centuries of death and despair from the fear of the wilt didn't help matters.

"All right, back to our lessons," Castor announced. We were locked in his quarters for the rest of the day, revisiting every detail about each kingdom, and I finally learned about some of the key players of Silver Meadows.

Their master-at-arms, Gunnar, was currently in command of Silver Meadows while Dax and Castor were away. He was orphaned as a child due to the wilt, losing his father, who fought under Daxton's command, and then, sadly, his mother, who died in childbirth. At an early age, apparently the youngest to date, Gunnar entered the Ice Gauntlet to earn his right to train as a warrior for Silver Meadows. His skill and hard work quickly caught Castor and Daxton's attention. They both personally saw to his training, and he quickly rose to earn their trust. Gunnar was young, but his success and leadership were remarkable, regardless of his troubled upbringing. What he lacked in magic, he made up for with a cunning military mind, determination, and loyalty.

Zola, who served as spymaster for Silver Meadows, was just as mysterious as her job title. Castor's description of her was brief, but from what I could infer, she was different from any other High Fae alive. Zola was born a citizen of Crimson City, but the wilt had changed her. She was a member of the scouting party that Castor and Daxton's mom led, but Cas wouldn't say much more. He told me that I would have to ask Zola when I met her. He did tell me that Daxton helped save her life, and since that day, he had her loyalty.

"We shall now work on the art of deception, Skylar," Castor announced.

"Oh, joy," I said with a heavy dose of sarcasm that I knew Castor heard but decided to overlook.

"That's the spirit." He grinned. "Now, why the long face? I'm going to teach you one of the most valuable lessons there is. You may not master this, but you will learn enough to keep that pretty little head on your shoulders."

"Pretty little head … Did you just give me a compliment that wasn't drenched in an inappropriate sexual undertone?"

Castor rolled his eyes, ignoring my comment entirely. "Pay attention."

The seriousness in his expression told me that this was not the time or place for games. I groaned, but I knew he was right. "All right, let's begin."

"Now, males and females naturally deceive one another by omitting information, denying the truth, or exaggerating details. Or they might agree with others when they don't in order to preserve a relationship or try to gain the favor of one. Self-serving lies, on the other hand, help us get what we want, make us look better, and can spare us blame or embarrassment."

Okay, Castor really had a knack for this. Now, I understood why Dax was insistent that I study this with him. Even if I picked up on half of what he was trying to teach me, it would help. I was good at reading true intentions, but I was also naive when it came to lies and deception.

"Now, when you are trying to conceal the truth, the best thing to do is base your story on simple facts."

"Like how, exactly?" I asked.

Castor leaned back in his seat with his elbows resting on the armrests and laced his fingers in front of his pinched mouth. His dark eyes glimmered with anticipation and perhaps a twinge of excitement. This was clearly his playing field of expertise. "I'll give you a firsthand example of how deception can be used to your advantage. Ask me a question, any question, Skylar."

An open-ended question with no barriers. Was it my birthday or something?

"All right." I leaned forward and met his stare, but I was panicking and didn't necessarily know what to ask. So I thought of the first thing that popped into my head. "What is your favorite breakfast?"

"I give you a blank canvas, and *that* is what you ask me?" I nodded, and he sighed heavily. "Of course, a meal is the first thing on your shifter's mind. I assume it is a good place to start. Very well." He unlaced his hands and relaxed his shoulders. "My favorite breakfast meal is an egg cooked over toast. But not the traditional slop that is planted on top, with the yolk running along the plate. I enjoy it the way my mother made it for me and Dax each day when I was younger."

"Your mother cooked for you each morning? That's endearing," I answered, thinking about what young Castor and Daxton were like.

"Yes, she did. Don't all mothers care for their children and devote the morning to making sure they have the best chance to begin their day? What did your mother do for you?"

"Well, I didn't have my birth mother with me, but Julia taught me how to cook for myself. I loved sharing that time with her in the kitchen. We would spend hours together making meals for the family. Neera would always bring us fresh ingredients from the garden, and Magnus happily devoured each creation I managed to put together. Even if some of them weren't the best, he always ate them with a smile. We … Hey!" I exclaimed.

That grin on his face was met with my narrowed eyes. He had asked me one thing, and somehow, I had trailed off on a tangent. I hadn't even realized I was doing it!

Castor bowed his head and flung his arms out to the side. Humility was not on his list of characteristics. "And now, I have learned vital information about you … while presenting you with a lie."

"Okay, now I have to admit, *that* was impressive," I said while still glaring at him. "So, where was your lie?"

"My mother did cook me and Dax eggs on toast on the rare occasion, but we employed help in our palace. I falsified my own upbringing and then asked you about yours. A key lesson is that regardless of who you are talking to, they always want to talk about themselves. And fae are known to have a crippling vanity streak."

"So, how did the lie help?"

"I learned that Julia was not your birth mother, and if I ever needed to gain your favor, I could use that treasured experience of cooking with her to manipulate you. I could ask you to join me in the kitchen, and we create something together, later gaining your trust and allowing you to reveal even more than you already divulged." That was a complete mind-fuck. My mouth practically fell open and onto the floor. Did all fae think ten steps ahead, or was this just a special Castor trait?

"Now, let's try again."

Castor and I spent the next hour practicing how to manipulate conversations and how I would respond to questions about my past or anything I knew. I focused on simple key elements that were true but spun them in a different direction so I didn't give anything away. This was a new way of viewing the world for me because I was raised with honesty as a virtue.

"Think of this like armor—but for your mind," Castor instructed me. "You will get better at it the more you practice, and I'll make sure your mind stays sharp."

The door handle turned, and Dax stepped inside. My heart fluttered inside my chest as he entered, despite my best intentions. He tilted his head at us both in a silent greeting as he closed the door behind him. His presence consumed the room, isolating the attention of every freaking fiber of my being, making me lose focus and almost miss Castor's closing statements.

"Do you suggest I do this all the time?" I asked, trying to divert my gaze from where Daxton waited. "Because that would be exhausting, and I would never feel right in myself."

I wanted to be me. These mind games were not appealing, and if I was going to compete in the trials, I knew I needed to be true to myself.

"This is where your shifter instincts will come in handy," Dax answered, and Castor nodded in agreement.

"From what other champions have shared with us, you have a sixth sense that can help guide you when it comes to trust and identifying allies," Castor added.

Dax stepped closer to our table and placed a hand on his own chest. "It's a feeling you have when your animal is aware. She will guide you. All you have to do is listen and ask."

"Ask her? You both know we can't actually speak to one another, right? It doesn't work like that."

"But you can feel each other's emotions and presence." Dax came closer to me, and on cue, I could feel my animal perk in my middle, along with other things. "I can sense the power in you and your animal spirit, Spitfire," he said with a grin.

"As shifters, your animals respond to power … strength, magic, authority—all of the above," Castor added with a wave of his hand. "You must learn how to listen to her when encountering others. She will let you know whom you can trust."

"How?"

"Ask her," Dax said plainly like this task was as easy as walking. "Try it now. Ask her."

Easier said than done. I did find it amusing that these two were trying to teach me what I could or could not do regarding my animal. All right, well, they hadn't been wrong so far, and with over five hundred years of life experience over me, it wouldn't be the worst thing to try. I settled in my seat as Dax crossed his arms in front of his chest and gave me an inquisitive look. I closed my eyes and tried to reach out to connect with my animal. She instantly responded, causing me to practically jolt in my seat. Her power flowed through me, and I could feel the heat migrate along the length of my limbs.

"Good," Dax said encouragingly.

I opened my amber eyes and took in each of their faces. *Can we trust them?* I asked in my mind and waited for a reply. A warm, tingling sensation flooded my middle, making me feel safe and warm. It reminded me of home, being wrapped up in a blanket in the loveseat Neera and I shared, with a good book and nothing but time to spare.

"Well?" Castor questioned.

"I think I did it?"

"Think or know? Those are two very different things." I glared at Castor and stuck my tongue out at him. He laughed. "I think we have the answer then."

"You two seem to be getting along better and better each day," Dax teased. A horn sounded, and both Daxton and Castor stiffened. "The veil. Cas, did you get a chance to tell her about what would happen when we cross through?"

"The drunken high paired with adrenaline rush and overflowing emotional whirlwind?" I cast him a smirk paired with a wink and my trademark thumbs-up. "Yup. Should be a fun ride."

"Do you want to see it firsthand?" Dax asked me with his hand outstretched. "Castor will stay in here, I imagine, with his companion from the previous night. I didn't think you would want to be here for that … Or—"

"Oh Gods, no. The other night was more than enough." I willingly accepted Dax's offer not to be anywhere near here when crossing the veil.

"Don't be a prude, Sky … Haven't you—" Before Castor

could finish his sentence, Dax teleported us out of Castor's room and placed us on the front of the ship.

"Thanks for the rescue," I said, noticing that Daxton's hand was still intertwined with mine. I swallowed a loud gulp. Feeling his body's heat pressed against mine was intoxicating, and it only made me yearn for more.

"Happy to help." Dax grinned, but it didn't last long as he turned his focus to the sea before us.

"I don't see anything," I admitted, still very aware of our close proximity.

Daxton's grip on my hand tightened, and I could sense his anxiety beginning to rise as the ship continued forward. "You won't see it until we start to cross, but you can feel it in other ways," he spoke in a low, hushed whisper.

I didn't understand at first, but suddenly, my animal surged inside of me. I felt her react to the magic that was apparently swirling everywhere around us, so I closed my eyes and tried to sense where it was coming from. Straight ahead, I connected with a powerful wall of magic, the force of which contained the energy of an exploding river dam. My eyes snapped open in the direction Daxton was looking only moments before.

"There … you feel it now. Come, stand over here." Dax guided me to stand in front of him as he took both my hands in his own. His touch was gentle, opposite from the roughness of his calloused palms that were earned from centuries of fighting. I relished in the tenderness he was able to show me and sank into his open arms, ignoring all the warning bells that were fading into nothing inside my head.

"I'm going to release my powers to create an opening. Would you like to feel the magic of the veil with me?"

"It's not dangerous, right?" I asked cautiously.

"No. Not with me," Dax said. "I'll keep you safe. Do you trust me to do that, Spitfire?"

"I trust you, Daxton." I stared into his stormy eyes that softened at the corners with a spark of longing I hadn't noticed before. Dax grasped my hands and moved in closer behind me. I felt his body flush against mine, and his head tilted to the side, just above my shoulder, to see around me. The warmth of him surrounding me sent waves of excitement thrumming through my middle. I knew this was not the time or the place to pull focus, but I couldn't help it. He was a ripped wall of muscle and strength. And not only that, but he was patient, respectful, and kind to me. He was everything a female would want and more. So why was I fighting this? Why was I trying to deny my feelings for him?

Daxton's hips shifted slightly as he pulled me in closer to his chest. His muscles tensed, and I knew we were about to cross into the veil. "Here we go."

Dax held out his left hand with mine, and I experienced the first kiss of raw magic caressing my skin. It felt like fireflies were dancing along my nerves as goosebumps formed over my skin. The ship moved forward through an invisible illusion, and it wasn't until we passed through the outer barrier that I finally saw it.

The veil sparkled and shimmered in a white crystalline color that glimmered all around us. I took in a deep breath as my legs shook from the waves of pure, uninhibited emotions that crashed into me. I was overly ecstatic with glee and devoured by my thundering carnal hunger the next. I wasn't able to properly ground myself, and my emotions were wildly trampling through every corner of my mind. The magic ignited my senses, like diving into an ice-cold pool of water. It swirled around us like a tornado, highlighting every touch, smell, and feeling I had ever had.

Through all this wonder and chaos, however, this magic somehow felt familiar. I couldn't seem to put my finger on it, but I could have sworn I felt something like this before. Maybe in a dream? Or perhaps I was just feeling the effects of the overflow of power that was rolling through my body.

Dax gripped me tighter, and I could feel the thrum of his heart beating rapidly against me. The smell of his fresh winter mountain pine scent filled my senses, quickening my breathing and awakening sensations across every inch of my flesh that his arms wrapped around. Gods … this was amazing. *He* felt amazing. I was flying without ever having to leave the ground.

"Daxton," I whispered his name with an intense need that I no longer wanted to hide. He dipped his head toward my ear, lightly brushing his beard against the soft curve of my face. My knees wobbled as a strong pulsing began thrumming between my thighs. He was so gods-damned desirable. I didn't know if there would ever be another that could compare to him.

"Skylar." The same heavy tone of lust thrummed in his voice as his breathing quickened to match mine.

A hungering need begging to be satisfied built inside me as I moved my hips back, rubbing my backside against him. I couldn't help the reaction my body was having, and I didn't think Dax could either. The friction building between us was euphoric and almost unnaturally pleasing. Daxton could quickly become my addiction. I knew the dangers of this fact, but right now, I mentally told all my concerns to fuck off.

I released one of Dax's hands and reached backward to grip the back of his neck. I threaded my fingers into his voluptuous shoulder-length hair, pulling him toward me as I melted further into his embrace. His free hand swooped under my arm to clutch my breast, causing me to moan in delight. The sound I made encouraged him to continue exploring the curves of my body, and Dax didn't hesitate to do so. He swept my hair to the side, lightly brushing his lips over the sensitive skin on the base of my neck and up toward my earlobe.

"Daxton …" I shuddered with blissful delight.

My apex throbbed, dying to be devoured by his touch. The yearning I felt for Daxton made me crumble to my knees with just the whisper of a kiss. I was barely able to think through the intense waves of pleasure rolling through me. I turned around to face him and took his face between my hands.

*Desire.* That was the emotion I saw reflected in his heated gaze, and I knew mine were saying the same. I didn't care how naive or foolish this might be. I was done holding back how I felt or what I wanted. I was about to enter the Inner Kingdom and compete in the trials that would likely lead to my death. No one had survived before me. So, with this knowledge, why was I hesitating? Why was I so scared?

Daxton swallowed. His delectable lips were only breaths away from mine as a heavy wave of arousal swirled through me. I wanted to kiss him. No, correction, I was dying to taste his lips on mine. I felt every fiber of my being lean toward him as my animal surged with a flush of power. It felt so right like I was exactly where I was meant to be, with him. With Daxton.

Suddenly, the air cleared around us as the magical veil disappeared. Still, I didn't shift away or relinquish my hold on Daxton. My breath halted as I felt his arms resting around my hips, his hands tracing along my back before reaching up and brushing a strand of wind-blown hair from my face. We had successfully passed through the veil.

The intense hunger in Daxton's eyes told me everything I needed to know. I was done second-guessing my feelings and denying the possibility that he felt anything for me. This was my moment to take the leap of faith, and I was not going to let this opportunity pass me by.

I boldly tugged on the back of Dax's neck and brought his lips crashing down onto mine. His arms pulled me in close, our bodies pressing against each other with growing need. The kiss only intensified as I parted my lips and allowed his tongue to begin exploring the inside of my mouth. I moaned as he sucked in my bottom lip, nibbling on it before devouring my mouth once more with his. I was overwhelmed by the high induced by the veil combined with the sweet taste of Daxton's kiss.

His hands groped my backside as I tightly encircled my arms around his neck, pushing my body against his and reveling in the seductive friction that was downright sinful. His kiss was everything I had ever dreamed it would be, and more, if that were possible. Ice trickled across my skin, sending sensual pulses of pleasure through my core. I moved my hand to his chest, admiring his perfectly sculpted pecs before reaching up to cup his bearded face in my hand.

A loud horn sounded across the deck, announcing a successful crossing of the veil. Our kiss stopped and we pulled our lips apart. I pressed my brow to his, wrapping my arms around his broad shoulders, desperate to remain close. Dax didn't seem to mind as his arms encircled my middle. I tilted my head to the side to lightly kiss his bearded cheek where I knew a dimple lay in wait. Slowly, my lips traced over his jaw, moving down to his neck before I nuzzled my head into the nook on his shoulder. Dax traced his hands up my back, entangling his fingers through my hair before grabbing my chin between his fingers and pulling my lips to his once more.

This kiss was different. It was tender and soft, reminding me of his gentler side that he had to hide from the rest of the world. This time, he opened his lips to let me taste him, and I could hear his moan of pleasure as my tongue entered. I was lost in a sea of pure bliss, and I knew this male would be my undoing.

I felt Daxton tense as he suddenly paused and pulled away from me. "Look at me, Skylar," he commanded.

I strained to open my eyes, still lost in the trance of his kiss. The magic of the veil had made its way through our systems, and I no longer felt the same rush or high from the raw magic as I had before.

Fuck … I was panicking. *Was he only kissing me because of the veil?* I pulled away from him, placing my hands behind me on the railing, bracing for Dax's confession of regret. I closed my eyes and looked away, embarrassed about how rashly I had just acted.

"Look at me, Spitfire," Daxton said again with a commanding yet gentle voice.

I knew that I couldn't hide from this. I needed to swallow my pride and accept what had just happened. So I bravely looked at him, but to my surprise, I didn't see one ounce of regret on his face. In fact, I saw the opposite. He was relaxed with a confident, beaming smile of hope that I couldn't break away from.

But then, it changed. "Skylar … I'm conflicted," he said with a furrowed brow.

"Conflicted? How?" I asked as I watched his muscles flex along his chest and arms as he ran his finger through his free-flowing hair. The tattoo that decorated his shoulder peeked out from under his shirt, and I couldn't help my wandering mind as it flashed to moments before this when his hands were all over me. Gods be damned, I could no longer deny my growing feelings for Daxton.

"Don't do that," Daxton said with a low growling sound deep in his throat. The sound of his growl was meant to intimidate me, but like always, it had the opposite effect. "Gods, we need to teach you how to shield yourself," Dax said as he gripped the railing of the ship. If I didn't know any better, I would have guessed he was holding himself back as well. "Your arousal is intoxicating, Spitfire, and I don't know how to stop myself from …"

"From what, Dax?" *Again … why is he conflicted?* He never answered my question, and I was so tired of the secrets and avoidance. I wanted there to be no games between us. I could manage to play pretend with everyone else here, but I needed something to be authentic and real. I wanted Dax to be real.

"What's going on, Daxton Aegaeon?" I arched my brows, using his full name to try and get his attention.

He took in a deep breath to try and steady himself. "I need to prepare you for the trials. Surviving should be your main focus. This," he said, pointing between us, "this is a distraction. I cannot be a distraction for you. I would never forgive myself if … If I were the reason—"

"The reason?"

"The reason you fail the trials."

I staggered back a step, my brows raised in surprise as I sucked in a breath through my teeth. He did have a valid point. Even if my body disagreed, my mind identified the sound logic in what he said.

"All right." I sighed heavily, looking down at myself, embarrassed by my reaction to the veil's magic. It had lowered my inhibitions, and apparently, it was the same for Daxton. "I'm sorry, Daxton. I shouldn't have crossed that line."

"No, Skylar!" His voice pitched. "I didn't intend to make you feel this way about our kiss." He reached for my hand, but I hesitated and moved it away before he could latch on. The look on his face said that I might as well have slapped him. "I deserve that, I guess."

"What do you want from *me*, Daxton?" I asked the same question he said to me earlier on this ship. "I don't like these mind games you're playing with me. I am learning what I can from Castor, and I expect the banter and confusion from him—but not you. I expect honesty and openness." I was practically yelling at him, and I didn't really understand why. He was conflicted because he didn't want me to lose focus and miss out on learning any skillset that could make the difference between me dying during the trials or winning.

That was the whole reason I was here, wasn't it? But I dared to ask myself, was that enough? "I guess I'm conflicted too," I said with a lowered voice, wrapping my arms around myself tightly. "So, we are both on the same page with our feelings in that respect, at least."

He gave me an empathetic toothless grin while huffing a breath and leaned on the railing next to me. "Yes, it seems we are."

"Do we have to make a decision about this right now?"

"Not if you don't want to. No, we don't," he replied.

"All right then, let's agree *not to talk* about us right now. And focus on the chaos of everything else happening around us."

"I will respect your wishes, Spitfire. Always." He was oddly quiet for a moment, so I dared to glance sideways at him. "Even though I will be reliving that moment in my mind over … and over again." My mouth practically hung open with a look of shock and embarrassment flushing my cheeks.

"What?" Daxton shifted, turning his shoulders toward me. "Am I supposed to deny that I find you attractive or that our kiss was something I will forever cherish? You just stated that you expected honesty and openness from me." That smug grin revealing one of his dimples ignited my core for multiple reasons. "There it is."

"How do you do that?"

"What exactly?" Daxton asked as he arched his brow with a gleam in his eyes. I shook my head and stared back out toward the sea. "By the way, have you even noticed it yet?" Dax asked, nudging me to turn around and look at what was ahead of us.

"Noticed …" I stopped, realizing I had been so preoccupied with our conversation that I had almost missed it.

There it was, the Inner Kingdom. The first landmarks along the shoreline reminded me of my own home, but instead of a tan sandy beach, this one was black. The forest behind it was dead, with wilting plant life surrounded by shadow. Thick veins of black vines threading through the landmass beyond the blackened sand.

"Is that the—"

"The wilt. Yes."

The lush greenery that should have been bursting to life from the long branches and thick tree trunks was gone. The meadows, the forest … it was all gone. There was so much decay it was difficult to fathom or look away. I swallowed a thick breath, understanding that this was the fate of our worlds if I did not succeed.

"I can't believe this is what you are all living with," I said in a low whisper.

"This is the most recent area that was overrun. Fortunately, this is not the state of every realm in our lands. Crimson City, Silver Meadows, and Aelius are all warded with most of our queen's magic. She cannot heal the land that is destroyed, but she can help prevent it from spreading. The magic replenishes her wards that fend off the wilt."

"Why didn't she stop this?" I gestured toward the shoreline.

"It appears in different areas, spreading like wildfire once it has a hold of the earth. This northern area was overlooked because it was isolated with little to no fae kind residing here."

"But there were some." Dax nodded, and I shuddered, thinking about the fate of the fae who didn't make it out in time. "Where will we dock?"

"We will enter Niamh Bay, but we will not venture into the city itself. I'm sure word has spread about your arrival, and the faster we reach Crimson City, the better."

"Couldn't you simply teleport us all there?"

"Since the queen siphoned my power, I have limited access to my gifts—for now. I cannot travel that far with this many passengers without draining my well of power dry."

"I see." I leaned over the rail and quietly watched the shoreline pass us by.

We remained at the front of the ship for the next few hours, silently watching the scenery as we sailed with the wind. The Inner

Kingdom was different from what I had imagined. Eventually, the decay of the wilt stopped, and the landscape began to change. Trees sprouted to life once more, with thick vegetation stretching as far as my eyes could see. To the right spanned a massive mountain range with the tops still painted white with snow despite the warm climate.

I knew the veil surrounded the island of the Inner Kingdom, but I was still surprised by the illusion it produced. You could see a faint difference when looking toward the magical invisible barrier, but only if you were searching for it. As we sailed into the night, Daxton kindly retrieved us some food, and we dined together on the ship's deck under a blanket of stars.

"So, what was it like?" I asked him as I took a bite of my dinner.

"I believe you will have to be a little more specific with your inquiry," he replied as he shifted to lean back against the ship's side.

"Before the wilt. What was your life like?"

Daxton hummed to himself in quiet contemplation. "That is an interesting question. I have not dared to look back in quite a long time."

"How long?" I eagerly asked. His sense of time—of his lifespan—was drastically different from my own. He was immortal … while I was not. This was a very real fact that I also needed to remember. While I would eventually age and die, Daxton would live on for centuries.

"Since the day the wilt took my mother," Daxton answered as he took another bite of his meal. "But now that you ask … I would be happy to think back and share it with you."

"I would love to hear about it," I said with a coy smile.

Daxton shared his memories from his former life with me as we dined together underneath the darkening starry sky. He fondly told me about his first training sessions with his father and, not surprisingly, his mother as well. Khalon was a skilled warrior, like Daxton, but his mother, Arabella, was also very skilled with a blade—and deadly with her bow. I couldn't help but admire how he described his parents' dynamic. They were the epitome of a mated pair, working together to help strengthen their partnership and seeing each other as equals. He described how proud his father was when his ice magic developed, and then, only a few years later, how his mother's gifts manifested. They were overwhelmed with hope for the future of their people, telling Daxton that he was the prince that was promised to unite them all.

Castor was conceived and born by the time Daxton had already mastered the Ice Gauntlet and earned his first mountain peak emblem of the Silver Meadows warriors. He was so happy to have a sibling and vowed the moment Castor was born that he would always be his brother's protector.

"That is a lot to be thankful and happy for," I said, recalling my own fond memories of my home. I watched Daxton closely as a glimmer of joy flashed across his expression, the dimple on the side of his face making a rare appearance.

Daxton tilted his head to the sky and relaxed the handsome features along his face. "Looking up at them reminds me …"

"Reminds you of what?" I asked as I stared at the beauty revealed only by a shadow of darkness that lingered in the sky.

Dax shifted his gaze, his eyes watching me with a mesmerizing, glossed-over stare. I succumbed to the need I felt to be near him and shamelessly curled up against his side.

His arm draped around me. "That you don't have to know what they are to be amazed. Sometimes, the beauty of the moment is enough."

"The beauty of the moment. I like that." I smiled and allowed my head to rest against Dax's chest, staring up at the stars that were full of wonder and grace, just like him. Wrapping his other around me, I snuggled into his lap, sitting between his legs and leaning back into his embrace. I felt our bodies relax as we lost ourselves in the beauty of the moment together, allowing the world around us to disappear.

# Chapter Twenty-Eight

Footsteps announced another's presence, interrupting our secluded bubble of bliss. Castor casually strutted up to Dax and me and lightly bumped into my shoulder with his knee.

"It's nice to see you two are getting along better and better each day." He winked at Daxton, repeating his brother's taunt from earlier this morning.

"Seems that way," Dax answered, giving me a tight squeeze around my waist. He didn't seem to care that Castor saw us together, so I decided to do the same. Regardless of our conflicted feelings and undeniable attraction to one another, the reality of our situation couldn't be ignored. Still, some things just couldn't be helped. I knew developing feelings for Daxton was unwise, but I didn't know if I was strong enough to resist it—or if I wanted to.

What the hell, let's be honest, I was already there, and denying it wasn't helping anyone.

Trying but failing to hold back a shy smile that reached my eyes, I asked, "Are we leaving tonight?" Dax and Cas both answered with a nod. "Well, with everything I have been through these past few months … I think I can handle anything this world has to throw at me."

"Trust me, you will handle the courts just fine," Dax whispered, giving me a strong vote of confidence. "We need to say farewell to Fjorda before we teleport to shore," Dax said as he shifted and released his hold on me.

I immediately regretted the loss of Dax's warmth, and for a second, I swore I saw him wince with the same hesitation. It was so blatantly clear to me now that his concern for me was deeper than simply protecting me as his ward. But how much did he care for me? Was this simple attraction, or was there something more? These were questions that required time, and unfortunately, time was not in my favor.

As the three of us wandered to the wheel of the ship, we found Captain Fjorda. "I was anticipating the three of you leaving tonight," he said as we approached.

"Thank you for all that you and the crew have done for us, yet again," Daxton said, lowering himself into a slight bow.

"No, High Prince Daxton." Fjorda shook his head and stepped around the wheel. "It is us who should be thanking you. We know of the sacrifices you are giving … and continue to give on our behalf. You and the other princes of our Inner Kingdom have our eternal gratitude. Young champion," Fjorda said as he turned his seafoam-green eyes on me.

He held out his hand for me to take, and I hesitated for a moment before accepting his gesture. Testing out my shifter instincts, I called upon my animal to help me navigate instead of relying solely on Daxton or Castor's opinions of Fjorda. My animal stirred and gave me a reassuring feeling of warmth that was similar to the one I felt with the Silver Meadows princes, and I internally sighed with relief. My shifter instincts told me that Daxton was carefully watching me, knowing that he was ready to step in if there was even a whisper of a threat or foul play from the sea captain.

"You, fair shifter … are a bright beacon of hope in a dark, deserted land. I believe you will be the one to succeed and surpass the trials. If you ever have need of me or my ship, do not hesitate to call out for me." Fjorda's eyes sparkled like the sun rays reflecting off the calm ocean seas.

"How should I call upon you?" I was still skeptical, even if my animal said I could trust him.

Fjorda turned my hand over and brought my palm to his lips. He brushed the skin of my hand across his soft mouth and whispered an incoherent chant that was laced with magic. My skin tingled as the outline of a circular white opal stone appeared on the palm of my hand, tangled with whisps of ebony wind.

"Speak the name of my ship and its captain into the marking, and we shall answer your call." He removed a glove on his right hand, revealing the same tattoo that was now on my palm.

Daxton was immediately at my side, inspecting the marking made by Fjorda. "This is a very generous gift, Captain."

"All for our champion. I believe great things will come from her. It wouldn't be the worst thing to know the *Opal* could one day be in her favor." He winked at me, and a spark of hope ignited in my chest. They all believed I was different and that I was the salvation they had been waiting over five centuries for, and it was hard not to feel the weight of their hopes resting atop my shoulders.

"Thank you." I smiled and closed my palm into my chest.

I was preparing myself to be the champion not only for the High Fae but for all of Valdor. *No pressure, right?* If I died in the labyrinth, they would set out in one hundred years and find another shifter. However, the state of the shoreline from when we first crossed the veil was devastating to see. The decay of the land was spreading faster than the queen could manage. It was already encroaching on the mainland, and no one was able to stop it back home. If Valdor had to wait for another hundred years for a champion … there very well might not be anything else left.

"Where's mine?" Castor playfully held out his hand toward Fjorda. "I believe I have negotiated a deal or three for you in the past, Fjorda. Where is my special summoning mark?"

The captain merely looked at him in annoyance with a hint of trickery hidden beneath his smile. "Perhaps you should ask my first mate if you are worthy enough for this gift."

Castor immediately glared and stuffed his hands into his pockets. "I guess I will have to wait for another time then."

Daxton reached out and placed a hand on his brother's shoulder before opening his hand to take mine. It took me a moment to center myself, and Dax waited patiently for me. I was about to take my first footsteps on Inner Kingdom soil, the land of my ancestors.

The trials were weeks, no, perhaps only days away from beginning. It felt like I was standing at the base of the tallest mountain, being forced to scale the sheer cliffs with only my hands and feet. A daunting task that seemed like an impossible climb. I missed my friends. Rhea and Shaw would know exactly what to say to get me going at a time like this. The reality of it was that they weren't here, so I put on a brave face and reached out to take Daxton's hand.

My eyes traveled from our intertwined fingers to his gray stare that bore into my soul. It was like Daxton was peering into the depths of who I truly was at my core. Despite the lack of time knowing him, he had become one of my most trusted companions. I knew without a shadow of a doubt that he would do everything in his power to keep me safe and to help me achieve anything I set my mind to. This reassurance was like a shield of armor I could utilize to take on the world.

"Ready," I said with a wave of confidence.

Pride beamed in Daxton's eyes as silver flashed around us, and we were teleported off the ship and onto the shore.

"Welcome to the Inner Kingdom," Dax announced.

In the dead of night, it was difficult to get a feel for this place, but one thing was for certain: magic was in the air. I could feel it with each breath my lungs inhaled, in the earth beneath the soles of my feet, and in the beauty of the land that stretched out all around us. The thick, luscious forest reminded me of home, but the trees here were stronger, older even. It had likely been growing for centuries, with the strength of the wild magic reinforcing its lifespan. The stars shone brightly above our heads, highlighted by a dimming crescent moon in the eastern sky. The world seemed to come alive around me, with different smells and sounds of creatures I had never heard before.

Out in the bay, I could see the white gleam of the *Opal* turn and begin sailing east back where we came from. "Where will they go?" I asked. They were trapped inside the veil along with all the other High Fae.

"Starfall Island," Dax said as he checked over the supplies that he teleported with us onto the mainland. "They dock within my kingdom's domain, residing on the island off shore to grant them access to lives surrounded by the sea. It is the least I can do, asking them to ferry us across the veil each century."

"He is being modest like always." Castor sighed.

"Are you pouting because you lost the company of Fjorda's first mate this evening?" I teased.

Castor spun around and gave me a boisterous grin. "It is not my loss, but hers. I mourn for her. My skills in pleasuring those I choose to bed are legendary. I am known for my silver tongue in more ways than one."

*Dear … Gods*, I thought with a loud eye roll. If there were an image of confidence tied with arrogance in the dictionary back home, it would have a portrait of Castor's face.

A thin shield of ice materialized around Castor's mouth, and I couldn't help but fold over laughing as he tried to claw at the muzzle that silenced his incessant boasting. He was able to breathe properly, but despite his own magic, Castor could not overcome his brother's.

"That's enough for now, Cas." Daxton was trying his best to conceal his amusement. And to my utter delight, he was failing miserably at it. "Don't panic. I'll release you once you calm down and take your post. Skylar and I don't need to hear about all the things you can do with your silver tongue. You are on rotation to keep watch first."

Castor glared at Dax and finally gave up fighting his ice gag.

He stormed off near a boulder and perched himself on top, slouching over his legs with his chin resting in the palms of his hands.

"You're never going to hear the end of that one." I laughed.

"Only if I release his muzzle."

"I still need him to teach me, and he needs to speak in order to do so."

"I know." Dax reached into a pack and began to unfold two bedrolls and spread various weapons along the ground. "It's already gone. He's just pouting. Would you mind gathering some kindling on the edge of the woods over there?"

"Sure thing." I began walking toward the tree line when I suddenly got a chill running up my spine. "Do I need to be cautious about someone or something attacking me out here?"

Dax paused, and I could see he was genuinely considering my worries before answering. "No. Not this far from the wilted area; we should be fine. Castor and I won't be out of your line of sight, so you're safe."

Trusting in his logic, I ventured off to gather smaller kindling and other various sticks for a fire. The forest seemed quiet, almost like it was alive and watching me as I arrived on the outskirts of the darkening woods. As a shifter, I could see in the dark, but there were regions of these thick woods that even I had difficulty deciphering. It gave me the creeps, and I had that all too familiar feeling of a predator watching me. I peered deeper into the darkness, but nothing answered. The silence was baffling to me, but all of this was new. Perhaps the woods of the Inner Kingdom were always this quiet? Gathering as much wood as I could, I returned to Daxton and Castor.

"Is it wise to have a fire tonight? Wouldn't it alert anything lurking in the woods to come and attack us?"

"Not with Castor and I standing guard," Dax said with confidence. "What weapons are you comfortable with? I already laid a bow and quiver of arrows near your bedroll. Would you be comfortable with a dagger as well?"

I nodded as I accepted a lightweight dagger that would strap easily to my upper thigh. But that wasn't what held my attention. My eyes darted over to my bedroll, which had one of the most beautifully crafted bows I had ever seen in my life. It was simple yet elegant, with dark smooth wood along the grip decorated with silver swirls.

"Did this weapon come from your kingdom?"

Daxton smiled. "It did. It belonged to a fierce female warrior of my people who died in battle protecting those she loved. I believe she would be honored if you carried it."

I blushed and carefully pulled back the string, testing its stability and strength. From the looks of it, this bow had seen its fair share of combat, but it was well taken care of. The lightweight and flexible frame was astonishing, the absolute perfect bow, in my opinion.

"I'll make sure I take good care of it."

"I trust that you will and that it will serve you well. There are creatures in our land that you need to be cautious about, Spitfire, but nothing that will haunt us tonight."

"What types of creatures?" I shifted the pile of kindling next to him and worked on building a fire. "Come on. You had to know by now that I was going to ask." I winked at him, and even in the dark, I could see the hint of his smile in return.

"Dryads can be bothersome," Daxton said. "Especially in the thick woods leading to Crimson City and all around Silver Meadows. I don't know how many times I have accidentally harmed a tree they were protecting when I was younger and had my ass almost handed to me as a result." He sighed heavily, recalling his various encounters throughout his long life. "They can be a handful to negotiate with, but I was thankfully able to repair my mistakes."

"Interesting." I hummed in contemplation. "I've read about these creatures."

"I'm sure you have," Dax said, flashing me a half-grin.

"Is it true that if the tree a dryad is protecting is killed, the dryad also dies with it?"

Dax nodded. "We have been working closely with the population in Silver Meadows, trying to save their trees from the wilt or relocate them. But sadly, many do not survive. Their devotion to protecting nature is remarkable, combined with their wrath to all those who threaten it."

"It sounds like you know from experience." I huffed a laugh, reading the grimace on his face as an indication that I was correct.

"I tend to learn things the hard way and have to experience life firsthand for it to really sink in," Dax admitted freely.

I lit a small spark with flint rocks and encouraged it to grow with dried grass and long exhales of breath under the larger broken branches I collected. The flames burst to life, and I could see Daxton moving his fingers, allowing his magic to help encourage the flames. "Okay, what other creatures should I know about then?" I asked.

"Water nymphs," he answered quickly. "Also known as

merfolk. Their main colony resides in the depths of Sterlyn Lake—the largest body of freshwater in the Inner Kingdom that feeds many of the rivers and streams throughout the island. Nymphs keep to themselves mostly, but every so often, there are stories of a male or female High Fae falling for their beauty and being taken under the waters of the lake, never to be seen again."

"Have you ever seen them?" I asked as my curiosity piqued. I enjoyed hearing and learning about these creatures and the world I was now in, but most of all, I liked hearing it from Daxton.

"I have, yes. The trick to water nymphs is that they are gorgeous in their element. But once they leave the water, their beauty drips away as well. They are terrifyingly hideous on land, with elongated fangs, sunken eyes, and very foul tempers. It is best to conduct business with their kind in a shallow river or stream."

"Why is that?"

"They keep their natural forms that don't creep into your nightmares, and they also can't lure you into the waters to drown you."

"They would do that?"

"Everything must eat, Skylar."

My eyes widened, but eventually, I just shrugged. I was not naive and understood the nature of life and the hierarchy of the world. There were predators, and there were prey. It was pointless to be angry at the natural flow and balance of their world.

"All right, hit me with one more that I should know about," I said as I lay back on my bedroll. Daxton smoothed his roll out so our heads were next to each other, with our feet pointing in opposite directions, allowing us to remain close while keeping watch.

"One of the most dangerous creatures created by the wilt …" He paused for a moment, looking out into the dark woods. "They are called nalusa falaya— also nicknamed the fallen."

"Why … *the fallen*?"

"You remember me telling you about casualties due to the wilt? That some were lost and did not escape in time?" I nodded, remaining deathly quiet, intently listening to every word he was telling me. "The fallen are long, gangly ebony-black beings of pure death and shadow. They are a byproduct of High Fae and other fae-type creatures coming into contact with the dark magic of the wilt. It changes them, destroying the beings they once were and mutating their bodies into creatures whose sole purpose is to kill. And trust me from experience … they are also very difficult to kill." Daxton twirled a blade of grass in his fingers concentrating on his description. "They hunt along the borders of the wilt's territory, searching for any living thing they can find to curb their appetites. If you are bitten or scratched by a fallen … their poison seeps into your body, and you are changed into them. Almost all who are infected by the wilt's magic choose death rather than succumbing to the change and transforming into a fallen creature."

Daxton flipped over onto his stomach to look at me, and I did the same. He reached out and lightly grasped my arm, his eyes shining against the warmth of the fire. "Please, Spitfire." His demeanor changed, and I was surprised by the genuine plea I was hearing in his voice. "Promise me if you ever see one of these creatures, you'll turn … and you'll run. No questions asked. There is no healing what is already dead inside."

"But they can be killed, can't they?" I asked. "You just said you knew from experience."

"They can, but it is not easy by any means. They are gifted with dark magic, making them stronger and faster than a normal creature. Decapitation is the only way to stop them and end their existence in this world." The night was quiet as I gazed into Daxton's eyes, holding onto him as his grip tightened on me. "For me, Skylar, please promise me you will turn and run from this threat."

The look I saw within him was impossible to argue against. Underneath his mask of a warrior, I saw pure fear lingering behind his eyes. Fear for my safety. "For you, Daxton, I promise. I will turn and run." If *he* was afraid of these creatures, then I knew I should be terrified.

"Thank you." He sighed heavily as he squeezed my arm and propped himself upright. He bent his head downward but then stopped himself. He looked at me and inhaled a sharp breath, almost like it was killing him not to be closer to me. Yet he remained where he was. "Not the best idea talking about these creatures right before we sleep, is it?"

"There are worse things that keep me awake at night," I said, gazing at the fire. Dax was deathly silent, and if I hadn't heard him breathing, I would have sworn he disappeared.

"I-I … didn't mean to cause you any distress, Spitfire," he said with a somber expression. "What else keeps you awake at night?"

"I'll survive. I mean, I did. But sometimes it's hard to move on from it." I didn't want to talk about my nightmares right now. If I spoke about them out loud, I was afraid the nightmares would return and swallow me whole despite all the progress I had made with grounding and facing my fears.

"Tell me about things that bring you joy in your life, Skylar." Daxton flashed me a kind upside-down smile as he laid back down, gazing up at the stars.

"Only if you do the same." I grinned, turning on my side so we were facing each other. "What is your favorite color?"

"Would it be too cliché if I said silver?"

"Really?" I sighed heavily and slapped my palm to my face. "That's your favorite color? Yes, it's cliché. Pick another one."

"Very well, green or orange."

"And I can tell there is a story behind that one, so lay it on me, Dax." Even though he was draped in shadow with his back to the fire, I could tell he was amused. I was beginning to anticipate his reactions and understand his mannerisms. And I would be lying if I said I didn't enjoy it.

"I enjoy gardening and working with my hands. I imagine that if I were not born as the heir of Silver Meadows or leading our armies, I would enjoy the simple but important work of a farmer."

I tilted my chin up. "Seriously? All right, I need to hear the rest of this story."

"Absolutely." Much to my amusement, Dax playfully mimicked my expression perfectly. "I like the color orange because it reminds me of the warmth and beauty of the sunrises over the mountain range near my home, and some of my best work with the plants occurs in the early hours of the morning. The color green reminds me of the herbs and vegetables I enjoy tending to in the gardens around the palace. My mother and I used to spend time together there. It was our sanctuary of silence in the busy, bustling world around it. She was the one who taught me to sing. The plants love it."

I could practically hear Daxton's smile as he fondly recalled his memories with his mother. "So, you only sing to your plants?"

"They are the only ones who don't taunt me for my efforts," Daxton said with a wink, knowing that wasn't the case at all. My mind raced to the memory of the song I heard while I was captured by the hunters and the deep gravelly baritone voice that carried me away from my horrors. And then, again at the beach, when he hummed the same melody to me. "I have also read countless logs and manuscripts to try to improve our crops in Silver Meadows to adapt to the changes caused by the wilt. It is a fascinating subject that I have the opportunity to research to help my people. I have even dabbled in creating crops of plants that utilize moonlight to grow." Dax shifted, propping his hands behind his head, and his fingers lightly brushed against my hair. "Here is a question for you."

"All ears."

"What would you be doing right now if you were not chosen as our champion?"

This was an interesting question for me to answer. In all honesty, I hadn't really thought about what-ifs. I hadn't had the time to really wonder about that. "I was training to be a healer for our pack. It made the most sense due to my gift, and I did enjoy helping people, but just for fun … let's say I didn't have my healing magic?" I paused to really give this some thought. "I would open my own bookshop," I said with a smile. "I envision opening my own special place where I could create different meals or treats that would cater to a place of knowledge and imagination with a vast collection of different stories and histories."

"That sounds like your own personal piece of paradise."

"And the best thing about all of it—"

"The unlimited supply of delicious food for the owner?" Daxton asked with an amused tone in his voice.

"Yes!" I exclaimed, followed by a heartfelt laugh. "Hey … you're starting to understand what makes me tick."

"If the food is anything like the meal you prepared at your family's home, I'm sure you would sell out each and every day."

"And then there would be the food of the mind when the real sustenance is devoured." This was a fantasy I hadn't really been brave enough to admit to myself, let alone another person. I would never put my gifts on a shelf to be forgotten about, and I would always use it to help heal those who needed it. But it was nice to dream.

"Favorite anything … else?" Daxton asked.

"Anything, huh? That is a very broad range you are giving me. Could you narrow down your inquiry there, Princey?"

"I want to know everything about you, Spitfire." His tone changed, and I could sense the magic around us beginning to spark in the air.

"Purple is my favorite color," I said quickly.

"And why is that?" His voice dropped low into that smooth, irresistible baritone that sent goosebumps dancing across my skin. Would I ever just be able to sit and listen to him without feeling like this?

"I believe that the Mother and Father created the shade of purple in this world to catch our attention and force us to take a moment from our busy lives to stop and appreciate it … To take notice."

Only Rhea and Neera knew the real reason why I loved the color purple, and now I could add Daxton to that list. Others, like Gilen, assumed it was simply because it was pretty. But those who truly knew me knew there was always depth behind my choices. With Dax, it was easy for me to be open and honest. There was no explanation for why, but I could tell that my animal also agreed with me.

"You fascinate me each time I learn something new about you, Spitfire." I didn't know if it was a compliment, but I intended to take it that way. "You mentioned when we first boarded the ship that the fireweed that was painted for you … is not your favorite flower. Do you mind me asking what is?"

I was about to answer when a sound from beyond our campfire light startled me.

Daxton immediately sprang up from his relaxed position and was on high alert, crouching low and balanced on his feet. A long silver sword materialized along his back and he pulled the majestic weapon free from its sheath with one swift movement.

I reached for my bow and nocked an arrow along the string, keeping my eyes locked on the tree line. "Do you see anything?" I whispered.

Dax shook his head no, but lightly tapped his ear and twitched his head toward the right. He could hear something from behind the thick brush. I listened carefully and faintly picked up on the sound of rapid breathing coming from the woods. It was erratic and haunting, like the creature it came from didn't have a proper nose or mouth to take in air sufficiently.

Castor appeared at Daxton's side with slender, curved twin swords in each hand. He looked at his brother with blacked-out eyes that gradually transitioned back to their normal state. I had seen Castor's eyes change just like that once before when I was about to approach Queen Minaeve and Daxton in the alpha's house. It didn't appear to alarm Dax as they silently exchanged hand signals with each other. Unable to decipher what they were saying, I scanned the tree line with my shifter's sight.

Dax turned to me and whispered in my ear, "Garmr. Vicious hound-like creatures created by the dark magic of the wilt."

*Fuck. That didn't sound good.*

Dax held up five fingers, and Castor nodded silently. "They are fanned out along the tree line. The female in the center is the lead, with two males on either side."

"Take out the bitch, and the rest will run home," Castor sneered before he crouched low and silently stalked out to our right. He moved into position with his twin blades drawn and ready, waiting silently for Daxton to give him the signal to attack.

Dax crouched behind me once more and whispered with his free hand clutching my shoulder, "Do not let them bite you. Their jaws hold venom that paralyzes their prey. They are the gatherers for the fallen we talked about earlier."

I nodded in understanding. "Where is their weak spot?"

"Just below the neck, above the rows of spikes along their spine."

Holy Gods, these hounds sounded grotesque—spikes along the spine and a paralyzing venom in their bite. *Welcome to my new hell.* The wilt had a strange way of turning the beauty of nature upside down. These creatures sounded like they were created from a child's nightmare.

"You can do this." The confidence in his voice left no room for question. In that moment, I understood why he was such a successful leader for his people. He very well might be afraid, but when the time came, he didn't back down, cower, or hint at his own shortcomings—if there were any.

I pulled back the fletching of my arrow, holding my draw. "Give the signal."

Daxton immediately teleported, giving Castor the go-ahead to charge forward, drawing out the five garmr hounds lurking in the woods.

The first hound on the right lunged out of the brush, followed closely by another on the far left. I hesitated for a second as I saw for the first time the horror the wilt had created. I now understood why the forest was deathly silent when we first arrived. It was because the hounds were prowling the lands, looking for any sign of life to drag back to their masters. The smell in the air was foul, like the stench of rotting, burning flesh mixed with charcoal. My hands trembled, but waiting any longer would seal my fate before the trials began. I loosed an arrow, aiming to the left, while Castor attacked the hound on the right. It flew straight and true, colliding with the base of the hound's neck and instantly dropping it to the ground. Dax appeared next to my kill and sliced his blade clean through at the base of its head to ensure it would not rise again from the ground. His eyes met mine for a brief second before he darted back into the thick woods with his mighty silver sword leading the way to our enemies. I looked left to find another hound, nocking another arrow with my black and silver bow.

The sounds of the forest suddenly came alive. Every animal screeched an alert, warning as many others as they could about the evil lurking in the brush. The sounds echoed and vibrated off every surface, distracting me from the three other hounds that were slowly encroaching upon my position.

I heard a snarl from behind me and turned to see a set of four glowing red eyes staring back at me. I couldn't believe I fell for a distraction and allowed an enemy to approach from behind like this. The garmr was larger than I expected, towering well over five feet tall on four powerful legs equipped with three-inch long talons on each paw that would shred any enemy to pieces. The spines along its back were jet black against a tan coat of coarse stubbly fur. I staggered backward a step, frozen in fear and unable to draw my arrow in time with the space between us. The hound lifted its snout and opened a mouth filled with rows of jagged teeth, with two distinct canines dripping with green paralyzing venom.

Castor and Daxton fought against the other three hounds off in the distance, and my stomach dropped at the reality that I was alone. Somehow, I knew the hound could smell my fear, and it seemed to enjoy the taste of it as it licked the air. I withdrew the dagger from my thigh and took a defensive position with the blade in my right hand. I remained balanced, holding my ground, not giving away any sign of where I might move next.

*Gods, help me.*

Before I could finish a silent prayer to the Gods, the hound launched toward me. I recalled my training with Dax on the ship and punched outward with my blade, ducking and rolling underneath the underbelly of the creature. I was tall, but with the creature leaping into the air, I was able to duck underneath it in time. The tip of my knife sliced through the soft underbelly of the beast as it soared over me. The blackened blood of the hellhound dripped onto my skin and face. I quickly brushed it away from my eyes, preparing immediately for it to turn on me again. The creature snapped its four crimson eyes toward me, baring its teeth and releasing a loud snarl that twisted my insides. It crouched, ready to pounce again, but its legs suddenly collapsed. A long silver blade sliced through the animal's hindquarters before severing its spinal cord at the base of its skull. Daxton towered over the creature, holding only minor scratches from his combat with the remaining hounds. His eyes were hard, and he looked absolutely terrifying as he stared at the beast at his feet. Realizing that the menacing Silver Shadow now stood before me.

Castor appeared from the brush, crashing through the trees with his swords ready at his side. Dax's sword disappeared once more as he quickly scanned me for any injuries. I gave him a thumbs-up before he peered down at Castor, looking at an open wound on his brother's leg. "Did she bite you, Cas?"

"No, just her claw." Castor boasted as I watched his eyes blacken again. It made Daxton tense and caused my heart to skip a beat as those ebony eyes swiveled in my direction.

"What is it?" The sound of flapping wings encroaching from behind me. The rapid beating paired with a snarl and sharp pang of talons opening to grab their intended prey.

I didn't even have time to breathe.

In a silver flash, Daxton materialized behind me, shoving me aside and standing in my place. He stretched out his arms and shielded me from talons that shredded into his back before embedding deep into the flesh of his shoulders. The winged creature screeched a high-pitched cry and with one beat of its wings carried him off into the darkness, toward the land infested by the wilt.

"Daxton!" I screamed into the night.

My animal roared inside me, urging me to follow him and not stop until he was safely back in my arms. Crimson blood stained the ground around me, and I knew it was Daxton's. He was gravely wounded, and since his powers were drained from the queen and passing through the veil … Gods, no.

"Daxton!" I roared again as I pushed myself up onto my feet. "Daxton!"

I didn't hesitate as I took off at a sprint. Blindly following Daxton and the winged creature from the ground as they soared through the sky. I didn't care what had captured him. All I knew was that I was going to get him back.

Castor managed to catch up to me even with his injured leg. I was about to argue with him, but I stopped when I saw the same decision echoed in his expression. There was no other option. We were going into the wilt. And we were going to rescue Daxton.

# Chapter Twenty-Nine

"It's a fucking harpy," Castor cursed between pants of breath, with a slight unbalanced sway to his stride. I offered to heal him, but he refused, insisting it was not worth the time or energy.

I could tell his injury bothered him more than he let on. Otherwise, he would be a good three lengths ahead of me. "A what?" I exclaimed.

"A half-fae-creature that is thriving in the wilt. It hunts with the hounds. Typically, one of them oversees a troop of garmr. Gods. Above," he swore. "We knew better. We should have anticipated one of them lurking nearby in the sky."

"Forget about what should have happened and focus on what we need to do now!" I was screaming at him even though I knew I didn't need to. But I was scared. Watching Daxton being taken away like that awakened a very primal instinct inside of me that I didn't expect to feel. It was like Daxton was pack and threatening him was a direct threat to me.

"What is the harpy doing? Where would she take him?"

Castor suddenly skidded to a stop and reached to grab my arm. "You … You should stay behind. Dax will skin me alive if anything happens to you."

"He has to be alive for that to happen," I snapped as I glared at him and shook my arm free. "I am going with you. And *we* are going to find Daxton. You can't do or say anything to stop me from going after him, Castor." I dared him to try and buck against this. I was even willing to ask my animal to help tap into that command magic I had used on him in the past.

"Daxton can handle this. Once she drops him, he will kill her, and then—"

"I'm coming with you!" I yelled, interrupting him.

Castor gave me a firm glare, pursing his lips together into a thin line. "Skylar, I have personally witnessed my brother annihilate and tear through his enemies regardless of injuries acquired in a battle or his powers drained. Harpies, humans, shifters, and even fae—anything that stands in his path is dead. Shit, I have even seen him kill someone with a gods-damned butter knife at brunch."

"I. Am. Coming. With. You."

He pursed his lips again, twin lines forming between his brows as he met my stare. "Fuck. Fine." Castor turned and looked up into the sky. He analyzed our surroundings and plotted the best route through the forest and into the wilt. "This way … you better not die or get hurt. Daxton will bury me where I stand if that happens," he snarled with a menacing tone, gesturing toward the southeast. I knew he hated the fact that I was coming along, but nothing was going to keep me from finding Daxton.

In a flash, I sped off in the direction Castor pointed, with him only a few steps behind me. To be honest, I knew where I needed to go to find Dax. I didn't need Castor to tell me the way. Something pulled at my chest, guiding me.

*I will find you. We will always find each other.* His words flashed in my mind, and I wondered if it wasn't all just for show.

"Damn you, Daxton," I swore under my breath. "You had better be alive when we find you."

We crashed through the thick, overgrown trees, slowly making our way through the forest until it began to thin and fade away. We stopped at the edge of a clearing where a distinct line was drawn in the dirt. On one side, where we stood, was life, green grass with the sweet smell of open, clean air. Looking across to the other, it was the polar opposite. It was one thing to see the wilt from a safe distance from the deck of the *Opal* and another to be inches away from stepping into its border. Death was only one word to describe the feeling from the wilted side. The smell of sulfur was strong in the air, along with the overwhelming feeling of unease. This place felt wrong. Unnatural in every way possible. Shadows lurked around corners of dead fallen trees like they were awake and searching for the next victim to swallow whole. There was no light, no life in this place. There was only … death.

This was a place that embodied destruction and decay. Materialized and manipulated into shadows and broken dreams of fear that paralyzed you from within. Fear gripped my chest, but I couldn't give in to its crippling grasp. Daxton was in there. My animal surged up inside my center, causing me to fold over and clutch at my heart, which seemed like it was on the verge of exploding.

"Skylar?" Castor was at my side in an instant, looking me over for any sign of visible injury.

I waved him away. "I'm fine."

"Bullshit," he sneered, glaring at me. "Are you sure you want to do this?"

I whipped my head around and knew my amber eyes were blazing with power pumping from my animal. We would not shift while the mark was on our arm to complete the trials, but it would not stop her from fueling me with the strength I needed. And right now, I needed every drop of it to rescue Daxton. "Yes."

Castor took a step back and nodded, his lethal twin blades out and ready at his sides. "They wouldn't have carried him far past the border."

"Good," I said as I stepped forward into the land of the wilt.

I clutched the bow in my hand and reached back for an arrow to hold in the other. We jogged together slowly, our eyes and ears constantly scanning every step we made before daring to take another. It was slower than I wanted, but we had to be cautious. With that harpy creature's talons embedded into his shoulders, I knew Daxton could not free himself through his teleporting magic. Wherever he would go, that monster would follow.

Not too far ahead, I heard a loud thundering clash. "There!" I exclaimed, knowing without a doubt that it was Daxton.

As we approached, the commotion increased. Multiple pairs of beating wings combined with the clashing sound of a sword slicing through flesh. My heart leaped at the knowledge that Daxton had not stopped fighting. No, he would never stop fighting. That fact alone stirred me to run faster, with Castor only a few paces behind me. I clutched my bow in my hand and nocked an arrow across the string. I was no physical match for these creatures with my dagger, but I could do some damage from a distance. That would give Castor the opening to return Daxton to safety so I could heal him.

"Up there." Castor pointed to a small plateau, and we hurried up the side of the sandy hill. I could hear Dax fighting and felt the pulse of his ice magic fending off not one but three harpies that were bombarding him on all sides. I crested the side of the plateau and pulled back on my bow to take aim.

One harpy lay motionless to Daxton's left, with a shard of ice penetrating through its feathered chest. I knew from the coloring of its feathers that this was the creature that intended to capture me. Three other female harpies were still circling Daxton, who held them back with a magical shield of ice, attacking with his sword if they dared to come closer. I could see the bloodied gashes along his neck and shoulders staining the ground from the wounds inflicted by the talons of the first harpy he'd slain. The sharp points penetrated essential muscles and tendons that he needed to wield his sword above his head to fend off his enemies. We had arrived just in time to help him.

At a closer look, the creatures were a grotesque combination of fae and animal. It was like a shifter had been caught halfway through their transition between their human and animal forms. They had long, free-flowing golden hair with elongated pointed ears that stretched the length of their heads. The gray skin covering their faces looked almost sickly, with a dreaded hunger reflected in their large, ominous black eyes. Tan feathers coated their middle, leading to their bottom halves, which resembled the legs of an eagle or other bird of prey. Long, dark talons replaced their hands, and on their backs were a pair of sandy-colored bird-like wings that carried them through the air.

I took aim at the back center chest of one of them, hoping that if these creatures had a heart, my arrow would find it. Releasing my bowstring, Castor charged toward his brother. The female I aimed at saw me release my arrow and quickly dove out of the way, fiercely flapping her wings to retreat from the battle scene. *I didn't kill her, but at least that leaves only two.* Castor leaped from a nearby boulder and flew through the air with twin blades slicing through one of the wings of the harpy that Dax had frozen between walls of his ice magic. She was trapped and unable to escape.

The creature's scream of pain was deafening as it sliced through my ears and split my skull from the inside out. I dropped my bow to cover my ears, desperate to block out the sound, struggling to right myself. The world was doubled over, and I couldn't concentrate on anything but the mind-numbing sound the harpy was creating. Daxton lashed out with one powerful swing of his sword and sliced through her neck, effectively ending the screeching melody. The ringing stopped in my head, and I sighed in relief as my vision stopped splitting in two. With the absence of screeching, I immediately grabbed my bow again and began searching for the remaining harpy that was still circling us in the sky.

Even though I could see in the dark, the magic of the wilt somehow interfered with my ability to see. I closed my eyes and listened for any sign of her approach. To my right, I heard the faint whisper of a wing flap and snapped my eyes open to the night sky. There she was, soaring through the air, diving straight for Castor and Daxton. I pulled back my arrow and released the string, aiming for the empty space I calculated she would be when my arrow reached its target. There was a loud thud as my arrow sank deep into the harpy's chest. The female flying monster crashed into the ground, skipping over the top of the plateau until coming to a stop at the feet of Castor and Daxton. I remained still, my bow arm still extended and my release hand close by my cheek. My heart was thumping so loudly in my ears that the world around me seemed to disappear. I killed her.

I watched Daxton give Castor a command, and he took off over the top of the plateau. Very carefully, Daxton made his way over to where I was still standing with my bow. He held up his palms and whispered something, but I was still unable to hear much of anything. Coming to my side, I could smell the blood seeping from his open wounds, and that triggered me to snap out of my trance. I immediately dropped my bow, frantically throwing myself into Dax's open arms. I didn't care that he was bloodied from battle. He was alive, and he was safe. His arm encased me in a blanket of security as he pulled me in closer, one hand running through my hair while the other wrapped around my waist. My forehead rested against his cheek as we both refused to allow the other to move away.

*He was all right.* I almost didn't believe it. If he wasn't holding onto me, I didn't know if I would have believed it. I released my hands and carefully moved them to the gaping wounds on his shoulders, ready to heal his wounds, but he made me pause as he cupped my face in his hands.

"Are you injured?" Dax asked while inspecting me from head to toe.

"No, but you are," I said. I could smell the fresh blood pouring from the open wounds on his back, but Daxton didn't even seem to notice. "Let me heal you, Dax, or else we won't get out of here alive."

"I don't want you wasting any of your energy on my account. Trust me, I'm fine."

"Liar." I gave him the most disgruntled glare I could muster. "Turn around, you stubborn ass fae, and let me heal you."

He grunted in disproval, but eventually turned his back to me so I could inspect his wounds. I summoned my healing magic, and it immediately answered my call. A golden hum of power appeared in my palms as I began to mend what was broken. I ran my hands over the deep gashes that scraped across his back, slowly migrating to the puncture wounds the harpy utilized to carry him through the air. I didn't miss the fact that these wounds were meant for me, and I was astonished that Daxton was alive … and still able to fight in this state.

"There," I whispered, wiping my brow to examine my handiwork. "Feel better?"

"Much. My healing would have been able to repair these wounds, but—"

"But the veil and the queen have drained your magic. I know, Dax. You hide it well, but you didn't allow me to heal everything the night she accepted your offering. There is no use trying to fool me."

"It seems that way." Dax rolled his shoulders and cast his gaze out toward the direction he sent Castor. "My brother is hunting for any others we missed. We don't want a fallen or others coming to hunt us."

"I should've—"

"Don't," Dax answered, turning to face me. "You ventured into the unknown dangers of the wilt and managed to slay a harpy diving out of the sky. You saved my life, Skylar." His rough palm cupped my cheek once more, forcing my eyes to focus solely on his. "You found me."

I smiled, knowing exactly what to say next. "We will always find each other."

Dax leaned into me, and I couldn't help the longing I felt to melt into his arms and allow him to help me carry the weight of the world that was resting on my shoulders. My eyes began to water, with a single tear falling to my cheek. Dax bent his head and gently pressed his lips to my brow, washing away my moment of weakness, allowing it to disappear without a hint of judgment or pity.

"It's normal to be afraid, Spitfire. I would try to convince you that everything you are feeling is normal, but then again, you charged into the deathly wilt without hesitation. There is a wild streak of insanity beneath that wickedly beautiful face, isn't there?"

*Beautiful? Did Daxton just say that?*

"It's not this place that frightened me," I said with a stone in my throat.

"What was it then? You can tell me. I won't judge you."

I looked into his eyes, which made my hard exterior melt away like there was nothing there. "I was terrified …" I blinked as another tear fell, but Dax was there to catch it. "I was terrified I would lose you."

"Skylar—" He whispered my name as he leaned in, our lips dangerously close to one another's. The tension between us becoming irresistible, both of us realizing it was becoming impossible to defy.

Dax suddenly stilled, his body becoming rigid as his eyes snapped upward, scanning the area behind us. His expression hardened like stone as he gripped my arms tightly, protectively throwing me behind him. Silver Shadow was reemerging and ready for blood. He released a long, high-pitched whistle with his two fingers in his mouth and frantically looked east. "Castor is heading for the border. You're going with him."

"I … What?" There was no time for me to argue.

Silver flashed, and Dax teleported us east, just below the raised plateau we were standing on. His legs shook underneath him, even though he refused to buckle under his fatigue. Castor was by our side no more than a second later. Daxton passed me to his brother, and he gripped my arm tightly. Castor refused to let me go even after I tugged, trying to free myself from his grasp.

"Dax, what is going on?" My heart sank as I whipped my head around to see Castor's ebony eyes appear once more. "Is it …"

"Yes," Daxton snapped, his eyes scanning the area around us. "We don't have time. You know how the shadows and fog interfere with my magic, Cas."

Castor began to tremble for a brief second before he forced on his mask of composure once more. The whites of his eyes returned, but a darkness lingered beneath. What was going on? What came next after harpies and death hounds? What could possibly be worse than … Oh, Gods, no. It dawned on me once the shadows streamed in from all sides. Daxton reached out and pulled me in behind him while Castor sandwiched me in from behind.

"Dax." Castor's eyes were locked onto his brother's.

"Don't move, Cas." Daxton's magic began to coat my skin in a thin sheet of ice.

I glanced to the side and noticed Castor doing the same, manipulating Daxton's ice with his own powers, utilizing the shared gift of their father's magic. A dense black fog encased us, blocking every escape path we could take. There was nothing, but we knew something was lurking behind the curtain of blackness.

Daxton and Castor both locked their sights on top of the plateau where Dax and I had been only moments before. A dark stream of black mist tendrils crawled over the sides as two midnight-cloaked creatures floated over the sands. They came to a stop mere feet away from Daxton, who pushed me backward toward Castor.

A pale, gangly hand extended from the blackness of one of the creatures and it pointed a bony finger directly at me. "*Shifter* …" its raspy voice said.

"Touch her, and you die." Daxton's voice was low and calm, more terrifying than the deafening roar of a battle cry. He stepped into my view, intercepting the attention of the cloaked creatures. His long silver blade was drawn in his left hand, while his right was wrapped behind him, trying to shield me.

"Dax?" His eyes were locked on the creatures with a cold, deathly stare.

"*Not you* …" It spoke again, but I'm not sure I would accurately describe it as speaking.

The voice sounded like someone had been screaming for days, weeks, or months on end. There was a gravelly sound that made me want to curl my toes and run as far away as I possibly could. Sadly, I understood how painful it was and how long you had to be screaming for a voice to get to this point.

"Remember your promise, Skylar," Daxton whispered under his breath.

"What?" I pinched his arm, but he was unmovable. Hyper-focused on the enemies standing before us.

"Your promise, Spitfire."

Gods be damned. *These* … These were the fallen. "I am not leaving you, Daxton! Get it through that thick head already. I will not leave you. You're going to have to force me."

His eyes fluttered back at me for a moment before focusing on the nalusa falaya, the fallen monsters hovering before us. The moment his gaze lingered on mine, I understood more than I cared to admit as tears appeared in my eyes. I refused to let them fall, because I was not leaving his side. *Fuck that.*

"Castor," Daxton murmured.

I looked to Castor to try and read his emotions. He was usually a master at hiding them, but not here, not now. His eyes showed pure terror and fear, not just for himself but for his brother. What crazy fucked-up plan had these two come up with? I was not on board if it meant leaving Daxton to fight this creature and inevitably die while Castor and I ran away to safety.

Shit, I realized that was exactly what they intended to do.

"I will *never* forgive you," I swore at Castor, but it didn't make a difference. I could see it in his eyes that he didn't want to do this either. My threat held no hold over him because he wouldn't ever forgive himself either.

"Castor!" Dax roared.

"Why have they not attacked us yet?" Castor asked.

"I don't know," Daxton replied. "But I'm not wasting more time trying to figure it out. Go. Now!" Castor hesitated, but Daxton yelled again, "Go now!"

Silver flashed, and Daxton teleported toward the creature on the right and attacked with his ice magic, followed by a swing of his silver sword. The fallen creature screamed, materializing its long, gangly fingers and turning them into claws that would tear Daxton's head clear from his body. Tendrils of shadow began encroaching upon him, opening a small window in the fog surrounding us. It was a distraction.

"Move now!" Castor yelled as he tried to grab my arm. With the help of the thin coat of ice on my skin from Dax's magic, I spun in place and slipped away from Castor's hold. "Skylar! Dammit, no!" Castor yelled at me like a parent does when their offspring is about to do something incredibly stupid and possibly get themselves killed.

But I couldn't let that stop me.

The clang of Daxton's mighty sword echoed off a blade drawn by one of the fallen creatures. His ice daggers and shield walls combating the dark shadows that crept behind him from the creature's dark magic. I prayed to the gods to keep him, and Castor, safe. I wouldn't stand by and do nothing while those I cared about were in danger. It wasn't in my nature or my animal's. These fallen creatures were the most terrifying monsters that I had ever seen, giving the garmr hounds and the harpies a run for their money.

I technically wasn't breaking my promise to Dax. I did exactly as I said I would. I turned and I ran. While Daxton handled one of the creatures, I would take care of the other.

My animal stirred inside me, encouraging me to charge forward and call upon my healing magic. My palms glowed with a warm orange and gold color, illuminating the surrounding area of darkened fog. The shadows from the fallen that spoke to me retreated from my glow, and the creature slowly turned its cloaked head in my direction. There was no time to think.

Closing my eyes, I extended my palms and placed them on what I imagined would be the face of the fallen if I was able to see inside the shadows of darkness that concealed its body.

I felt the pull immediately.

My healing powers flowed into the creature, pulses of magic washing over me and the fallen as I grasped onto its face. As my magic flowed into the creature, the scenery around us changed. The barren, dried, cracked ground beneath my feet started to soften and spring small green blades of grass. The shadows and fog that encased us dissipated into nothing, and the foul stench of death faded into the wind. Hands, actual living hands, no longer grotesque claws, grasped onto my forearms. With one final push, I poured every ounce of strength I had left into the fallen creature.

Daxton appeared behind me with his silver sword coated in black blood that I knew was from the decapitated head of the other nalusa falaya. I released my hold and staggered backward into Daxton's embracing arms. He knelt on the ground with me in his lap as his body tensed.

"Spitfire. What … What have you done?"

I didn't know what he was talking about. Honestly, I hadn't been brave enough to open my eyes and see what was happening the entire time I attempted to heal the nalusa falaya. "Please tell me I didn't make anything worse."

Daxton scooped me up in his arms and cradled me close to his chest so I could feel his heart beating against me. He lightly kissed my forehead and tucked me securely into the nook of his neck along his collarbone. There was a long, fatigued inhale of breath as he squeezed me tightly, and it took everything I had not to drift off into my shifter sleep right then and there.

"Open your eyes," Dax whispered. "I can feel you start to drift, but before you do, please, just look."

I cracked open my eyelids to see what he was talking about and gasped. "What? Where did she come from?"

Laying on the ground in a black shredded cloak was the alluring, breathtakingly iridescent face of a female High Fae. Her once gray, sickly flesh was now healthy and full of life. Her fair skin contrasted beautifully with silky ebony hair that cascaded down the length of her petite figure. Double eyelids surrounded rounded eyes with a deep brown coloring that almost looked black. Her slender, delicate nose matched her narrow jawline and small face, giving her a unique beauty and gracefulness that I had never seen before.

"Where did she come from?" I stammered.

"She was the fallen creature. You … healed her." I shook my head in disbelief at what Dax was telling me.

The female High Fae struggled to push herself upright, but Castor was there in an instant, offering her his hand. He looked at her with the same mesmerized stare that I'm sure we all had plastered on our faces.

"What's your name?" Castor asked in a hushed whisper.

She was silent. The female looked to be in shock, glancing around at us and her surroundings. She panicked for a moment and looked down at her body, feeling her face for any sign of the teeth or claws she once had.

"You're safe." Castor's voice was gentle and soft.

*This is a new side to him*, I thought as my vision began to blur. "Dax …" I whimpered, struggling to hold onto my consciousness, fighting with the fleeting strength I had left to try and stay awake.

Daxton stood up with me cradled in his strong arms. "Sleep. I've got you, Spitfire." I wanted to argue, but there wasn't any fight left in me to do so. My head tilted back as Dax adjusted his hold on me so I could snuggle in against his chest.

"Thank you," he said in the final moments before I fell into my shifter sleep. "Thank you for keeping your promise."

I grinned. "For you, anytime."

**End of Book 1**

# ABOUT THE AUTHOR

J.E. Larson is a born and raised Alaskan, with a passion for being active and outdoors while daydreaming in her own worlds. Wife to an ever-patient husband and mother to a princess, and a unicorn. J.E. Larson has been writing and creating stories since she was very young (#2 pencil and spiral notebook paper style). And now, she finds the time to write in the quiet five a.m. mornings and secluded night hours after bedtime.

Social Media

TikTok: j.e.larson8

Instagram: j.e.larson8

*Skylar Cathal*

**"A Trial of the Heart"**
***Valdor Series Book 2.***
***Coming 2025****

**The trials begin.**

Fate is a fickle master of the unknown,
and yet, fate has led me here–

I chose to take my cousin's place as the shifter champion of the trials.
I chose to come back from death's doorstep in the hunter's keep.
I chose to deny Gilen's claim as my mate.
I chose to travel to the Inner Kingdom with the High Fae.
And now, I choose to follow my *heart.*

Where my heart will lead me, however— that is still unknown.

Made in the USA
Monee, IL
24 December 2024

74cd464b-57b0-47ac-83b3-904356553561R01